John Saunders

Hirell

A novel

John Saunders

Hirell
A novel

ISBN/EAN: 9783337044466

Printed in Europe, USA, Canada, Australia, Japan

Cover: Foto ©Andreas Hilbeck / pixelio.de

More available books at **www.hansebooks.com**

CHEAP WORKS OF FICTION.

Each in one vol., crown 8vo, cloth, price 6s.

Gideon's Rock, and other Stories. By Katherine Saunders.

"Especially worthy of commendation."—*Queen.*

Joan Merryweather and other Stories. By Katherine Saunders.

"Interesting."—*Daily Review.*

"Intensely powerful tale."—*Guardian.*

Margaret and Elizabeth: a Story of the Sea. By Katherine Saunders.

"Powerfully told . . . A very beautiful story."—*Pall Mall Gazette.*

The Confessions of a Thug. By Colonel Meadows Taylor, C.S.I., M.R.I.A. With a Frontispiece.

"A story so powerfully and graphically narrated does not soon lose its hold on the imagination."—*Daily News.*

Tara: a Mahratta Tale. By Colonel Meadows Taylor, C.S.I., M.R.I.A. With a Frontispiece.

"We should deliberately place 'Tara' first among all books ever written to illustrate native life, and in the very front rank of novels."—*Spectator.*

Culmshire Folk: A Novel. By Ignotus. New and Cheaper Edition. With a Frontispiece.

"Charming throughout."—*Spectator.*

"Cleverly written, and in a brisk and dashing style."—*Morning Post.*

Beatrice Aylmer, and other Tales. By Mary W. Howard, Author of "Brampton Rectory."

"These tales possess considerable merit."—*Court Journal.*

By Still Waters. By Edward Garrett. A Story for Quiet Hours. With Seven Illustrations.

"It has more than pleased—it has charmed us."—*Nonconformist.*

'SHE WAS VERY LOVELY.'

H I R E L L :

A NOVEL.

BY THE

AUTHOR OF 'ABEL DRAKE'S WIFE.

'If the first among the problems of life be how to establish the peace and restore the balance of the inward being——

'I know not what true definition there is for any age or people of the highest excellence of any kind, unless it be perpetual effort upward in pursuit of an object higher than ourselves, higher than our works, higher even than our hopes, yet beckoning us on from hour to hour, and always permitting us to apprehend in part.

'It is, I think, an observation of St. Augustine, that those periods are critical and formidable when the power of putting questions runs greatly in advance of the pains to answer them. Such appears to be the period in which we live.'

W. E. GLADSTONE.

HENRY S. KING & CO., LONDON.

1876.

(The rights of translation and of reproduction are reserved.)

TO THE

AUTHOR OF THE MOTTOES

WHICH APPEAR ON THE TITLE-PAGE OF THIS WORK,—

TO

THE RIGHT HONORABLE W. E. GLADSTONE, M.P.

ETC. ETC,

THE FOLLOWING PAGES ARE DEDICATED

BY PERMISSION

WITH THE PROFOUND RESPECT

OF

JOHN SAUNDERS.

HIRELL.

CHAPTER I.

JOHN RYMER CUNLIFF.

THERE are no dreamers like unimaginative people. With such persons dreams remain to the last pure dreams. They have no power to make the actual grow out of the ideal; and Nature, in a kind of divine foresight and pity, compensates them by keeping up this inner light; which, however feeble and discoloured, warms and cheers, even though there be no window in the sanctuary of the soul through which the rays may pass out to guide the benighted steps. Faithful to the last they dream, touchingly unconscious of the process. They could not tell anything, perhaps, if asked. But not the less do they dream, and dream on, of what will never be; and thus assert their share in the profounder instincts of humanity. But they also toil on, along the roughest, the dryest, and the dustiest of roads; patient and enduring; and never think to complain that such things should be in their hearts if they may not realise them.

But there are men whose dreams, no matter how wide and glorious their scope, are ever monitions to duty; who see their thoughts return to them, as the messenger returned to Joshua, laden with tokens of the Promised Land, and who know they can go and take possession if they will. Not without heroic discipline of self, perhaps; certainly not without great and protracted effort. But they can do it. They do not. Again they are tempted, and yet again. Every faculty cries out to them for leave to do its own proper work, to grow strong, healthy, victorious. But the reluctant feet still cling to the familiar soil. The eyes, dazzled for a moment, turn away, and see all things more dubiously. The lips answer, ' Yes, but not now.'

And Nature deals with these men, too—justly, not pityingly. They are the worst of traitors to her ! And she so loved them ! So poured upon them her choicest gifts ! She leaves them to their fate. And they are, or try to believe themselves to be, happy ; for they no longer dream those disturbing dreams.

She leaves them. Yes, as the sun leaves the tropical forest at eve, stifling in its own rankness, a prey to a thousand unclean things. And yet how beautiful many of them are ? One doesn't see them properly in the open, harsh, unsympa- thetic daylight. It hurts the eye, too, so much looking at the sun. We see well enough here, after all. The soul, like the eye, soon accommodates itself to a soft, luxurious gloom. Who knows but it may shut out unpleasant objects, and bring nearer to us things we may like ? Besides, we are modest, and prefer that some things should be veiled. Let us look around and enjoy while we can. Let us take the goods our toiling sires provide. What wealth we have ! What leisure ! What infinite opportunities for active gratification ! What delicious couches for repose ! And—yes, once more we can dream sweet dreams, from which it is a pain to awake.

The light streams from the little conservatory on his face— on John Cunliff's face, as it bends over his writing-desk in his luxurious bachelor apartments, overlooking one of the parks. The light, being that of the September noon-day, is strong, and shows the face more truthfully than flatteringly, thus :—A long face, with a colourless complexion, light hair, parted in the middle of the head, and falling rather long, as in the earliest Anglo-Saxon portraits ; not golden hair, or chestnut brown, but only pale, dead brown. A straight, long nose ; lips full, firm, well-shaped, flexible, expressive. A long chin, with a small, pointed beard. Surely there must be large and brilliant eyes to ennoble and glorify so seemingly common- place a countenance ?

He looks up from his writing towards the flowers in the conservatory. The eyes are not even blue, nor dark, nor large. Grey, with green lights in them as they look towards the sun ; keen as an eagle's ; bright, and, like the lips, expressive ; a little darker and more tender in colour when bent again contemplatively on the writing, but not handsome eyes at any time, if studied only for themselves ; and yet the face as a whole is good, original, and in some of its aspects has a certain massive and melancholy beauty, caused by no particular feature ;—unless, indeed, by the broad, smooth, finely-rounded brow—but due to the perfect harmony of all.

What is he doing ?

It is a question that apparently he would not care to have put to him even in look, for when the man-servant enters with coals, Mr. Cunliff slides his letter under the hollow of his desk-slope ; and appears to be busily engaged, with elbows propped on the desk, studying a large photograph from one of the Hampton Court cartoons that he has just purchased, and mounted straight before him beyond his desk, by the aid of a pile of books, at a suitable angle for examination ; and towards which his eye had unconsciously turned at every pause in his letter-writing, as if with a true artistic love. When the servant has gone out he draws forth the letter. Then, after a pause, he rises, goes to the door, and locks it. Still dissatisfied, he unlocks it, rings the bell, and when the man comes, says—

' Mind ! I am at home to no one to-day.'

' Except, sir, I suppose to—'

' To no one ! '

' Very well, sir. I'll take care.'

This time the door was not locked after the servant, and the work at the desk recommenced.

What is he doing ?

Can we discover for ourselves by watching him ?

The human face is always one of the most attractive, but also one of the most perplexing, of problems. Lavater, no doubt, was right enough in his theory that the character is to be seen in the countenance. But then we need an angel to read it for us, and keep us from making the most dangerous mistakes. What, we might ask, could be clearer than the passions that express themselves in the looks and gestures of two men engaged in a deadly struggle ; deadly to life, or to reputation, or to one's dearest hopes ? Surely there, if anywhere, we might hope to find the perfect outward manifestations of those inward forces which so jealously shun the light ?

But no. Neither of the combatants forgets, for an instant, that the other's eye is upon him; and that consciousness modifies, perhaps even falsifies, all expression.

But there is a position in which the student of physiognomy may revel to his soul's content. It is that of a man who, believing himself free from observation, is writing a letter which stirs his nature to the depths, and which may affect his whole future. And such a letter, it is impossible to doubt, John Cunliff is now engaged on.

Can it be that he is in debt and serious danger? No. Men don't lock their doors, even for an instant, against a servant in order to answer a creditor. Nor do they spend half an hour over the turn of a single sentence in writing to him. Neither do they tear up sheet after sheet, and pause again and again, as if hopeless of self-satisfaction in style; and pace up and down the room with nervous irritable gestures, before sitting down once more to the apparently unconquerable task.

No, John Cunliff's difficulty is not one of debt. What then?

Is he discovering that the beautiful fruit which was held to his lips when he entered the world eight years ago—independent in purse, radiant with youth, energy, enthusiasm, and the honours of a successful University career—this fruit of pleasure of which he has been eating ever since, with palate growing less keen, but habit growing more exacting,—is he discovering, at last, as he gets to a core, having exhausted bloom, rind, and pulp, that the essence of all is but a bitter ash? Is that his discovery? And is he sitting down in the first hours of remorse to unwind the toils that hold him fast; and beginning to tell the truth with all fit considerateness to others whose fate is involved with his own? No. For even the most considerate of beings will, at such times of domestic revolution, think chiefly of themselves, and make short work of others' sacrifices while striving to complete their own.

But may not this still be his true position, only that there is an addition to be made? Perhaps he intends to reward himself for his self-denial. Or rather he, perhaps prudently, won't over-estimate his own heroism; and intends, while turning from the Delilahs of life—the typical Delilahs only, let us say—to take to himself a beautiful and virtuous spouse, provided only she will consent? An excellent resolve—but not in the least resembling John Cunliff's. Else why the lowering expression of that naturally frank face; the almost furtive glances towards the door of so fearless an eye; or the peculiar colouring of his cheeks, that has partly driven off the ordinary pallor, and which seems to suggest, you hardly know how or why, the idea of a man engaged in a terrible struggle, that yet has nothing in it of the noble, or even of the self-respecting? Never did a man sit down to write an honest and manly love-letter and bear the while an aspect like John Cunliff's.

He must have been insulted; or, worse still, have himself given mortal offence, and he now offers or accepts a challenge. But the days of duelling are past; and men either summon or are summoned to the Divorce Court; accept or compel refuge with the police: or arbitrate their rights and wrongs at Nisi Prius. They don't agree to fight. Besides, there breaks through the powerful restraint that one sees John Cunliff imposes on himself occasional glimpses of an extraordinary change of feeling. Chaos suddenly changes into creation. All his unpleasant thoughts seem to die, and pleasant ones to spring up into vivid and attractive life. And then he walks about the room with an elastic step; glances at his favourite pictures on the walls, which always send him with new zest to his Raphael photograph; or he goes into the conservatory to see what new plants the florist has brought in the weekly exchange for those gone out of bloom; but pauses unthinkingly, and yet full of thought, over a rose so long, that one gets the notion he has forgotten all anxieties, and is abandoning himself to some fascinating day-dream.

What, then, is he doing? Why, simply writing a short, and surely very innocent letter; if this be all:—

‘ I hear you have half accepted Lady Sellon's invitation to go back with her into the country after her hasty visit to town; that she goes very early to-morrow morning; and that she thinks you will come to her this evening *prepared* to stay If she does not see you this evening, she will conclude you refuse to go. I ventured to say you had expressed so much pleasure at the thought that I was sure you would accept. If so, may I not hope to see you later in her drawing-room, that I may explain how I have fulfilled the slight commission with which you honoured me? Or, as I must myself make a call in your neighbourhood about eight o'clock, may I, if I should have the good fortune to come across your carriage on its way to Lady Sellon's, venture to ask to be taken in ? I shall not add much to the weight of your trunks. By-the-by, what an exquisite *carte-de-visite* of yourself was that which you showed so reluctantly yesterday ; and which, but for Lady Sellon's kind treachery, would have remained unknown to us all ! You gave away copies, but did not give one to me. I did not ask then, it is true. Now I do. I wait anxiously to know if you forgive the request.'

Surely an innocent letter ! But why is it unsigned ? Why is there no indication of the name of the lady to whom it is addressed ? Obviously it is a lady to whom John Cunliff writes.

He must be one of the least conceited of men, to be so unwilling, even now, when he has got a fair and completed copy after innumerable failures, to read it over and over so many times, and always with increasing dissatisfaction. To judge from his attitude—his head supported on his left arm, which is elbowed on the desk, looking sideways at the letter which the right hand has drawn away and holds up just a little while, resting on the farthest part of the slope—there is not a sentence or a thought in it over which he does not hold a mental cavil ; and which he only leaves unaltered because he dares not embark on a new attempt, and is hopeless of improving the texture if he did.

' It must go as it is—or not at all,' he says to himself.

One more pause—the open letter on the slope, elbows on each side, hands clasped and drawn down over the eyes as if to shut out the too brilliant light from the conservatory—and shut in the letter while a last thoughtful look at it is taken.

Suddenly he breaks the pause ; encloses the envelope, addresses it, and two minutes later drops it in the post-office letter-box, saying to himself, with half a smile —

' That settles my part of the business, at any rate. Six hours will tell me all the rest.'

CHAPTER II.

WAITING FOR AN ANSWER.

WHEN the letter had been dropped into the box, Cunliff stood for a moment in the street, irresolute—then turned towards a shop to purchase some gloves, but suddenly hurried back to his rooms, as if wishing neither to see nor to be seen. On his way he met a respectable-looking man, evidently fresh from a journey, who stopped and bowed with marked respect.

'Jarman! You in London! Anything the matter?' asked Cunliff, stretching out his hand.

'No, sir—no. But as you were so anxious about the payment into the bank to-day, I thought I'd come myself, with all I have been able to collect.'

Cunliff looked as if he could have dispensed with this personal attention on the part of his obsequious agent; whose inclined head, subdued attitude of deference, upward side-glance from a brown bright eye, and respectful words, only called forth a rough, 'Oh, very well!' and then Cunliff turned on his heel, leaving Mr. Jarman to follow as he pleased. That gentleman accordingly hung back just enough to admit of conversation without seeming to claim intimate acquaintance.

'And how much have you got for me?' demanded Cunliff, the moment the door was closed upon them in his own room.

'A little less than sixteen hundred pounds.'

'You mean beyond what must go to the mortgages?'

'I am sorry to say, sir, inclusive of that.'

'You didn't sell the timber, then?'

'The best of it; but it only fetched four hundred and ten pounds.'

Cunliff looked at the agent, and his face darkened.

'I assure you, sir,' said the agent, 'I have done my best to force in all arrears, even under painful circumstances—'

'I told you, Mr. Jarman,' interrupted Cunliff, in a rapid, impetuous tone, 'I did not wish to hurt deserving people among my tenants.'

'Yes, sir, I understood that; and I hope I have drawn the arrears I refer to with as little damage as was possible.'

'You must go into this matter more fully with me.'

'Oh, certainly! Now?'

'N—o, not to-day! I'm busy.'

'Of course, sir, any time will do for that.'

Cunliff glanced at the agent, then turned away moodily. Nothing could the agent say that did not jar. His employer looked so thoroughly dissatisfied that it was a wonder he ventured on his next theme: 'I had, sir, I must confess, another motive for presenting myself to you to-day.'

'Then why the devil didn't you say so? What is it? The fact is, Mr. Jarman, I'm thoroughly disappointed. I expected at least five hundred more. And when I intimated to you that I might possibly travel, and not find it convenient for a long time to wait for remittances, I did expect you would have managed better. Sixteen hundred pounds! Absurd! Why, half goes for things that, as you know, must be provided for! But what's this other matter?'

'Pardon me for what I am going to say. I have been thinking you might be put out at this unsatisfactory result, and as I have a thousand pounds lying idle, if you will allow me to anticipate your next rents, and—'

'Jarman, you surprise me! I didn't expect this. No, thank you. It's very kind—very! Excuse my ill-temper; I'm out of sorts. But I don't think I can avail myself of your kindness.'

'Why, sir, may I ask?' And Mr. Jarman's attitude of respect and upward side-look of enquiry compelled Cunliff to ask himself the same question—'Why?' Not getting any decisive answer, he said—

'Mind you take interest, till you have repaid yourself.'

'Yes, sir; I'll mind that!' said Mr. Jarman, with a rich smile overspreading his face, which seemed to say for them both—As if he were the man to forget!

'You won't care about my being inhospitable?' said Cunliff. 'If I do decide to go, I shall start this very evening.'

'Pray don't mention it, sir!'

'Of course you noted my request?'

'Not to say anything about your journey?'

'Yes: not till you know I am off.'

'I have been, and will be, very careful.'

'Oh, it's merely this: two or three different things are tempting me into new expenses at home, and so I'm half inclined to join a military friend on a Continental tour, and economise.'

Something tickled Mr. Jarman's throat, and caused him to cough ; but he only looked red and discomposed when Mr. Cunliff stared at him, and said—

' Have wo done for the day, then ? '

' Hem ! yes. One thing I will just mention—merely that you may, when at leisure, kindly take it into consideration.'

' And that is—? ' asked Cunliff, wondering at the agent's hesitation.

' The cottages, sir—the labourers' and the workmen's cottages—' Mr. Jarman spoke in a low and confidential tono that particularly irritated the listener.

' Well ? '

' They are getting bad, and people talk, and there's some illness—not much, but a little. You'll forgive my mentioning it, sir ? '

' Of course. Quite right. I ought to have attended to this before. But I couldn't see my way to doing the business effectually. So, Jarman, I must get you to draw me up a comprehensive report, and add your own suggestions.'

' I beg pardon—I did so, and sent it to you about a year ago.'

' Did you ? Oh, very good. I can't stop now ; neither can I just now spare a sixpence. But it shall be seen to. Say so if you like.'

' And the money ? '

' Pay all into the bank, instantly. Thank you ! I wish you good-bye in case we don't meet again for the present.'

Mr. Jarman shook hands as he always did with his ' superiors,' that is, he managed by the very set of his shoulders, and the movement of his apologetic hands, to express how highly he felt the compliment, without at the same time doing aught that a bystander could have charged against him as fulsome or unmanly. Indeed, Mr. Jarman gave the impression of a gentleman who had only bent his mind to circumstances, but with a little more than ordinary determination as to the *bend*, and as to to the subdued and graceful dignity of its manifestation.

It was an odd thing that when Cunliff had got rid of his visitor, happening to entangle his feet in the crimson wool mat at the threshold of his door, he sent it flying towards the open conservatory, and had the satisfaction to hear a crash of falling pots and plants, which made him grind his teeth as

he waited for the end—but when it was over, his only comment was—

'I couldn't refuse without insulting him. Excellent man,
and thoroughly detestable!' He then shut the conservatory
door, and forgot all but his immediate cares. And in some
such fashion as this was the fabric of his thought:—

'Six hours. One gone. What on earth am I to do with
the other five? Five hours, twenty quarters, three hundred
minutes—no, I won't go into the seconds, lest I should turn
wild, and lose what little reputation for sanity this day may
leave me. And yet, in the name of Heaven, how am I to get
through five hours of this?'

To keep down the irritable fit that was taking possession of
him, he found or made things to do which in a measure engrossed him. He read a French novel—a rather exciting one
—for a few minutes, then threw it away, walked till he was
tired, and then read again, and so got rid of a couple of hours.

Then he went over his banker's book; and no worn-out
clerk of an old-fashioned private bank could have done it
more slowly, methodically, or painstakingly. It was as if he
felt he was in the mood for mistakes, and mistakes should *not*
be made. His strong will carried him successfully through.
When he had finished, he dallied a little with his cheque-book
in his hand, thinking :—

'If I draw the cheque, I needn't do any more till I know.
I must draw it close. The bank won't mind—I may when
I'm far off.'

He drew the cheque, examined it with minute care—went
twice or thrice over it as if conscious of failing attention, to
be sure that no accidental violation of form might cause embarrassment at the last moment, and was about, when satisfied, to put it in his pocket, when he remembered something,
and rang the bell.

'George, did the tailor send the things?' he said, as the
man entered.

'Yes, sir. They are in the dining-room. Would you like
to try any of them on?'

'No. Yes! Bring the waistcoat. The last fitted badly.'

The servant brought the waistcoat, and left it on the table.
When he had gone, Cunliff, without even a single glance at
the shape or quality, changed it for the one he wore; slid his
hand into a pocket inside the breast which he had specially

ordered ; and there ended the trial of the waistcoat, with entire satisfaction to the owner.

Into that coveted pocket he put the cheque ; and then, as he stood musing, his eye happened to fall on his ivory card-case, and some loose cards bearing the words—

'MR. JOHN R. CUNLIFF.'

He gathered the cards up into the case, and put that with the cheque in his new pocket.

One thought leading to another, he began to hunt for some plain cards and a less showy case ; and having found both, he dropped them carelessly into his coat-pocket. He looked at his watch and spoke aloud—

'Two hours yet ! They will pass ! But it isn't easy to believe it.'

A spasm of disgust of his own voice drove him to silence, and to the study of the map of the Continent, which hung over the back of a chair in a corner. This interested him. So much so, that he began to make memoranda in pencil, partly from the map, partly from a Murray's Handbook. And thus, and by beginning to sort the papers taken from his pocket—a week's accumulation—while casting a sort of half-comic, half-helpless look at the medley in his desk, and instituting an *auto-da-fè* with a wax taper for stake, he whiled away another hour.

Then he could no longer engage in any occupation. He could read nothing ; look at neither plants, pictures, nor photographs. He could not sit still at the table, nor stand still at the window, whither he went determined to watch the doings of the world without, while comfortably secure the world could not watch his doings within.

To and fro, like a wild beast in his cage, he moved. And, like the beast, seemed to take a desperate pleasure in feeling the bars, by always touching with his foot as he reached it— the touch being very like a kick—the skirting-board that bounded his walks.

'This infernal hot sun ! How hot it is ! ' he once exclaimed, and drew down the blinds. And then, on his next coming to the spot, he drew them up again, and with a change in his manner and aspect, ' Somehow, one always needs light in this queer world. And I'm a pretty fellow, to have the impudence to say so, just now. Well ! Only forty minutes more to the time when the postman generally makes his rounds. I can fix him to a nicety. I'll bet he's here within the thirty-seven and the forty-two—that's giving him five minutes' grace. Yes, and what'll you bet he brings you ?'

Silent, John Cunliff? Yes, he is absolutely silent.

The door opens. The servant enters on tiptoe with a confidential smirk.

'I saw Mr. Arnold coming—'

'Not at home! Didn't I say so ? ' almost gasped Cunliff below his breath.

'Yes, sir,' answered the frightened man. 'But, sir, I thought I'd run up and tell you before he spoke—'

'Quick then ! '

The servant hurried out; a little too fast, it seemed, for presently he was heard apologising. Then, as Cunliff advanced to shut the door, he met at the threshold, Mr. Arnold, with his brown, healthy vigorous face, volunteer garb, and a superb new rifle in his hand.

'Cunliff, how are you ? I found the door open—the hall empty ; so I thought I wouldn't stand on ceremony.'

'Delighted, I'm sure ! But you haven't enlisted—taken the Queen's pay for life, have you ? '

'Oh, the rifle and uniform ! Just fresh from Wimbledon— on my way home. Private match. Such an exciting one— such a scene ! We were done for when they told me to go in and lose, for to go in and win was simply impossible. Cunliff, old fellow, I did it ! I won !'

Mr. Arnold was a tall, robust man, who found it only a sort of profitable and honourable recreation to guide a lucrative business, and become a popular M.P., and who was therefore able to devote the serious business part of his life, with all its responsibilities, to volunteering and manly sports. He was the crack shot of his corps.

To Cunliff's extreme discomfort, Mr. Arnold began to give, in fuller detail, a glowing, almost boyish recital of his triumphs that morning, when he had won the superb Mountstorm rifle he carried in his hand, after a most critical and exciting contest. He finished by saying :—

'But I'll tell you what really did please me. When the thing was done—and, by Jove, I wish you had only heard the shout, and felt the grab, as I was carried off my legs, in spite of most energetic remonstrances of fist and foot—that Lord

Bullyblow, as we used to call him at school—Don't you remember him? Why you polished him off after half an hour's struggle, having previously very kindly disposed of me.'

'I remember,' said Cunliff, with a laugh.

' Well; though he and I always hated one another as boys, and though he's now a furious Tory, and I—'

' Am now a bitter Radical.'

' Perhaps—perhaps not. Well, he was one of the most uproarious. He's left his mark, I can tell you, on my right thigh, with his tremendous grip. I like that, and honour the fellow now, though I held him only as a snob before. But, I say, Cunliff, what's the matter with you ? '

Glad to see his chill responses growing effective at last, Cunliff said :—

' Then you don't know ? '

' What ? '

' That I'm off this evening to the Continent—that is, if certain preliminaries are made easy for me. Travel's expensive, and—'

' For how long ? '

' Can't say. Most likely a year or two.'

Mr. Arnold gave a low whistle, and began to look so much concerned that Cunliff wondered.

' Haven't heard worse news, old fellow, for a good while. I didn't come to tell you all this bosh. Don't you give me credit for being such an ass. No, I came to ask you, have you had enough of this kind of life, a very arduous one, I should imagine ; and are you willing, say only for the novelty of it, to try another ? '

' And that is ? '

' Politics.'

John Cunliff shook his head, and laughed, as he replied :—

' Politics don't interest me. Not now, at least. What do I care which side is in or out, when I see both sides are substantially the same ? Wait till the American war is over, and then let's see. If the North wins, there'll be a tremendous shaking of the dry bones all over the world sooner or later,* and then, perhaps—'

' And then, where shall we be if we don't prepare beforehand ? '

---

* Written during the earlier portion of the great struggle.

'Who are the *we* ? '

'The Independent Liberals.'

'Independent ? Yes, so independent that they can never, by any chance, be brought into working union against the enemy. A mere mob of sharpshooters—not a disciplined corps. However, that's not my reason for keeping aloof.'

'And what is your reason ? '

'Arnold, you know very well that, apart from yourself and a few men like you, there isn't in the whole House of Commons, just now, a particle of earnest faith in any one great or good thing, unless it be in that supremely good thing, the English gentleman, sublimated by squirearchy, and by an undying devotion to game-laws.'

'Grant all that, and then ? Do you think that if I am in earnest, and if there may be a few others also in earnest, we ought to be left alone—a prey to the Philistines ? '

'Hang it, Arnold ! you come too close. And, besides, I haven't time even to think to-day.'

'Well, it may give you a twinge or two—I hope most heartily it may—to know that I came to offer you one of the nicest boroughs in England—a place where, if you once get in, they'll never turn you out, nor make you bleed profusely, either, every time you must be re-elected.'

'Seriously ? '

'Seriously. And if you think our long-standing acquaintance justifies the request, pray pause. I'll say no more, but wait till to-morrow to see whether you go or stay. If you stay, I shall believe the House will obtain a man who can, if he pleases, delight it with his chastened and vigorous eloquence, and yet at the same time obtain and retain the hearts of the people by a breadth of sympathy rare among politicians. The want of our time is a union between the unspoiled but also untrained instincts of the many with the culture, knowledge, and experience of the few.'

It was impossible for Cunliff to listen unmoved. At first he thought his friend was speaking so wildly that he asked himself if his speech were not a bitter jest. But he knew why Arnold said these things. He saw in Cunliff not the man of to-day, but the man of the debating club, and of the solitary walk, and of the students' 'oil and lamp' of Oxford. Besides, Arnold's tone and manner, so light and conversational, could not prevent Cunliff from understanding they were the ring of true metal ; the man's heart was in his words.

Cunliff's face flushed with pleasure and surprise. It was pleasant for the moment to find that if he had forgotten what might have once been supposed to be his true self, others had not. That was his feeling just for a moment; and then a shadow swept across the face that made Arnold unconsciously turn to see if anything was passing the windows, and darkening them. But the cloud was from within, not from without. With an emotion he did not for once attempt to hide, and which, from its infrequency, was only the more striking to the observer, he said, as he shook his friend cordially by the hand:—

'You are partial. I do not deserve—I could not justify that—that which you say of me. Even the little good you knew of me at college, and which you remember so generously now, has, I fear, died out. The soil was poor, perhaps, and so the showy sprouts have dwindled in the sun. However, that I do value your friendship and good opinion, let me show by saying I will do what you ask.'

'You will? You'll think it over? Even now, before you commit yourself to anything else?'

'I will.'

'Thanks! Good-bye! Stop, Cunliff; do you know people are talking about you and Mrs. Rhys?'

'Damn people!'

'Hem!'

'Let them talk—the idiots!'

'That's very well for you, but—'

'Of course; I didn't mean to be selfish.'

'Of course, of course. And I know there's nothing in it, or I should fight shy of this talk.'

'Nothing in the world. I am bound to say that for the lady's sake.'

The men looked at each other, shook hands, and parted.

'He'll know all, I suppose, to-morrow,' was Cunliff's secret comment on this. 'Pleasant!'

He looked at his watch and started. Only ten minutes now. Ten. The postman was due in that time. Could he do better than spend the brief interval in weighing Arnold's proposal? He felt more disturbed about it than he could quite understand. He took up his waiting place. It was the top step of the conservatory. From thence his eye commanded just a few yards of the open space across which the postman must pass. He never moved till he saw the man, but leaned his back against the lintel of the door, and drew out a cigar, intending to smoke it, as he often did, in this place; but he never lighted it. He only, in the intervals of his painful thought, pierced it with his penknife—stopped, and then again, after a while, resumed the work.

It was a trying time. What he had undertaken to do involved a retrospect inexpressibly painful and humiliating. His instinct had only too accurately warned him to keep off such themes altogether. And the future? Suppose he were even yet to draw back, and use this very election business as an instrument of extrication? Did he feel the spring, the energy, the clearness of aim and faith that would give him reasonable hope of success? No, no, no! He doubted everything, and most of all, himself. He doubted success, even if that which is called so were obtained. Doubted, therefore, whether he ought to succeed; doubted the way he was going, but also doubted whether it would be any gain to change the direction; and if it were, he still doubted whether the gain would be worth the inevitable struggle. The fatalism of the time in English politics and in English society had in John Cunliff an adherent whose obedience to the cause was only equalled by his contempt for it.

What fine things Mr. Arnold had managed to say of him, without seeming to be insincere! But Arnold was a fine fellow, and saw in his friends what he wanted to see, and had in himself. But there might be grains of truth in the appreciation. Was that all to go for nothing! Could it be—and Cunliff's face changed a little at the thought, and looked decidedly belligerent; could it be that Arnold knew more than he had chosen to reveal? Was there a special—and so to say friendly meaning in this visit, which, if fully understood, would explain such unusual demonstrativeness of word and wish? Was he consciously interposing at a critical time? Then, with an effort to forget Mrs. Rhys, and reverting to Arnold's words, Cunliff tried in a sort of abstract way to look at himself, and judge whether it was likely he could, if he tried, fulfil such expectations.

Finding little satisfaction in this, he passed, as by an effort of will, to a different theme—what other men thought of him and his 'tastes.' These were said to be exquisite. And of himself there had been circulated the remark, that to make an idle gentleman the world had lost a true artist. If he remembered these things now, it was only to ask himself why there seemed ever such a principle of death in his tastes, as well as in the gifts for which Arnold gave him credit. Was he, then, the man to teach the world how to live? Absurd! If, indeed, the answer he expected every instant was unfavourable, then— An almost audible laugh burst from him—bitter and self-mocking—and distorted his face, as he saw the sudden exposure of his logic. He could not while he looked one way; he could when he looked the other! And though he didn't like to confess it, he saw that, after all, that solution might be true, however uncomplimentary.

Very well: he accepted it. If she—but that hypothesis needn't be pursued farther; for he was then committed to her by all the ties of honour. But if the answer were not of the kind he had—perhaps absurdly—anticipated, then—

'There he is!' he ejaculated aloud, and there was an end to all speculation. The blood came in a rush to his face and brow, as he turned back into the room to meet his man with the letter, if letter there were. There was time enough for an answer—that he knew. He knew, also, that the lady was so occupied as to be sure to have been at home. If there were then no letter, the silence would mean—what? He could not tell—not just then.

Aware of his own agitation, and of the violent heat in his brain, he paused, and quelled it so thoroughly, that by the time the servant entered the face was not merely pale, but so unnaturally white, that the man fancied his master was ill, and forgot what had brought him.

'Are you ill, sir?'

'No!' was the stern reply. 'George, why the devil do the police allow those vagabonds to squat all the day on the seat there, just in front of my window? Have them rooted out.'

So saying, he held out his hand to take the letter from the tray, and only thus did George know that his master was conscious there was a letter. When the servant had gone, and not till then, did Cunliff open the delicate pink envelope, and turn suddenly with his back to the light that he might better gaze on that which he had drawn forth, a card portrait.

'Only this!' his face seemed doubtfully to ask, and then its sudden illumination told all the rest. He understood it well enough. Presently he was in a cab, the horse galloping under the excitement of the cabman's whip, who knew he had got the right kind of fare, when told to drive fast, and to go to ' Coutts's Bank.'

CHAPTER III.

A LONDON TWILIGHT.

LONDON is not beautiful, that must be owned; neither is it grand or picturesque. It is not even convenient. The ' practical ' men to whom we are indebted for it have not yet carried out in architecture the rule they enforce so vigorously in their ordinary transactions; they have not found out and discharged the incompetent—themselves.

But even this gigantic medley of buildings loses its hardness, ugliness, and incongruity when twilight hangs like a veil over the whole. Inexpressibly tender then steal forth a thousand objects, animate and inanimate, and we can gaze on and question them, as if suddenly set down in a new world.

That twilight lull is now existing in all its force and beauty for John Cunliff. The sky above, from which the sun has quite vanished, seems yet full of his presence. Wanderers gaze on the fine opal tint with a sense of its pleasantness to the eye; and as they gaze a star appears in it, the first and only one, sparkling, palpitating, wondrously beautiful. Below, at the same time, the artificial lights of the park begin to appear in bright succession among the trees, and Cunliff takes an almost personal interest in the movements of the unseen man who kindles them. The trees themselves, grouped in darkening masses, but forced forwards at intervals into publicity by the lamps, take new shapes; suggest unfamiliar glades and coverts even to those who know them best; and lend a kind of romantic background to the persons walking in the road, and to the carriages that roll dreamily along. The never-ceasing roar of the three millions of people who make up what we call London comes to Cunliff's ear as if some dim thought of the hour possessed, quite unconsciously, for a single instant—for a passing mood, the whole of that diverse mass of humanity.

Hark! It is the clock of the palace tower that strikes with its deep musical and prolonged boom. Before it ceases there

comes faintly borne upon the wind, which changes for a
moment its direction, the answering voice of the bell of St.
Paul's. And then, short and menacing, from the farthest
City bounds eastward, comes, also borne upon the breeze, the
sounds of the Tower cannon. And to the fancy, the three
structures seem to take gigantic life, and to cover London
with their far-stretching arms,—religion from Wren's magnificent dome brooding in the centre over all, and having the
law and the sword, representatives of existing civilisation, on
either hand, keeping watch and ward, within sight alike of the
city and of the distant boundaries.

Amid his final preparations John Cunliff comes every now
and then to the window to look out. His own thoughts are
dream-like as the scene; but with no twilight lull, no twilight
peace for their atmosphere.

He hardly seems the same man that we have seen so much
of during the last few hours. A sense of spiritual intoxication
seems to expand his whole being; though it is so controlled
by the Englishman's habitual reticence as to be perceptible
only in the softened tone of the voice when he speaks to
his servant; in the springy yet cautious step; and in the
sparkle of the eye, which, as it glances from time to time
towards the brilliant star in the heavens, appears to borrow
an unearthly lustre.

He answers now such letters as must be answered. He
puts off engagements; declines invitations—and always on the
same plea, his foreign tour. When they are completed, and
he is about to send them to the post, he is struck by a sense
of the ridiculousness of his position if aught should affect his
purposed journey. What if he had made a mistake, after all?
Nonsense! he knew better than that. There should be no
mistakes. But he might as well retain the letters to the last.
So he put them into his pocket, and in order to make occupation, finished the sorting of his desk papers, by selecting
the few he cared to preserve and by burning the rest.

While thus engaged he came upon a single leaf of manuscript in his own handwriting, and which yet seemed fresh—
as if unseen for many years. As he gazed on it his thoughts
were carried back to an altogether different and long-forgotten
world of daily aims and occupations. He could hardly credit,
for the moment, it was he who had written, when about
eighteen or nineteen years old, the verses before him.

STUDIES.　No. I.

Black boughs at night, just arching o'er
　A little hall themselves have made ;
Where spectral leaves upon the floor
　Dance through the light, dance through the shade ;
While in the branch-built roof the Moon,
　Great world to little, holds the lamp.
The soft light wakes the toad too soon ;
　He eyes askance the leafy tramp,
Until his brightening eyeball sees
　The silvery slime-track of the snail ;
Then squats ; to take him at his ease,
　And hold him linked by his own trail.
He squats ; and heaves his glistening sides,
　And sensual throat in stifled mirth.
The adder sees, and rears, and glides :
　The red worm lengthens from the earth.

Cunliff paused a long time over this paper, looking at it, and not seeing it, but seeing instead the world beyond it, of his vigorous and manly college life, of which these verses were a mere passing mood.

'It's well I had the sense not to go to No. 2,' he said at last as he carefully put by the leaf.

He would go out and freshen his blood, and shake off these morbid tendencies.

He went out. The first thing he saw through the increasing dusk was the family of vagrants on the seat, whom he had ordered to be driven off. He felt in a different mood now. Poor wretches, how desolate they all looked ! Had they really no home ? Would they sleep there ? Were they very hungry ? He wished they would ask him for help. He couldn't go to them, it looked so ostentatious—just as if he were on a philanthropic hunt.

While these thoughts ran through his mind he was able, unnoticed, to see something which touched him keenly. The family seemed to have been waiting for the return of a boy, who had been sent somewhere—perhaps to beg. The boy came. Cunliff saw, from the angry gesture of the father, and the pleading attitude of the mother, that the boy's honesty was suspected. The man searched his pockets. Cunliff could not refuse the inviting shelter of a tree-trunk, which enabled him to get close to them, and see the end of the search. The little pockets were all turned out, and from the last of them emerged a hard, dirty crust of bread. The boy burst into tears as he gave up his hidden treasure. Cunliff's heart seemed to give him a sense of stifling, as he thought of the depth of misery the incident revealed.

He ought to stop and go a little into their history, before doing aught else, he knew that. But he was in no mood to embark in such mental adventures ; so he slipped the biggest coin he could feel in his pocket—a crown piece—into the man's hands, and said,

'Take this, my friend, and get yourself and family something to eat. Good-night.'

He heard no thanks, no loud ' God bless you, sir ! ' follow him. He only heard the woman's passionate cry and the man's terrible silence.

He passed on and soon forgot the affair. He wandered about, neither knowing nor caring whither. He revelled in dreams that were only the more delicious that no human being could guess at their existence, even though many might wonder what caused him to stroll to and fro so aimlessly.

Still he wandered—still he dreamed. He was at one moment so lost in thought, that when a cab came rushing past, at the turning of a corner, and the cabman seeing he had muddied the gentleman's overcoat, grew angry and abusive, Cunliff only laughed, and said to him,

' I assure you, I didn't intend to do it.'

He was to be roused from this amiable mood and these pleasant dreams. As he approached his home, thinking it must be dinner-time, he saw his man standing outside, bare-headed, looking anxiously in every direction but the right one.

' He wants me. There's something wrong.'

That was Cunliff's instant thought. An instinct warned him that all his glittering bubbles were about to burst. He walked fast, then faster, though still preserving that personal dignity of bearing which was a part of him—which he valued —and which he, a little too artificially, perhaps, always maintained.

' There's a man in the hall, sir. He brought this letter, and said he was told to wait till he knew you had got it.'

' Very well.' He took the letter. ' Keep the man five minutes. Then, if I do not ring, let him go. Give him a shilling.'

Cunliff went slowly up-stairs with his unopened letter; waited patiently while the servant lighted the lamp; saw the man close the door after himself as he went out, and then he read this:—

' Five o'clock.

' I have this moment received a letter from R., and copy for you a few sentences:—

' " I have had a letter from a very aged maiden aunt, who tells me that some one, whose name she is not at liberty to mention, has told her that you and a Mr. Cunliff are very often together; constantly meeting at the same places; and that she believes you are to meet him at Lady Sellon's country-house; and, in a word, that she wishes me to hurry home and judge for myself. I shall hurry home undoubtedly, but for any reason rather than the one suggested in my aunt's letter. She is an exceedingly old woman—nearly ninety— and I let her say what no one else, I think, would dare to say to me. But if you want, my dear Catherine, to know what I think, I say then go to Lady Sellon's by all means if you wish to go, whether Mr. Cunliff or Mr. anybody else is, or is not, to be also there. My trust, dearest, is in you; not in the place you happen to be at or in the men into whose society you may happen to be thrown. I do trust you, darling, with all my heart and soul. Old as I am, I am young enough in heart to feel the tenderest affection for you. One that will never fail you while you do not wish it to fail. God bless and preserve you, my own ever dear, dear wife. Within three days I shall be with you."

' Cunliff! do you read this as I read it with streaming eyes, with a sense of shame that can never, never fade away, yet with a cry of transport to God that we are awakened in time ?

' Farewell for ever and ever ! You will not, I am sure, wish to violate this my only and parting injunction.

' I reopen this to say, do not blame yourself alone. God bless you ! Again, farewell ! '

When Cunliff had read to the last word, and he read very slowly, he raised with a painful gesture his long-bent head. Finding the light of the lamp too brilliant, he stretched forth his hand to moderate it, and, whether intentionally or accidentally, put out the light.

CHAPTER IV

EXHALATIONS OF THE DAWN.

AT the age of twenty-two John Cunliff had quitted, as he had come to, the University under peculiar circumstances. He had entered it as a lonely, studious, friendless youth, not long after the death of a beloved mother; and when he was dependent upon a harsh and unsympathetic father, who kept him on the shortest possible allowance; scarcely ever saw him or wrote to him, and seemed to think it not of the slightest importance whether his son studied or no. Thus he entered the University. When he quitted it he was surrounded by troops of friends, including some of the very best men of his college, who exulted in the honours he had won, and predicted what they were to lead to; his father was dead, and had left behind him an estate of two thousand a year, without a sixpence of mortgage upon it; and another relative having also died, young John Cunliff became the presumptive heir to a baronetcy, and a property of at least six times the value of his paternal estate.

That was his position when suddenly launched into the great world of society, with appetites keen as youth and health and the associations of a rich and cultivated nature could make them; and where he found glad faces and seemingly warm hearts welcoming him on every side. Such a man, with good birth, manly and attractive person, eloquent tongue, a spiritual something not easy to describe in the general style of his conversation, and with a kind of stately chivalrousness in his peculiarly gentle demeanour to women, became the cynosure of female eyes; and made the face of many a dowager grow almost ideal as she received the answer to her eager question, 'Oh yes, it was quite true—two thousand a year, unencumbered, and with some prospect in the distance of nearly thirteen thousand a year, and a baronetcy!'

He entered London in the first flush of his University successes. Yet it was remarkable how seldom he spoke of them—how unwilling he was to be spoken to on the subject. The Alps he had climbed only showed him the greater Alps yet to be surmounted. He was modest, earnest, hopeful; and in heart and soul the student and the scholar.

Thus, at least, he seemed to his few intimate associates at the time of his introduction to London society; perhaps even to himself. But there was another and still more remarkable trait of his character that must not be passed over. Though no one ever heard him speak in the language of Utopia, it was impossible to listen to him when engaged in any earnest discussion on political or social subjects, without seeing perpetually bright gleams of ideal light and Utopian fancy flashing across the arid regions of fact and figure; and suggesting that the young John Cunliff had gone far and wide in his wanderings after those central truths which promised to transform the world. Yes; he was then young enough and hopeful enough to believe in the divinity of his own instincts, which seemed ever to whisper to him. 'Go forth, thou, too, to the fight! Error, and vice, and crime, and misery are *not* the inevitable lot of man—they are only the inevitable lot of man's unorganised—half-barbaric past. It is habit, precedent for precedent's sake, and the slavishness of soul these two create—that sustain the existing evil of things. Destroy *them*—build on new foundations a place for the aspiring soul to labour—and, then, indeed, shalt thou see this world become a temple fit for the gods, with men only less than gods inhabiting it.'

Perhaps it was the very magnitude of his secret desires, and the sense of unreality which exaggerated expectations and high-flown visions inevitably bring home to us, that sobered him in his communications with others, and suggested the propriety of due pause and preparation. The fashionable world soon settled all the rest. It did not treat his dreams with ridicule, for he took care it should know nothing about them. Silently, day by day, he measured its forces for resistance on the one hand, and its many seductive attractions, on the other, for those who are content simply to enjoy and ask no inconvenient questions, till he gave up the whole problem with a bitter laugh at his own absurdity; and then—why then, the world went on as usual in its own serene course, knowing nothing of its noble victory, or of the fresh victim offered at its shrine.

Thus speedily died out John Cunliff's notions of the possibility of his becoming a sort of literary prophet of a new social era, and with it went more than he or the world could have easily suspected.

What remained ? He would, at least, play the part of an English gentleman. Unbounded was Cunliff's faith in that character. Nor was he, perhaps, destitute of a strong hidden belief that he was himself, so far as natural powers and tendencies were concerned, no unfit representative of its truthfulness, high personal sense of honour, magnanimity, fortitude to bear, reticence in speech, dignity in serious act; and all these springing from the belief in, and feeling for, the greatness of the English name, history, and destiny, as individualised in the said English gentleman ; with his nature deepened and heightened by the reflex of the religious sentiments that had permeated, at critical periods, his family's historical life. A character that, at its best, needs only the flower or crown of all—chivalrous abnegation in the weightier things of life—to become the exemplar of the world ; but which, at its worst, becomes one of the most insufferable specimens of humanity : egotistic, priggish, hard, cruel.

This dream shared, to a certain extent, the fate of the other. It may be very inconvenient, but certainly the scheme of Providence does not consist in giving us a complete nature with many separate parts which we may divide as we please— select, reject, or accept as we please—and so John Cunliff found, when, after a little coy dalliance, he threw himself with open hands and heart into the world's arms, as represented first by society at large, and then by some of its baser elements. In a word, society—which arrogates to itself the idea that it is the very flower of all civilisation—did not know how, or did not even care to try, to appeal to the purer and nobler elements in the young man's nature ; which, if received in a natural and wholesome atmosphere, would have added new lustre to itself. And as to what it did offer of material or sensual enjoyment, John Cunliff preferred to go elsewhere ; where he could, without any sort of social hypocrisy, please himself in his own way, and run riot to his soul's utmost content.

It was not long before John Cunliff's appearance at public and private receptions became less and less frequent ; and when he did come his presence ceased to create the old flutter, for the prophet had spoken—he was not inclined to marry.

Thus eight years passed away, each one of them leaving its own special mark upon him, till he became little better than

an habitual sensualist, a bad landlord, an idle and utterly
useless man ; and with little of the true gentleman remaining
below the surface or shell.

Happily for him his pleasures were to a certain extent
antagonistic. Poetic instincts of purity survived in him
through all his worst degradations ; and made him feel at
times as keenly the true character of his life, and shrink back
from it with a loathing as intense, as if some powerful religious
belief had suddenly risen within him, and thrown his whole
nature into a kind of revolutionary convulsion. What religious
feeling might have done for him Cunliff knew not, and never
even dreamed of asking. What his poetic tastes left him he
had little pleasure to see.

At thirty years of age he already felt as if his capacity for
enjoyment (once so boundless) needed to be economised
thenceforth. He therefore became thrifty in his pleasures ;
restricted in his range of vision ; ceased to see always so
many beautiful and attractive forms flitting before him, as
parts of an infinitely extending aërial perspective, and fixed
on one of them. To do him justice, John Cunliff's love for
Mrs. Rhys was certainly the best feature in a continuously
bad life, if we may speak so paradoxically. It was only since
he knew her that he had given the first real check to desires
and tastes perpetually wandering, under obedience to no law
but that of an unceasing thirst for pleasure.

<hr>

CHAPTER V

PASSING GLIMPSES.

DURING the day following that on which our story begins, a
gentleman got out at Shrewsbury from the train going towards London, and immediately took his place in the down
train for Wales, thus retracing the way he had come.

The official, as he looked at the ticket given up to him,
wondered why the gentleman was sacrificing so coolly, over a
ride of a few miles from his country seat, a ticket taken for
London. He appeared to be well known on the platform.
Porters touched their caps as he passed. The guard of the
Welsh train put him into a compartment by himself, and
locked the door.

The traveller shut down both windows, and threw himself into a corner with the air of a man worn out with fatigue and anxiety, and who felt he could now enjoy his miseries in his own savage fashion. He threw his feet with their muddy boots on the opposite seat; opened the breast of his coat, and drew a long deep breath; flung his hat to the farthest corner; and then sat still for a minute or two, staring at the flying trees.

'What a superstitious ass I grow! I put it all on the question whether I should or should not reach Shrewsbury in time for this train. I did reach; and here I am, going, not to London, but—whither? To the devil, most likely. With all my heart. And I had better, now that I am in for it, entitle myself to his most respectful consideration.'

Thus ran the first turbid current of thought; the actual evil of the speaker's heart consciously exaggerated in his bitter irony.

By-and-by he became quieter, leaned back his head, closed his eyes, and for a few minutes seemed to sleep; but suddenly he started up, and stared as if he saw some horrible thing; then laughed, struck out his arms with a sort of gymnastic movement, till he was thoroughly wakened from his drowsiness, when he sat down again, as still, and holding as stern a command over himself, as if not a single seat in the carriage had been vacant.

He was soon interrupted by the guard, who said, in a low, deferential tone—

'Very sorry, sir, but we've no room elsewhere. Quite a gentleman, and—'

'Now then!' shouted the station-master; the guard sounded his whistle; the ponderous train began slowly to move; and then, leaping in so as to compel the gentleman inside to draw up his limbs in an undignified hurry and posture, came the new passenger. The door was banged to. They were off.

'I really beg pardon,' began the new-comer, out of breath. 'Rather a sudden entrance. We had a run for it. I didn't know anybody was inside. I—'

Here he stopped abruptly, noticing that no kind of response was forthcoming; stopped; took one steady look at the corner where the silent person sat, and said aloud, with inimitable coolness and enjoyment—

' Really! I am sure I thought I saw a gentleman somewhere ! '

And then, as if entirely convinced of his mistake, took out
a cigar ; lighted it without gesture or apology, which obviously on his theory could not be required ; opened the
window on his own side, and was about to do the same on
the other, when the silent gentleman found it necessary to
interfere with a decided lift of the hand, and a—

' No ; I thank you ! '

Again the new comer looked, and his look was answered
with interest. And then, before either knew what he was
going to say, both broke out into a laugh.

Five minutes later the two young men were engaged in
more genial talk than either of them had ever had before on
so slight an acquaintance.

The silent traveller had felt attracted by the intruder's face
even in spite of his boorish reception of him. Subsequent
glances more than confirmed the impression. He thought he
had never before seen so handsome a countenance to be so de-
void of pretension and conceit. There was nothing scholarly
about it, nothing intellectually noble ; just as there was
nothing sensual, nothing mean. It was manly. It was
picturesque, with its short, thick, curling, chestnut-coloured
hair. But its great charm was an indescribable healthiness
and happiness of expression, a perfect sunniness of content,
that obviously did not spring from any temporary cause—
recent good-fortune, or recent gratification of long-cherished
desires,—but seemed to be native. The very sound of his
laugh—low, joyous, but quite undemonstrative—would, of
itself, if you shut your eyes, tell you the kind of man,—a man
who needed only to be. In person he was of middle height ;
shorter and stouter than his fellow-traveller ; easy, graceful,
and unembarrassed in manner, though not, to the critical eye
of his neighbour, polished. That personage set him down as
a gentleman farmer, and so he proved to be. He was from
Kent, which he soon gave his companion to understand was
the finest county in England.

' Yet you do find a change desirable sometimes ? ' was remarked to him.

' Change, sir ? '

The young farmer laughed ; glanced at the scenery they
were passing, shrugged his shoulders, and looked at his com-

panion with eyes brimful of merriment at the idea of his needing a change.

'I had something to do to make up my mind to come away, I can tell you!' he said. 'I haven't been away before at this time of the year since I was a boy.'

He had a peculiar mode of speaking, in brief, quickly-uttered sentences, with a meditative pause between each, and the words that came after the pause were often rather a continuation of his silent thoughts than of what he had previously said.

'Why, it's just in its glory! No rains over there yet. Roads cracking in the sun. Hop-pickers pouring in night and day. Ditches nice and dry for 'em. Corn-fields up to the hedge-tops. Nights pretty well light all through ; and so hot with gipsy fires, and so noisy with corncrakes and crickets, and with apples falling crash, crash, on the cabbage-leaves, you can hardly sleep. No, sir, I haven't come out of Kent, in September, for the sake of a change.'

'Nor for health, I presume ? '

'Not exactly.'

'Business, perhaps ? ' suggested the other, tempted on by the farmer's own interest in, and liking for, the conversation.

'Yes ; and not very pleasant business.'

'Indeed ! '

'I have a cousin in Wales—a small farmer with forty acres of thin mountain land—only rents it—been as poor as a rat all his life. Six months ago he came into a legacy of nigh seven thousand pounds, and now I've got to tell him it's all moonshine.'

'How's that ? '

'Do you happen to know the firm of Morgan and Garnet, curriers, Bermondsey ? '

'No,' said the other, with a slight smile.

'Well, Morgan, a Welshman, who made that business, retired twenty years ago from the management, but kept his capital, twenty-seven thousand pounds, in the concern. He died last April, and we, who were his nearest relatives—there's four of us in all—thought we had come in for a good thing. I bought a hunter—a prime bit of blood—on the strength of it. Luckily, I'm not obliged to sell him. Two days ago, when I was expecting a summons as executor to meet the partner, and receive the transfer of the capital so long invested, I got, instead, a letter inviting me to a meeting of creditors. Didn't my lawyer go off in a terrible hurry! 'Twas all true. Two-and sixpence in the pound for the ordinary creditors—nothing to the dead man's relations, for he had been a partner, and his capital long since lost—which he didn't know or suspect.'

'Sharp practice—eh? to keep you all in ignorance so long.'

'That's what I can't get over. For myself I don't care; but I never felt so cut up for anybody as I do for my cousin Elias Morgan. He's rough, but true as steel. One in a thousand, sir.'

'But as he has never, it seems, been other than poor, won't he soon get over it?'

'He may. It's a cruel business. Just one bit of sunshine in his whole hard life to show him how gloomy it had been, and then everything back in the old state.'

The listener's look was sympathetic, but he said nothing, and the young farmer went on :—

'I'm afraid I made matters worse by being over-sanguine. When the rascals—who wanted, they tell me, to inveigle another partner—kept up such a show of prosperity as to pay us a year's profit, eight hundred pounds—two hundred apiece—which had been for some time due, and when my lawyer said it was a most respectable firm, is it very wonderful I was taken in? So when I sent Elias his two hundred, I congratulated him on his being easy for life, and I told him I should soon have to send him all the rest, nearly seven thousand pounds.'

'Then he may be incurring liabilities on the strength of it?'

'That's what I'm afraid of. He was so cautious as to write me back a special letter of enquiry. It ought to have warned me. It didn't. I told him the money was as safe as in the bank.'

'Hem! Very awkward that! He may be drawing cheques on this ideal bank in the shape of orders for goods, that are really promises to pay.'

'Well, it's done, and can't be undone. If he's very hard upon me, I must grin and bear it, as one of my ploughmen says when he is pulled up suddenly by a big root or stone in the furrow.'

'Then you are equally disappointed?'

'Oh, it won't hurt me.'

'Are you so very rich?' was the query in the other's eye.

' It won't hurt me,' he repeated. ' In fact, I've got a hunter out of it. I shouldn't have had him else. Now I mean to keep him. Mine's only a bit of a place ; but it was my father's, and my grandfather's, and, I believe, my great-grandfather's, but I won't speak to that. A hundred and nine acres. That's all. But such land that I'd rather have an acre of it than ten of this foul stuff we're passing.'

The companion looked out with a curious expression of interest at the land they were 'passing,' but said nothing, perhaps through the stoppage of the train.

' We're in for more company,' said the farmer. ' Shouldn't you set this down for a doctor ? '

A gentleman with splashed leggings came and took his place in the seat nearest the platform, and turned round instantly to speak to some one who had accompanied him. His first words made the farmer smile significantly :—

' You'll keep her quiet, my man, and bo careful about the medicine.'

' Ay,' answered a gruff voice, while eight thick dirty fingers hooked themselves over the door. The platform was too low for the face of their owner to be seen by those farther in the carriage. Only the top of a grizzled rough head was visible to them ; and sometimes a bit of red forehead full of wrinkles ; and a pair of eyes bleared and bloodshot, and wildly intent on every word that fell from the doctor's mouth.

' Keep the children away as much as you can, you know.'

'Ay ! And the light stuff in the queer-shaped bottle to-night, aint it ? and the dark in the morning ? '

The doctor nodded.

There seemed to be no more to say ; but the fingers still clung obstinately to the door ; and the bleared eyes still looked up into the doctor's face. There was apparently something more he wished to ask, and which the doctor did not wish to hear. He looked up and down the platform. The man's eyes followed the direction of his, and the grizzled head turned listening intently to the puffing of the engine.

Suddenly a broad pair of shoulders filled up the window. The man had set his foot on the step, his arms over the door, and brought his face close to the doctor's. A repulsive-looking face, with a square chin covered by a prickly beard of a week's growth. He said something which the others could not hear, but they saw the doctor look boldly at the face, and heard him say—

' Well, and if it should be so ?   We are doing our best.   If
a ter all it should be so, you are a man, arn't you, and a father ?
You know, you musn't forget that.'

The arms uncrossed with a heavy, awkward haste.   The
fingers hooked themselves on the door again.   The grim face
and unfragrant breath were gone.   Then the fingers also disappeared, and the window was cleared.

The doctor unthinkingly put out his head to look after him,
but drew it in quickly, and kicked his carpet-bag farther under
the seat.

In a minute the fingers were again on the door, and the face
came close up.

' Doctor ! '

' Well, my man ? '

' Jarman said as he was a comin' over to-morrow, agin, for
the rent. If she's better, by the Lord ! I'll see him, and speak
him civil.   I will, Doctor ; but if it's *that*—'

The thick voice died off into hard breathings.   The eyes
looked round the carriage at the two quiet occupants on the
farther seats, encountering their eyes without seeming to see
them.

' If *it's that*, Doctor,' continued the thick voice, ' keep him
off o' my place, will you ? Keep him wide of it, Doctor !   He
was there o' Thursday, and that set her off.   She was by herself, and he went on at her ever so long, and when he was
gone, she skirled out with a silly laugh, and's been so ever
since.'

' Be off, my man !   The train s moving,' said the Doctor.

' Jarman said as the landlord's kep' writin' for the money.
If he writes agin, tell Jarman—will you, Doctor ?—to write
back and say his d—d rotten pig-styes can't, and never won't
be paid for in flesh and blood and money too.   When we can
live in 'em, instead o' dying in 'em, p'raps we can pay for 'em ;
but we can't pay house-rent and coffin-rent, too, all the year
round !   What do they mean by a saying we don't pay ?   By
the Lord ! we pay that as they'll be made to give us the
receipts on, some day. Yes, yes ! good-bye, Doctor.   God
bless yer ! '

The Doctor turned to look at his fellow-travellers.   One
was gazing out of the window ; the other, with a face full of
sympathy, seemed to ask the same question that the miserable husband had been determined to have answered.

But the Doctor, though reticent as to his opinion of the woman's chance, could not help showing something of that which was in his thoughts. He explained to the young farmer that he had been called in to a bad case of typhus; and that it was a chance if he saved the poor woman's life, who had seven miserable children dependent on her, and on that poor desperate creature, her husband.

'Nice thing, isn't it,' he asked, 'for a gentleman to keep cottages on his estate that breed pestilence and death; and then himself spend every shilling he can wring out of his tenants in all the enjoyments of society?'

'And is this his land we are passing?' demanded the young farmer, with quite new interest in the state of the soil.

'It is.'

'What's his name?'

Before it was possible for the surgeon to reply, the gentleman in the corner turned from the window full faced upon the surgeon, who then first saw him, slightly coloured, hemmed, and took advantage of the slackening of the train to cry out, with his head at the window—

'Here—porter!'

'What may be the gentleman's name?' again asked the unsuspicious querist.

'Cunliff!' was the stern reply from the far corner—the occupant of which again exchanged glances with the embarrassed, but not exactly ashamed surgeon, who, lifting his hat, said—

'I wish you good-morning, sir!'

'Good-morning!' said the gentleman, as he responded to the courtesy with a menacing expression of face.

The young farmer followed with his eye the retreating form of the surgeon along the platform, then turned to ask more about this Mr. Cunliff and his land; but his new acquaintance was settling himself for a nap, and saying with a half-smile, as he shut his eyes—

'Excuse me; I scarcely slept last night.'

And thus suddenly broke up the pleasant relations that had been growing between the two young men. This was much to the regret of the Kentish farmer, whose freshness of feeling, contrasted with his very limited intellectual experience, had caused him to look on his companion as a marvel of knowledge and eloquence; and to listen with so much earnestness,

faith, and admiration visible in his large, bright, joyous eyes,
as to give new zest to the operations of the speaker's own
mind; and apparently he had felt in return a counter influence working on himself. However, it now seemed all to go
for nothing. Hardly a word more was said till the train
stopped at Llansaintfraid; and there, when they both found
themselves standing on the platform, about to separate most
likely for ever, with the rain making so great a noise on the
glass overhead that they could scarcely hear each other speak,
it seemed a question for the moment whether they wouldn't
even part as absolute strangers. But the young farmer, even
though a little hurt, could not help putting out his hand; and
it was grasped warmly just for a moment; then something
was muttered about hoping to have the pleasure of meeting
again somewhere or other, and the two separated—the one
to go, as he said, to ' the Town,' the other to take the 'Major's
coach' just about to start for Dolgarrog. They separated, not
even knowing each other's name.

The young farmer paused on the platform just for a moment,
looking after his late companion; and seeing he was mistaking his way, ran after him, and shouted—

' To the left ! '

Thanks ! ' was shouted back, and then they were rapidly
lost to each other in the distance.

———

CHAPTER VI.

OVER CRIBA BAN.

To the farmer's surprise and vexation the coach was full.
While he had been thinking of his late acquaintance, and
obeying the impulse to set him right on his road, other
passengers had hurried to secure the seats, and the train
being a heavy one, the Dolgarrog portion of it soon filled the
coach.   There was a general outcry among the Welsh
passengers to have him up or in somehow; but the driver, a
gentleman who owned the coach, said it was quite impossible;
they were overloaded already.

The disappointed man looked black, and growled aloud—

' Pleasant voyage ! ' and hurried back out of the rain to the
platform, from whence he went off to the town, which is at

some distance, fearing he would be obliged to stay over
Sunday, when the coach did not run. Before entering the
inn-yard he was overtaken by a man who had been hanging
about the station till the coach was out of the way, and then
hearing of the gentleman left behind, had run after him. He
had come from Dolgarrog with a party of tourists, and was
going back when the horses had rested.

'How much ? '

'Five shillings, sir.'

'All right. Quick as you can.'

About half an hour later, and while the farmer, whose
spirits had sunk a little, was trying to congratulate himself as
he sat before a fine cold sirloin of beef and a preposterously
tall glass of ale, on his good fortune—'so economical, too ! '—
the driver re-entered.

' Wild night, sir, to cross the mountains. No idea of stopping here, I suppose ?'

'Certainly not. Are you ready ? '

'Would you mind, sir, a gentlemen going with you ? '

'Oh, I see. As I'm not to be got rid of, I must have a
companion. And he pays five shillings too, eh ? '

The driver laughed.

'Who is he ? '

The driver handed a card, on which there was writing in
pencil. It was a neat, almost elegant hand, though that
perhaps was in a measure due to the care and minuteness
compelled by the limited space.

'Mr. John Rymer begs to apologise for the liberty he is
taking, and trusts the occasion will be his sufficient excuse.
He is most anxious to reach Dolgarrog to-night ; but there
are no horses obtainable either at the other inn or at this. A
share in the return carriage, which has been pre-engaged by
the gentleman he has the honour to address, is therefore his
only resource. May he then venture to ask so great a
favour ? '

'Give my compliments—Mr. Robert Chamberlayne's com-
pliments—to Mr. Rymer, and say I shall be glad of his
company. Perhaps he will like to come in here. I shall soon
be ready.' Then, as the driver moved off, he called after him :
'I say. no more passengers ! It'll be "No" next time, even
if, as I expect, you bring me a benighted woman and child ! '

The driver only laughed his answer, and went out.

A minute later the gentleman came in. How shall we paint the expression of the two faces? The annoyance—almost shame—on Mr. Rymer's, to be so unexpectedly caught and exposed in his secretive arrangements; the genial, broadening mirth on the other's, who had risen to receive his visitor, and could not help exclaiming—

'Hang me, if I didn't think so!'

Mr. Rymer, with admirable self-possession, began to explain. And then Mr. Chamberlayne could no longer restrain himself within the bounds of courtesy and good-breeding. He laid down knife and fork and roared again.

Mr. Rymer joined in the laugh, or tried to do so, then he said—

'But I thought you were gone by the coach?'

'It was full; they wouldn't have me.'

'I see. How absurd! How very ridiculous! But I asked the man if it was a gentleman in a dark overcoat, and he said, No.'

'I wore two—they're very thin—and I was getting so hot with my walk that I took one off before the man came up to me. So you also are going to Dolgarrog? How very odd!'

'Very! And how fortunate we should thus meet again!'

'Yes; but why the deuce didn't you think so before?' was the question in Chamberlayne's expressive eyes. Rymer didn't choose to notice them. They got into the coach and were driven off.

'I assure you,' said Mr. Rymer, after a pause, 'I am really glad of this meeting again—quite apart from its convenience to me.'

Chamberlayne needed some such assurance to recover his former interest. He smiled. And then Mr. Rymer, as if conscious of his false position, evidently determined to have it soon forgotten, by regaining his ascendency over the mind of his companion. So he promptly forced the conversation into particular and agreeable channels, and again delighted the young farmer.

But he was not quite successful in making Mr. Robert Chamberlayne forget. He saw that that gentleman was getting more sensitive, reticent, and cautious. No wonder. How could Chamberlayne overlook the fact that Mr. Rymer, even if he had not liked to go by the coach to Dolgarrog,

might have said he was going there, and might have offered a
share in the carriage he had been intending to take? What
did it mean? That he had been standing on his social rank?
Confound his social rank! Chamberlayne was inclined to
cry, if his social rank was mean enough to encourage other
men to talk of their affairs, and then when they exhibited in
return equal interest in his, to coolly make them a bow, and
walk off.

So mused Chamberlayne, in spite of Rymer's pleasant talk.
But, somehow, the latter gained upon him nevertheless. He
liked him, gentleman or no gentleman. Perhaps he had
mistaken altogether the cause of his reticence. Perhaps he
had mistaken even his social position.

A bright idea strikes him. Isn't he a speculator in the
gold mines, of which so much has lately been said? Of course
he was! Why they were both now on the direct road to
them. Bod Elian itself, Elias Morgan's place, had four or
five gold mines within its immediate neighbourhood. That
hypothesis needed only to be true to explain all. Was it true?

'I suppose,' he said to Rymer in the most artfully quiet
way he knew how to assume, 'you have heard of the new
mines?'

'Ah, yes. The British Eldorado! Anything in them?'
The words were indifferent enough—but there was quite a
promising ring in the voice, Chamberlayne thought.

'I fancy so,' was his answer. And there he stopped, and
turned away a little to show his indifference. And both were
silent.

'Which is said to be the best of these mines?' asked Rymer
after a little pause.

'The Duke of Cornwall's, I think.'

'You don't happen to know—do you? the present value of
the shares, the amount of paid-up capital, and the likelihood
of success?'

'No,' said Chamberlayne, 'but it would be easy to learn.'

'Ay, but so that one might trust to the alleged facts—if
one were inclined to speculate?'

'I think so.'

There the subject dropped, but Chamberlayne could not
help saying slyly to himself, 'Aha! I thought I'd find him
out! He doesn't want to buy a pig in a poke, nor pay too
much when he does buy. 'Cute fellow! I may help him if

he's on that scent.' Then he said aloud, 'What are your plans on reaching Dolgarrog?'

'Plans! I haven't got any that I know of.'

'I am going to a private house—Butty Hughes's! I'd rather be there than in the tourists' hotels, which must be still very crowded—though the season's nearly over.'

'I don't know but I am in the same mind. Who is Butty Hughes? What a name!'

'You musn't call him so—he's a most respectable old gentleman. When I was pupil to the Reverend Daniel Lloyd, whom I hope to see to-morrow, I used to sit in the parlour at Mr. Hughes's, and eat bread and butter every time I came into Dolgarrog. His invitation (always the same)—" Have a bit of bread and butty?" was a standing joke. I and the little Lloyds called him among ourselves Butty Hughes. But he's a very respectable old gentleman. Shall we see if he can accommodate us?'

'With all my heart,' responded Rymer.

'The rooms are ridiculously small, but clean and comfortable,' added Chamberlayne.

From that moment Mr. Rymer, as if he had, on second thoughts, discovered special advantages in an intimacy he had previously striven and manœuvred to shun, threw off whatever even of occasional reticence his manner had previously exhibited. He seemed now to accept Chamberlayne's first advances in a thoroughly genial spirit. In a word, there was, thenceforward, a perfect tone of equality.

They were still ascending, as they had been doing almost from the first mile or so of the journey. The sharp mountain air penetrated to every corner of the rickety carriage. Chamberlayne, as he grew more comfortable about his companion, fell asleep. A heavy drowsiness had also for some time been stealing over Rymer. But the cold would not let him give way to it, so he remained in a state of miserable half-consciousness—personal and mental—patiently pushing back Chamberlayne's heavy form, as it kept falling against him; patiently listening to the rattle of the broken windows; to the bleating of a sheep lost somewhere in the black watery chaos without; and to the sudden fall of masses of slate, that seemed to him as if the very foundations of the hills were shaking and shivering away into fragments.

As he leaned back, to escape the drifting rain, with half-closed eyes, he saw lights twinkling, now down in giddy depths, now up on what had before appeared to be dark rolling clouds.

The noise of waters was everywhere, trickling, babbling, leaping, roaring. There seemed to be a kind of water jubilee that night, in which river shouted to river, sea to sea, the waters under the earth to the waters above the earth; and yet they were now on the highest ridge of a shoulder of the Criba Ban; and Rymer would have seen, if there had been light, a wondrous panorama of mountain tops, with mountain valleys squeezed in between them—or looking so.

Once they stopped in front of an inn. Rymer, at the sight of the red firelight streaming from the door, felt inclined to get out, and stretch his limbs, and warm himself; but Chamberlayne was so sound asleep, and the interior of the house looked so strange and uninviting, he fancied, that he preferred to remain where he was; so while a boy came out to give the horse water, and the driver went in, John Rymer took his first look at a Welsh interior.

A flight of rough stone stairs faced the door, and on these stairs an army of black shadows coming from above, and an army of lurid fire gleams from the room on the side, met and struggled for possession. Now the red light ascended in triumph, pushing off the darkness, and showing more and more of the stained damp stones. Revealing two tiny children tired and dirty, eating their oat-cake supper, side by side, on the stairs; revealing, first, their little wooden brass-toed shoes; then, the dirty, dimpled knees; their arms; the lovely little faces leaning cheek to cheek; the great round oat-cake, with two mouths closing on its thin edge at the same moment; the tumbled, glittering curls. Then back would fall the red light, and down would come the darkness, swallowing stair after stair, till bright curls, baby faces, fat knees, wooden shoes, all were gone from sight, and there was only a worn step or two left visible, and the room to the right, where three solemn men, watched by a solemn long-nosed shepherd-dog, were drinking, and talking in a strange tongue. A young woman was nursing a child in one corner; while a stiff old dame with short petticoats, and with her knitting in her hands, came stalking out to look at the strangers, to whom she vouchsafed a bobbing courtesy.

The young woman began to sing to her child a soft little

Welsh air, to which the old dame's flapping cap-frill kept solemn time. Two voices, small, fresh and clear, from the dark stairs joined in the song.

'What's that?' cried Chamberlayne, waking, and staring about with his wide blue eyes.

By this time the driver had resumed his seat. The firelight gave Rymer one more glimpse of the stairs, and the tiny mouths opened to the shape of a round O, and two clumsy wooden shoes raised to beat time to the tune they sang, and then began again the rattling of windows.

'N's da'!' (Nos da'—good night), said the old dame.

'N's da'!' answered the driver, and they went down into the windy, watery darkness.

Down, still down, mile after mile, between dark woods, which in the light of day are so inexpressibly beautiful, with their fern-covered ground, surface teeming with wild flowers, and low guardian wall, where the moss, most delicious of natural cushions, may be felt several inches deep on the rounded stones of the top.

Down, still down, through the pelting rain, till the lights in the sombre and low stone houses on each side tell the travellers they are in Dolgarrog. And there, to the driver's great relief,—who had been ordered by Rymer, when starting, to drive to his own hotel,—he was directed by Chamberlayne to take them to Mr. Hughes's, at the Council House.

This was a long, low building, at the very bottom of the market-place. Rymer could see nothing striking about it in the darkness and rain, and was glad to follow Chamberlayne into the shop. A single flaring jet of gas lighted it and its contents, which formed the oddest mixture Rymer had ever seen. The shop was paved with bright red bricks, which a stout young woman with her hair over her eyes was mopping vigorously. Tarpaulin hats, untanned leggings, tin kettles, onions, and dried hams, hung from the low ceiling. On the deal counter smoked a batch of bread, hot from the oven; and behind the counter, sorting the loaves, stood a woman of about forty, with a worn, amiable face, and soft dark eyes, which continually glanced to the far end of the shop, where, in a little parlour, and seated by a roaring fire, the master of the Council House was taking his supper. He was a fine-looking old gentleman, fair faced, and with blue eyes, full of gentle, childish enjoyment of his food and of everything that was going on. There was a softness and oiliness about him that made Rymer smile as he thought of the name that Chamberlayne had given him.

There was a great fuss over Chamberlayne when, after teasing the good folks for some time to discover who he was, he made them remember Mr. Lloyd's young gentleman, who used to come there for bread and butter.

The little room upstairs was vacant and quite ready for their use, for the hotels which sent their overflowings to the Council House were not just then full. The gentlemen were both glad to retire early.

CHAPTER VII.

DOLGARROG.

DOLGARROG by the light of morning confirmed all that Dolgarrog by night had suggested of melancholy grayness, barren breadth, and straggling architecture.

To Mr. Rymer, as he looked down from the window of the old Council House, while Chamberlayne piled the fire to keep out the damp, the town appeared inexpressibly dreary. The low stone houses seemed utterly deficient of window-sill and balcony, door-step and portico, and of all those innumerable little hints and promises of interior comfort which ooze out of English homes. In the intricacies of back streets, perhaps, some little flannel-weaver might have his flower-pot or his blackbird at the window of his one-roomed factory, but no hint of such luxury found its way, in odour or in song, to the gray market-place.

Unadorned, stiff-backed, austere, yet not without a certain pathetic suggestiveness, and built of the same sad-coloured stone that covered the graves in the churchyard, the houses seemed to belong to a solemn Puritanic community, who regarded their town and their churchyard as two chambers of one dwelling; two chambers, in one of which they spent their day, the other their night.

The rain fell, as Rymer stood looking out, seeing no signs of life in the King's Square, as the market-place was called, except now and then a half-dressed slipshod woman, running across to fill her jug or kettle from the swollen little spring.

There was a large covered way over the opposite shops, where, last night, gas was flaring, and legs of mutton, and linseys, and wooden shoes, were cavilled over ; but now, on the rainy Sunday morning, all was silent and deserted, only a miserable outcast of a dog had gone under for shelter, and was looking up and sniffing at the empty meat-hooks.

When breakfast was over, Mr. Chamberlayne sent word to his landlord, that if he had no objection his friend and himself would come down and hear the Dolgarrog news ; and Mr. Butty responding most heartily from the little parlour at the foot of the stairs, the two gentlemen presently joined him there.

A delicious little parlour ! They saw it down there below glowing and glistening at the stair-foot—a queer little three-cornered bit of a room—as they descended by the steep stairs which led right into it, and saw doors in different parts opening out. A room where Brobdignagdian roses blossomed on Lilliputian walls ; where the tiniest of windows were darkened by the highest of cacti ; where the heavy furniture would only fit in one particular way ; where the woolly, yielding hearth-rug reached farther than the middle of the room, making it seem all fireside ; where there was not a square inch of oak-panelling, or a twisted chair-leg, but was in a state of warm, blushing polish ; for the parlour was, in fact, the object of everybody's best and brightest handiwork, the very idol of the old house.

They found the master, who was as little in proportion with it as everything else, seated in an elbow-chair by the fire, with his wife's apron pinned over his shoulders, and his Sunday toilette being performed by Mrs. Hughes in bits and scraps between her more pressing household duties ; Butty having long since been too stout to undertake so arduous a task himself.

He rose and blushingly apologised to the gentlemen for the state in which they found him ; while his wife set them chairs, and placed two steaming tumblers beside that one from which Mr. Butty occasionally sipped to sustain himself during the fatigues of his toilette.

Mr. Rymer stood at the window a minute, looking at the people crossing the King's Square on their way to the church' and to the many little chapels.

'Well,' said Mr. Butty, reseating himself, and resigning his

silver locks to his wife's hands again, ' I supposo you young
gentlemen are going up to Capel Illtyd Church this morning,
to hear your old master—eh, Mr. Robert ?   Mrs. Rhys has
come home, you know, and there will be English service.'

' Yes, indeed, Mr. Robert,' added Mrs. Hughes; and those
words, always so sweet and characteristic from a Welshwoman's
lips, lost none of their force now. 'Yes, indeed, Mr. Robert, you
must go.   And eh, dear me !—why he'll never know you a bit.'

' I was thinking of going,' answered Chamberlayne ; ' but
I didn't know whether Mr. Rymer would care to walk a
couple of miles in this weather, though it is clearing a little.'

He looked inquiringly at Mr. Rymer, who stood at the
window, with his back to them.   He had happened to be looking at his watch when he heard the lady's name mentioned,
and the question put to him. He looked at it still, as he paused
before answering, and by its aid gave himself exactly half a
minute for thought.   Chamberlayne wondered if he had heard
the question.

Five more seconds.   Mr. Rymer almost felt that if they had
been no longer than ordinary seconds, he never should have
seen the inside of Capel Illtyd Church ; but they were long
seconds, full of evil leisure, as if some imp of wickedness had
leapt astride the little golden hand, and was holding it back,
and gaping at the pale face bending over it in an agony of
hesitation.

' What do you say ? ' asked Chamberlayne. ' Shall we go ? '

' Decidedly,' answered Rymer, turning round in his quick
way. ' I shall like it, of all things.   Do we start at once ? '

' Not for a quarter of an hour or so,' returned Chamberlayne.   And then taking his boyish low seat in the corner, he
began his inquiries about old acquaintances ; which Mr. Butty
answered with a pleasant twinkle in his eye, at seeing he
remembered so many of the tribes of Jones and Evans,
Williams, Roberts, Rees, and Hughes, that almost exclusively
peopled Dolgarrog.

The twinkle became mischievous presently, and both
Butty and his wife sent amused expectant glances at Chamberlayne, as if waiting for a name that the young gentleman felt
some reluctance to mention.   At last Mrs. Hughes, while
giving her husband's hair a little pull, said—

' Eh, dear, Mr. Robert, sir, the master's waiting to hear **you**
ask after your little *curiad* (sweetheart), **Miss Hirell.**'

Chamberlayne coloured slightly and laughed.

'I didn't ask, because I am going to Bod Elian myself to-day, Mrs. Hughes. They're all well, I hope?'

'Yes, sure,' answered Butty Hughes, his fat face dimpling with smiles as he exchanged significant glances with his wife. 'And your uncle Elias is a great man at Dolgarrog to-day, Mr. Robert.'

'Indeed! How is that?'

'Why, don't you see the country people coming in?' asked Mrs. Hughes. 'There's all Capel Illtyd chapel-people, and the folk from up in the mountains behind, that'll be here. The master's counted twenty from Aber. Eh! there'll be a chapel full.'

Chamberlayne stood up and looked out of the window in astonishment.

'Why, what has all this to do with Elias Morgan?' he asked, and Butty's tongue was now unloosed.

Didn't Mr. Robert know? There was the great Calvinistic Methodist minister from the Welsh chapel in London had come down, and was going to preach at Dolgarrog, that morning, in aid of a new chapel that Elias was building near his own home.

'Elias building a chapel!' echoed Chamberlayne in undisguised alarm.

'Yes, indeed!' exclaimed husband and wife in chorus, though it was Mrs. Hughes who went on—'And's put a hundred pounds to it, and is responsible for all it will cost. Two hundred and fifty pounds, they say! Yes, indeed!'

Chamberlayne stared at the couple in blank dismay. A gentle glow of excitement overspread the face of his host, who, to heighten the effect his news produced, went on to give more illustrations of Elias Morgan's expenditure.

While Mrs. Hughes unpinned her apron, and took it from his shoulders, and dusted him with it, he told Chamberlayne how Elias was sending his young brother away to college to-morrow, with an outfit which David Jones, the little tailor, had been at work upon for the last three weeks; how Hirell, Elias's daughter, was to be sent to a sort of finishing school at Liverpool; and how she and Keziah were working their fingers to the bone to get her dresses made; how Elias growled and groaned over the fine silks and ribbons as vanity and vexation of spirit, but how, notwithstanding his preaching,

he had been very kind and generous to the young people, as if
he had not the heart to spoil the first glow of good fortune
for them. Butty told how a great sum had been laid out on
Bod Elian itself—Elias having built two new rooms to the
house, and bought a red waggon and a second horse.

All this Butty told with a cheery, childlike excitement, sometimes losing himself in the middle of a sentence, and being
obliged to look for help to his wife, who was a little, a very little,
better acquainted with the English language than himself.
Now and then they had a little gentle, coquettish discussion
over certain points, and would stop to have it out in Welsh ;
and between-whiles Mrs. Hughes would call up the stairs to
her two nieces, who were dressing for chapel, to hasten, and who
presently came down with their hymn-books in their hands.
A shrill dialogue in Welsh was carried on between them and
Mrs. Hughes as she buttoned her husband's gloves, and put
the finishing touches to his collar. In the midst of it Mr.
Rymer, who had been for the last few minutes feeling a good
deal of sympathy for Chamberlayne, said to him in a low voice—

'You ought almost to see your relatives before they go into
chapel.'

Chamberlayne started to hear this unexpected confirmation
of his own thoughts.

'Yes,' he muttered. ' I must if I can.'

'Then I shall have to find my way to Capel Illtyd Church
alone,' said Rymer, as he prepared to move.

' I hope not. Wait a bit for me,' replied Chamberlayne.

' Good morning, gentlemen ! ' said Butty, turning back to
bow politely, as he joined the girls at the door ; and, kissing
the tips of his black kid gloves to Mrs. Hughes, went forth,
guarded on either side by a blooming damsel, and followed by
the admiring eyes of his wife, who stood on the wet stones at
the door, with her head a little on one side, and the sweetest
of smiles on her worn, kind face, looking after him as if he
had been a child ; and, indeed, Butty's fat face, when it looked
back to nod to her, was as fair and fresh, in spite of its silver
hair, as full of beaming simplicity and radiant consciousness
of being good, as any child's.

They had not gone many steps before one of the nieces came
running back to say that the Morgans were all coming over
the bridge, and that Mr. Ephraim Jones, the great minister,
was standing in the King's Square waiting for them.

Chamberlayne took his hat and went out. Mr. Rymer wished Mrs. Hughes 'Good morning!' and followed. He found Chamberlayne standing still a few steps from the door, with his handsome face so bewildered that he hardly knew it as the same he had sat opposite during so many hours yesterday.

The church bell had ceased. Chapel people took the benefit of its warning silence and began to stir. Yes; the great London minister was indeed there, and a most prominent figure he made in the market-place. He was a thick-set, burly, Cromwell-like man, with rough, pimply face; a man who seemed to have been battling through all his long life with the eternal enemy, whether intrenched within or encamped without, and to have grown strong, bristling, antagonistic; his very attitude of repose a defiant poise—victorious on the whole, but scarred—and obliged to hold his very conquests by the tenure of perpetual watch. He—the Reverend Ephraim Jones—now stood in the middle of the market-place conversing with Dolgarrog ministers, and watching the approach of four persons.

These were Elias Morgan, his young brother Hugh, his only child Hirell, and his housekeeper Keziah Williams. The slim, youthful figure of Hugh, on whose shoulders Elias's heavy hand now and then fell, as if to give additional weight to some admonition, attracted little attention. It was the elder brother—it was Elias himself, towards whom all eyes were turned.

A short man, but broad-chested, supple-limbed, powerful treading, and with a certain rough dignity in his bearing that compensated for an utter want of grace, both in form and feature. His eyes alone, dark and bright, and shaded with long thick lashes, might have been comely but that there looked out of them a spirit so inscrutably stern, so piercing and alert, yet withal so immovably calm. Little passing emotions, such as give most human eyes their wondrous variety of expression and light, must have been crushed dead in Elias's broad chest, before they had lived long enough to trouble the stony calmness of his eyes. His square chin, and his lips, thin and firm-set, had the same unflinching look.

When he first came within view of the market-place, Elias was wholly absorbed in his brother, and the counsel he was giving him, as to how he was to meet the snares and temptations of the great world, for which the lad was to leave his mountain home to-morrow. Presently, as he saw Hugh's eyes looking excitedly forward, his own followed them, and he suddenly became aware of the stir his approach was creating. His hand dropped from Hugh's shoulder, he slackened his pace, and a scarcely perceptible colour rose in his swarthy cheek; his mouth somewhat relaxed; his eyes softened. Chamberlayne watched him in deep anxiety. There was more of happiness in his cousin's face than he had before seen there. Yes; Elias Morgan's cup of bliss—bliss after the thirstings of his own stern heart—was full. What! Did the elect of God honour him for this little humble edifice he was raising on the mountain slope? How much more would he not yet—God willing!—do for them!

And the poor mountain farmer, who had been used to earn his bread from hand to mouth till his fortieth year; Elias, with his narrow notion of things and his boundless faith in God, felt his coming inheritance of seven thousand pounds to be a power in his hands, by which he was to accomplish all sorts of great and divine purposes. He could venture now to snatch a little leisure, in which to perfect the conquest of his own stubborn heart. He was not usually thought a charitable man—for none knew how much he strove to accomplish for those in his own household with the barest means—and therefore could not know the strength of his motives for resistance to ordinary appeals for charity. Now he felt he might be better understood. Hitherto he had had to stint himself in food to spare a penny to a starving tramp. Now! —but he closed his firm lips suddenly with an expression that seemed to say ' Thou knowest! '

With the solemn glory of his dream about him, he advanced into the market-place, to take the two hands Mr. Ephraim Jones, the London minister, stretched out, even while his friend was yet distant.

Chamberlayne did not understand what had caused Elias to quicken his pace; and feeling he must make an effort to deliver his ill news, he went hastily towards him.

' Cousin! Cousin Morgan! '

Elias, strange to say, had either known him at the first glance, or was too much preoccupied to express any surprise when enlightened by the words addressed to him. He gave him his right hand cordially, while with his left he made a motion towards the group in the market-place, as if to show him he could not then stop.

'Cousin Chamberlayne, is it you?' he said. 'Have you come to stay at Bod Elian? You are welcome. Come up to-night, if you like. Only no business, Robert, till to-morrow. The Lord's day this;' and then his half-closed eyes, and moving but mute lips, seemed to say he, of all men, ought to remember that.

'But, Morgan,' began Chamberlayne, hurriedly. His cousin instantly stopped him with a sort of stern good-humour.

'Cousin Chamberlayne, we are late. Bad roads made us so —and the vanities of dress.' And he motioned with his broad hand towards the two women behind him.

To these Chamberlayne, in his despair of any useful effort with Elias, turned, only to have his wits still more confounded. The slender form and fair face of Hirell were familiar to him, but now he found the familiar image painfully, yet bewitchingly, strange to him, by the new and wondrous beauties which breathed from it and surrounded it.

No childish, pouting, country beauty, with glowing glances stealing the admiration under which she blushes—for thus had Chamberlayne, with his Kentish experience, and not too brilliant imagination, painted her—and yet no pale statue, coldly perfect, was the daughter of Elias Morgan. Her loveliness was neither of marble nor of roses. Her beauty was a mysterious beauty, which alike puzzled and charmed Chamberlayne, but which he could not succeed in comprehending. Hirell's form was lithe and slender, and full of wild natural elegance. Its little, wavering, flower-like movements were very pretty, and suggested a constant recollection of its native mountain breezes. But it was not her form that so bewildered Chamberlayne, nor her hazel eyes that glanced up to him full of sweet, fresh dewy light, like sudden gleams of morning; no, it was the thought of her name which had often puzzled him, and which he felt for the first time he understood. Hirell— beam of light—angel! Yes, he felt that since he had last seen her, that wild, restless soul of hers had become moulded to her name. She was no longer the same being who had run wild races with him in the stony fields of Bod Elian, or sat in the little room at the old Council House, laughing at Butty Hughes. They had taken her away, he felt, her father and those grim old Dissenting ministers, and lifted her from her

half-melancholy, half-boisterous childhood, and placed her in a
sort of saintdom, where he, at least, could hold no commune
with her. He felt as if he could not speak to her. He could
only stand before her, and feel pain at her entire forgetfulness
of him.

He was thinking of her still while Keziah spoke to him.
He was wondering if Hirell ever had those sudden fits of sadness that used to come over her when they were children
together, or those wilder fits of passionate restlessness and longing to break through the iron restraint of her poverty-pinched
lonely mountain home. Surely nothing of this ever troubled
Hirell now ! Sweet saintly gravity was on her lips, her eyes
were full of joy. Had it all gone from her, this restlessness,
he wondered ? Was the beam of light a pure beam, free from
all discolorations and dust of earth ? Or—and the thought
brought him fresh pain—was this bright joyousness caused by
the supposed change in their fortunes ? If it were this indeed,
how could he meet her to-day or to-morrow ? How look in
her eyes when his news had sent all the sweet light out of
them—perhaps for ever ?

At her father's half jocose allusion to her vanity, which had
drawn upon her the sudden looks of Chamberlayne and his
friend, the beautiful Calvinist blushed and trembled, and let
fall her carefully upheld dress ; and in her confusion at seeing
the fair, pale silk slip to the wet stones, and herself revealed
in all her rich attire, she glanced up and met Mr. Rymer's
half-smiling gaze of admiration and of pleasure in what he
felt must be Chamberlayne's pleasure at the sight of her. He
lifted his hat and bowed when he saw her look at him, and she
blushed most painfully, hesitated, then courtesied—so rustic
a courtesy that she blushed again to think of it when it was
done, and turned to follow her father, quite unconscious that
she had neither spoken to nor shaken hands with her kinsman
and old playmate, Robert Chamberlayne.

The two young men stood apart, watching the moving
masses of figures in the market-place. Elias was holding the
minister's hands ; and the latter, seeing a strange look of
inquiry in Elias's earnest, weather-beaten face, said, in his
burly, loud voice, which seemed, however, softer than usual—

' Yes, friend Elias ; I am reminded I didn't come here for
the rest I so much coveted among my old friends, but to do
His work. He knows what He is about when He says, " Take

this sorrow," and wrings out the cry in answer, "What is it Thou wishest me to do?" Elias, my little boy—my only one—is dead! so this letter has just told me. God help and comfort the poor mother! She is too old to have another child. You can guess, then, how it must have been with us—how it now will be. Enough! Courage, Elias! God is thinking of you and your plans to-day. He means to make me speak out for you. He fills my heart—how, then, can I help but speak? Your cause won't suffer through my loss. It is I who tell you so, but it is He who tells it me. Come!'

Elias had been holding one hand during these words, with a sense of strong, almost passionate yearning to the stricken but brave man. He now relinquished the hand, and took the proffered arm, and he said in a voice so low and dream-like in tone that it hardly seemed meant for the minister (whose first hearty words of congratulation as to the change of fortune were still ringing in Elias's ear)—'The Lord giveth, and the Lord taketh away.'

'Is that all, friend Elias?' sternly asked the minister, stopping at the threshold of the chapel-door to look in the other's face. 'Thou art over-considerate. Dost thou think *I* cannot say what thou art secretly saying—"Blessed be the name of the Lord!"'

The hard voice that for its pain might have been the voice of one speaking from the rack, was followed by a burst of children's voices singing in the school-room, before the service began, a hymn prepared for the occasion. So fresh and soaringly did it rise, that it seemed as if the little singers, unknown to themselves, were charged with God's tender answer to the words wrung so sternly from the stricken heart.

The minister and Elias lifted up their faces and listened: stirred like veteran soldiers by the trumpet-call to battle. Hirell looked at them, and from their rugged faces drew to her own a new glory. Forgetful of her fair silks, she folded her hands, and glided in between the two burly figures—a beam of light, indeed!

The inner chapel-doors closed. Rymer and Chamberlayne turned, and silently crossed the bridge, on their way to Capel Illtyd. Once more the market-place was gray, sombre, and deserted.

CHAPTER VIII.

DOLA' HUDOL.

THE gray house fronts of Dolgarrog were drying in patches as Rymer and Chamberlayne crossed the bridge leading out of town, and entered upon a road the beauty of which endures even the test of the old Welsh motto, which says, ' Nothing is excellent but that which cannot be excelled.'

The whole way from Dolgarrog to Aber, where the little river winding through the valley ends in the sea, the road gently ascends. The breeze blows with increasing freshness as you advance. The old walls, built of large stones, are held together by no cement, but only by the roots and stems of innumerable plants ; conspicuous among which are the ivy, fern, stone-crop, and the vigorous and healthy penny-wort, whose round fleshy leaves mimic the size of every coin in existence, till they become so small and minute that only fairies can need to put such money into their purses. And these old walls grow more and more rich as we recede from the town, till every square yard becomes a kind of inexhaustible treasury for the artist, the poet, and the lover of nature to stand before and study.

And still as the road ascends the openings in the craggy banks on the right show glimpses of fresher green ; the valley on the left broadens ; Criba Ban, stretching its vast bulk above it, and above its many tributary mountain-vassals for a distance of many miles, assumes more distinct and majestic forms ; the magpies flash their dazzling white and black more frequently before the eye ; while the rougher and the more full of obstacles the stones of its shallow bed become, the louder and more determined is the triumphant song of the little river.

Through this road the two men move in an almost unearthly silence, after the first few and faint flashes of conversation have died out. Chamberlayne's eye scarcely quits the line of the road before him, and even of that he sees little more than the ground upon which he treads.

It is very different with his companion. He, too, is deeply absorbed ; but, unlike Chamberlayne, who can follow but one stream of thought and emotion at one time, Rymer cannot help but see and feel, even though it be almost unconsciously, the influences around him. And thus, while the secret thoughts that so strongly possess him keep his spirits fluctuating like jets of flame in unwholesome air, he cannot help but stop now and then, gaze round half-incredulously, then, with a quick, impatient step, rejoin his companion, and then once more let his eye and fancy go free through those exquisite regions of earth and air.

It is strange how differently these glimpses of the landscape affect him at different moments—deepening his sadness when he is sad, increasing his exaltation of spirit when some flattering surmise happens to elate him—or making more restless and feverish his ordinary mood, which is one of the deepest anxiety.

About a mile from Dolgarrog he stood still before a scene, the charm of which, to an eye like his, was as sudden and potent as a strain of exquisite melody to an unexpectant ear. And truly all the chords of beauty were here gathered to one perfect, silent, harmonious work, by the Divine Musician.

Two mountains stood near together—one a little in advance of the other. The farthest was of tender purple; the other, clasped by the sunshine bursting from the clouds, was of deep, bright green; and they stood so leaning together as to form a sort of mighty gateway to a world of mountains beyond, the edges of which could just be individually seen, and all of which repeated the colours of the two in fainter and more exquisite tints, till the curving lines—purple beyond green, and green beyond purple—ceased against the sky. As Rymer stood before this mountain gateway, and looked in upon this mountain world, it seemed to him that, from its wondrously dewy freshness, and freedom from all trace of life but that of trees, clouds, waters, birds, and sunlight, and of all which helped to make its beauty, it might be appearing from under the rising mist for the first time since its creation. The faint rainy sunshine met the majestic heads and the coloured slopes, and crept from one to another as if bewildered by excess of beauty—now fainting on the bosom of the hill where it lay—then awakening, and with sudden passion clasping all. Still Rymer stood and gazed upon the scene. He only gazed. There was not a thought dared to enter.

He had chosen actual darkness in the first agony of his disappointment, and had chosen to consider himself in the dark ever since. Could he dare to see now ? If he allowed himself to remove this mental bandage he had put before his eyes, to perceive the majesty of these heads—the colours of these slopes—the inexhaustible tenderness of the valley depths between—must he not see more, much more, which he did not wish to see; which he dared not, would not, see ? But for one moment the 'seeing' had come ; and with it an indescribable sadness. Then back into the darkness and onward again.

And the darkness had begun to have a subtle charm of its own : he turned towards it with a glad exhilaration, to which the freshening air and increasing wildness added every minute, and seemed to give a false glow of health and naturalness.

The wind—its wings no longer clogged by the rain that had weighed it down so many days—rose and swept on with exultant voice ; tearing the white mists from the valleys, and the blue mists from the mountains ; creeping, conspirator-like, into the woods, and setting the friendliest trees by the ears ; dividing itself into millions of genii to seize and shake dry each blade of grass in a whole field, and making the solitary little flower on the hillside laugh its blue-bell empty of tears ; pausing now to make a loud, jubilant song to the waterfall's music; then, like a careless shepherd who suddenly remembers his neglected sheep, hallooing to the grey straggling clouds, and driving them before him with a tyrant's fury, till his own strength is exhausted, and he lags with weak, puffing breath behind.

Presently there appeared, above the wall on the left, a bit of rich swelling park land, on which Robert Chamberlayne's eyes rested with a pleased look.

'That's Dola' Hudol,' said he ; 'most likely the people from there, with a tourist or two and ourselves, will be all the congregation at the English service this morning.'

'This place, then,' asked Rymer, 'is owned by an English family, is it ? '

'Mrs. Rhys is English,' answered Chamberlayne, without noticing the light that kindled his companion's eyes as they both drew to the other side of the road, and stood on a low wall the better to see up a slope to the knoll of trees in the distance, where, all but completely hidden, stood the plain Tudor mansion built of the grayest, coldest stone.

'Yes; and they make enough of it,' answered the farmer, a little contemptuously; 'they have even named the house from the fields. Dola' Hudol means the "fascinating meadows," I have heard; but there's some story connected with these Hirell Morgan once told me—I forget all about it now though.'

One of the paths—the beginnings and endings of which Rymer's eye was busily trying to discover—came winding from the house to a little door in the wall near where they stood. Down just before the door was a stone placed over a noisy little channel of water. It was green underneath, and on the top thickly cushioned with moss. It was like a tiny antique drawbridge to some fairy castle.

'What exquisite moss!' said Rymer, and stooping he took up a little piece from the old stone, and raising it as if enjoying its fresh peculiar scent, he bent over it as it lay in his palm some time, touching it with his lips with a stealthy tender reverence.

A little later, as the two went on, leaving Dola' Hudol behind them, he crushed it in his hand in a sort of scorn of himself. What foot could have trodden upon it? The little door was not in use—the ivy grew about it in chains and bars—but as he crushed it, it thrilled him, and by some strange power kept his fingers from unclosing and casting it away.

They were now on Capel Illtyd bridge, looking down on the old Roman causeway, as it lay visible beneath the beautiful water; and Chamberlayne pointed to where, low down on the right, lay the old Abbey farm, where he had spent his schooldays. The smoke rising above the trees—a few cows grazing in the fields—a woman in a blue spotted jacket washing potatoes in the river, using an old basket as a sieve—these seemed at first to be the only signs of life visible. But looking up the gray mountain-sides, Rymer saw a few dreary stone cottages, and two or three miners sitting at the doors—English probably, thinking of English homes, by the way in which they sat gazing across the valley and over the crowding mountain heads. From here the two men could see in the direction opposite to the mountain gateway to the end of the valley; where the turbulent little river met the sea, whose black swollen lips spat at it livid foam that blew hither and thither, scarcely distinguishable from the white seagulls. The meadows all the way were dotted with lakes by the last rough tide. A heron stalked upon a sandy little island by itself. Clouds of strange birds were glutting on the drenched pastures—the whole scene was wild, watery, and desolate.

At the top of the steep bit of road they were ascending stood the toll-gate, to the left of which is the village of Capel Illtyd ; and to the right the church. Turning towards this they entered upon a road like a Swiss mountain pass, and in a few minutes came upon the church, a very small and primitive looking building.

The chief part of the little congregation attending the Welsh service had gone, and were seen dotting the far-away road to Aber, which appeared cut like a shelf in the mountain ; but Rymer and Chamberlayne met a few solemn-looking communicants leaving the churchyard—some grave, old men, and soberly-attired women in their long cloaks and high-crowned hats. They stood aside to let them pass, then looked along the road for signs of the English congregation, but saw none ; and Chamberlayne began to have a doubt as to whether there was to be au English service at all.

They paced up and down the gray slate paving-stones for a few minutes, looking at and trying to read the inscriptions on the graves, and glancing expectantly along the quiet road—Chamberlayne carelessly, and almost hoping to see no one, that he might the sooner join his old friend and tutor, and confide to him all his trouble and perplexity concerning his relatives ; Rymer with a studied indifference, beneath which was hidden a torturing suspense that made him feel as if time were standing still by his side, and waiting with him.

The wet September foliage rustled against the dark little church windows ; a few yellow leaves fluttered about the gray tombs and green grass, and suspense cut it all much too sharply on his heart for the picture ever to be effaced. Every time they reached the little square porch, as they paced up and down, they heard a dry, patient cough from the clerk within ; and every time they reached the gate they heard nothing but birds and running water—no sound of wheel or of foot-fall on the road.

'I think no one will be coming now,' said Chamberlayne, at last ; 'we had better walk on towards the Abbey farm till Mr. Lloyd overtakes us.'

He led the way out of the churchyard, and Rymer followed him. He still held the bit of moss, crushing it in his hand with a fierce grief, as if, having come from her door, some pith or hope might be wrung from it.   He walked on, and the lovely still life of that road was hateful to his straining eye and ear.

Midway between the church and the toll-gate they heard a strange sort of call ; and, looking back, they saw a man standing at the gate of the church, beckoning them.

'That's old Jones, the clerk,' said Chamberlayne, looking annoyed and perplexed.

'We must have made some mistake—they are there; they must have come some other way, the English family you mentioned,' said Rymer, hurriedly.

'There is another door; but they must have been waiting in the churchyard ever since we've been, if they are there; for there's no other road from Dola' Hudol,' answered Chamberlayne.

'Let us go back; they must be there!' Rymer said in a sharp, decisive tone, which he often used to conceal some strong emotion.

The gaunt old clerk, in his threadbare coat and spectacles, beckoned determinedly, almost angrily, till they came up to him at the gate.   Then he went to the porch, and beckoned till they reached him there.

Then they entered the church, and, in a minute, made the discovery that, with the exception of the clergyman and the clerk, they were the only persons in the building.

Rymer was horribly annoyed, and glanced round more than once in the hope of retreat.   But Robert Chamberlayne's old tutor began immediately, leaving them no choice as to staying or going; and it was as strange a thing as either had ever experienced to feel that the service had really begun and would be gone through entirely on their behalf.

There was a humorous side as well as a solemn one to the position, and the men both felt the humour more than the solemnity.   The clergyman felt it a little also, and there was an odd twinkle in his eye that showed a certain enjoyment in his task.   The Reverend Daniel Lloyd had two gifts seldom found in one man ; great energy of mind and extreme quietness of manner.   His energy was not of the feverish, dry, exhaustive kind ; but was a bright, dewy, refreshing energy, which seemed to have no end.   His small gray eye shone as bright in his dry-skinned, sunburnt, hale-looking face as a clear spring of water in a rock ; his voice was sweet, and had

a rich sort of grit in it, and had a dry mellow music peculiar
to itself; his hair was gray; his form tall and slight, but
erect and hardy. He did not read the prayers, but prayed
them, and the Psalms he read as poems. He did what scarcely
anybody else could have done that morning—drew Rymer's
thoughts from himself.

But this was not for long. As he sat, his attention divided
idly between Daniel Lloyd's small vigorous head and the
quaint primitive funereal plates of metal that decorated the
walls, there was a slight sound at the door.

A rush of heat that no power of will could hide came to
Rymer's face.

What was it? Was it not the branches that he had heard
brushing against the windows and door, as he paced up and
down the churchyard with Chamberlayne? No—the clerk
was rising; he saw some one then.

The clerk walked to the door. Then Rymer heard his
footsteps and those of another. Yes, of another, that made
his very throat swell and throb with a strength that threatened
to break the silence. Then he heard a pew-door opened and
shut some way behind him; and the clerk returned to his seat,
and the next minute a new voice was joining Chamberlayne's
in the responses; a sweet, rich, young, tremulous voice, that
held Rymer's mute, and for the moment so filled his soul with
joy, that he felt repaid for all he had suffered in that little
gray-tombed churchyard, in which a grave had seemed to lie
waiting for his last fragile, darling hope.

Robert Chamberlayne, in his impatience to transfer some
of his own anxiety concerning the Morgans to Daniel Lloyd's
shoulders, was hoping he would not think so small a congregation worth a sermon; for he remembered he had sometimes
omitted it on such occasions; but his former tutor had no
such intention now, and never had Chamberlayne heard him
preach with more vigour and homely eloquence. He spoke of
the smallness of his congregation, and as in nowise regretting
it. He even said that, were only one present, that one might
perhaps receive more good than great numbers; for, as he
would have no neighbour to whom to pass on Christ's
message, he must perforce take it to himself.

When he finished, the clerk, who had been fast asleep, woke
with a start, and got up and opened the door of the pew where
Chamberlayne and his friend sat.

They came out and followed him down the aisle, Chamberlayne, engrossed in looking for half-a-crown for the clerk, who was an old acquaintance of his, followed him to the door ; and Rymer came after them—slowly—very silently and slowly.

He had to approach a large square pew, with armorial bearings on the panels, before turning to the door.

He approached the pew very slowly, and as he did so was looking into a face that was regarding him with amazement, fear, and agitation.

The pew belonged to Mr. Owen Rhys, of Dola' Hudol, and the face which looked over it was that of his wife, Catherine Rhys.

It was a full Saxon face with large blue eyes, fair hair, and a rose-like richness of complexion ; and there was in its beauty an indescribable depth, like the folded mystery of a rich garden-rose, the power of whose hidden graces breathes through the visible beauty, till that which is apparent appears less than that which is felt to be concealed.

It was a face which had in it the same kind of loveliness that pervades the earth in very early summer, or rather, in full and perfect spring, when the softness, and bloom, and perfume of all things are richest ; when the wild hyacinths rise under the trees, between the thickly-spreading surface roots, in gleaming lines of azure ; when the yellow cream of May has settled thickly on the fields ; when the breath and blush of the first rose offers consolation for the fading lilacs, and the falling of the fragile hawthorn ; when the green Guelder rose is but half blanched, and the honeysuckle has just opened the end of one of its clusters of tiny bugles, and blown its first sweet joyful *reveillé* in perfume to the summer.

The very spirit of this time was in her face :—the softness, the bloom, the fresh abundant health and life—nothing lost or lessened, but all deepened and intensified by being human. There was nothing of the ethereal part of very early spring, the childlike innocence, or arch wildness ; and there was nothing of the wearied heaviness, the fierce splendour or voluptuous languor of July ; it was all bright May—eager, fervent, passionate, but dewy and healthful as the morning breeze.

Surprise seemed to take from Mrs. Rhys all power of concealing the agitation which the sudden appearance of

Rymer caused her. The colour in her cheek at first paled; then, under his fixed and passionate gaze, returned, and burned in it with angry vividness. As he passed, he saw her anger and surprise lessening, her lip quiver, her deep blue eyes fill and droop. He went away towards the open door, listening with the air of one who is certain of a coming step. Then he heard the sound of her pew-door, and with almost unnaturally keen perception, knew it was herself had opened it.

The expected and waited-for step came—weak—uncertain. He did not look back, but all the light that was mounting before his dazzled eyes over Criba Ban, and showing him for the first time the grand range, bare of cloud and mist, to the very summits—seemed caused by that step's approach; which, from the long-hidden heights of his hope, was sending the mists flying, and lightening all with the old warmth and beauty.

He stood just without the church-door; the step was almost on the threshold, when it paused, and his heart seemed to pause too, as on the threshold of something to which it yearned, but could not move save with that step. Yes, that step was still; then he heard the sound of a faint rustling, like the dragging of a weary wing, not *to* the door and to him, but away; back into the silent aisle! He turned, he listened; looking with wild eyes into the cold, still place. He saw nothing, but, as he looked, heard a long-laboured sob, and in it a name—and the name was that of the clergyman to whom he had just been listening.

He understood then. She had turned back and appealed to him.

CHAPTER IX.

THE ANSWERING CHORD.

During the next two or three hours Mr. Rymer wandered about irresolutely.

Going back towards Dola' Hudol, he met a man whom he had seen crossing the fields from Dola' Hudol. To this person he addressed himself.

'Excuse me, my friend, stopping you, but I want to ask you whose house that is just before us?'

' My master's, Mr. Rhys ! '

' You are—'

' His gamekeeper.'

' And who is he?—some fortunate millowner from Lancashire, or—'

' You had better not ask him that question,' said the man dryly.

' Why ? '

' Of course,' said the gamekeeper, ' you're quite an Englishman, and with the usual Englishman's knack for showing his ignorance of, and contempt for, the people among whom he happens to be.'

' I fear so, except as regards the contempt,' said Rymer, taking off his hat, and bowing with a mock humility that only increased the gamekeeper's irritation, ' but I am very willing to learn.'

' Mr. Rhys, then, is the descendant of a Welsh prince, whose ancestors ruled a brave, happy, and illustrious people, while England was little better than a flock of silly sheep, and worried by Danes, Norwegians, and Saxons at pleasure.'

' The Welshman, also, I think, gave us an occasional early taste of the amenities of genial neighbours—did they not ? ' asked Rymer; and the gamekeeper became so eloquent in his answer, that by the time he had come to a full pause he had discovered the English tourist was certainly a good listener, and had possibly therefore learnt somewhat. So he said to him,

' Are you fond, sir, of old books and manuscripts ? '

' Very. Is Dola' Hudol rich that way ? '

' Stuffed full ! and they're of immense value—heirlooms. They've one manuscript there,—the green book of Dola' Hudol they call it,—that no Welshman would exchange for the crown of England ; no, nor give away its least precious leaves, leaf by leaf, in exchange for gem by gem of the Regalia.'

' And is the house visible ? '

' Not now. Not since yesterday ! '

' What's the matter ? Some tourist outrage ? '

' Oh dear no ! Mrs. Rhys has come home—that's all.'

' That's all,' echoed Rymer. ' It is shown then when the family are away ? '

' Oh yes.'

' Well, my friend, let me tell you, I admire, more perhaps

than I ought to do, these old families and their old homes, and shall be inclined to tread most reverently the halls and corridors of the descendant of a Welsh prince. Take this,' he said, handing the gamekeeper half a sovereign, 'for a slight acknowledgment of the pleasure your talk has given. I wish honestly my man cared half as much about me and mine, or could speak as eloquently about them. But I don't know what ails you Welshmen. You seem all to me born gentlemen, whatever your station in life ; and as to your language, I cannot, for the life of me, understand the why or wherefore, but I notice if a Welshman speak English at all, he speaks it to perfection, and puts to shame the speech of the humbler among my own countrymen.'

This might be banter, and certainly was not spoken in entire sincerity. It may also be a question whether such truth as there was would have been so demonstratively expressed under any other circumstances. Anyhow, he spoke of real facts he had noticed ; and consequently there mingled with the unreality of his tone something deeper and more genuine. The effect was irresistible. The gamekeeper coloured with pleasure, his eye laughed, and his voice rang out as he apologized to the stranger for his previous expressions.

'And now,' said Rymer, 'can't you get me a peep inside ? It's Sunday, I know, but your curate, I have heard, once showed on a Sunday the old abbey where he lives to a friend who could not wait for Monday. That's just my case. I am going back to England immediately, and feel a strong desire to see what I call a typical Welsh gentleman's house. I dare say you think I could find no more favourable example ? '

'That's very certain, sir, and thank you for your liberality ; but if it's given with a view—' and he held the coin out, as if to return it.

'It's not given for anything in the world but to enable me to please myself in pleasing you, if you are not too proud to accept it.'

'Well, sir,' said the Welshman, as he pocketed the half-sovereign with considerable satisfaction, 'it seems a trifle to refuse you, and perhaps it might be managed ; but great offence was once given to Mr. Rhys by a party of visitors, who were, as a special favour, allowed to see the principal ruins while the family were in residence—'

'But he is not here, is he ? '

'No, and to be sure that makes a difference!   For his lady
wouldn't say a word against our admitting a stranger—if he
were really a gentleman—except for the sake of disobedience
to orders.   Well, sir, I think I'll venture, if I may be sure
you will keep close to me, so that there may be no risk of
annoyance.'

'Don't doubt that.'

'Well, sir, I think, knowing the place and its ways so well as
I do, I may manage to show you what is best worth seeing,
without coming across my mistress.'

Rymer heard, but said nothing, and followed the gamekeeper silently.

As the stranger became more reserved and silent, the gamekeeper became only the more chatty; and told the history of
a certain family, the chief member of which had committed
suicide through finding himself unable to pay a debt of honour
—a touching piece of domestic tragedy, which Rymer would
have listened to with interest at any time but the present.

He was now feeling the full significance of his position—
was realising the nature of the perilous path along which he
strode as if no giddy precipice were on either hand, no termi-
nation to the vista beyond that even the boldest spirits might
be unwilling to face.

Thus they reached Dola' Hudol; when a new trouble
affected Rymer that he had not, in the intense preoccupation
of a determined purpose, previously thought of.   Was he now
being seen by Mrs. Rhys, as they approached?   Would she
again fly from him?   Or would she not feel so deep a resentment as to arm herself against all further consideration for
him, and denounce him, and expose him before her husband's
servants?'

'To his great edification!' said Rymer, grimly to himself.
'Not a bad stroke of policy on her part, if—'

He did not finish his sentence, for they had now reached
the house, and without—so far as Rymer's keen eyes could
discern, as they ranged incessantly from window to window—
attracting the least attention from any one within.

It was a great infliction to him to have to deal with the
intelligence and zeal of his companion.   He would have given
the diamond ring from his finger—her gift—so he felt, to have
exchanged the gamekeeper for the ordinary showwoman,
with her monotonous cut and dry sentences, and utter careless-

ness as to what he thought, how he looked or moved, so long as he did not linger too long, nor touch forbidden things.

Through half an hour of almost intolerable torture did he vainly strive to listen to talk that he knew he ought to attend to, if only to keep off suspicion ; while, in fact, every sound was full of pain and alarm, for it confused what he was striving to make clear with all the faculties of his soul—those other sounds all so soft and remote, which whispered to him of the rustle of a dress, or the fall of a light foot, a distant word of direction, or a question put to a servant—sounds so delicate, that he feared to lose them in the thicker stream of the gamekeeper's voice.

Suddenly he was startled into consciousness by the remark—

'You are tired, sir, I see : and can't take much interest in the place.'

'No, no, you are deceived ; I never was more interested in my life. Talk on, and don't mind me.'

For a few minutes Rymer managed, with great effort, to preserve a manner more obviously suitable to the character he had assumed ; but it wearied him so much that in a wanton spirit he threw all further attempt aside, and stalked on, gloomily listening to everything said, but perfectly unconscious of any one fact whatever, except this—*she* was near him ; and yet he was failing to find her, or even to get the slightest trace of her whereabouts.

'What's that ?' he said suddenly, in a voice so low and significant, that the gamekeeper was startled, and fancied the stranger had caught some sounds that he too ought to hear and did not.

'I—I mean—the—singing !' said Rymer, with an attempt at indifference.

'Oh that! I couldn't imagine, sir, what you heard. Oh that's only Mrs. Rhys singing : she's a fine singer, they say— though an Englishwoman.' The Welshman said this with a sly smile.

'It does indeed seem exquisite. I wish I could hear it more plainly.'

'Do you ? Well, I have a message for her, so I'll go in, and leave the door open behind me—then you'll perhaps get half a minute or so.'

'Stay What if she were to come out while I am here ?'

' She will not do that. I shall tell her what I have done ;
she's sure, then, not to be angry.'

' Very well.   Give me as long as you can.   The air is one
I should like to hear through, if it were possible.'

' Please, sir, to be very silent, and do not move at all till I
come back ! '

' I will not.'

The gamekeeper went to the other end of the corridor, in
which they stood, and tapped lightly.

' Come in ! ' said a voice that seemed even still richer in its
own natural music than in aught that it had artistically
learned.

Rymer stood listening ; breathless, moveless, gazing at that
opening door which did not reveal her when fully open, and
which was then partially reclosed.

He could not hear distinctly what the gamekeeper said to
her, and yet felt certain from the tone that he began by giving
his own independent message, and that it was to that the
pathetic voice replied, wearily,

' Very well.'

Then again there was silence for a moment.

And then, while Rymer wondered if the gamekeeper's
courage had failed him about the intruding visitor, and
whether she would begin again the singing, he heard the
man's heavy step moving not towards, but away from him,
Rymer.

' What on earth does that portend ? ' he asked himself.

' You will find it, James, I think, on the dining-room table ;
I am sorry to trouble you,' Mrs. Rhys said, in a raised voice.

She had then sent the man for something.

Truly Rymer felt it to be a wonderful piece of good fortune ;
he might venture in, and in half a minute might do that for
which alone he had come hither.

But even as he moved with fixed resolution to his purpose,
he heard Mrs. Rhys's voice rise again, very falteringly, it
seemed, then grow stronger, and then it sang to Welsh words
the exquisitely pathetic air, *Ar hyd y nos*, but not to the end;
there was an inexplicable sinking and diminishing of the rich
full tones—then fresh effort and struggle—almost a conquest—
then a low cry of intensest anguish, and—then what Rymer
dared not even to picture to himself, through the ominous
silence.

Unmanned for the moment by this, he changed his resolution, and wrote hurriedly in his note-book these words :—

'I am here, listening to you, but quite unknown and unsuspected, as a tourist visitor. Judge by that of the value of my word when I say I *will* see you—once—whatever may come of it.

'But that shall be our last interview, if you choose.

'Hear me then, as I must also hear you, once for all. Then I accept, absolutely, your decision, however fatal.

'Come alone to the place called the Maiden's Lake, at dusk this afternoon. There is a catchpenny gold-finder there on week days, whom people go to see make experiments in washing for gold-dust. He will be absent to-day. We may meet there as strangers, without risk to you ; and find no one but ourselves.

'Strike a chord upon your instrument to say yes ; I will not take no—not even if I have to seek you here again after your husband's arrival. Destroy this.'

While this was being written, Rymer expected every instant to be stopped by the returning gamekeeper, till he remembered his own request to the man, and saw how easily the slight commission given to him by Mrs. Rhys might be, and no doubt was being consciously, used for Rymer's benefit.

Tearing the leaves out, he strode stealthily towards the still partially-open door—paused—drew himself up—seemed to hesitate as to the shock the sight of him might give Mrs. Rhys, —perhaps also as to his promise to the gamekeeper ; so he hastily rolled the leaves round the only convenient weight he could find, a half-crown, and threw it against a part of the wall he could just see.

Glass crashed, and was followed by a slight scream, which was instantly interrupted, as if in sudden consciousness of the possible meaning of the incident.

It was the glass of a picture that had been broken. Strange enough, too, the drawing was a water-colour drawing of Mrs. Rhys herself.

Rymer seemed to hear each separate beat of his own heart, as he listened to hear how she would act.

He was not long left in doubt. Of course she could not choose but deal some way with an incident so compromising.

She crossed the room. Rymer saw her, and saw her stoop—saw how carefully she chose not to see him—saw that then she went away back, and most probably to her former seat at or near the piano.

The gamekeeper—who had stayed to the utmost verge of what he dared—now returned ; and Rymer, who was standing so much nearer than before, could hear him give his not very confident explanation about the visitor outside.

A long and embarrassing silence followed, before Mrs. Rhys made any kind of comment. Then she said, with a tone of severity through which Rymer could feel every thrill of her heart—

'I shall say nothing now, James, but if this happens again I am sure Mr. Rhys will discharge you. You need not wait.'

Scarcely knowing how best to excuse himself, James uttered a few faltering words and hurried away ; and being already angry at the reproof he had incurred, was still more angry to find the tourist almost close to the door, instead of being where he had left him—a long and respectful way off.

'I have got into trouble on your account, sir, and must beg you to hasten your departure,' he said somewhat roughly.

'Many thanks. You may want a friend some day—if so I shall remember this.'

The gamekeeper was mollified, and even showed him certain other objects of interest that did not involve further penetration into the recesses of the mansion ; and he found that his visitor seemed to linger more over these comparatively trifling articles of vertu than he had done while examining the most priceless of the heirlooms of Dola' Hudol.

At last, though most unwillingly, the man was obliged to repeat his warning to Mr. Rymer, about his too long stay ; and though again the latter, by his coolness and presence of mind, was able to say something which obtained him another minute or two, all resources and expedients were failing, and he was at the door, and still he had not heard the chord he had demanded in sign of acquiescence.

But when the door was opened—and it was a door that could only be noisily opened—Rymer understood the delay ; for as its harsh, jarring sound, as it was thrown back against the wall, ceased, there came through an open window one loud, wild, stormy chord from the instrument, then sudden silence ; and then the sharp, impetuous closing of the window a moment later, which suggested to Rymer thoughts so confused and intricate, that he could not even in fancy disentangle them.

'No matter—she *will* meet me!' he muttered to himself.

CHAPTER X.

THE MAIDEN'S LAKE.

THE intervening hours were spent in wandering about in places where Rymer thought himself most secure from observation. As sunset drew on he loitered before a lane about three miles along the road to the right of Capel Illtyd toll-gate.

It was a fine golden October afternoon; but he looked impatient with its very brightness, as if that for which he waited and watched would not appear till the evening, and yet he could not help waiting and watching, though the sun still burnished the spare autumnal boughs above him, so that they shone like wreaths and wands of dusky Indian gems.

He strolled up and down, and time lagged heavily. He grew sick of the thin-looking crops of the corn-fields, where children were gleaning on his left, because the shadows were so slow in creeping over them; sick of the tiny river flashing through the trees on his right, because its restless silver was still stamped with day's bright image; sick of the burnishing transforming sun, because it was so long in gathering to itself its beamy offspring, that lay sleeping on tree and field and dell, in such heavy languor.

He watched, and paced, and wearied, and as he looked at his watch often doubted if the hands really moved at all.

But the slow reaper and his scythe came on, as surely as slowly, and cut the day down like a flower; and as it lay dying and flooding the earth with sweetness, even in death, Rymer left the road by the lane on the right, and entered into a wonderful labyrinth of sylvan passages; airily roofed and walled by hazels, aspens, and willows; and paved with moss, red leaves, white stones and gray; lights and shadows all mingling and blending in mosaic richness.

Some slight sound meeting his ear made him start and pause to listen with head inclined forward, and eye kindling and dilating. Then he pressed on with a rapid noiseless step, till he reached a small and beautiful sheet of water, walled on one side by the bending trees, dropping their foliage across like a curtain ; and on the other by a quaint little bridge, from which the ivy hung so low as to touch the surface of the water.

There was a dainty elfish elegance about the spot ; the blocks of rock that rose from the water in stately forms were as smooth and polished, and almost as white as alabaster, and suggested the idea of their having been the resting-places of some troop of tiny bathing nymphs. The lake itself was clear as glass, shallow, and paved with smooth fair pebbles.

Rymer stood at the water's edge, and listened till the faint sound he had heard became nearer and more distinct. It was, as he had thought, the sound of footsteps.

He listened as they fell—now light on the stones, now crisp on the dry leaves, now silent on the moss ; and he never turned till they paused very close to him. Then with an expression in which mingled tender welcoming, self-abasement, fear, and reproach, he looked round into the face of the person who had come to keep this appointment with him at the Maiden's Lake.

It was Mrs. Rhys.

As he turned towards her she lifted her veil, and he saw that her cheeks were very white, and her blue eyes and rounded lips were contorted with an expression of scorn and bitter grief.

From old habit he held out his hand, but she refused it by a slight, ever so slight a gesture, and looked steadily into his face.

'And is this you ? ' she said in a voice whose trembling weakness she tried to turn to sternness. 'Is it possible it is John Cunliff who has brought me here to meet him, by this —this honourable letter ; this delicate threat which he knows I can no more help trembling at, than I can help despising it and him now that I *have* come.'

Cunliff was silent. He was reminded at that instant of how he felt when, a child suffering from ghostly horrors in the night, he had cried aloud and brought the household to his room ; his relief, his acute shame, and acute joy, then resembled that which he now experienced.

'Why did you not let me see your true character before ? '

continued the voice that made his heart tremble with its sweetness and anger. ' It might have saved me some misery. I thought you braver, more humane, more chivalrous than most men ; and what must I now think of you—you who could write this letter, threatening me, threatening my husband's peace, your own life, anything—anything to frighten and terrify my already most miserable heart.'

' Oh Catherine, Catherine ! have *you* been brave ? Must it not be a cruel and unjust judge who passes a sentence she dares not deliver with her own lips ? '

' Well, I have come now. I will deliver it with my own lips if you demand it. This is to be the last time we two meet. Is that plain ? '

He looked down on the grass and repeated the words as though they were of a language but half known, and he was uncertain of the accent of each—

' This is to be—the—last—time—we meet.'

' And may you be forgiven,' said Catherine turning away her face, ' for bringing upon us the bitterness of such a last meeting.'

He did not reply, and she moved as if she would leave him.

At the first few steps his eyes looked up with a gleam of water in them ; then, as if drawn towards her in spite of her stinging words, which chained his feet, he fell or threw himself after her retreating form, and his clasped hands fell on the edge of her dress, as it swept the grass, and detained her.

She turned and looked down upon him. Her fair girlish forehead was drawn up in such lines as belong to age, her round under lip was held from quivering by the pressure of her teeth.

' Take care,' she said in a voice of great anguish ; ' Cunliff, we are not alone.'

' No ? Who is here—Rhys ? With his pistols, perhaps ? Is there any such merciful end in store for me ? ' ·

' Mr. Cunliff, one is here without whom I dared not have come.'

' Ah ! your confessor at the church, to whom you have exposed me, I suppose ? '

' No, he knows nothing—shall know nothing, but that you are one whom it is not for my soul's health to be permitted to stay here.'

'And this meddler is near us now?'

'He is.'

'I thank you, Catherine.'

'Oh, don't make me repent more than I already do having obeyed your command!'

She seemed to feel how deeply he was stung and humiliated, for she said in a softened tone—

'It is useless to speak of my regret in giving you this pain—must not everything that brings us together be painful now? There, I will wait—I will sit down.' And gently drawing her dress from his hands, she sat on a piece of the beautiful white rock that rose from the moss. 'Say what you wish to say, I will be patient if you will be generous. We will part as friends—as dear ones if you will; only I conjure you reflect well beforehand on all you say to me. The present is very, very, bitter—the past has been humiliating—let us leave some possible consolation for the future. We are neither of us very fervent Christians, Mr. Cunliff, but we have I think a little real faith in a life to come, where the evil or the goodness of our acts here will be of consequence to us.'

'Oh yes! how glibly a woman can talk when she is mistress of herself, when she knows and acts out all her own secret purposes with the most admirable self-command; when, in a word, the man loves her with his whole heart and soul, while she only loves him with strict attention to the proprieties.'

She seemed about to answer him in his own way, but the angry impulse died out: she sighed deeply and said—

'You shall not offend me by this wild talk, for I can only too well understand it. But I must tell you my husband is at this moment not many miles away. It is dangerous for me to be here, he is so likely to arrive during my absence. Do not then, I entreat you, waste the time in meaningless reproaches.'

Then, as he lay, he began to pick up the small pebbles that lay about him, and throw them into the stream, now with an affectation of utter indifference, now with a quick, passionate, vindictive gesture; and as one after another fell into the water, and sank, deeper grew the gloom in both their hearts, sadder the sense of their utter hopelessness. Cunliff was the first to renew the discourse—

'I have found a profitable occupation, you see, but still it is not half so profitable as the one you taught me—that of throwing every thought and faculty, every energy and hope into the unfathomable gulf of a professing woman's love.'

Did I *profess* to love you ? '

No, you only made me think you professed it.'

Did I even do that ? ' she asked.

God knows, I cannot say ! The upshot of the matter is, we have been as two gamesters playing for a great stake ; but I did not know you played with false dice ; and so, now that I have lost all I played for, you need not wonder if I am sore and complain.'

She was about to rise, but his look restrained her. There was something terrible in his face. Her own face changed as she saw his, her eyes dropped, and for the moment she felt as though all her senses—kept so long on the rack—were about to leave her.

He on his side saw, and had seen the passionate resentment slowly gathering in her heart ; and he had consciously fed it, yet not without a certain quickening sense in his blood of the perilousness of the process, which presently assumed the mastery, and impelled him to change his manner and tone, which became full of an inexpressible tenderness and melancholy, and made the tears for the first time rush to Mrs. Rhys's eyes, as she sat with averted face listening to him.

' You asked me, I think, why I brought you here. I do not know whether I can tell you, without much more talk of myself than I find it agreeable to contemplate. Let me own, however, I am not the brute I have seemed. I did not bring you here to punish you for giving me some gleams of happiness, some fancies and hopes of so winning a nature, that, even now that I understand their hollowness, I am fool enough to wish, like a child, that they might all again return to me, to mock me once more. Do you know what I was when we first met ? But I am mad to ask the question. A pure heart and soul like yours—'

An agitated voice interrupted him—

' Do not say anything like that again to me. The punishment is greater than I can bear.'

' You would I suppose refuse to believe me if I told you, as I do now, with a calm voice, in quiet and deliberate words, and speaking, I hope, with entire possession of my sanity, as yet at least, that it is because you are so pure, so sweet, so intrinsically good, that I compare you with the mass of your fellow-women, and wonder no longer at my own love and worship, or, if you will, at my own infatuation. I have found but one bit of solid ground, one real, true, beautiful, divine thing, one influence of good springing up, I scarce know how, into wondrously productive activity. But this is all mere words —words; what shall I say of it that can even distantly shadow forth its miraculous powers; what but this, it transformed even me? Call it by what name you please, but do not deny that we have known love. Catherine Rhys, look on me—here, grovelling at your feet, and believe what I say, that even if you desert me, still it behoves you to let me know henceforward I have known one true woman, have had the grace to love her, and in my heart-felt devotion to her, have thus some claim to be satisfied, that I too am not utterly beyond redemption. The worst has come and must be endured, I know that—yes, I know it—we cannot undo what is done, then let us draw out of it whatever of benefit we can. You love me, Catherine, or you have bitterly deceived me. You have known what has been passing within my heart for many months—you will not deny *that?*'

'No—you know that I cannot—and you ask it to make me hate myself still more than I do already,' Mrs. Rhys answered bitterly.

'No—only to make you do me one last act of justice, Catherine.'

'Justice! we have both forgotten it towards ourselves and towards—him. What justice can I do you, Mr. Cunliff?'

'Tell me that this very misery with which I go away is not come of an empty dream—a mockery—tell me you *have* loved me. We have been so silent in our hours of happiness. We have felt ourselves so wise in reading each other's thoughts. I may have been misled, or may fancy I have. Don't think it will weaken me to have the sweetness of the truth as well as the bitterness. Since I go, Catherine, give me the words that staying I might never have asked for, and I will go with such terrible contentment as is alone possible for me, if only I might bear with me the unchallenged possession of my one jewel, my sweet amulet, my precious talisman, my only—only earthly possession that I can care for, and gloat over, and draw light and comfort from, in the dreary awful years to come. Catherine, you know what that is—the knowledge of your love.'

'Cunliff, you press me hardly, inconsiderately, cruelly. I think of another beside you. I must think of him—will think of him. He deserves all I can give him—and shall have it.'

'Ay—curse him! No—do not be angry. Doubt not I curse myself with infinitely keener tongue.'

Again she essayed to rise, and again he detained her, but with so much of pleading, passionate entreaty, that she once more yielded with the murmur—

'Cunliff, see how the evening darkens. It is impossible I can stay many minutes longer.'

'What! give him all—all—for evermore—and deny me even these bitter moments which I see you are resolved shall leave no other taste behind. Ah, you are indeed heartless.'

She looked down at him as she echoed his word in tones of bitter reproach, then suddenly—so suddenly that he was shocked into forgetting himself in alarm for her—she burst into tears; and in that moment of weakness and uncontrollable childlike passion of grief, she sobbed out his name with so much tenderness that the instant after she drew in her breath, and stood as if aghast at the revelation she felt she had made.

A secret thrill of joy ran through his veins—even beneath all the unquestionable agony and conflict of John Cunliff's soul—and shook his whole frame. But with the lover's instinctive cunning, which is never more true, inventive, or daring, than when love is in the highest state of spiritual exaltation, he remained silent, as if finding naught that he desired in her passionate invocation. The trick was only too successful. As she saw him despondent at her feet, she could not but feel steal over her—in vivid succession—the remembrances of their first meeting, and the gradual and unsuspected growth of their attachment; favoured as it had been by the general habits of society, and of the people among whom they had been thrown.

And though it was no longer with secret delight she nourished her many remembrances of that time of illusion—though she had no longer pleasure or satisfaction in marking the almost daily processes of change—still, as Cunliff lay there, prostrate, and the consequences were brought home so vividly—she could not help letting her thoughts run back—

even were it only in wonder—or with the hope to draw some comfort out of them for him.

She saw how they had dallied with talk which rarely failed to bring the blood into her cheek. How they had exchanged opinions, and always with the same result; that the opinions insensibly passed away and were forgotten, while leaving something behind too sweet and mysterious to be prudently looked into. She remembered their few but coveted solitary walks together, where even the commonest acts of courtesy insensibly assumed a strange and attractive meaning; their half-accidental, half-managed visits to the same country house, or the same London drawing-rooms, at the same time; where each of the hypocrites of love played the same well-acted part of glad surprise at the unexpectedness of the meeting—she from the woman's instinct of safety, he to cover her design while feeling he thus strengthened the claims he might one day urge.

She saw all this now with changed eyes, and would have given some of the best drops of her heart's blood to wipe away from her soul the stains such a career left there.

But she saw also, with almost a new sense, how strong and irresistible a love had grown up under those evil conditions. How her present scorn of the conditions, and of the miserableness of the whole array of temptations, proved the strength and reality of the love.

And so step by step she was driven back to look into herself—to note what a creature of impulse she had been—what a plaything every one had made of her from her earliest years—spoiled by her parents at home, her teachers at school, and most of all by her husband, who saw in her a beautiful idol, and treated it as if half of his own creation.

Then again, when she had gone forth into society, what new and fascinating changes were rung on sweet-sounding bells to the same old theme, her gracious goodness in consenting simply to look and to be; when she became the especial pet of fashion; the favourite object of court by hosts and hostesses who wished to invest their dreary dinner-tables with a new charm; the day-dream of young men for her beauty, talent, and fascination; who fluttered numerously about her and made her the constant centre of a most brilliant circle.

And had Catherine Rhys been no more than she thus saw in herself her career would doubtless have been that of a thousand others—the career of a woman who has no inconvenient scruples against any kind of enjoyment, provided only all be done with due outward decorum and respectability.

Catherine had soon found herself to be quite another woman, when her strong though undeveloped passions and affections began to be called forth by a new influence. Looking back at herself, she seemed now for the first time to understand herself, and could not resist the fascination of collecting together, as into one focus, all the scattered traits under the new light. She had always been kind-hearted, and rarely thoughtful in her kindness ; pure in feeling and desire, but with no fixed basis of religious or moral principle ; worthy of admiration for her many real and charming qualities, but spoiling all by the practical habit of dissociating cause and effect ; and demanding worship for herself, whatever that self might choose to be, in any moods, however wilful and fantastic.

And if all these things are changed, and for the better, how can the heart of the woman but acknowledge the author of the change ? How refuse to him what he asks, as his sole repayment ? She turns her brimming eyes full upon him, takes his hand, kisses it, and then says to him—

' Did you not know in fact, beyond all possibility of honest denial on my part, the true state of things with me, no power should now draw it from me.'

' No ! ' she added, with uplifted eyes, and with the smile of a martyr at the stake, at the moment she feels she is about to triumph and make the eager soul resist and keep down the shrinking and coward body—with a smile like this on her face, even while the big drops were falling heavily on his hand, ' No—God, who sees into my heart, may best judge me—but I think I could keep my secret in spite of you, John Cunliff, had I any secret the keeping of which was humanly possible. But as it is not—I can but own to you that I am not ungrateful ; that if I am in any way less frivolous than I was, less heartless, less inclined to see all creation as a kind of magnified image of myself—but rather to ask why, amid so sad and yet so sweet a world, where there is so much good to be done— why I, so pitiful and useless a being, exist—it is to you I owe the change. Aye, wonderful as it may sound, it is you who would have led me away from God, who have carried me, and are now carrying me nearer to Him ! Dear friend, if you wish then to hear the truth—which can only shame me by its existence, not by its declaration—I will no longer deny you the poor satisfaction.'

' You love me ? '

' I do.'

For a time that seemed to both as if centuries of thought and feeling were sweeping over them, they were silent.

Then she spoke very softly—

' Have I now satisfied you ? '

' I cannot thank you. I suppose you know that ? '

' You do thank me. I am sure you do. Well now, Cunliff, it is your part to be generous, manly, considerate. If our love be such as we have both, with unconscious flattery perhaps, painted it, it is a love that will not allow you to attach evermore a breath of any kind of reproach or dishonour to my name. So also is it a love that will make me yearn not to see you, nor in any way, for a long time to come, to communicate with you. No—hear me out !—but that will make me watch unceasingly, to learn of your good works, of your growing fame, of your recognised power and influence among and over your fellow-men.'

' Dreams ! ' ejaculated Cunliff, and turned as if he would no longer even look upon her.

When he again turned, he was startled to see how unconscious he had been while she had risen and walked away homeward.

Swiftly he pursued and overtook her.

She, however, resolutely moved on towards the slope in front, which had to be ascended, and he was obliged to content himself with pouring out the last bitter flow of speech as he walked by her side.

' And is it possible that you can thus dismiss me to my fate ? Can you see me return, perhaps, to the base life from which only an angel could have drawn me ? You are, you must be —the instrument of my salvation ! Live for me—and I will be to you what man never yet was to woman. I feel I could write my name and yours so deeply in the world's heart, that they should never be forgotten. I am no philanthropist, yet I could, I think, under the inspiration of your ever-present love, move the men of my time out of their ceaseless talk into serious action—for the benefit of the recking mass of miserable humanity that lies all about us. The beauty of such work would impel me on when the duty of it might seem too weak. But I need your eyes to refresh my dulled ones—if the sense of that beauty is to keep alive and be fruitful. Catherine, dearest, is there no hope for me beyond aught you have yet said ? It is your love I need. With that I will play my part worthily before God and man.'

'That love shall be yours so far as I can in honour give it. Honour! God help me—for even His common words fail to express my sad state. But He will pity me, I think, if I act by the light given—and that light, dear friend, says—I must go this way, and you that !'

She pointed as she spoke, first downward towards Dola' Hudol; and then to Dolgarrog, and the mountains behind it, through which lay the road to Cunliff's own home.

They were now on the edge of the hill they had been ascending, and stood almost on a level with the dimly-seen mountain-tops, across the valley that lay below in misty distance, winding in large, grand undulations from Criba Ban on the left, to Snowdon on the right. Looking towards Snowdon, the valley appeared almost straight; and down it, as Cunliff turned his eyes that way, there came sailing through the sky, where the golden haze of the sunset had left just a last suggestion of its warm radiance, a single heron—gaunt even at a distance—stately and steady in flight, unswerving and swift. With that unconscious superstition that in moments of great import makes trivialities become as the signs of fate, Rymer looked at the bird, and felt that if it continued coming straight down over the valley, and passed where they two were, as certainly must this bitterness pass his lips. As he stood and looked, Mrs. Rhys came close before him, holding out her hand, as if taking her final leave. He received it, but dropped it again ; and sat on a bit of low broken wall beside her, his hat off, his hands clenched between his knees, his eyes on the patch of dark cloud sailing out of the faint but still golden distance.

As Mrs. Rhys looked at that white face, and that broad brow, where the lines seemed to have marked the minutes instead of the years that had passed over it, there came a rush of warm, brave pity into her heart. A mother's comforting power and sweetness was in her touch and voice as she laid her hand on his shoulder and said—

'I should suffer more than I do if I did not know that with you things are better than with me. *My* existence ! What can it be now at the best? Patience, endurance, success in hiding the only living thing in my heart. This is suffering! But with you it is all different. You have a comforter. Do you think I have not seen it? Call it the dream of your youth—your first ideal—what you will; I shall call it as Christ did, 'the spirit of truth.' You *have* seen truly; *I* never did till I knew you. You may again see truly. And oh, Cunliff, may these tears that dim your eyes at this parting be the falling of the mist that has blinded them so long. This very suffering itself should help you; for you know that for such minds as yours there is a rebound from deepest misery to highest and noblest bliss. And you will let this be so now? If you wish there should be one link between us still, if you would let some light and hope into my dark life, you will let me hear this has been so with you.'

He felt that she bent down towards him; he saw the lonely heron—his messenger of fate—coming steadily, swiftly on through all the clear spiritual beauty of the evening sky, growing larger and more gaunt and sharp in outline.

It came—it passed. He cowered on the ruined wall.

Mrs. Rhys stooped and kissed his brow, but he did not stir, for he thought the kiss was not for him, but for that spirit within him, of which she had spoken, and in which he had no faith.

He knew then that she was going from him, but could not stir or speak; there was in the quiet, gentle step, as it receded, something that told him no gesture, no word could stop it.

But suddenly it did stop, and his heart seemed to stop beating at the same instant. Yet he did not dare to look up or to move.

The steps came hastening back, and he could but look up now with a certain fear, for they were like those of a person running from danger.

The next instant Mrs. Rhys was clinging to his arm, trembling, panic-stricken.

He looked beyond her for the cause of her alarm, and saw it slowly ascending the path through the firs—a gray figure, tall and courtly, a grave, long face, pale and bearded. He did not recognise it, but knew that he had done so. He needed to ask her no question, he needed only to think how to help her, as the great blue eyes and white trembling lips appealed to him with a child's helplessness—a woman's agony.

Selfish as he was, Cunliff at that moment would gladly have had the earth swallow him for her sake. For himself and his own danger, in meeting the man who was approaching them, he cared little. But for her his very soul yearned to do the thing that was best. He conquered his own strong longing to let things so chance as to drive her to him for protection. He gave a quick, scrutinising glance at the coming face, and saw that it was at present looking down. Was there hope still that he had not seen them? No sooner did the thought come than he saw it was the one to act upon.

He looked at her, and said quickly, but decisively—

'He may not have seen me. You must meet him as if he had not. Have courage!'

His look and voice had complete command over her. Her cold hand was firm, even before it left his, with one tight, icy pressure.

'Have courage, dear life!'

'I have—I will have,' answered the white lips. 'God bless you! Go—go quickly!'

And they parted, Cunliff going to the little wood, and Mrs. Rhys hurrying to the brow of the hill to meet her husband.

Cunliff could not, to save his soul, have kept out of earshot of that meeting. He could urge her on to save herself; but if it were too late, she should not stand alone to meet that man's rage. Whatever his interference might cost him, or her, interfere he would if he suspected danger.

So he crept along inside the firs, as she went with a sickly miserable smile on her face down the path up which the form he could not see was coming.

The firs now were too thick to allow him to see her, but he heard her footsteps, and his own kept pace with them. Soon he heard also the ascending footsteps, and wondered whether they were not more than usually measured and deliberate. Was *she* thinking so, poor soul, and trembling? he asked himself.

They have met—he has heard the footsteps stop.

'Dear Owen!' says the sweet, hysterical voice.

Cunliff can just see through the trees that her husband has taken both her hands and kissed her.

'You are looking very pale, darling—are you not well?'

The tone is rather politely kind than tenderly anxious or shocked. Is it natural to him, Cunliff wonders; or is it

strangely unnatural, and filling her with alarm, as it fills him
with alarm for her sake ?

Then they turn and move on slowly together towards Dola'
Hudol, Mrs. Rhys murmuring some inaudible reply to her
husband's question ; and Cunliff is left in wretched suspense
—suspense that is not to be passively endured—that makes
it impossible for him to withstand following and watching the
two figures. Gliding along in the shelter of the firs, he
descends the hill with them ; gliding on inside the rude road
wall, he goes with them till they reach the carriage-gates of
Dola' Hudol. But no movement of theirs shows him what he
so much longs to know, and he is never near enough to over-
hear their words.

The great gates are open, and still remain open after the
master and mistress have passed through them ; but now
he dare only follow them with his eyes up the broad, rising
carriage-drive. They stop at the little side door of the Tudor
arch, and then he loses sight of them.

But he lingers about the place, watching the windows as the
lights appear in them one by one, with a passionate dread
that will not let him go—that drags back his feet when he
takes some paces homeward.

The park trees are black, and the owls of Dola' Hudol are
filling the sweet, still night-air with their melancholy cries
before he has forced himself to take his way back to Dolgarrog,
to his little close lodgings at the old Council House—to struggle
there with his remorse and his miserable suspense as to
Catherine's fate.

<hr>

CHAPTER XI.

THE HOME OF THE PEACEMAKER.

DAYLIGHT is spreading slowly down the long valley below
Capel Illtyd, driving the clinging river mist before it. There
is light enough for the miners as they cross the little bridge
to see part of the Abbey ruins, even if another light did not
fall redly upon them—the light of a turf fire burning in the
great refectory, which is now the centre of a straggling farm-
house, hidden from the bridge by trees.

As the light streams from the hidden window, and flickers

across the yard to the roofless chapel, with its nail-studded doors and mouldering jagged walls, there is such an air of stillness and solemnity about the place, one could half expect to see some monkish form among the shadows. Approaching the yard by the muddy little path beside the stream, one perceives on the fresh breeze a slight odour of musty antiquity. The wooden stile by which the yard is entered is so rotten, great crumbling splinters can be picked from it; and the moss on the wall is deep and rich with age.

The chief door of the farm-house is directly opposite the decaying doors of the old chapel. It is iron-plated and nail-studded, and opens right into the great refectory. The window is a little to the right, and shows this morning an interior worthy of Rembrandt.

The span roof of black oak, still in perfect preservation, seems to mock, by its grand proportions, the lowly fortunes of the family, gathered now round the wide chimney-place.

Two small tree-trunks are blazing there, giving out a pleasant, pungent smell; giving out also a red light, that leaps to the rich black oak of the roof, and to the fair brown oak of the dressers and cupboards, which glow and deepen in colour as if blood was rising to their surface at its kiss.

Old-fashioned polished chair legs throw their shadows on the gray stone floor; on the homely blues and yellows of the dinner-ware; on the shelves, and the breakfast things on the little table by the fire; and on the bright irons and brasses of the garden tools and cooking utensils, hung up indiscriminately in the chimney-place.

On one side of this chimney-place, which is all sooty shadow and vivid light, sit two great boys, squeezed together in one elbow-chair, their whole attention centred in a little pipkin of milk, placed on the logs to boil. A shaggy little terrier, on a high stool beside them, fixes his greenish-brown eye on the same object, and with no less interest and watchfulness, perhaps with a keener appetite. On the other side of the fire, with a baby of two months old on her lap, sits a girl in a black dress and square-bibbed apron. That is Nest, the curate's eldest daughter. Her fair, simple face and light hair, her blue eyes and wide laughing mouth look pretty in that dark old chimney, whatever they might look elsewhere.

Two tiny girls sit at the table, waiting for the milk, and comparing the fulness of their basins of cut bread; and opposite these, with a three-days-old ' Times ' in his hands, is Daniel Lloyd, the curate of Capel Illtyd.

His eldest girl sends anxious looks at him from time to time, for she sees that there has been some addition since yesterday morning to his many anxieties and troubles.

'What's the matter, Nest—another stray ?' demands one of the boys, looking eagerly at Nest, as she rose in haste, and went to the window, as if to look at the pigeons strutting on the ruins.

' I do believe, papa,' cries Nest, in sudden animation, 'there's Robert coming across the fields ! '

' Robert ! ' cried the curate. ' What !—not Robert Chamberlayne, surely ? '

' Yes—it is him ! He's waiting on the stile now ; he can't get across for the sheep.'

The curate rose, his face illumined with sudden warmth and gladness, and came to the door ; while the boys rushed out delightedly, and Nest put off her nursing-apron.

The yard was crowded by an immense flock of sheep, which Chidlaw, the tenant of the Abbey farm, and the curate's landlord, with an old shepherd, and two long-nosed dogs, were trying to drive into the chapel, whose ancient doors stood open, showing a roofless, grassy little hall, which was often used to confine the sheep in while they were being marked.

The curate and his boys looked across the, as yet, impassable sea of wool, and saw Robert Chamberlayne sitting with one leg over the stile, looking down upon the sheep with lazy perplexity.

' What, can't you get across to us, Bob ? ' said Mr. Lloyd, laughing. ' And how are you, Bob ? Well ? '

' Yes ; jolly enough, thank you, sir,' shouted back Robert's voice, with the mellow ring of health in it.

' God bless him ! ' said the curate to himself ; ' he's just the same as ever.' And he stood looking across at him with kindling eyes, feeling as if a bit of the brightest and healthiest of the outer world had come suddenly to his home in that handsome face of Robert's. The very sight of his fresh light clothes was pleasant to Daniel Lloyd, who was used to looking down on the same rows of coats Sunday after Sunday, and year after year.

The boys shouted out no end of information to him, a little of which he heard, but the greater part of which was lost in the loud lamentations with which the whole place was distracted. He did not appear at all troubled at the delay, but sat comfortably with his cigar between his fingers—in amused patience—laughing across the noisy yard.

' So you haven't had much of a harvest here ? ' he shouted.

' No,' answered the curate. ' And how goes farming with you, Bob ? '

' Splendidly,' roared Robert, half despairing of being heard above the increasing tumult.

But the curate did hear, and thought with a sigh of the failure of his own potato crop.

' I don't know how you manage to tear yourself away from it all just now, Bob. I hope it's a good wind that blew you here, eh ? '

' No ! confoundedly bad.'

' Ah ! '

' Yes. Halloa ! the tide's beginning to turn now.'

By fair or foul means Chidlaw had got one of the sheep into the chapel, and the others began to awaken some fears in the minds of beholders as to whether they would not smother each other in their blundering haste to follow.

The latest stragglers nearly threw Robert down as he came across the yard.

' I can't act patience on *that* monument any longer,' he said. ' How are you, sir ? I was at church yesterday, and you did not recognise me.'

There was a deep respect and affection in the manner of the young man, as he came up to him and grasped his hand, that moved the curate very much.

' No, Bob ! ' he said, ' I shouldn't have known you. It is a long time since we met. I scarcely expected to see you again.'

' Or wished, sir ? ' asked Robert.

' Ah, Bob ; I often do that.'

The young man held out his hand again, colouring with pleasure. They passed on into the refectory, Chamberlayne, by the way, pulling the ears of the boys, and greeting Mrs. Chidlaw, the curate's landlady, with a compliment that made her for some minutes oblivious to everything around her. There was a touch of gentle reverence in his greeting to Nest, as she met him with a child in her arms and one at her skirts —looking, he thought, like one of the tender virgin mothers of the old pictures—fair, and sweet, and placid. Her black dress, and the black frocks of the little girls, reminded him how one kind face, that had always grown kinder at his coming, was no longer there to meet him. The remembrance put a sudden quietness and constraint upon him, which lasted all the while he was drinking the coffee Nest made for him ; and when at last the curate took him into the study, the boys were both agreed that Bob was not nearly so jolly as he used to be, and went out together to discuss the fact with Chidlaw.

The curate had winced a little when Robert asked if he would go with him into the study, for it was a spot to which the gentle care of Nest had not penetrated since her mother's death. The window-plants, which the still hands now crossed over the still heart had tended so lovingly for the sake of him who worked here, were dead and dry ; and the very walls of the room seemed to weep for her ; for the damp she used to keep from it by her skilful care, now oozed through the bright papers and discoloured the low ceiling.

Daniel Lloyd did not trust himself to look round, but waited at the door till Robert came in, and then sat down and kept his eyes upon his face.

'I thought there must be something the matter, Bob,' he said ; 'at least I was half afraid there was—by your coming here before you went to Bod Elian. Sit down, my boy, and tell me all about it.'

Robert knew the room well, for it was here he used to pore over lessons during the three years he was the curate's pupil, and he was at once conscious of an indescribable dreariness about it he never noticed before.

'Yes,' he said, 'it's the most confounded sort of business I ever had to deal with in all my life before ; and, if it were not so terrible to Elias Morgan, would be the most absurd !'

'Elias Morgan !' echoed the curate, with a look in his eye that rapidly changed from wonder to sudden enlightenment, and then to deep concern. Robert went on—

'Let me see. I've got the lawyer's letter somewhere. Oh, here it is ! Read that, and you'll know the best, or rather the worst, part of the business.'

In silence Mr. Lloyd took the letter, went to the window, and there read it slowly and carefully. After that he did not need to ask many questions in order to learn the true character of the calamity impending over his neighbour, and of his pupil's unfortunate share in bringing it about.

'Poor things!' he said, 'the blow will be very terrible!' Then, seeing the pain on Chamberlayne's face, he added: 'My dear boy, I really feel for you.'

Robert sat down on the broad window-seat, saying—

'I'm as wretched about it as a fellow well can be!'

'Elias is my neighbour,' said the curate, 'though he hasn't spoken to me of late. For many many years we have trodden the same ground; our footsteps have perpetually crossed, yet he keeps himself now more rigidly aloof than ever, as if he thought it not merely impossible for two men to lead by different roads to the same God, but that my road must be to a very bad end indeed! Yet I can but feel for him—I can but feel for him! He is a proud, austere man; he'll think that the scorn of his neighbours will be turned upon him. The blow will, indeed, be awful to him! The poor children, too! Yes, yes; it's a sad business altogether! Bob,' he said presently, 'I'll go up with you to break this to Elias. At the worst, he can but turn me out of the house; and if he did that, I should be tasting a little of his humiliation, which will do me more good than sitting here thinking of him.'

'I was going to beg you to do so, sir,' said Robert wonderfully relieved, 'but I was half-ashamed to show you how cowardly I feel about it altogether. You see, it makes it so much worse, my cousin being what he is. He's not one to let the blow be softened for him a bit. I know he wouldn't take a penny from me to save himself from starving.'

'Well, Bob, I have a letter to write, and one or two things I must see to before I can be ready to go with you to Bod Elian. There are the boys wild to be at you, I know. You must give them a few minutes, and remember the accumulation of gossip Nest has for you.'

So Robert went back to the refectory, and had just seated himself comfortably opposite Nest, with his favourite little Margaret on his knee, when the curate called him back.

'I want to ask you a question, Bob,' he said; 'and mind you're quite at liberty to decline answering it if you like to do so. It's about your cousin Hirell!'

Robert coloured, and looked with an air of deep interest at a cart lumbering past the window.

'You have changed your mind; you have given up all these old fancies, possibly?' asked Mr. Lloyd.

'No sir!'

'May I ask, then, Robert (and mind you needn't answer if you'd rather not)—may I ask how you think this change will affect you with regard to her?'

'I think it will play the deuce with me altogether, with regard to Elias, and everybody belonging to him,' answered Robert gloomily.

'You think it would not be right to her to say anything under these circumstances?'

'I'm afraid,' said Robert, 'she would think I wanted to take advantage of their difficulties.'

'I think so too, Bob,' said the curate rising; 'and this is what I want to say to you—if you *do* think of speaking to Hirell, do *so before* they know of this. Now go and talk to Nest.'

CHAPTER XII.

BOD ELIAN.

BOD ELIAN (the abode or dwelling of Elias, an ancestor of the Morgans, from whom the house was named in the days of its prosperity) lay up the mountains on the right of the Capel Illtyd road.

Daniel Lloyd and Chamberlayne ascended the path through a thick wood, so thick that, in spite of the rains of yesterday, the ground they trod was almost dry, and crumbled under their feet.

This led them to the foot of another hill, one far more rugged and steep, where the wind blew fiercely, and the wild hungry-looking sheep tore great patches off their coats, and lamed themselves in getting to the little bits of storm-blackened vegetation on which they fed with utmost wolfish voracity; looking up, some with half-threatening, others with pleading and pathetic faces, at the intruders crossing their wretched pasture.

'I know the poor fellow who rents these fields,' said Daniel Lloyd; 'his own food is as scant as that of his sheep.'

'Why doesn't he come to Kent?' said Chamberlayne.

The other smiled without answering; and they went on till

they had left the sheep far below, tearing at the half-bald hill-side, like ravenous children at the breast of a mother dead of famine.

And now the hill, as they continued to ascend, became more barren, and seemed leading to a region utterly destitute of all life and beauty, till suddenly there appeared before them, on the hill's summit, a fringe of foliage against the sky.

'I think,' said Chamberlayne, 'I know where we are.'

'Yes,' answered Lloyd, 'that is the garden of Bod Elian.'

The very word 'garden' seemed strangely out of place. The garden of Bod Elian, looking at it from where they stood, far below it, had an ethereal, unreal aspect : its trees might have been but fringes of the dusky cloud that hung over them and seemed mimicking their shapes. The path did not lead them to this, but curved round the hill till they came to a spot where they could see the house of which they were in search, and where they had the garden below them on the right.

They were now descending a green sloping field, in which sheep and a few cows were grazing. Below this was another field, level and brown ; and therein, with the garden trees on its right, and a wet heavily rutted road leading to it from the left, stood Bod Elian.

It was even more austerely simple than the Dolgarrog houses, as if its builder had had in his mind the thought, 'I want a house to shelter me from rain, and storms, and sun, and nothing more ;' and had said to all manner of comfort and beauty, as Thomas à Kempis would have a true Christian say to happiness, 'I can do without thee.'

It stood alone, detached from the garden trees ; and the sun, shining on its flat, dark face, took from it none of its coldness and solemnity. Some of the windows were open, but no snowy curtain or blind flapped in the breeze ; the windows were dark, no brightness from within welcomed the brightness without. And the sunshine lay on the house-front, like a smile on a dead, stiff face.

As they came upon the road leading directly to it, Mr. Lloyd suddenly stood still ; and Chamberlayne, looking at him inquiringly, saw a gleam of kindly emotion in his clear gray eyes. He looked in the direction of their gaze ; and beheld, in the distance, on the slope of a stony field, Elias Morgan's new chapel ; the roof just finished ; a flag flying merrily in the morning breeze.

Robert examined it with his tourist-glass. There was no creature near, except a dog asleep upon some clothes of the workmen, who had probably gone to dinner. There was such an air of stillness around it as seemed to belong to a ruin rather than to a new building; and almost as a ruin the two visitors to Bod Elian, knowing what they did of its builder's fortunes, regarded it. It was a simple building—so small and humble that John the Baptist might have raised it in the wilderness, and preached there in his garment of camel's hair.

The two stood gazing at it silently.

'And this was his great ambition,' said Chamberlayne, deeply moved; 'this is what we must show him to be his castle in the air.'

Daniel Lloyd did not make any reply as they turned towards Bod Elian. He was the curate of Capel Illtyd, and his feelings concerning this chapel were necessarily of more mixed a nature than Chamberlayne's. The bit of hardy colour on his cheek grew deeper as they approached the house.

'I confess to you,' he said to Chamberlayne, 'I feel anything but sure that my interference will be welcome to Elias.'

'Oh Mr. Lloyd, but what is it to me?' cried Chamberlayne earnestly. 'I am more of a coward every step I take. Look at that flag; fancy them all going out to see it hoisted this morning; there's the new red waggon Hughes was speaking of, I suppose; and what's this? Oh, the two new rooms, see, built out at that end. By Jove!'

He slashed at the grass and weeds by the road with his stick, as if each thing he had mentioned had increased his indignation against himself and his unwelcome news.

'I am no longer in doubt, sir,' he said, suddenly turning to the curate and speaking in a low voice, 'as to what we were talking about. I will try and see Hirell, if you will talk with Elias a little while before he is told.'

'There's someone in the hall,' remarked Mr. Lloyd.

'It is Hirell!' said Chamberlayne, slashing away at the weeds harder than ever.

The ground was sodden, and their footsteps fell noiselessly upon it, so that they approached the door without being perceived by two persons just inside it.

These were Hirell and Kezia Williams. One side of the hall was crowded with large packages, and by one of them

knelt Hirell, drawing aside the cover to peep at the velvet
cushion of the arm-chair it enclosed. Kezia was feeding some
linnets in a long cage, and listening with a gentle flutter to
Hirell's exclamations of delight. Though she spoke in Welsh,
Chamberlayne knew the meaning of the girl's joyous tones
too well ; and concealed pity gave his own voice and manner
a deeper seriousness and gentleness than he had meant it to
show, as he entered the door, meeting her face to face, and
calling her by name.

' Hirell ! '

' Robert ! '

And then he was holding her hand, listening without
understanding, as she spoke apologetically of her coolness
yesterday.

Hirell's mode of speech was peculiar. She was frequently
seized by hesitation, almost painfully apparent in her face and
manner, but she never allowed herself to go on speaking while
this lasted. She would be suddenly silent and confused in
the middle of a sentence sometimes ; but during that silence,
and while the listener pitied her, would recover herself, and
then she would continue her speech with a grace and firmness,
a sweet dignity of voice and look, that at times was noble.

'Nay, be not afraid for your child, my friend,' the old
minister, Ephraim Jones, had once said, in reply to some
tenderly expressed misgivings of Elias ; ' her very voice speaks
within her like the ringing of a bell that is sound.'

Robert Chamberlayne could hardly realise what it was,
whether voice, eyes, old memories or new hopes, that charmed
him so as to deprive him almost of the power of speech as
Hirell spoke. He only knew that some strange spell was over
him.

' I am so glad to see you, Robert,' said Hirell ; ' Hugh was
afraid you would think wo were not pleased to see you yesterday, but we were indeed—all of us were—but—'

She stopped as she noticed Daniel Lloyd talking to Kezia,
and moved to him slightly, then went on speaking with quiet,
genial confidence.

' You find us just at the beginning of a great change. But
you knew. And have you thought about us—did you fancy
how all would be altered here ? '

' Well—yes—I supposed it would alter things for you,'
answered Robert with a desperate effort.

'Father,' said Hirell, 'is in the new parlour with Hugh. He is writing a letter to the master of the college where Hugh is going ; and some other letters to friends he once knew in London, and who have been very kind in their congratulations on this change.'

'Oh !' said Robert, his gaze straying from the sweet direct eyes to the little fingers playing with a gold chain, the only bit of yesterday's finery Hirell wore this morning. 'Then your father is engaged just now ? '

'Yes, but not for many minutes, for he is expecting company. Mr. Ephraim Jones, the minister you saw us with yesterday, is coming to see the chapel, and to have prayers for Hugh. Kezia, won't you bring Mr. Lloyd in ? '

She led the way as she spoke towards the *old* parlour, which Robert remembered well enough.

Mr. Lloyd did not follow them, but stood in the hall, talking with Kezia about certain poor people to whose houses they both were in the habit of going on the same errand.

It was a damp, faded, commonplace room into which Robert followed Hirell. The window was shut because Hirell's dresses were lying here. The table was covered with pieces of silk, and near it stood two chairs in which Hirell and Kezia had sat at work till the arrival of the new furniture.

Every bright ribbon and shining fold of silk added to the disturbance of Robert's mind. Presently Hirell said—

'I am to go to London for a little while, and one must do as other people, you know.'

As she sat down and carelessly took her work in her hand, Robert dropped into Kezia's chair on the other side of the little round table, and watched her nervously, feeling as if every stitch she set were a fresh knot for him to undo in this tangled web.

He looked at Hirell as she sat and stitched; and her hand, like a soft little bird held captive by a string, flew to and fro from her work; he looked at her, and all his honest wish was in his eyes.

Hirell felt his gaze on her face, and drew from it the knowledge that Robert found her much changed from what she had been when they were together last; and she knew well that the change was not for the worse, but was one of the many delights which were just now being showered upon her. She was beautiful; the knowledge was not new to her, but it came with exquisite freshness from Robert's honest eyes. She bent her head and trembled, for she knew that her childish joy had risen in soft blushes to her face, and in tears to her eyes.

'Will you forgive me, Hirell, if I ask you a question that may make you very angry with me?'

Robert's voice trembled; his arms were on the table flattening the crisp silk, and Hirell knew that he was looking upon her with very bright and eager glances. She vaguely supposed it was one of the old silly gallant speeches he was about to make, and tried to overcome her confusion, and smile as she said—

'If your question makes me angry, Robert, I promise to forgive you; and if it does not, as I don't believe it will do, there is no forgiveness needful, I suppose?'

'No, I suppose not—not in that case; but I'm afraid it won't be so. I'm afraid it will make you angry, Hirell. I shouldn't ask it just now, not till we had seen more of each other, after such a long separation; but I have no choice as to time. I must go away to-morrow unless—well, I want to ask you, Hirell, if you remember—if you ever think with any pleasure of the old days when I was here, when we spent so much time together?'

Hirell could not quite see why so much earnestness need have been put into the question. It was one which she had often thought she should like to ask Robert; and now he had asked her, but not exactly as she would have asked it of him. She was puzzled, but on the whole pleased that he should think so seriously of a time which was very dear to her.

'Yes, Robert,' she answered, 'I have a great delight in thinking of that time.'

'And do you ever wish it back, Hirell, as I do?'

Hirell paused in her work, resting an elbow in the palm of one hand and her chin in the other, looking dreamily, without one pang of regret, on the silk that Robert was crushing.

'Do you?' she said in a soft, wondering tone. 'Do you wish it back, Robert? I don't—I can't—sweet as it was. I can't wish it back. As one gets older one sees so many things coming so much more wonderful and happy than anything one has known before! But don't think me ungrateful, Robert, or changeful,' she said more earnestly, looking up at him and smiling. 'I would not have that time cut out of my life for the world. It was like what nothing else will ever be again. I remember it as one in a rich orchard full of ripening fruit remembers the blossoms—they are lovely to remember ; but one would not wish to have them back instead of the fruit.'

'No, that stands to reason,' said Robert, bluntly and sadly —'and I don't know that I mean I should care for the old state of things altogether. I'm too lazy now to satisfy Mr. Lloyd's idea of a morning's work ; and—but that's nothing to do with it, Hirell, it isn't the time I want back—it is my old friend of those days, Hirell—it is you ! '

Hirell's hands fell in her lap, her cheeks turned pale, and her eyes, as she raised them to Robert's face, had a chilled, blank look in them.

'Robert,' she said, ' I suppose I know what you mean.'

' I mean, will you be my wife, Hirell, as you promised me when you were a little girl, and my dearest friend, though not half as dear as you are now ? '

Hirell sat silent. She felt cold and choking. All her bright life seemed threatened by sudden dulness and mono-tony. She felt like a child who, hastening gladly to some gay feast, is asked to turn away with a dry crust. What! marry Robert—honest, commonplace Robert Chamberlayne —-for so she could not but look upon him, without stopping to ask as to the justice of the opinion—and live all her life long in his boasted county, crammed so full of corn and hops, or, as Hirell looked at it, of bread and beer, that one could scarcely breathe !

Was this the thing for which she was asked to give up all the new delicious dreams that were enchanting her life day and night ?

She looked at Robert's large hands thrown half-clasped across the table in his eager, hearty earnestness, and rising laid her own hands, cold and trembling, on them.

'Robert, you asked me to forgive you if your question should be one to cause me pain.'

' Was it then, Hirell ? '

'Yes,' answered Hirell, selfish in her intense desire to throw off the chill weight his words had laid on her heart. ' I wonder you should have asked it, Robert. But never mind ; whatever pain it has given me I forgive freely.'

' Thank you,' said Robert, taking her extended hand, and looking in her face with a deep regret. She would not have been flattered had she known what an unselfish regret it was ;

how much he was thinking of *her* loss by her refusal, and how little of his own. His evident pain, as he clasped her hand and looked at her, gave her much trouble.

' I wish,' she said, with tears, ' I could forgive myself as easily for causing you disappointment, Robert.'

' Now, don't you think of that,' cried Robert, with sudden relief and heartiness ; ' don't you, for a moment, think of that, Hirell. *I* sha'n't hurt; I mean I shall throw it right off, and forget it in very little time. Before I've been back a month, you shall hear of me being as jolly as ever. Don't you have a grain of uneasiness about me. Now promise me you won't.'

And holding her hand in one of his, he laid his other on her slight shoulder, and looked in her face with a smile that seemed so simply bright and genial, that Hirell could but smile too at her own fears concerning Robert's heart-wound, as she answered with perfect sincerity, and with the slightest touch of contempt at his utter want of romance—

' No, I won't be uneasy about you, Robert. I don't think there is much cause for uneasiness.'

' Not the slightest ; and now let's forget it. I shall go and speak to Kezia, or we shall have Mr. Lloyd converting her.'

As he passed out of the door a dog came in, and he turned his head a little to look after it, remembering it as an old acquaintance ; and Hirell, whose eyes were following him, saw that his face was full of trouble—so full as to make her feel for the moment she had hardly understood him. In spite of all that he had said then, he was suffering, she thought—even a nature like his was not to be easily read.

But she soon forgot him ; for her pale-blue silk, the most beautiful of all her dresses, at which Kezia and herself had worked so hard, was now finished ; and Hirell stole up to her own room to try it on, intending to come down in it and dazzle Hugh and her father—both of whom enjoyed such pretty surprises of Hirell's after her own manner.

<hr>

CHAPTER XIII.

ELIAS MORGAN'S FEAST.

In honour of the expected guest, the Reverend Ephraim Jones, an unusually bountiful repast was being prepared in the kitchen of Bod Elian.

Before the two new parlours were built, the kitchen was the

principal room in the house. It was a large long-shaped room, with low ceiling, and smoke-blackened beams, thick set with iron hooks, on which almost every suspendable thing in the kitchen was hung. There were old market-baskets, hams and flitches of bacon, jugs, hats, kettles, horse-collars, and old sets of harness ; strings of onions, bags of seeds, bunches of dried herbs, and coils of stocking yarn. But to-day the beam hooks were crowded beyond their wont by the provisions for the great chapel feast which was to be given by Elias to-morrow to all the members of the Dolgarrog chapel. Large joints of butcher's meat—a rare sight in Bod Elian—kept the noses and tongues of the three farm-dogs in a state of perpetual unrest, as they prowled about the kitchen in spite of Kezia's gentle scoldings, and the vigorous flappings of the rough servant-girl's apron. The morning sun shone on nets of rich russet apples, that had plainly never ripened in the windy little orchard on the hill behind; and the dresser was crowded with parcels of grocery, and cakes and sweetmeats. Hampers half unpacked stood about, bewildering Kezia, as she moved gently to and fro over her work.

Robert Chamberlayne found her here, frying 'lightcake,' as she called some heavy preparation of batter, very popular in her country. Mr. Lloyd sat near the fire, chatting to her about the domestic affairs of the farm. He looked at Robert with a kindly anxiety. The young man laid his hand lightly on the curate's shoulder, and as Kezia was bending over her cooking, said in a low voice—

'We were both mistaken, sir.' Then Mr. Lloyd looked up into his eyes more scrutinisingly, and Robert nodded and smiled, and the curate nodded, as if saying he understood, but did not smile ; and then Robert went to the other side of the fire, averted his face, and they both sat as if quietly watching Kezia's cooking.

Kezia Williams, Elias Morgan's housekeeper, was a soft-eyed, fair-haired woman, about twenty-three, but seeming older; for her manners were peculiarly grave, and her face wore a look of peaceful wisdom, as if she had seen through all the great mysteries of life, and would never let herself be disturbed by a single worldly hope or fear. Her soft gray eyes had a kind of sympathy in them for the griefs of others, however trivial ; and her placid lips a dreamy smile for all who smiled at her ; but she did not allow her thoughts to dwell on

the bitter sufferings of the world, she kept her meek eyes on
her own narrow path, and followed it with patient cheerfulness,
thankful that she had just light to see it.

'Elias is still engaged, then ?' Robert said to Kezia.

'He is, Master Robert,' she answered. 'And I was saying
to Mr. Lloyd, I hope you will not think us rude not telling of
your being here; but he wished not to be disturbed while
writing this letter for Hugh.'

The tone in which Kezia said 'he wished' expressed as
much respect for the injunction as if it had been a command.

Chamberlayne showed no more signs of impatience, but sat
watching Kezia as gravely as if she had been preparing a
funeral feast.

While his eyes were resting on a basket of new spoons and
forks, engraved with Elias Morgan's initials, Kezia pointed
out to him an object he had not yet noticed.

It stood at one end of the room, the farthest from the wide
old chimney, wrapt carefully from dust and smoke, and for the
last hour Kezia's eyes had kept turning towards it with a
tender pleasure. It was a present which Elias intended for
his young brother, and of which Hugh as yet knew nothing;
for it had arrived while he was out, and had been concealed in
Kezia's own room till this occasion, on which it was to be
presented to him.

It was a new harp, and its purchase was, next to the building of the little chapel, the greatest extravagance of which
Elias had been guilty.

The old one, which had been in the family many years, had,
under the young man's touch, been the source of the only
pleasure the grave elder brother allowed himself to enjoy.
And his enjoyment of Hugh's music had been deep; so deep
and exquisite, that he no sooner possessed the means than he
felt he must give expression to it; and he chose to do this by
this gift, 'which,' said Elias to Kezia, 'will thank him in
language he best understands.'

There it stood, and Kezia pointed it out to Robert, and related its story; and he looked at it gravely enough.

Yes, there it stood, veiled music, like their future, which
when they came with joyous impatient hands to try it, was to
startle them with its mournfulness.

The long deal table was spread; and Kezia laid out the
bright new plate, and ranged her dainties on the shelf before

the open window, through which they could just see the new chapel with its merry flag, and the workmen, who had returned to their tasks and were making Moel Mawr (the great mountain) faintly echo with their sawing and hammering. Seeing all this, Kezia smiled and brightened with a gentle excitement, that brought a faint rose on her cheek, and gave new light to her eyes.

Robert had assisted her to draw up the heavy stiff-backed oak chairs to the table, and to bring in benches and stools so as to make up the necessary number of seats, when they heard, at last, a door opened, and the feet of Elias and Hugh approaching.

They came in together. Elias held the letters he had been writing in his hand. Both brothers had on their faces a tender gravity which seemed to speak of but lately subdued emotion, and gave them for a moment a faint likeness to each other, though Hugh was thin and slight, and had a small oval face and brown eyes like Hirell's.

As they came in at the door, Elias resting his hand in his old way on Hugh's shoulder, there was a touching contrast in the expressions of the two faces; in the lingering anxiety of the elder brother's as his eyes rested on Hugh with a deep fatherly love, and the bright furtive self-confidence that lay behind the respectful attention in Hugh's downcast look. It was sad wisdom and happy ignorance, loving, but doubting, each other.

Kezia had placed a clothes-horse before the harp, that it might not be seen by Hugh till the moment Elias should think fit to present his gift.

'See, Elias,' said she, going to meet them as they entered, 'here is Robert Chamberlayne come, and Mr. Lloyd with him; they have been waiting for you nearly an hour.'

While Hugh and Robert shook hands, the keen gray eyes of Elias rested on the curate's face inquiringly. He had a few secret grievances against him. A member of his chapel had been drawn away to become one of Mr. Lloyd's congregation; one of his labourers had been made drunk at the fair by a ploughman of the Abbey farm; and, worse than all, to Elias's certain knowledge, Mr. Lloyd had not only allowed some English tourists to visit the Abbey ruins on the Sabbath-day, but had actually conducted them himself, and given them all the information he could.

Elias could not look into the curate's face without seeing these three transgressions written plainly upon it, and his gaze was at first severe and repelling. But on different parts of the curate's apparel was traced in certain hieroglyphics—such as a darn in the white necktie; a chalkiness round the button-holes of his coat; a patch on the toe of his boot—a word which had far more effect on Elias Morgan's heart than all the curate's crimes put together

Poverty—yes. *He* was still poor; always to be poor. *His* children—*his* home—*his* heart knew none of the sunshine that was flooding Bod Elian, where everyone moved about in a sort of delicious blindness—where Elias himself at times could only think calmly when he darkened his eyes to pray.

They approached each other. Daniel Lloyd's face was very sad. Elias, little dreaming it was the shadow of his own calamity that made it so, bowed himself before the superior dignity, which, it seemed to him, sadness and poverty gave even to his misguided and much erring neighbour.

The obstinate, rigid head, so unaccustomed to bend before anyone save One, bowed stiffly as he held out his hand.

'You do me an honour, sir,' said Elias. 'I thank you for this visit.'

Mr. Lloyd had been prepared for coldness—suspicion; for anything but being received by Elias warmly and humbly, and his voice was not quite steady as he said—

'And I am grieved—grieved more than I can express, to tell you my visit is a very sad one.'

Hugh, who was standing by Robert, turned hastily, his attention arrested by something in Mr. Lloyd's voice.

Elias, whose perceptions were not so quick, thought the curate was alluding to some trouble of his own, and was beginning to be filled by a new hope and pleasure. Had Lloyd come to him for help? Would ho let him help him? If so, how could he do it most humbly, most effectually? How could he anticipate what his neighbour was going to say, and spare him the anguish and humiliation of saying it?

Hugh's eyes had seen in their hurried, searching gaze at the curate's face that something was wrong, and they flashed back to Robert questioningly. Robert's lip was unsteady; he bit it, and moved his hand vaguely towards Mr. Lloyd, which was all the answer he could give to Hugh's silent question.

Then, as Elias stood praying in his heart for light to see his neighbour's need, he was startled by hearing Hugh cry out behind him—

'Mr. Lloyd, for God's sake speak at once! Something is the matter! What is it?'

Elias looked round bewildered, but sternly reproachful at Hugh's use of that holy name.

Daniel Lloyd was about to ask to speak with him alone, but seeing that Kezia had left the kitchen, and no one was there but Elias, Hugh, and Robert, he saw no good in further delay. The blow which he had to give seemed as if it would take all the strength out of him. He looked about for a chair.

Robert came round and gave him one. He sat down while Elias stood before him, his face grim with sudden foreboding, his form rigid as a rock.

'Morgan,' said the curate, 'I think I can understand now, for the first time, why I have always had a sort of wish to shun you. I believe it was because Satan warned me that if I became intimate with you I should have presented to me finer and harder lessons than I should care to learn. But now I am so placed by the hand of the Allwise, as to be obliged to come here to learn of you such a lesson as I speak of. And this is what I have come to learn: If a man, after a life of poverty—and depression, and sadness, through poverty—is made rich in all that he desires for himself and those dearest to him; and if, just while the joy of his good fortune is at its height, he is called upon by God to resign all, suddenly and completely, how should he bear himself under this blow? Elias Morgan, *you* are to teach us this lesson. God requires it at your hands. He wills that you should teach it to all within your house—to your young brother Hugh, to your child Hirell, to your faithful servant Kezia, and to all here who have been glad with you in your prosperity, and must suffer by your loss.'

Elias remained still, his eyes cold and hard-looking as flint, fastened on the curate's face.

Hugh had thrown himself into a chair, and was sitting with his arms on the back, and his head bowed down on his arms.

Then Robert Chamberlayne came to take his part in explaining, and Elias turned his flinty eyes slowly from Lloyd's face to his cousin's.

'Morgan,' said the young man, 'I take great blame to myself for writing you that letter. Till last Wednesday I thought nothing, not the Bank of England itself, safer than our shares in this affair.'

An almost lion-like glare came into Morgan's eye as it scanned Robert's flushed and troubled face. He stood still; his chest heaved. He said with manifest effort, and in a voice that made even Hugh start, stricken as he was—

'Had I been *you*, Robert Chamberlayne. I had rather have cut off my right hand than have done this thing. Facts! Facts!' he almost wailed in his strong voice. 'I asked you for them before, and you gave me—opinions—it seems. Tell me the truth now; the whole truth, though it be more bitter than gall, and sharper than a sword.'

'This is the whole truth, Morgan,' said Robert. 'The firm is ruined; they paid us a year's profit to deceive us, as they wanted to keep all quiet to get another partner in. I never knew a word of it till Wednesday, when I was asked to a meeting of creditors. Here is my lawyer's letter, which tells all.'

Elias took the letter, and read it through with the same strange glare in his eye, a glare of wrath—of wrath at the world's crookedness which had brought this thing to pass. When he had read the letter he gave it back to Robert.

There was silence then for a minute; neither Robert nor the curate feeling fit to cope with the difficulty.

A bitter sob from Hugh stirred him at last. He half turned his head towards him.

'They will all want comfort from you, Elias,' said Daniel Lloyd, gently.

Elias looked round at him.

'Comfort!' he repeated, grimly. 'No, sir, my family will expect of me that I do my duty. *You* come to see how I do it in this sore strait. You *shall* see; you shall see me do it according to my light—according to my light.'

The light was a narrow one, but intense. First of all it showed him the well-filled table where the new plate was shining.

'Kezia!'

She had just come into the room, and was standing like one petrified, as she looked at Elias.

He stood at the head of the table, and motioned with his hand as he said sternly—

'Gather these up; pack them as they were before. They go back; they are not mine.'

'Elias?' cried Kezia. 'Mr. Lloyd; oh, mercy! what is the matter?'

'Obey me!' shouted Morgan.

The letters which he had written for Hugh to take with him to London lay on the table close to his hand. His eye fell on these next. He took them up quietly and tore each in two, and dropped both to the ground.

Just then a soft rustle of silk drew his eyes to the door, and in a moment Hirell entered, coming quickly, conscious of having loitered over her new dress. She noticed nothing strange at first, for she was full of tender expectancy of the surprise and pleasure of her father and Hugh.

They all watched her approach, and trembled for her at the cruel severity of the voice that went to meet her and arrest her step.

'Hirell!'

She stood still; her colour went, and she turned her soft startled eyes from one to another; then they returned to her father's face with a look of great fear and trouble.

It did not soften the indomitable sternness of that face—only a sharp spasmodic quiver passed over it; as Elias stretched out his arm, and pointed to her dress.

'Take it off!' he cried; 'go, take it off!—and these gauds,' touching her necklace with a cold trembling finger—'off' with them. Kezia, take them off!'

Kezia, with her usual prompt obedience, came in timid haste, unclasped the necklace, and laid it on the table before her master.

He looked from it to a large trunk that stood by the wall, partly packed, ready for Hirell's visit to London.

'Go with her,' he said to Kezia, pointing to Hirell; 'and take off that gown, and bring it here, and all her other finery and your own; all that has been bought with this money.'

Hirell, in her great perplexity and terror, allowed Kezia to lead her away, and as they went Elias turned upon Hugh.

'Brother! if I am not to have help from you, at least let me have obedience. If you must grieve as a child, obey like a child. Those clothes that you had made at Dolgarrog, put them up—all of them. Give me that watch.'

Hugh roused himself, and threw the watch on the table by Hirell's necklace.

'That pin in your handkerchief.'

While Hugh was taking it out, a heavy marching tread was heard along the passage—a form stood in the doorway, and all but Mr. Lloyd recognised the burly figure and strongly-blotched face of the Calvinist preacher, the Rev. Ephraim Jones.

'Well, friend Elias,' he cried, in his loud, hoarse voice, wiping the moisture from his face, 'here you are, feasting like Job among his brethren, when the days of his trouble were passed. Well, shall I, like them, condole with you over the evils that are gone, or rejoice with you for the peace and plenty that have been showered on your house ?'

Elias looked at him, his clenched hand on the table—his nostrils distended.

'Do neither, friend Ephraim,' he answered, in a voice of hard, calm agony. 'Since you are come, assist me to set my house in order; for God hath commanded that Mammon shall depart from it! and I am sorely tasked in destroying his idols, and tearing his bonds from the hearts of my children.'

Robert Chamberlayne, seeing the minister stand amazed, went to him, and told him the truth, entreating him to prevail upon Elias to deal more gently with Hirell and Hugh.

As he was speaking with him, Hirell and Kezia entered, pale and trembling. Their arms were full of things, with which they timidly approached Elias.

Hirell wore one of the very oldest and poorest of the dresses that were hers before the sudden change from poverty ; for all the better ones had been given away by herself or Kezia to the poor. It was a dingy blue print, with white spots, made loose and fastened with a coarse cord girdle. She had only been used to wearing it for milking in on wet mornings, and on churning days, and had seldom sat down to any meal in it in the presence of her father and Hugh. Having now to come into the presence of so many in it, seemed to her to add greatly to the strange and sudden humiliation that had fallen upon the house. She had resisted, but Kezia in her great fear of Elias had been strong, and had forced her to do his will. Her white, stricken, terrified face, as she crept in at Kezia's side, with her beautiful dress in her arms, touched

Robert more than all her joyousness had done. His heart ached for her as she stood waiting for, but trembling to meet her father's look.

That look came upon her and Kezia, and on their gay load, quickly and sternly. It made Hirell's tears pour forth. She dropped her burden on the ground, and hid her face on Kezia's shoulder.

The sight did not move the pity, but roused the anger of Elias.

'What!' said he; 'is this a child of mine—shedding tears over such gauds as were worn by the daughters of Zion? Put them by!' he cried, turning to Hugh, and pointing to the heap of things on the table and to the open trunk. 'Let them go out of my sight—out of my house—back to where they came from; back to the world of vanity, and deceit, and snares. Hirell, if you will not, or cannot assist, go; but do not hinder. Kezia, help Hugh to put those things in.'

Kezia gently withdrew herself from Hirell, and went on her knees before the trunk, meekly laying in the things as Hugh gave them to her.

Hirell, as she stood alone, seemed to see every form and object before her begin to swell and sway; a chill crept over all her limbs; and she would have fallen but for the rough grasp of the minister's hand on her shoulder.

'The child is sick,' he said, looking down at her kindly.

She struggled with her faintness for a moment, then turned deadly white, and fell against him, cold and powerless.

Hugh and Kezia left their task, and went to her then; while the minister rested his foot on the open trunk, the better to support her.

Elias stood looking on with folded arms and compressed lips.

Robert and the curate could not take their eyes from her face till they saw the sweet faint colour returning to her cheek, and the little mouth struggling for breath. She opened her eyes, and looked at the minister gratefully. He was moved. He had no thought but that her distress was for the loss of her fine clothes—as Elias had so spoken; but her anguish, and her pure and exquisite beauty penetrated to his rugged heart.

He glanced into the trunk, and shook his head as she opened her eyes upon him, and said with a rough tenderness in his loud, harsh voice—

'Foolish maiden! what need hast *thou* of these things, thou lily of the field?'

Kezia led her to a seat in the chimney-corner, and Mr. Lloyd came and sat by her, trying to give her words of comfort.

'You must let my daughter come and see you,' he said; 'she is wiser in sorrow than yourself. Your garb is the garb of poverty—so is hers, poor child! but Hirell, it is black.'

Kezia and Hugh were again at work, under the direction of Elias; and the Reverend Ephraim Jones, seeing there was no staying the turn of his friend's mind, and having, moreover, a secret exultation in the spirit of stern integrity that was ruling him, tendered his hearty assistance; and fell to cording the hampers with as much vigour, good-will, and grim satisfaction, as if Satan himself were confined in them, to be banished piecemeal out of the world.

Hugh had been sent out to give orders for the red wagon to be taken back to its maker; and to stop the two gardeners, who were at work making paths, rooting up old shrubs, and planting new ones. Kezia was still busy, though even Elias and Ephraim Jones had paused, and were standing wiping their brows before the open window.

For a moment there was a pause and a deep silence, broken only by the stifled sobbing of the poor frightened servant-girl, as she assisted Kezia.

In this pause and quietness, there came to the ears of all, with sad significance, the distant noise of the workmen at the chapel.

'Friend Ephraim,' said Elias, turning to him with gleaming eyes, 'the chapel shall *not* bo stopped! What I have bought with this money for the uses of the flesh and the devil, I take back from the flesh and the devil; but rather than take that back which I have bought and consecrated for God's uso, I will beg—I will beg!'

'And I, too, Elias;' answered the minister, extending his hand, red with the labour he had just ceased from. 'I will beg for you rather than stop that work. One triumph you *shall* have—one sweet drop in your cup of bitterness!'

Hugh now came in with money in his hand, which had been given to one of the men entrusted to make a purchase at Dolgarrog. He gave it to Elias across the long narrow table, on opposite sides of which the brothers were standing.

While Hugh was out, the servant, in fulfilling Kezia's orders, had moved the old clothes-horse from before the harp.

Elias, as he took the money from Hugh, glanced round and round, and saw the instrument standing there. He glanced back at Hugh with the ferocity of a tigress who would defend her young from pain, and saw his eyes were on it with a great light in them.

Then the eyes of the brothers met. Elias dropped into a chair, covered his face with one hand, and flung the other across the table towards Hugh.

The lad's slim fingers for an instant quivered in a sort of agony over the clenched hand of Elias; then his young face and form became suddenly inspired as with the spirit of the ancient Celtic warriors. He rose, he touched his brother's hand with a light thrilling pressure, he spoke clearly and musically:

'Elias, do but lend it to me to show you how I thank you, and it shall go back at once.'

Elias lifted his heavy head to look after him as he went and uncovered the harp.

The minister watched him, and gave a sort of grunt of assent as he sat down.

'Ay, play to him, young man,' he said; 'comfort him if you can. Comfort his heart, as David comforted the heart of Saul.'

Hugh seated himself on a box beside the harp and began to play.

His prelude was rough, chaotic—stormy. The minister liked it, and half-groaned now and then, in sympathy with its strength and mountainous rudeness. Minute after minute passed without one sweet strain coming. Robert Chamberlayne began to think he did not like the harp; but Hugh's other listeners were all Welsh mountaineers, and knew well to what loveliness they were climbing so laboriously. The change was sudden—instantaneous. All at once, out of that tumultuous, crashing winter of sound, the summer of his music stole upon them—perfect, fresh, dewy, full-blossomed, balmy, intoxicating.

In one minute Hugh had made a heaven, and drawn every soul present into it. Hirell came and sat on a low box near him, her sweet face lifted like a flower, athirst for dew. Elias kept his hand before his eyes. Kezia watched him with the joy of a mother who has seen water in the desert for her perishing children.

Workmen from the chapel, who had come to ask questions about their work, crept near the open window, keeping out of sight.

Young god of the world he had made, Hugh sat glowing with triumph, and smiling with happy scorn on the baskets of the upgathered feast of fortune from which he had been driven.

He stopped—gave up his godhood, and became—a man? No, a boy—flushed, trembling, abashed.

Elias slowly moved his hand from his eyes.

'Hugh!'

In an instant Hugh's hand was in his. Then a cry of more passionate love went from Elias:

'Hirell!'

The girl cried out and ran to him.

'Come,' said the curate, softly to Robert; and they went out.

The Reverend Ephraim Jones stood irresolute, then went towards the door.

Before he reached it, a broken voice called after him—

'Nay, friend Ephraim, do not leave us. I had prepared to receive you a table on which was spread good silver plate and wine. But stay with me now, I entreat you, and eat at my table, though my " silver is become dross," and my "wine is mixed with water." '

<hr>

CHAPTER XIV.

ROBERT CHAMBERLAYNE DOES ELIAS YET ANOTHER SERVICE.

WHEN Robert Chamberlayne left Bod Elian, he went back to Abbey Farm with the curate, and did not return to Dolgarrog till the shops were closing, and the guide to Criba Ban was driving out his hard-worked ponies into the meadow behind the town.

A group stood round the door of the old Council House. Robert recognised the little tailor to whom Hugh's clothes had been sent back. He was reading the list of things he had

made for the young man, to the gentle amazement of Butty
Hughes, who sat near the door of the little shop, enjoying the
freshness of the evening air, the salutations of his neighbours
as they passed, and the gossip about Elias Morgan's change
of fortune, which was the theme of the day. His wife stood
knitting behind his chair, her soft dark eyes ever ready to
answer his upturned look of childlike wonder, and her lips
always replying with a gentle sympathetic—

'There, master! Only to think!'

His eyes brightened with fresh anticipation at the sight of
Robert, at whose approach the others moved aside; and he
became almost tearful with disappointment, when the young
man strode in, merely nodding as he passed him.

Robert went through the shop across the tiny parlour, up
the steep little stairs, and entering the sitting-room he shared
with Rymer, found his friend lying on the sofa apparently
asleep.

'He has been overdoing it to-day,' he said to himself, as he
noticed the air of utter exhaustion which Rymer's figure and
pale face wore as he lay.

Robert seated himself at the open window, and lit a cigar.

There was nothing pleasant to look upon now in the King's
square. The covered market-place was empty, and the gas
turned out. The night came darkening down, soft and calm,
but starless.

But for a reluctance to wake Rymer, Robert would have
rung for candles. If he had any poetry at all in him, he
certainly cared nothing for its shady side; his spirit throve
not in that. He suspected 'blight' in every sunless day. He
felt his own weakness in this respect as he sat at the window
of the old Council House, looking on the dull gray buildings,
the darker mountain lines, and still darker sky. 'I know,'
he thought to himself, 'I should have a devil of a temper if
things went wrong with me.'

And he felt that his mind had lost its balance as it was.
Hirell's scarcely disguised pain at the thoughts of a marriage
with him, Elias's sharp bitter tones, still caused him not a
little disquietude and humiliation.

He had relieved his mind a little by sending an anonymous
subscription for the chapel; and there was another matter in
which he hoped to serve his cousin, and it was the thoughts
of this that made him glance impatiently towards Rymer.

It was not till Mrs. Hughes brought up the candles, that the latter opened his eyes and got up.

'So you are back,' he said, coming to the window.

Then Robert brightened, and told him some of the results of his communication to Elias; and it was not long before he brought out what had been in his mind concerning Rymer for some hours.

'You said you had some thoughts of spending a month or two up among the mountains.'

'I was thinking of it, certainly,' answered Rymer, vaguely; 'but why do you mention that in connection with your cousin?'

'Well,' said Robert, 'I have promised Kezia Williams, his housekeeper—that stiff nun-like woman you saw with them on Sunday—I have promised her to try and find them a lodger, as they intend to let the two new rooms that they have just built. She came down about it to the Abbey Farm this afternoon. She thinks of furnishing the rooms with some things she left at Aber, when she came to live at Bod Elian. I was thinking if you wanted, as you said—privacy and quiet— you'd get enough of both there.'

'I thank you. I'm sure I should like the sort of place,' replied Rymer, 'but my plans are changed, I fancy; however, I'll let you know to-morrow morning.'

That question of his staying or going was one he was forced quickly to decide, irrespective of Chamberlayne's proposal. For his own part he would have been glad to go—to leave Wales, England, Europe—to give way to the feverish restlessness that possessed him, and made stillness unendurable. But could he leave while so uncertain as to what the consequences of his selfishness might have been to Catherine Rhys? He could not—he knew he could not. No, he said, he *must* stay —and yet he dared not stay here in Dolgarrog, too many eyes were on him, too many strangers coming daily through the town. He would seek concealment among those solitary mountains—he would be Elias Morgan's lodger.

'I am sick of this place,' said he to Robert, after they had been smoking their cigars in silence for half an hour—almost forgetting each other's existence. 'If I decide on staying, I might want to move to-morrow, and you say the rooms are not furnished.'

'I could soon see if Kezia couldn't accommodate you some-

how,' said Robert.   'I'm almost sure she could, if you would
not mind sharing with the rest for a few days.'

Rymer felt anxious now to decide the matter at once.   He
took some letters from his pocket, and appeared to consult
them, then looked up with a quick dry cough, and said to
Robert—

'Upon my word, I don't see any use in leaving it uncertain.
I think I'll say that, if you like to arrange it with your people
to have me to-morrow, I'll come.'

'Very well,' said Robert. 'I'll walk up to Bod Elian before
breakfast to-morrow, and settle it all with Kezia.'

CHAPTER XV

MR. RYMER'S FIRST NIGHT AT BOD ELIAN.

IT was past nine o'clock when the young men arrived at Bod
Elian ; and Elias Morgan had already given orders that the
house door should be closed and supper delayed no longer for
the new inmate who had been expected since noon.

Robert took him round to the back, where they saw light
coming from an open door.

'Ah, here is Nanny,' he said ; 'you must make friends with
her. She's the belle of Capel Illtyd. Listen—she sings well.'

Rymer looked in and saw a young woman ironing in a large
un-English-looking outer kitchen. There were rude farming
implements hanging on the damp walls and standing in
corners—a low fire burnt dimly in the chimney, and sent puffs
of smoke over the girl's head as she stood with her back to it
and her face towards a young man who leaned indolently
against the empty dresser. A little stream of water from the
leaking tap ran along the sloping stones to the door, over which
a piece of the roof was broken through and a long garland of
ivy trailed down from it.

'So, Nanny,' said Robert, 'you had shut us out.'

Nanny stared, and took a sudden dislike to Rymer's pale
face and dull unobservant eyes.

'Lodger late, Mr. Robert,' said she. 'Elias Morgan very
angry,' and she stood with her hands on her hips regarding
the new inmate of Bod Elian with critical and somewhat dis-
dainful eyes.

'Come, Nanny, don't be cross,' said Robert, 'this gentleman takes a great interest in your country. I hope you'll do your best to make him comfortable while he's here.'

'Nothing to do with it, Mr. Robert,' answered Nanny, leaning against the chimney side, 'make no one comfortable here no more, going away'

She strode leisurely across to the door of the inner kitchen, which she flung open roughly ; and marching in a few yards, turned round with her fists in her sides, and surveyed the two visitors as they entered the room where Elias Morgan and his family were assembled ; and then she walked out again with a slow, contemptuous swing of her limbs, and without glancing to any of the family from whose circle she had been banished.

Elias Morgan had effectually cleared his house of all signs of the abundance and confusion which yesterday morning prevailed there. Austere order and cold poverty had once more linked hands, and taken command of his household ; and Elias sat at the head of his table, his old account-book and Bible before him, his sad gray eye sternly watchful of the drooping young faces around him, as if he would detect and punish even a thought that rebelled against the new and bitter rule. Yet the faces seemed all sufficiently meek and resigned, even to the Reverend Ephraim Jones, who sat writing at a little table by the fire, and who could not quite understand that watchful and almost cruel light in his friend's gaze, as it turned slowly from face to face at the narrow table. He did not know that the more gentle and complete their obedience, the more sharp became Elias's struggle with his own heart, and its passionate pity for them.

It was strange indeed to Rymer thus to find himself suddenly a member of such a household as he saw before him. The bare, low-roofed, black-beamed kitchen, with its long table, and the peculiar persons sitting at it, made a picture utterly foreign to all his experience.

As he looked vaguely round his attention was attracted by the eyes of Elias, who regarded him with such a severe scrutiny he could scarcely help resenting its length and fixedness.

He bowed.

Elias prolonged his gaze. Hugh rose with heightened colour, and Robert said, a little impatiently—

‘This is Mr. Rymer, Morgan.’

‘Yes, cousin,’ said Elias, ‘you mentioned his name before, but being entirely a strange one to me, I cannot see how your mention of it now is to serve as an excuse or apology for your and his arrival at so unseemly an hour. However, we have not yet had supper. Sir, you are aware that your private rooms are not fit for you to occupy as yet ; and that as you choose to come before they are made so, it will be necessary for you to conform to the arrangements of my family.’

Rymer bowed. Elias stood up and paused. He was not used to introductions, but he seemed to feel it behoved him to make the person who was to become one of his household somewhat acquainted with its members.

‘I should be very doubtful, sir,’ he said, ‘as to our power of making your stay here agreeable to you, if it were not for my housekeeper,’ moving his hand towards Kezia, who rose and curtseyed. ‘She will, I am sure, do her best for your comfort, as she does for ours. That is my brother, whose company I am very soon to lose ; this is my daughter.’

Rymer was standing near Elias on his left, and had acknowledged each introduction with the respect that seemed demanded by his host’s tone and manner. As Elias said ‘ This is my daughter,’ he glanced down at a form sitting at his right on a low seat, and so near to him that Rymer had not noticed it before. It rose up now, and he saw in a patched old gown and with some coarse needlework in her hand, the girl whose delicate beauty had seemed to fill the gray market-place of Dolgarrog with light. He looked into the same face now, but its sweet glad light was gone. The hazel eyes were clouded, the cheeks pale, the lips set in that firm, pathetic closure which seems to betoken the soul’s desire to lock itself in alone with its sorrow.

Rymer looked at Hirell with cold, vaguely observant eyes, bowed and turned away to the seat indicated by Elias.

Hirell sat down, penetrated with wonder and pity by the pale suffering face into which she had glanced.

Rymer stood with his hand on the back of his chair, looking on the people among whom he had chosen to make his home much as a mourner in a funeral-coach looks out upon the scenery and incidents of the road ; knowing that nothing can alter the sad purport of his journey. They were strange to him, and perhaps it was better for those restless thoughts that will stray away from sorrow, like children from the side of a mother who watches by a coffin—perhaps it was better they should come back laden with strange things rather than with tokens and memories of the dead.

At first the manner of Elias had annoyed him, and made him half inclined to turn his back on Bod Elian and all Robert Chamberlayne's strange Welsh relations at once and for ever. Then came the question, would any change of place or persons matter to him? His host's eye was stern truly, but would the most flattering of smiles make him less abhorrent of himself and his existence? The chair on the back of which his hand lay irresolutely was of hard, bare wood, but could he have found rest to-night on cushions of down? The barley bread which the meek, quaintly-attired young housekeeper laid on the supper-table was almost black, but was there any dish whose taste would not be bitter in his mouth to-night?

He sat down, finding the sad place none the less sad because he was convinced that the whole world contained none happier for him.

Elias now summoned the Reverend Ephraim Jones; who said grace, and seated himself opposite Rymer, scanning him frowningly.

Kezia placed a basin of warm buttermilk before each person; and Elias cut up the barley loaf, a slice of which he gave to each on the point of his knife.

Rymer took his slice, laid it on his plate, and looked at it in some perplexity as to what to do with it. He had not the slightest inclination to eat the solid, stiff, black-looking stuff; but seeing Elias's eye upon him, he took his knife and made a feint of doing so, to avoid notice, he told himself, but it was rather from a delicate reluctance to let them see his aversion to it.

He was vexed when he noticed Kezia's kind, attentive eye watching him; and his annoyance helped him to swallow a large piece of the distasteful food with apparent unconcern.

'I am sorry,' said Kezia aloud to Robert, by whom she sat, 'that I was not able to get to Dolgarrog to-day for some white bread. I am afraid your friend will not like ours.'

'What do you say, Kezia Williams?' demanded Elias, bending his eyes upon her so sternly that her face flushed.

She replied very gently in Welsh, but Elias said in a still sterner voice in English—

'And if you did, what of that? Do you think I would have better food on my table for this stranger than I eat, and my child, and brother, and you eat? No, do not trouble yourself, Kezia; when his rooms are ready he orders what he pleases, but while he shares our table he will content himself with the victuals that are upon it for our use.'

Ephraim Jones made one of the strange guttural noises by which he usually signified his approbation of Elias's blunt speeches. Hugh glanced at Robert with an annoyed expression, and Hirell and Kezia both looked troubled.

The whole thing was strange enough to draw Rymer's attention from himself; and make him look around him with something approaching to interest.

He looked at Elias, and was surprised to find his face calm and unmoved by any antagonistic feeling.

He saw nothing of the irritability or pompous self-assertion he expected to find there after such a speech. There was, as Elias looked at the faces round his table, a calm tragic watchfulness in his eyes, such as might be on the face of a captain preparing for a black voyage. Knowing what he did of this man's fortunes, Rymer could not help comparing for the moment his state with his own. Both he felt were tossed on a gloomy sea of disappointment and bitterness; but while the one was watchful and prepared, with eye alert, and firm hand upon the helm, the other drifted blindly into the darkness, helpless against rocks and storms, and perils of all kinds.

Looking where that steady, keen gray eye wandered, Rymer noticed for the first time the young man sitting at his left hand. He was dropping pieces of bread into the buttermilk with one hand, and leaning his cheek on the other, while he gazed across the table in a reverie that seemed at once pleasant and sad. It was a small, oval face, dark-complexioned, bright-eyed, with a boy's life and light in it, and a man's thought and vigour.

There was an impatient, bright sort of feverishness in it; a weariness, as of one cramped in too small a space; a yearning towards fate; a thirst for a deep draught of the cup as yet hardly tasted. Rymer could not help at once envying and pitying him; for he saw that his soul stood quivering like some prepared instrument, highly strung and tuned, ready to breathe music or shriek discord, under the touches of fate's capricious fingers.

On this face the eyes of Elias rested longest and most anxiously, as they traversed the two sides of the table. Rymer looked at the brothers, wondering what these delicate undertones of expression meant on the faces of two labouring farmers, for such he guessed them to be from their clothes and their domestic arrangements. But as he glanced about him with a more observant eye, he noticed a strange mixture of refinement with the primitive rudeness and simplicity of the household. It was altogether more like some high-born family of a far-off time, than of modern rustics. The women had gentle manners; and the men showed towards them a grave, unaffected gallantry.

Some of the vessels on the table were of very rare old china, precious heirlooms, through the delicate transparency of which shone, for the owners, a tender light of traditionary greatness; but time and poverty had brought them in contact with strange company; the delicate, thin-edged basin, in which some fair ancestress had placed a royal gift of roses, held now its owner's humble supper of buttermilk; a beautiful, fragile little cup rested on a plate of commonest ware, while on the wafer-edge of another reclined a pewter spoon. Among the clumsy horn and wooden knife handles were one or two of some antiquity and value. It was looking at these made Rymer aware that the one he held was different from all the others, being small and light.

He looked at it with a half unconscious curiosity, and saw that it was almost new, and that it had a pretty mother-o'-pearl handle, on which some letters were engraved. His lips moved silently with the name the letters made. It was '*Hirell Morgan.*'

Hirell saw the examination of the knife (her christening present) placed by herself and Kezia for the stranger's use, as the most modern in the house; and she saw also the lips moving over her name, and then the sad eyes glance absently across at her, showing she was remembered in connection with the name: and though they were so absent, and looking out as it seemed from such vast distances of sorrow, she could not help dropping her own confusedly, and blushing under his gaze.

'Young man,' said Ephraim Jones, suddenly looking over his spectacles at Hugh, 'listen to this.' He spread out a letter he had been writing, and cleared his throat.

' It is,' said he, ' to my friend, James Griffith, the manager of Messrs. Tidman's, and I hope it fittingly expresses your desires and intentions.'

Hugh looked from Rymer to Ephraim Jones with a glance of quick, eager remonstrance; and the minister saw and understood it, but in his bold and downright way of dealing with things, he had little patience with such refinements of feeling; and he chose now to overlook Hugh's silent allusion to the presence of Rymer with grim sarcasm and indifference and began to read.

Elias listened with profound attention, Hugh with averted face, Robert with evident annoyance for Hugh, whilst Hirell and Kezia turned their faces reverentially but sadly towards the reader.

' DEAR JAMES,—Can you find a place in your office for a young man possessing some ability, but no business experiences whatever?　His age is twenty-one, his moral character good, and I doubt not, that he would, under strong discipline such as you have always been remarkable for exercising, prove of some use in a humble post.　He would be willing to place himself in some family of strictly religious principles and orderly habits, so that his services to Messrs. Tidman should not suffer in consequence of late hours, or through any of the evils which surround the young and ignorant on first acquaintance with the world.　I should not, of course, ask higher remuneration than would enable him to subsist with rigorous economy, and an unflagging self-denial, such as his youth and health render him quite capable of exercising.　He writes a good hand, but is a poor accountant, and quite unused to application.　This is, however, a quality he would soon gain at your hands; and I have no doubt, that with the grace of God, he would prove a useful and faithful servant to Messrs. Tidman, to whom have the kindness to convey my respectful remembrance, and show this letter.

' I shall speak of myself and my progress on this Welsh mission when I see you, which, God willing, will be at the end of the present week.　Trusting you will oblige me in the matter of which I have written, I am, dear sir, yours truly,　　　　　　　　　　　　　　' EPHRAIM JONES.'

The minister as he refolded his letter looked at Hugh with eyes that seemed not asking but demanding his approbation of it. Elias looked at him in much the same way, but his gaze had also something of entreaty.

Hugh remained still with his face turned away from Rymer; his cheek was burning, his eyes were cast down in painful thought.

Ephraim Jones began to rap with his thick fingers impatiently on the table, and to lower his shaggy eyebrows.

'Well, young man,' said he, 'may we presume that you concur with the sentiments expressed in this letter, and intend to forward them to the best of your ability?'

'I hope you'll pardon me, sir,' cried Robert, no longer able to contain himself, 'but I really must say this is not business-like—it is not indeed. A fellow like Hugh, with his education and talents, to be spoken of in that way, why you couldn't say less of any ignorant shop-boy. Do let me try, Elias,' he said, turning to the elder brother eagerly, 'what *I* can do before this letter is sent. I am sure I could find him a situation better than any such a letter as that can bring him.'

Hugh's eyes filled with a grateful moisture as Robert spoke. Then he turned them entreatingly towards his brother.

'May this be so, Elias?' he asked. 'May Robert try for me, and may that letter be delayed?'

'Hugh,' answered Elias slowly, 'I am satisfied with that letter. Robert Chamberlayne!'—and all the wrath and bitterness of his sorrow rose in his voice and eyes as he turned towards his cousin—'have I had such good reason to be satisfied with your judgment as to accept it a second time?'

'I have done, Morgan,' replied Robert quickly. 'You know how to silence me, and you use your knowledge generously. Even for Hugh's sake I can say no more,' and he got up from the table.

'Come, come, friend Elias,' interposed Ephraim Jones, 'let there not be an angry parting between you and your young relative. He means well. If he condemns my letter for being unbusiness-like, it is because he differs from me in his notions of the quality and intent of business. *You* are satisfied?'

'I am,' answered Elias, 'and I trust that Hugh has more respect for our opinions and wishes than for those of a person even less serious and enlightened than himself. What do you say, brother?'

Hugh did not answer; but as Robert moved to wish Kezia

farewell, his eyes followed him with the yearning of a prisoner who sees his would-be deliverer turned from the gaol gate.

'Good-bye, Kezia,' said Robert, 'I musn't stay here, a wolf among lambs, any longer.'

Kezia's eyes were turned anxiously towards Hugh, to whose side she went when Robert had shaken hands with her, and gone round to Hirell.

'Hugh,' said Elias, with that peculiar thickening of the voice which came to him in moments of excitement, 'I have heard no word of approval or acknowledgment yet of this service which our friend Ephraim Jones is doing you.'

Hugh still remained silent, in sadness rather than in obstinacy or anger. Kezia, as she sat by him, gently plucked his sleeve and whispered,

'Dear Hugh, say something. Oh, think! has he not enough to bear?'

She had a tender winning voice, and eyes like it, and Hugh looked at her and received her persuasion passively.

In a minute he turned his head wearily to the minister.

'I thank you, sir, for what you have done,' he said.

'And will he take thanks from you, sir, so grudged?' asked Elias, with rising anger.

'Enough, my boy, enough,' cried the minister, extending his great arm across to take Hugh's hand. 'Elias, you require too much of the young man. Could the captives of Israel thank him who should point out for them the road of their exile?'

Robert leaned over Hirell's chair, and said—

'Good-bye, Hirell;' and she looked up at him with eyes so brimful of her own griefs, that they asked and won forgiveness for being too heedless of his. He even smiled as he pressed her hand, and all the pleasantness of his liking came over her.

Their friendship had been founded on simple knowledge of each other, and the habit of being and thinking together. As no admiration on either side made them exaggerate its strength, all that there was of it was genuine, and knit into their very natures. It was like that primitive mysterious link between blood relations, that is often never felt till it is suddenly broken by some bitter family dissension or death. Hirell's liking for Robert was as a stream that ran too deep and strong to make any of the murmurings by which a shallower one attracts and excites the mind. If her bright imagination had once looked down into it, it might have burst into sunny beauty; but as it was, it flowed silently and unseen—refreshing her without her knowledge.

'Good-bye, Robert,' said Hirell, and their hands clasped with clinging earnestness.

All had risen to take leave of Robert, except the lodger, who sat at the table still, either lost in thought, or anxious to appear unobservant of the disagreements that had taken place.

The simple hospitality of Elias would not allow him to sit while his guest and kinsman took his departure; but the attitude in which he stood at the head of the table, and the expression on his face of unmoved severity, did not encourage Robert to take any steps towards lessening the breach between them.

He had wished them all good-bye, and now approached Elias.

'Well, good-night, Morgan,' he said, and held out his hand.

'Good-night, Robert Chamberlayne,' answered Elias, as he took coldly the proffered hand.

Robert noticed the coldness, became flushed and irritated, then turned to go.

'The lantern,' demanded Elias, turning slowly to Kezia.

She brought it, and they were not surprised to see him follow Robert; for it was his common custom to light any one who went away at a late hour beyond the first white gate. Hirell and Hugh went after them.

Robert remembered the last time he left Bod Elian they had all followed him then, but not silently as to-night; the long, stone passages and kitchens had rung with blithe farewells, and entreaties that innumerable commissions with which he was charged might be remembered; that letters might be quickly answered; that nobody and nothing about the farm might ever be forgotten by him; and now he had nothing to do for any of them; no one had asked him to write, or wished to be remembered by him. He longed to turn back and tell Hugh that he might rely on his friendship when he came to London, but he dared not, for Elias was between them.

Hirell fully expected some outburst from Robert at the injustice with which he was being treated. It was like a dream to her to see him go—after once turning his face towards her —out of the gate and down the hill, and then to feel that he was gone.

Her father's harshness to Robert made her own thoughts of him kinder than they would otherwise have been. She laid her hand on the gate, and looked down in the direction of his footsteps sounding crisply on the slaty path, and falling into the rhythm of the fresh autumn night.

The light fringe of garden trees waved airily on her left, and seemed to lean and hearken after the footsteps with her ; and the water in the deep ravine to hurry and cry louder ; while the oxen in the field showed their breath in the faint starlight, as they turned towards the sound.

It went on, farther and fainter, and seemed to leave a chill behind it, and when it was quite gone from Hirell's hearing, and she took her arms from the gate and gazed round, the garden trees looked still and dull, the water plunged down the ravine with a crashing, gloomy monotony, the oxen lowered their heavy heads again, and tore and chewed the tough, dry grass. He who like the fairy prince would have changed it all, was gone, and the place left still under the dreary spell.

Elias had given Hugh the lantern, and was waiting for Hirell.

'Father,' she said, as she came up to him, 'I want to ask you if I have done right or wrong in some matter in which I have acted without asking your advice.'

'What is it, Hirell ? ' he said, gravely.

'Robert Chamberlayne has asked me to marry him, and I told him I cannot.'

Whatever Elias felt at the news, he kept concealed in his own breast. He said not a word till they had nearly reached the door, and then he asked her—

'Was it before—before this bubble burst, or after ? '

'After he knew of it all, but before he let us know.'

He looked at her—pausing in the doorway to do so, as they were entering—he looked at her with a keen, penetrating glance, and then across at the gate by which Robert had gone away.

'I thought of myself alone when I answered him,' said Hirell. 'If he had asked me after all this, I cannot tell but perhaps that, for all our sakes, I might have been tempted to give him a different answer.'

'And he saw this when he decided to speak to you first! I honour Robert for it, Hirell. I shall write and tell him so.'

'I care enough for him to be very glad to hear you say that, father,' answered Hirell gratefully.

They went into the house, and Elias shut the door, and followed her into the kitchen.

They found there Ephraim Jones and the lodger, by no means in a friendly attitude towards each other, and Kezia looking on with much distress.

'I maintain, sir,' the minister was saying, ' that it is utterly beneath the manners of a Christian—or what I suppose is a stronger word in your vocabulary—a gentleman.'

'May I trouble you for my candle?' said Rymer to Kezia.

'What is this, Ephraim?' inquired Elias.

'Friend Morgan,' said the minister, 'have I not rightly informed this person in telling him that everyone under your roof is expected to be present at evening prayers?'

'It is my rule,' answered Elias.

'And one which by no means should you permit to be broken,' cried the minister.

'My candle, if you please,' repeated Rymer to Kezia, who stood looking hesitatingly from one to another.

'Your candle,' said Ephraim Jones; 'and what candle, sir, will light you in the darkness of a night unhallowed by prayer?'

'Shall we begin at once, friend Ephraim?' proposed Elias, 'as Mr. Rymer appears anxious to retire; and, indeed, it is growing later than I thought,' he added looking at the clock.

'You are very kind,' said the lodger; 'but pray do not alter your arrangements on my account, for I am going at once to my room. Oblige me with a candle.'

And he took it with a bow from Kezia's yielding hand, saying, 'I fear I must trouble you to show me what bedroom I am to occupy.'

She turned a perplexed look on her master.

'Elias,' said the minister, 'it is your duty to uphold, like the ancient fathers of Israel, the statutes of your house.'

'Surely, sir,' interposed Hugh, who had just entered and seen how things stood between their guest and lodger, 'Mr. Rymer can do as he likes. He is not under the obligation of a visitor. He buys a home of us, and I cannot see how our share in the bargain is to be fair unless we give him a home with all its privileges and liberties.'

'And one of the privileges and liberties he is to enjoy,' said the minister, 'is letting Satan find a passage through his heart to your very fireside. Take heed, Elias ! May not the exposure of one sheep bring the wolf into the fold—or the carelessness of one soldier betray a whole garrison ? '

The word of the Reverend Ephraim Jones was law at Bod Elian, and all stood irresolute and perplexed. Everyone, even Elias himself, would have been glad to let the lodger have his will, and relieve them of his presence, yet no one dared volunteer to show him the way to his room.

Rymer's position was even more embarrassing. He stood with the candle in his hand determined upon going, yet not knowing in the least which way to turn.

At last he remembered Nanny, and, instantly he did so, went towards the kitchen where he had seen her.

Hirell and Kezia were thankful to hear them going upstairs together ; and to see by the manner in which Ephraim Jones flung into a chair, and opened his Bible, that he had given up the contest.

'Perverse and stubborn spirit,' he cried, shaking his head at the door by which Rymer had gone out ; ' God grant that this night sleep alone may visit him, for if death got hold of him, sharp indeed were its sting, and great "the grave's victory." But come, friends, come, fellow-soldiers, maimed and weary—before we leave the battle-field to rest under the tent of night, let us kneel down at our Commander's feet, and make known to him the defeats and triumphs of the day, and ask of him that he will enlighten us as to the duties of to-morrow.'

They all knelt, and he prayed—specially mentioning Hugh in his prayer—and setting forth such a terrible vista of temptations to be passed through by the young man as to make the women tremble, and redouble the anxiety of Elias.

Hirell knelt where she could see the minister's face ; but it was not while he was praying that she cared so much to look at it, but when his prayer was finished. Then, as if the loud voluminous tones of his own voice had acted like a kind of thunder on his mental atmosphere, and cleared it of the evils which filled it, keeping him for ever watchful and antagonistic, his face grew calm, peaceful, radiant.

His eyes swam in glad light, like the eyes of a soldier who descries through the battle's smoke, and lines of interknitting steel, the green hills of the land on which he would set his foot as a conqueror.

Hirell gazed at him in childlike wonder and reverence as he knelt there, his large red face slightly raised, his thick lips firmly set, his nostrils distended, his blotched forehead updrawn in thick lines, his eyes full of tender ecstasy.

Did he see his little boy who had been taken from him, Hirell wondered? Did he see him on those glorious shores to which he looked? The look was so humanly as well as divinely happy, she almost thought he must.

She would have liked to ask him when they rose from their knees, but it was not permissible at Bod Elian to hold any converse after the last prayers of the day. She could not forbear touching his great hand with her lips when he wished her good night and blessed her.

Then Elias went first with the one light which was to be set in the passage before the partly-open doors to serve for all.

They were all on the broad oak staircase together, Elias foremost with the candle, then Hirell and Kezia, then Hugh with his two dogs, who always lay at his door, and Ephraim Jones came guarding the rear, his great Bible in his hand.

As he passed Rymer's door, he could not himself forbear breaking the silence by a deep groan, which so startled Hugh's dogs that they growled ominously, till silenced by their young master's foot.

Rymer heard both sounds, and felt as strange in his bedchamber as he had done at the supper-table of his new Welsh home.

─────────────

CHAPTER XVI.

HIRELL.

THE autumn rains set in now with persistent force, making the slow monotonous days at Bod Elian pass still more slowly and monotonously, and impoverishing Elias Morgan's scant harvest fields.

In spite of the wet weather, the lodger spent most of his time out-of-doors, and when he remained in shunned the

family, **and** shut himself up in his own room. He was so
irregular in his habits, as to cause Elias no little annoyance.

On some mornings he would not come from his bedroom
till nearly noon, on others Elias met him returning before
breakfast from the barren hills behind Moel Mawr. He was
an inexhaustible theme for gossip and speculation in the
village of Capel Illtyd, where every morning a group assembled at the little post-office to compare notes and discuss
him. At Bod Elian no such gossip was permitted. Elias,
while in his heart resenting his lodger's apparent contempt for
his rules, sternly silenced all curious comments and speculations concerning him.

Before Ephraim Jones left Wales, Elias gave him a simple
account of what he had himself observed about Rymer, making
no mention of reports that had come to him, and the minister
had answered—

'It is manifest to me he is at war with the enemy of the
world. Bear with him while this appears so ; honour him if
he seem to you victorious ; cast him from your house if you
see signs of his being conquered, for Satan will use him there
for no good purpose.'

Elias, while much impressed with this view of the case, did
not see exactly how to deal with it, finding it impossible to
tell by his lodger's moods whether he or his supposed antagonist was enjoying the best of the conflict.

But Elias had little time and few thoughts to spare away
from the hard duties of his farm and household, and it was
much the same with everyone else at Bod Elian. Kezia was
busied with preparations—very humble ones this time—for
Hugh's departure. Hugh intended to be of wonderful assistance to Elias with the harvest work, but he was restless and
preoccupied—as most people are on the eve of a great change.
Elias was very patient with him, and never told him he was
doing him more harm than good.

The lad had already recovered so much hope concerning his
prospects in London, that Elias began to have less anxiety
about him.

His greatest care was Hirell. It was the thought of her
that so often kept his weary eyes from closing at night, and
that made his meagre harvest bitter to him.

She was drooping daily—in spirits and in health—he saw it
—he had seen it from the very day when the great shock had

come to them. He watched her in perplexity and fear. If she had fretted and complained he would have understood that as the natural effect of disappointment. But he never saw her in tears ; and if she sometimes spoke impatiently, it was never on the subject of their poverty—but generally to Kezia for showing too much concern for her.

Sometimes Elias returning with his little cart full of spare sheaves up the field in front of the house, would see Hirell between the garden trees standing lost in sad thought. He would have given up his best acre to know what kind of thought it was. Did the girl reproach him in her own mind, he wondered, for letting her enjoy too much the fruits of their brief prosperity ?

One day Nest Lloyd, the curate's daughter, who had visited them two or three times since their trouble, called and left some books for Hirell.

Elias watched her when Nest was gone—taking up one volume after another and throwing each down again impatiently. He went over to the settle where she sat, and looked at the titles.

'And did the child of a minister of the gospel advise you to read *these* ? ' he said. 'They are novels, the work of those who think the world so deficient in wickedness and vanity they must needs imagine more. Hirell, you will not read these ? '

'Very well, father,' she acquiesced, wearily.

He was touched by her passiveness. It rather pained him, appearing as if she had no interest in anything. He felt himself growing weak enough to wish she would ask leave to read one of the books, and detecting the weakness, said sternly—

'Such works are most pernicious.'

'It is a pity, then, that some of them are so beautiful,' answered Hirell.

'Then they have corrupted your mind already, or you could not think so,' said her father.

'Perhaps that is it,' she returned, sadly, but quite simply, and without a touch of satirical meaning in her voice.

Elias was more and more disappointed. He now quite longed for her to ask for one of the books ; and was so angry with himself for the feeling that he put them aside and said—

'See that these are sent back and no more of their kind allowed to enter this house.'

' Yes, father,' said Hirell, without looking a bit distressed
or disappointed.

' And do you take a pleasure in reading such things ? '
asked Elias, hoping still to draw a request from her.

' While I am reading them—yes,' answered Hirell ; ' I have
found the greatest happiness I have ever known in reading
two or three—but I think it must be a kind of fool's paradise,
for I find my own life so much duller afterwards. At all
events I know I am the sadder for reading them. I know it
is better for me to give them up.'

The sight of the books going away cost Elias far more
regret than it did Hirell. He could not understand her. She
was a mystery to him, but he had a deep faith in her ; he was
certain that the mystery hid something good and beautiful
that his mind was too dense to understand. He had no wish
to see her mind brought to the level of his own, nor did he
ever once tell himself she was better left to her own thoughts,
and that there could be nothing in common between them.
The more saintly and beautiful she seemed to him, the more
his heart cried out that she was his child—the more his
mind yearned up to hers. He was frightened of his love and
reverence for her—frightened that they might weaken his
hand as a father and guide, and in this fear he often dealt
more harshly with her than anyone else.

He was sitting one morning at his bureau, in the close little
parlour, busy at accounts, when the door opened and closed,
and without hearing a step on the carpet he knew that Hirell
stood near him.

' Are you very busy, father ? may I speak to you ? ' she
said.

His hard fingers fluttered nervously among the bills in the
bureau. It was an unusual thing her coming to him in this
way.

' Surely, Hirell,' he answered, half turning towards her.

She sat down on one of the old horse-hair chairs, and fell
with a grace indescribable for its gentle naturalness into her
customary attitude, her elbow in one hand, and her chin in the
other.

' Father,' she said, ' Ephraim Jones was talking to me the
other night before he left us about my going away from
home and doing something to earn my own living.'

Elias turned his face towards the bill-file, and moved the

papers up and down. After a minute he moistened his lips, and said—

'Well, Hirell?'

'I have thought a great deal about it, and I feel it would be better, much better if I did.'

Her cheek was flushed, and her hazel eyes were very earnest as she met her father's slow, puzzled gaze.

'You wish to go away from home, Hirell?' he asked her, slowly.

'I wish it very much.'

She had no thought of paining him. She had conjectured he might disapprove of her wish, that he might refuse to gratify it, but it had never occurred to her that he might be shocked or hurt. He had so carefully concealed his heart behind his conscience, that those belonging to him had almost forgotten it lived and felt. Hirell had great veneration for his character; he seemed to her to embody all that was grand in the old puritans, of whom she delighted to read. She had also a strong love for him; but this she looked on from childhood as a useless possession, for ever since she could run alone she had been taught to do all that she did for duty's, not love's sake. To her he was faultless, but cold and unmoved by human weakness as a rock.

When she watched him moving the papers in the bureau, she was disturbed by no fear but of her wish being denied to her.

'Will you tell me, Hirell,' asked Elias, very gently, 'why you think it better for you to leave home?'

'I'm afraid I cannot see all the reasons plain enough to tell them to you,' said Hirell, 'but one great thing that I want to go for is—'

She hesitated. Elias thought she doubted his power of understanding her, but Hirell's doubt was all of herself.

'What is the one great thing you want to go for, Hirell?' he asked.

'To see,' she answered, 'to see if life everywhere is as hard and dull, and unlike all the beautiful life in books as it is here.'

'No,' said Elias, a faint colour rising in his cheek, 'it is not. I can answer for that, Hirell. You might go far and find no place so poor as your father's house just now. It is no wonder you should wish to leave it.'

'No,' cried Hirell, her sweet voice ringing out with sudden passion, 'father, it is not that—it is not that. My want I cannot tell you. I do not know—unless it be I want the wish to live—but at least I cannot find it here. Oh, let me go, I want to find out not only for myself, but for us all, which is false—all the things I read and think of, or this life—this sad, sad life we all lead here.'

Elias leaned his elbow on the bureau, and his forehead in his hand, for some time, without answering.

At last he looked up with heavy, wistful eyes.

'I believe, Hirell,' he said, 'you have thoughts which I cannot understand, and I do not think it is because they are too foolish, but because they are too deep. In this case I had better leave it to your own wish to go or stay. If you think it for your good to go, then go, but—'

He stopped suddenly, and Hirell looked round in gentle surprise.

His head as he sat at the bureau, with his back towards her, was upright when she turned, but as she looked, it drooped forwards, and the hard hands received it, the fingers quivering as if they would reason with and uphold it against its weakness.

Hirell's eyes dilated, and filled with water and light—her heart swelled. She looked at the bent figure. Would it turn upon her angrily in a minute? Should she go out of the room? She felt he would wish she should.

She did go a few steps, but came back and stood near him.

She laid her hand upon his shoulder, requiring all her courage to do so. He was difficult to approach in his lightest moods. Was she not daring too much to come near him in his sorrow?

'Father,' she said, schooling her voice, that her yearning sympathy might not show itself, and annoy or startle him, and there was only perceptible in its music a faint breath of the passion she crushed down, that stole sweetly into his senses, like the perfume of a trodden flower, 'Father, have I vexed you? am I wrong in what I have asked?'

He raised his head slowly and looked at her. The tenderness in her eyes was like some strange transfiguring light upon her. He gazed at her as at something holy and far off, and shook his head.

'No, Hirell,' he said, 'if it seems right to you to go—go—but—I—'

The flinty eyes filled, and turned from her slowly, as he added—

'I was sorry, for I had need of you.   I had need of you.'

She stood a minute—her face streaming with large calm tears.

Then she knelt by him and clasped her hands on his knee.

'Father,' she said, 'how wise you are!   Oh I am amazed to think what wisdom God has given you.   You have lighted all my darkness; you have shown me what my want was.'

'My child! what was it?'

She put her arms up round his neck, and laid her wet face on his bosom, whispering with a deep joy,

'Oh, father, my need was that you *should* need me.'

CHAPTER XVII.

A BEAM OF LIGHT.

THE earliest step on the oak stairs of Bod Elian, next morning, was Hirell's.

The night had been one of awakening instead of sleep for her; she had for the first time been brought to understand how all the sternness and strength with which her father had encountered their late misfortune had been wrung from a nature sensitive as her own; less selfishly, more nobly sensitive she felt.   How easily had the blow struck her down!   How helpless, how weak she had been while all the houschold had been patiently and bravely bearing their increased burdens!   Poor Hugh was to be cast inexperienced, unprepared as he was, into the world, to make his own way as best he might.

Kezia, in addition to the heavier housework that Hirell's negligence had imposed on her, was earning a few pence a week by knitting stockings for the post-office shop of Capel Illtyd; and was so anxious over this private little scheme of hers that Hirell had once seen her fingers moving in her sleep as if busy with needles and worsteds.

'And I have done nothing since that miserable day,' she thought, 'but neglect what little work I did before, and add seriously to their anxiety.'

Then came the question, at first put passionately to herself, then fervently and entreatingly to God, 'What can I do? what can I do?'

Then she lay still and thought. She longed to be of great service to them all. She felt capable of achieving some act of heroism, if only it might be pointed out to her; but she at once saw the danger of any such dream keeping her from accepting humbly and with fitting earnestness the small, insignificant duties which alone were ready to her hand.

When in the morning she looked into her small dressing-glass nailed to the window-frame, the sight of her face, the beauty of which was intensified by the tenderness and enthusiasm that had sprung up in her heart, had a strange effect upon her. She took it as an evidence that the purity and light belonging to one of the elect were still in her spirit; and that her labours in the house, humble as they might be, were to be blessed by God.

With her feet unshod and her clumsy wooden shoes in her arm, that her steps on the bare oak stairs might not disturb the weary sleepers, she came from her room fresh, bright, noiseless as the sunbeams on the old stone walls; and, in so doing, startled back into his room a certain restless spirit who was slowly opening his door and meditating an escape from the house when the fair apparition appeared before him.

She did not see him, but sat down on the seat of the old window on the stairs to look at the sun shining over her father's fields. They had yielded nearly all their little harvest, and were looking empty and worn out; but Hirell's gaze rested on them tenderly, and found a pathetic beauty in what others would have seen but as stony barren wastes. There bloomed for her, at their corners and edges, memories brighter than the blue corn-flowers, and richer than the scarlet poppies of Robert Chamberlayne's Kentish fields. How many years had these black furrows and clods drunk the sweat of hands dear to her! By what hopes at sowing time, and disappointments at harvest, were they not consecrated! She wondered she could have longed so to leave them; her eye glistened with joy to think how gently she had been turned back. And, thinking this, Hirell rose and went down the stairs, pausing sometimes to feel how very still the house was; and to listen, with her finger on her lip, to the deep, calm breathing she could hear from the upper rooms. There was something strange to her in this feeling. She told Kezia afterwards that she thought God must have called her to show her how sweet and sacred He kept the house during their helplessness.

All the time she was descending, her face was looking up towards where the sleepers lay, with a smile of deep, reverential joy; and she whispered softly to herself, as she thought of all their trouble,

He giveth his beloved sleep.

The ticking of the old clock in the hall seemed to give no suggestion of haste, or even progression, but seemed rather like the measured tread of pacing feet, as if Time himself had turned sentinel to watch them. As Hirell took her hat from the row that lay on the bench by the door, it seemed to her a stranger might almost tell the characters of the owners by looking at them. There was her father's tall-crowned beaver, with a curve in its brim, which had a rigid, obstinate look peculiar to itself. There was Hugh's soft felt with the crushed crown, old and soiled, but with careless grace in every line as it lay upon the bench. There was Kezia's—of the ancient sugar-loaf shape—prim, and straight, and neat; and there was the large low-crowned beaver worn by the Reverend Ephraim Jones on his visit to Bod Elian; which, with its nap turned the wrong way, had caught the antagonistic expression of its wearer's face and form.

Hirell took her own from among them, and went out into the square flat field in front of the house, where the cows were standing by the wall waiting for Nanny to milk them.

There was a wild freshness in the morning, a joyous hurrying of water, gushes of birds' song glad and loud, flying armies of yellow leaves mad with liberty, a merry minstrel in every tree shaking music from it, and rain-drops that came dashing brightly down like tears shaken off by laughter.

Blithely as a child Hirell ran against the breeze, and came laughing and singing among the cows, which she caressed and spoke to separately with that soft drawl in the voice with which one often speaks to children or animals.

In the old times, when nothing but poverty and hard toil was expected at Bod Elian, Hirell had always helped Nanny with the milking; but she discontinued this directly the news came of their good fortune, for she had always disliked the task, and other and far pleasanter duties were thronging to her hand.

She had not resumed it when all that dream was over; and seeing her sad eye and pale cheek, they had not urged it upon her. Nanny had grumbled, but only with her face buried in the cows' sides, and would not have said a word about it to Hirell or Elias for the world.

This morning when Nanny went, gaping and rubbing her eyes, to where the two tin pails hung, she could not find them; and was uttering one of her not very refined maledictions on the person who had moved them, when, glancing round, she saw them standing ready with the milk in them.

In her surprise she glanced up to the little deep square window, and saw there a face looking at her with a sweet expression—pensive, amused, penitent. The little hand, in which the chin rested, was red with its labour; and the snowy forehead was moist under the half-rings of auburn hair that had been ruffled against the cows' sides; the hazel eyes looked deep, and full, and very bright.

As Nanny looked at that face her own became ennobled by a tender admiration and affection.

'Yes, yes!' she said in Welsh, with a rough fervour in her voice, 'they did right to call you so, Hirell, Hirell!'

The head, set like a picture in the square stone window frame, shook gently, and a voice answered, also in Welsh—

'No, Nanny; it is too holy a name for me. Angel! ah, what must the real angels think of me for keeping it.'

'Nonsense, Miss Hirell-*bach!*' [1] said Nanny, 'they know fast enough you've as much right to it as they have; and indeed more, for they know it's more to your credit to stay here, where angels are so much needed, than to sit up there twanging their harps and hallelujahing all their time away. *You* not an angel! Why what more *would* you do to be one?'

'My work as I used to do it, for one thing, Nanny; so mind you call me to-morrow, if I do not wake myself,' answered Hirell.

Then the face passed from the window—the beam of light was gone from before Nanny's eyes.

It came upon Kezia next, as she stood looking in amazement at the breakfast all prepared and ready.

[1] *Bach*—term of endearment.

' Is anything wrong, Kezia ? ' asked Hirell at the open door.

Kezia looked concerned—half frightened.

' Hirell, dear, you should not do this,' she said. ' Your father, what would he say ? he does not wish you to work hard; he will certainly be vexed.'

' He is coming, Kezia; let us go and meet him.'

Elias, returning from a far-away field where the plough was at work, saw them coming, and the bright fresh morning seemed to brighten and freshen still more. A sudden light shower had dashed down, and been caught by the glorious sunshine, that made it look as if there had been a fall of jewels.

Hirell approached him laughing and shaking the wet from her hat.

' Why, father, what a lovely morning ! ' she said, with a sweet gaiety that filled Elias with joy. ' The old year must be in its second childhood, for it's all tears and smiles, like April.'

Elias said—

' Good-morning, Hirell, God be with you.' And repeated the same invariable morning greeting to Kezia.

They went on towards the house together, Hirell's gaiety sobered as usual by her father's presence, but not destroyed.

Mr. Rymer was standing at the door watching the three as they approached. He had passed a restless night, and was for once thankful for the early habits of the house which enabled him to shorten the solitary self-communing which had in this particular instance become almost unendurable.

The long breakfast-table had, perhaps, owing to Hirell's deft hands, a more than usually inviting air ; or rather, a less than usually repellent one to Rymer. Hugh in the outer kitchen was mending a box to take with him to London ; and Nanny was chattering to him, trying to make her voice heard above the din of his hammering. The sunshine was streaming into the passage through the open door ; and with it a sweet sound like a voice singing, and coming nearer. Drawn by the sound, and the warmth of the sunshine, for he was chill with weariness and want of sleep, Mr. Rymer went to the door, and saw his landlord and the two women coming up the field.

The youngest walked a little in advance of the others on the side nearest her father; and was sending sweet peculiar notes half plaintive, half joyous, up the bright wet field before her. She was not walking trippingly, or as if any childish superabundance of spirits prevented her keeping pace with the others ; her step was elastic, eager, but quiet and even, and had more the gliding likeness of a spirit than mere youthful buoyancy.

As she approached near to the house and saw Mr. Rymer standing at the door, she fell back a little, so that her father and Kezia might enter first.

The lodger received from each a characteristic glance and salutation. His host's look was brief and severe as his ' good-morning,' Kezia's very gentle and full of humble solicitude at his pale, altered face, but Hirell's eyes looked into his with the modest boldness of perfect indifference ; they were so open, so dewy, so unflinching and un-selfconscious, that the man's sad eyes gazed back into them as if they were as insensible of his gaze or its profound sadness as two lovely flowers into whose depths it might comfort him to look. It surprised him to see them fill suddenly with sweet human pity, and droop as Hirell passed him on the threshold.

After breakfast Mr. Rymer found himself sitting in his landlord's dull little room listening to a voice talking and singing by turns—in much the same mood as he had looked into Hirell Morgan's beautiful eyes. He listened to it without thinking of the owner. It deadened the sharp aching of his head to rest it against the wall by the window, and listen to the strange language uttered by the sweet, peculiar voice. It blended so perfectly with the scene on which he looked—the tender outlines, and shading of grand heights, and soft depths —the poor simple houses scattered here and there, looking so lowly and plain, as if the builders had feared to blot God's work by theirs, and had therefore done no more than necessity required.

Hirell's voice singing over her work in the outer kitchen seemed the very music of these things, at one moment high and clear, dying off in soft, faint indistinctness, like those ethereal mountain points, then falling into depths of rich, dreamy tenderness, sweet and mysterious as seem the deep valleys in the distance ; then suddenly would sound the very key-note of sharp poverty —suffering, but enduring—patient, but pleading.

Mr. Rymer was not the only person at Bod Elian who listened to Hirell's voice just then ; Elias, harnessing his little rough-coated horse in the yard, heard her, and to him neither voice nor language was mysterious, but both inexpressibly touching and comforting; for he drew from them the knowledge that he was not henceforth to toil on his stony path alone, but to have with him a bright, sweet presence, surrounding him with flowers and light.

How bravely she was striving! For he knew that it was a matter of striving for Hirell to turn suddenly to these mean tasks from which she had thought herself for ever rescued. He knew this, even if her voice had not told him, as she toiled and sang.

She was packing the little market-cart, and as she passed to and from it and the kitchen, she burst out with a little antique Welsh song, with such a yearning in her voice that Elias felt his misgivings return, till he looked up and saw her bright face smiling as she dragged the heavy basket along and sang—

> Blithe is the bird who wings the plain,
> Nor sows, nor reaps a single grain ;
> Whose only labour is to sing
> Through summer, autumn, winter, spring.

'Now, Nanny,' cried Hirell, as she returned and laid her hands on a heavier basket, 'you must help me with this pork.' Then in sudden alarm—'What are you doing?'

Nanny replied by holding up a potato and knife.

'Goodness sake, leave off!' commanded Hirell. 'What do we want with them to-day, and father out, and Kezia making a bread-pudding?'

'Just a couple for the lodger—for the look of it, Miss Hirell-*bach*,' pleaded Nanny.

'Well, just a few ; but for goodness sake be careful, Nanny. How else *are* they to last the winter through?'

Nanny came and helped her lift the basket, and as they bore it to the cart Hirell went on with her song—

> At night his little nest he finds,
> Nor heeds what fare may next betide ;
> The change of season nought he minds,
> But for his wants lets Heaven provide.

She held the shafts as her father and Nanny put the horse in, and in moving quickly, tore a long slit in her dress ; and Elias, as he mounted and drove slowly over the rough ground, saw her look down at it ruefully as she walked back to the house, singing the last verse of her song—

Oft on the branch he perches gay,
Oft on his painted wings looks he !
And, penniless, renews his lay,
Rejoicing in unbounded glee.

CHAPTER XVIII.

THE WANDERER.

ONE evening Hugh and Kezia went to the chapel meeting at Aber. They were to stay the night with some friends there, that they might the next day pack Kezia's furniture ready for its removal to Rymer's rooms at Bod Elian.

Hirell and her father had spent a quiet evening together, for the rain had come on with increased violence, and put a stop to all work out of doors.

They were sitting at one end of the long kitchen table, Elias reading and Hirell knitting. They had no candle, they could no longer afford such a luxury ; but on the table over between them stood a curious little machine, that held, in something like a pair of nippers, a rush that had been soaked in common household grease. When one rush burnt out, which it did in a very few minutes, Elias would take another from a little bundle that lay close at his hand, light it and insert it in the place of the burnt one. He managed this so dexterously that Hirell never had to stop the rapid movement of her needles for the want of light.

As the rain beat on the long, low window, Elias raised his head with a troubled look.

' Are you sure, Hirell,' he asked, ' that Mr. Rymer is not in his room ? '

' Quite,' she answered, ' the door is opened. You can see right in as you pass.'

' Surely he must have sought some shelter ? '

' I hope so,' said Hirell.

' Is that the passage door ? Yes—listen—I think he has come in,' said Elias.

They listened, heard footsteps, a loud exclamation from Nanny, and then a faint shivering voice cry,

'My God! No fire?'

'Oh, father, go,' said Hirell, 'he is very ill.'

Elias rose and went quickly to the outer kitchen. The rush burnt down to the end, and Hirell, neglecting to light another, was left in darkness.

She went a few yards towards the open door, and stood still listening.

She heard Elias cross the kitchen and pause. Then she heard his voice speaking clearly and sharply.

'Go, sir, to your room and take off these wet things. I will come myself and light you a fire.'

'I cannot—I cannot move,' replied the faint shuddering voice. 'Let me be still. Leave me to myself.'

'I shall not,' said Elias with increasing sternness. 'I have left you to yourself too long. You are killing yourself, and you know it. I will no more permit you to trifle with your own life in this house, than I would with another's.'

Then Hirell heard her father's footsteps coming back quickly, and in a minute he met her where she stood.

'Give me a light, Hirell, in the lantern. I must saddle Gwen and go to Tan-y-Llyn for Dr. Robarts.'

'Is he very ill, then, father?'

'I never saw anyone look worse—quick, Hirell—send Nanny out to help me.'

She got them the lantern, and then stood alone in the great dark kitchen, watching the pale gleams of light across the window as her father and Nanny moved about the yard, and in and out of the stable and harness-shed.

In a few minutes she heard Gwen's quick, sure-footed trot on the wet road, and Nanny running beside it to open the gate.

Then Nanny came back and fell to chopping wood in one of the sheds, in order to fulfil her master's instructions to light a large fire in the lodger's room.

Meanwhile Hirell had heard several times something like a moan, and a sound as of teeth knocking together, which filled her with apprehensions.

Could she do nothing? she asked herself, feeling very helpless and very impatient at her helplessness.

Soon Nanny came in where he was with her bundle of sticks, and the next moment she heard her drop them, and cry sharply—

'Miss Hirell! Miss Hirell!'

Hirell was standing in the middle of the outer kitchen before Nanny had picked up her lantern.

Her steps had been swift and unhesitating as the impulse of pity and alarm, which the girl's cry had awakened in her heart, towards the miserable stranger.

She saw a form huddled together at the end of the long oak-seat near the chimney; and looked from it to Nanny, asking under her breath—

'What, Nanny?'

Nanny only pointed towards the bent form, and made a gesture of fright and perplexity.

The truth was, that Rymer had tried to rise, and had been seized with pain and stiffness, and thrown himself back with a moan of impatience and despair.

Hirell stood bewildered. What was she to do?

She was not at all experienced in cases of illness. Nest Lloyd had tried to prevail upon her to visit with her the sick people under her care about Capel Illtyd; but she was obliged to give up all thoughts of making a nurse or doctress of Hirell. She was like some wild creature in her extreme sensitiveness at the sight of physical pain. A consumptive cough made her tremble; a cry of suffering filled her with almost passionate alarm; the knowledge of some girl in the village being in a decline would cost her days of melancholy thought and restlessness. The wise, careful Nest was shocked at her want of discretion and self-control before such people; and thought it best to leave off taking her, for their sakes, as well as for Hirell's.

To Rymer's illness was added the fact that his reserve and isolation made it a great difficulty for her to approach him.

If she had found him in a fit or fainting, her hesitation to offer assistance would have been less; but the very dejection and wretchedness of his attitude showed his consciousness. And remembering how studiously he had avoided all contact with her family ever since he entered Bod Elian, even her pity could not overcome her reluctance to intrude herself on his notice.

'Nanny,' she said in a low, timid voice; 'I think you had better make a fire here, as Mr. Rymer seems too unwell to go to his room yet.'

Nanny set to work lighting a heap of dried furze and sticks

in the huge, sooty chimney; and while she did so Hirell came nearer, and stood in the smoke.

Rymer's form was twisted round on the oak settle; across the back of which his arms were laid, supporting his face.

When the fire began to give out a glow of light and warmth, he stirred, shivered, and turned towards it; stooping so that his arms rested on his knees.

There was such an animal-like gratitude and helplessness in the expression of the figure and white face as it watched the fire, that it gave Hirell courage to say—

'It will burn brighter soon.'

Rymer's gray sunken eyes looked up, and grew puzzled at the vision of grace and sweetness that stood in the smoke, looking at him.

The young bright eyes, with their fulness of charity, puzzled him. It was such pure charity, unsullied by reproach or inquisitiveness. So unquestioning and large it was, there seemed something angelic in it.

Who was it that looked at him thus?

Gradually he remembered who it was; he remembered Hirell, slowly and with difficulty, as one who, reading a stray line of beautiful poetry, might recall the poem to which it belongs.

Hirell had been almost fit to tremble at the sound of her own voice when she spoke to him. She fully expected him to answer her with anger; and the most she hoped for had been sullen silence. She was therefore very much surprised, and her pity became greatly deepened when he said, in a voice trembling with gratitude, as he cowered towards the fire,

'Thanks, thanks!'

At this she took courage and let a warm burst of pity out upon him in her voice and look—

'It gets so cold here now at nights; and the rain has been so heavy; and you have been out in it all.'

It was like part of the fire's delicious light and warmth to him hearing her speak so. As the warmth of the fire came penetrating through his wet clothes to his cold and aching body, so Hirell's voice and look, with its unquestioning kindliness and comfort, stole through the heavy clinging mists of loneliness and depression that had gathered about his heart.

The fire blazed, filling the windy chimney with its light and roar. Rymer leaned down towards it, and let his body and mind wake from their numbness, and for the first time for many days know something like comfort. He forgot the noises of the winds and waters, the cries of lost cattle in the solitary hills where he had wandered, and of carrion birds, and remembered only the crackling of the fire, and the sweet fresh sound of Hirell's voice.

As a dog may try to hide from a cruel master, and nearly starve in the attempt, and creep back, weary, famished, cringing for the driest bone, the meanest place at the feet that had so despitefully used him, so had Rymer tried to hide from the world that had grown so bitter for him, and had returned to accept gratefully its meanest comfort.

Hirell stood on one side of the chimney, knitting, and Nanny on the other, with her hands on her hips, and a look of broad sympathy on her face, and sometimes she stooped to pick up fallen brands, and threw them back upon the fire.

They were all silent; only the crackling of the fire or a shiver from Rymer broke the stillness.

And in this way more than an hour passed.

At last Elias came, and alone.

Dr. Robarts had been sent for to the Duke of Cornwall's mines, where an accident had taken place the day before.

Elias went straight up to Rymer.

'A lad at the mines has had his foot cut off,' said he bluntly; 'so you must do without the doctor till to-morrow morning. And, after all, you can do yourself more service than he can do you.'

The pale face bending down to the fire remained unmoved.

Hirell looked pained at her father's tone.

'You had better let me help you up to your room, Mr. Rymer,' said Elias. And he helped him to rise, and upheld him with a strong arm as he dragged his stiff, aching limbs across the room.

Hirell stood watching them, expecting, with childish eagerness, one parting word or look, but the sick man did not once turn his head.

'Ill-mannered English brute!' said Nanny, who had noticed her young mistress's disappointment. 'A fed dog wags his tail—but these English—ugh!' and she kicked aside the lodger's wet boots with inexpressible contempt.

Elias made his patient swallow some warm broth, and in half-an-hour came down and said he was sleeping quietly.

In this, however, Mr. Rymer had deceived him, for he had but closed his eyes in the hope of getting rid of his rough impromptu doctor; who had no sooner left him alone than he rose up on his elbow, and began to seek for something among his clothes by the bedside.

He took from a pocket a little note that he knew as well by feeling as at sight, and lay back on his pillow, with his eyes upon the note as if they read even in the darkness the words he knew so well—Catherine's last words to him—her little, almost illegible note she had been frightened into writing by his incessant watching and too evident alarm and suspense concerning her.

Waiting once, as usual, in the dusk, outside the wall of Dola' Hudol, by a spot where he knew she often stood at that hour, to watch the lights of the town so far below, and of the village so high above, kindling one by one—waiting at this place, Rymer heard her coming by herself. Then he heard her pause, and in an instant his arms were on the low wall, his eyes and voice chaining her to the spot by their misery.

'Catherine, I cannot bear it—I must know. How is he treating you? Did he see me? You are deadly pale, Catherine. Did he see me, then? Are you suffering for it?'

She stood still, her white face leaning a little forward, like the face of one who has had the voice of a dead person recalled to her memory, suddenly, startingly.

He held his hand out, but at that moment she started, turned, and walked quickly away. He lost sight of her as she went among a little group of trees. Would he see her no more?

Yes—the light dress fluttered out again. She came quickly to the wall, and went from it as quickly, without a word, a look to him.

But that little note had fallen at his feet. It contained few words, and none that gave him comfort—only such words, indeed, as drove him far from the only place he cared for in the world, and being banished from which made him hate every other place.

'I cannot tell,' Catherine had written, 'what he knows or thinks—he is kind, but seems different from what he has ever been before. Suspense is killing me. Keep away if you have any pity; do not add this constant alarm which your presence about here gives me to my other misery.'

For several days Rymer had kept out of sight of the walls and windows of Dola' Hudol; and had wandered on the mountains, exposed to all the fierce winds, and the frequent rains of the time, and only returned to seek the shelter of a home, when he found himself at the last stage of exhaustion.

As he had sat leaning towards the fire watching Hirell's five knitting-needles glittering iu its light, there came for him one of those intervals of peace and quietness which will come, and sometimes inexplicably, to the greatest sufferers; a breathing-space in which one can look upon one's own pain, and think of it almost as if it were another's. The delirious patient has some moment of the day or night when he remembers whose step has fallen lightest in the sick-room, whose hand has been most kind, whose eyes have longest kept awake for him— or whose heart has been wounded most by his impatieuce. It is a merciful subsiding of the waters, that we may see our own hearts for a little while, and discover there—and comfort ourselves with—the gifts of human grace and tenderness that sorrow's tide has brought us.

Such an interval had come just now for Rymer; and he found his heart's storm-beaten shore plenteously strewn with such gifts, and he looked upon and tried to count them with tenderness and remorse.

But he could not count them; they were innumerable—the delicate kindnesses that had been offered to and brutishly spurned by him, or churlishly accepted, since he first came to Bod Elian. To the gentle housekeeper, Kezia Williams, he knew that he owed many; to Hugh some; to Elias also a few; but he knew that the lightest step, gentlest hand, and most watchful eye in the sick-room of his soul all this time had been—

What was her strange name? he asked; and a second time he said it softly to himself—it and its meaning as Chamberlayne had told it to him—

'Hirell—beam of light—angel.'

CHAPTER XIX.

A WELSH ANTIQUARY.

WHEN Hirell and Kezia went to meet Elias returning from his work in the lower fields next morning, they both asked anxiously about the lodger; and Elias told them it seemed to him Mr. Rymer was in some kind of fever; that he was quiet, and willing to see Dr. Robarts when he should come.

'There is good in him,' said Elias; 'he entreated me like a child to raise the blind, that he might see Criba Ban from where he lay.'

Hirell and Kezia both looked at Rymer's little window, and from it to the mountain, standing, kinglike, above the rest; and both agreed there must be good in thoughts that could like to climb so high. Hirell felt, too, in her own heart, that they would hardly be content to rest there, for there was a flight of great snowy cloud-steps to take them higher still; and the morning sky seemed unfolding brighter and more intense depths of blue.

It was Hugh's last breakfast with them before his departure for London. All had been arranged by the Reverend Ephraim Jones for his entrance into the office of Messrs. Tidman, and his lodging with a Methodist friend, near the chapel where Ephraim Jones himself preached. Though he was not going till the evening, his two small boxes, and the old harp, already stood in the hall, packed and labelled 'London,' and Nanny, whenever she could spare time, went and had a cry by them. More than one of the farm-labourers put their heads in at the door to have a peep at the wonderful address; and several persons came up from Capel Illtyd, in the course of the morning, for the same purpose.

The gamekeeper from Dola' Hudol came with a message from his master, who had always been a sort of patron of Hugh's, to ask him not to go without paying him a farewell visit. So Hugh had to unpack one of the boxes, and put on his best clothes to go down to the great house for half an hour or so.

He went the nearest way, going from the road at Capel Illtyd and across the fields down into the valley, and in his walk he found how true was the old Welsh proverb, that parting looks are magnifiers of beauty. Never before had the grass seemed to shine with such emerald brightness, or the plumage of the magpies and sea-gulls flashed above it so dazzlingly white.   Was there any place in England where sea and land birds mingled as they did here, making such gladness and life in the air?   Even the children playing at holding a grand *Eisteddfodau* in a ditch came in for a share of his rekindled admiration.

Surely only mountain air, and only Cambrian mountain air could make such tints and outlines, such hardy delicacy of bloom and graceful strength.   Two farm-girls passed him, and before they had well got by, they heard him singing a Welsh song:

> Full fair the Gleisiad [1] in the flood
>   Which sparkles 'neath the sun ;
> And fair the thrush in green abode,
>   Spreading his wings in sportive fun ;
> But fairer look, if truth he spoke,
>   The maids of County Merion.

As he stood waiting at the little side-door at Dola' Hudol, looking at the sheep grazing in the rich swelling meadow, even they reminded him how clumsy and ungainly the English sheep, which he had seen at Dolgarrog markets, were in comparison with those graceful, agile little creatures, whose pretty intelligent faces were to be seen peering fearlessly over the most giddy heights, along which they ran nimbly as mice.

Hugh was shown into the library, and left there to await Mr. Rhys, who had sent word to him to amuse himself with the harp, or look at anything he liked till he came to him.

Hugh, however, remained standing just where the servant had left him, too much overpowered by the gloom and grandeur of the Welsh antiquarian's ' holy of holies ' to move hand or foot.

He had often been in that room before, and been made supremely happy by a sight of those precious relics of the ancient glory of his country.   Sometimes Mr. Rhys had read aloud to him from old manuscripts, sitting in his high-backed throne-like chair like a modern Don Quixote ; and sometimes he had made Hugh read, or play to him on the magnificent harp, while he leaned back with eyes half-closed, revelling in dreams from which he always rose with a prouder carriage of the head, and more haughty step and voice.   Hugh likewise

----

[1] The Salmon (Mr. Borrow's translation).

would go home with an air of grand melancholy, inspired by the contemplation of his ancestral greatness, and require some rousing words from Elias, before he became sufficiently reconciled to the existing state of affairs, to be able to take his part in the work of the farm.

But in spite of old acquaintance, the library at Dola' Hudol impressed him that morning as much as ever its owner could have desired that a lowly and young Bardic retainer should be impressed by such a sanctuary.

Perhaps the contrast between the great exploits of the noble wearers of those helmets bending over the door and window-frames, and his own narrow path of duty as carved out for him by the Reverend Ephraim Jones, made him feel more intensely his own humbled and their exalted state.

These relics and tokens of past greatness were not exposed in the common light of day.

Through the carving of an enormous piece of oak—part of a Gothic screen which blocked up one window, and through the stained glass of another window came such a light as should alone touch those rare mementoes of Kymric glory. It showed the antiquity of the books in the dingy oak cases without irreverently exposing their dilapidations. Yet they had been wonderfully well preserved. It was easy to see by the equal yellowness of their pages, and the general dry, crumbling look of their bindings, that no student had given them such destructive usage as Time himself.

Several of these cases had glass slides, which revealed, not books, but vessels of pottery dug up from a British camp; urns with human ashes; two golden sickles of the Druids— one broken, one only a little chipped; incense dishes; a breast-plate of richly embossed gold, and several curious drinking-cups. But the most famous of these, the Hirlas, was placed on the slab of slate supposed to be stained by the blood of a martyred warrior. This slab was supported by two blocks of stone, which also had their own marvellous histories engraved upon them in three or four lines of Welsh poetry, now perfectly illegible (with the exception of a name or two) even to Mr. Rhys himself.

Upon this rude but venerated sideboard stood the Hirlas— a long blue drinking horn, rimmed with silver, and having attached to it a piece of parchment bearing the following lines in Welsh, from Owain Kyveiliog's poem of the Hirlas—

> This hour we dedicate to joy,
> Then fill the Hirlas horn, my boy,
>   That shineth like the sea;
> Whose azure handles tipped with gold,
> Invite the grasp of Britons bold,
>   The sons of liberty.

Beside the Hirlas was another object on which Hugh's eyes rested with a certain wistful melancholy in their leave-taking glance.

It was not because he had any covetous desire for this ancient and most precious of all his patron's possessions, or any deeper regret in the thought that he might never see it again, than the same thought gave him with regard to all the other things in the room, but because it reminded him of many a boyish ambition, the recollection of which made the taste of his present lot very bitter.

In looking at that bar of twisted gold, four feet long, flexible, bright, and hooked at both ends, Hugh was not now so much inspired with enthusiasm at the thought of how many of the greatest of his country had worn such an ornament as a mark of their rank or valour; he had heard often enough from Mr. Rhys, how Aneurin the bard had worn one at the battle of Cattraeth: and Boadicea, when leading the Britons to fight against Agricola. Before his eyes, too, attached to the golden torque, was the boast of Llywarch Hen, Prince and Poet—

> Four-and-twenty sons I have had,
> Wearing the golden wreath, leaders of armies.

In Hugh's country, *Dwyn y dorch* (to win the torque) may occasionally be still heard as a household phrase for winning a prize; and the young man, who had ever loved to talk about the precious relic, had heard it applied to himself so frequently —*his* torque being fame and wealth—that now he could but look on the object before him with a sense of sharp disappointment and an irrepressible despondency, that made the grand antiquities of Dola' Hudol even dimmer to his eyes than the richly darkened windows made them.

But Hugh would not for worlds have had Mr. Rhys suspect him of any unmanly shrinking from a career his brother had with such difficulty opened for him; and in case he should come upon him suddenly while his throat was so uneasy in Kezia's new collar, and his eyes persisted in seeing the helmets of his patron's great-grandfathers nodding tipsily over the doors and windows, he crept quietly to his old corner where the harp stood on a sort of little daïs.

Kneeling on the step, and resting his cheek against the gold frame, his hands took from the strings a gentle and comforting sound ; and he was soon able to look round him with unflinching eyes, and take his farewell of the great spirits of the past, who seemed to him still to haunt the antiquary's room, swelling the gold breastplates and nodding the helmets. With the humility of the young and lowly bard of a great house, Hugh addressed them all in his wordless song. He told them that for the last time his soul drank to them humbly from the renowned Hirlas ; that he was to go forth to a contest arduous and inglorious ; to be no winner of the torque in this world, but a suppliant for it in that kingdom to which they had been gathered, and whose honours never tarnish, as that ancient torque, on which he looked, had tarnished.

Hugh's improvised farewell was very sweet and full of patient submission and subdued power.

The music reached the charming old morning room opening into the lawn, which seemed always to cast over it a reflection of its own soft, perpetual light.

Mr. Rhys heard Hugh's playing as he sat here, reading his ' Times ; ' and laying down his paper, listened attentively.

Mrs. Rhys was sitting near him, copying a faded little oil-painting, one of his most valued heirlooms. She was succeeding with her task so well as to give him much pleasure, and just now she looked tranquil, almost happy

She, also, heard Hugh's music, and glanced towards her husband with a smile, showing pleasant approval of his protégé's talent. His face, however, was turned from her as he leaned his elbow on the table, and his head on his hand, and gave his whole attention, as it seemed, to the unconscious Hugh.

It was not so much enjoyment of the music, as respect for the national instrument on which Hugh played, that the face of the descendant of the Welsh princes expressed, as he leaned back in his chair listening with half-closed eyes. It was a peculiarly narrow face now, but once, when the cheeks were fuller, must have been of a perfect oval shape ; the eyes were large, and almost black ; the nose and mouth undisguised by any moustache, and retaining still a noble and graceful contour seldom seen on so old a face. The thick iron-gray hair left bare almost too large and dome-shaped a forehead ;

the eyebrows were peculiarly fine-arched, and black; and a beard of patriarchal proportions hid the narrow chin, and half covered the broad chest.

Hugh's soft, distant music seemed to be burying the antiquary in profound thought.

'How well he plays,' said Mrs. Rhys, speaking rather to herself than to him, and scarcely expecting him to hear her; but at the sound of her voice the dreamy and somewhat sad face without looking towards her became attentive, anxious, wistful. It was like the face of a judge who feels that he must weigh the slightest gesture, word, tone, or look of a prisoner, as evidence from which to make a sentence of life or death.

Catherine had now become in a manner accustomed to this terrible judgment overhanging her; she had felt it, had suffered under it from the moment when Cunliff left her, to meet her husband alone, after that last interview at the Maiden's Lake.

Mr Rhys had hinted at no suspicion from that minute to this, when they sat together listening to Hugh's playing. Yet she knew as well what had been in his mind as if he had told her in words, how after hearing her talking with some one on the day of his return, his finding her alone had greatly surprised him; how he waited for some explanation from her, and how her continued silence on that point made him suffer.

She had striven, no human creature knew how hard, to ward off such an explanation, knowing it could bring forth only misery for both. She tried to forget her own suffering, and to make their reunion as happy as possible, that he might dread to sadden it by any expression of his doubts. And he did dread doing so; her timid advances were so sweet to him, hiding his suspicion as opening rose-leaves hide a thorn; so that it was only when his heart received them with the old passion that he felt it still there, and still sharp and poisonous.

Looking up from her task at her husband's trouble-averted face, she asked herself how long this could last, how long they could both bear it. And how must it end? Must she throw herself at his feet and tell him all before there could be peace for either? Perhaps he would not believe in her or forgive her, and then what would her life be? How then could her thoughts be kept from the one who did so well know her, and believe in, and love her? No, she must trust to her own courage and patience, and to time; confession, on the chance of her truth being doubted, was too desperate a risk.

Her greatest longing now was to do something to please him. She wished she could play to him like Hugh, or help him with his translations. How much she might do for him now that his young assistant was going away, if she had not been so ignorant of his beloved language, and all those things he cared for most!

'I am sorry your clever secretary is going away, Owen,' she said, bending low over her painting. 'I had almost made up my mind to ask you to let him teach me Welsh.'

The grave face lighted with sudden pleasure and surprise, which scarcely was perceptible in the voice as it said—

'Is it my ability or patience you doubt, that you don't think me fit to be your teacher, Catherine ?'

'*My* ability and *your* patience,' she replied, smiling.

'I don't think it would take many experiments to remove both doubts from your mind—but do you wish it seriously ? '

'Not only seriously, but anxiously, Owen. Will you teach me?'

And she laid down her brush, and looked full at him, with yearning eyes, tearful but strong, that seemed to declare how much more she would fain do, if it were possible, to remove the cloud that had come between them.

The expression of her face and voice moved him much. He rose and went to her.

'It used to be the custom,' he said, lifting her hand in a very courtly manner, ' for pupils to kiss their teacher's hand. Let me reverse the custom, Catherine, and thank you with all my heart.'

She smiled with almost all her old brightness, and rising, slipped her hand in his arm, saying—

'And now you must not keep Hugh Morgan waiting any longer. But I may come with you, may I not? I should like to thank him for playing for me so often last year ; and give him some little remembrance, that he may not go telling everybody his patron has a stingy English wife.'

Hugh heard their voices and brought his farewell rhapsody to a close.

He looked so slim and boyish as he came down from the daïs, that Mrs. Rhys felt quite a warm pity at the thought of what his family must suffer, at sending him alone into a world so utterly strange to him as London.

'You have been playing very charmingly, my lad,' she said. 'I am almost as sorry as Mr. Rhys to lose you.'

Hugh blushed scarlet with pleasure, as he made his bow.

'And so, Hugh,' said his patron, shaking hands with him, 'you are going the way of all our young men of talent—deserting Cambria at the call of England—eh?'

'Rather, sir, at the call of fortune. What can I possibly do here but starve?'

'Ah, yes; that is true. It was different though in the old days, when our country was as a very light among the nations; and when to come to Wales rather than to go from it was the aim of the young, the ambitious, and of those whom God had gifted with a spark of his own nature, that which we call awen—the English genius.'

'Ah, sir, I shall hear no more about those old days, but I am always dreaming about them, and wondering if they can ever be brought back.'

'Never, Hugh—never! But this you may do—help to make the world understand what we have been, and what we are. Ah—how we forget things! I remember now. I meant to have read you a little paper I have been preparing in my leisure hours, a sort of preliminary sketch for a more elaborate essay some day to be prepared.'

'Is it, sir, too much to ask that I might hear it now?'

'Not now, Hugh; not now. Mrs. Rhys loves Wales, I am sure—but she may be readily excused for not caring to hear prosy narratives about Britons and Saxons, and—'

'Owen,' she interposed, speaking earnestly, 'will you believe me if I say you could hardly give me a greater pleasure than to read this paper to Hugh and to me?'

He looked at her a moment in surprise, then a scarcely perceptible colour stole into his cheek; and when he spoke again it was with a smile of quite youthful unaffected gratification that she saw, and was in turn deeply affected by.

'But you know, Catherine—' he began, as if he could not even yet venture to realise as his own the pleasure he felt.

'I know, Owen, I have been very silly and ungrateful in past times, when you have sought to interest me in things that interested you. Let our young friend hear and condemn me for the confession if he pleases, that I have too often irreverently laughed, or indecently yawned, when, as I now see, I might have drunk in not simply instruction, but solace and agreeable occupation for those hours which pass so dangerously, if not profitably employed.'

These last words were said in so low a tone that Hugh

could not clearly distinguish them, but not a syllable—not an accent—not a tone was lost upon Mr. Rhys.

He gazed at her as if asking, as alone he could ask, with his eyes, what all this implied, and, strange to say, his gaze was the first to falter.

He went first to one cabinet, then to another, as if seeking his paper, but his wife saw he was struggling with the new hopes her words had conveyed.

Presently he came back stately, measured, composed as ever, and taking her hand as if to place her in a chair by his side, he pressed it for one moment tenderly, and felt that pressure responded to.

He felt half inclined to dismiss Cambria, the paper, and Hugh altogether, and use the blessed opportunity offered for trying to come to an understanding with his wife, whom he felt to be dearer than ever; but he controlled the impulse, while half afraid he should regret afterwards the testing her new docility and patience too much.

'Well, Hugh,' he said turning to him, as he took his own seat, which he turned away a little from his wife, as if not caring to risk the watching of her countenance as he read; 'well, Hugh, since Mrs. Rhys is so good as to indulge us in a bit of self-gratification, I suppose I must venture to read this sketch I so imprudently, perhaps, mentioned; not that I can hope it possesses the eloquence, the profound research as regards materials, or the literary skill that disposes of them to the best advantage, that adorn and vivify a subject; but simply in the hope that you, like another David, may find here and there among my facts and remarks, a pebble or two with which to hit that modern Goliath—Anglo-Saxondom.'

He had seated Catherine in his own stately chair at the end of the table, and taken his place opposite to her, while Hugh sat on the daïs step, his downcast eyes beaming with unbounded pleasure. It seemed like the days of bardic glory come round again, indeed, for him to be sitting there in the presence of the learned and proud master, and beautiful mistress of Dola' Hudol, and listening to a discourse on a topic of such inexhaustible interest to him.

The lad's simple enthusiasm, and the sweet attentiveness of Catherine's face, inspired the antiquary's calm, grave features and voice with unusual energy as he read, dashing at once into his subject.[1]

[1] See Appendix at the end of the book.

CHAPTER XX.

HUGH MAKES MISCHIEF.

HOWEVER weary older and wiser persons might have grown
during the reading of the paper, it is certain it had sufficient interest for the antiquarian's young listeners to hold
their attention throughout.

While Hugh sat in open-mouthed astonishment at some of
the facts he had just heard, Mrs. Rhys said, almost gayly—
'Well, Owen, you have made one convert at all events—Hugh
Morgan, be you witness, *I* am henceforward Anglo-Celt.'

Mr. Rhys was happier than he had been for many long
months. During the last hour all the threatening storm
seemed passing from above him, leaving serene beauty and
sunshine.

Hugh, to whom he felt he partly owed the pleasant opportunity by which he had gained, for the first time, his wife's
earnest attention and clear appreciation, was soon to feel the
effects of his patron's altered mood.

As he received his parting shake of the hand he found a
piece of paper left in his own.

Hugh coloured deeply as he opened it and saw that it was
a ten-pound note.

'Oh, sir,' he said, bluntly, ' would it seem very ungrateful
to ask another favour instead of this ? '

' Not to ask another favour, Hugh, certainly ; but why in
place of this ? '

He is discontented,' he thought ; ' of course, because I've
done so much for him, he thinks I ought to do more. Celt or
Saxon, they're all alike for gratitude.'

But he was wrong ; for Hugh was grateful to him, and
never thought there was any bitter inconsistency in his patron's
kindness for teaching him, first, that the whole charm and
essence of life lay in the love and cultivation of noble and
beautiful things—patriotism, chivalrous sentiment, music,
poetry, art—and awakening in his soul a passion for such
things that could only pass away with his life, and then letting him go to spend the best years of his youth on an office-
stool for fifteen shillings a week.

' I could not ask it, sir, unless you let it be in place of this,
that is, if you *can* grant it.' And Hugh coloured again, and
pushed the note farther on the table.

'Well, I suppose I must promise—out with it, then, Hugh; you have given me much of your time and labour, and must remember it's only due to me to let me know how I can best assist you.'

'Would you mind, then, sir—I am afraid it's asking a great deal—but would you mind not sending for the rent for some months longer, till Elias has recovered a little from his heavy losses? He is driven so terribly close, sir, I don't know how he will get through it.'

'My dear boy, rely upon my attending to this, and—' Mr. Rhys answered, but before he finished his sentence Catherine's generosity took fire, and she went to Hugh, and pressing her purse into his hand, said—

'I shall go up there and see them, Hugh, and do what I can for them—your pretty sister, Hirell—'

'Not my sister,' interposed Hugh, with a smile, 'but just the same.'

'Yes—I forgot—well, I have never seen her, but I intend to do so; I heard from my maid that she has not been well since this dreadful disappointment you have all suffered—now why shouldn't she come here for two or three days? I'm sure it would do her good.'

'It will give her such pleasure to hear you have wished her to come,' answered Hugh, 'but she's quite well, and I doubt if they possibly could spare her. Hirell's one that makes the very life of the house—no, I'm sure she couldn't be persuaded to leave Elias for a single day, just now, and as to any more help—' continued Hugh, growing rather frightened at the thoughts of the reception any charitable visitor might meet with at Bod Elian, 'as to any more help—it is not at all—at all—' He would have said 'needed,' but was too truthful, so stammered and broke off, blurting out again with 'They are getting on much better now—they've a lodger, you know, sir,' he said, turning partly towards Mr. Rhys; 'I dare say you have seen him—he's always wandering about—we often wish he knew you, for he's constantly grumbling about not being able to get at any books here.'

'I don't wonder at it, poor fellow—who is he, Hugh?'

'A Mr. Rymer.'

'Rymer,' echoed the antiquary, half carelessly, half musingly, 'it's familiar, somehow, yet I'm sure I don't know any man with such a name.'

'To say the truth, sir, Kezia and I don't think it *is* his real name,' said Hugh.

'I can't think how it is I seem to know it, Catherine,' he said, his whole face and voice changing to a strange tenderness as he uttered her name, and turned towards her.

But having turned, he stood still as stone.

She knew how bloodless her lips and cheeks had become, but as he turned she did not think he could know what had brought this deadly faintness over her—she expected some cry of surprise—fear—solicitude, but still felt that he was looking and was silent.   Did he remember Cunliff's second name? It was written in a book he had given her when they first knew each other, and that book she had sent, with others, to her husband, when he was in Italy.   Could it be that he remembered it?

Hugh watching them, thought Mr. Rhys must be paralysed with grief or fear at his wife's sudden illness, and seeing him so motionless, said—

'What shall I do, sir?   Shall I ring?   I have noticed Mrs. Rhys growing so pale, but I did not know she was ill.'

'I am better—I think the room is close,' came in a laboured whisper from the white lips.

'Well, good morning, Hugh, I wish you all prosperity,' said Mr. Rhys, in a cold, forced voice.

'Good-bye, sir, thank you for all your kindness.'

So Hugh passed out of the room where he had spent so many delightful hours, laying down on a book-shelf, as he went by it, the little purse Mrs. Rhys had given him.

When Catherine felt she was alone with her husband her deadly faintness came back; she closed her eyes and did not open them till the sharp shutting of the door made her spring to her feet, with a suppressed cry.

He had gone away!

She went to the door, then to the window, with a sort of weak, wild, hopeless impetuosity.

Near the window was a cast of a curious old cross—in which she had taken an interest when she had first seen this room a year ago.   It was from the 'Maen Achwynfan,' or 'Stone of Lamentation,' near Whitford.   She had heard from her husband how penances were finished there, and how tears of contrition and humiliation were shed there in olden times; earlier even than the ninth century.

As she faced it now in her inexpressible terror and anguish, she wondered whether the many burdened souls who had sought relief at its foot, had found what they sought. And then, without waiting to conjecture yes or no, she sank down herself before it with a cry as bitter as any pilgrim penitent that ever sought it could have uttered.

CHAPTER XXI.

A VISITOR AT THE ABBEY FARM.

IT was fair-day at Dolgarrog, and William Chidlaw, the young master of the Abbey Farm, had gone there with two of his men; and the Abbey farm-yard, in consequence, was shut in by its great gates, and was so quiet and sunny that the Reverend Daniel Lloyd found it a pleasanter study than his damp little parlour, or the great refectory where his boys were buzzing over their lessons.

He was pacing slowly up and down, from the refectory door to the nail-studded doors of the ruined chapel, when the yard dog woke and began to growl, looking menacingly towards the stile.

Mr. Lloyd glanced absently in the same direction.

The intruder was Mr. Rhys of Dola' Hudol.

The curate's look of quiet thoughtfulness changed to one of subdued anxiety, almost distress. He looked down at the sheet of manuscript he held, while he recovered some presence of mind before meeting his visitor; and the last words his pencil had traced happened to be such as came to him far more impressively than he had hoped could ever affect others for whom they were written.

He had earnestly desired to keep the secret of the poor young wife, if it were possible to do so with honour to her and to himself. And though he had refused to be present at her meeting with the stranger, unless she gave him permission to tell her husband all he knew, if he saw such a course was best, he had earnestly hoped it would not be necessary to take advantage of her promise.

The countenance of his visitor gave him nothing but the most gloomy forebodings; and turning his eyes from it to his page of manuscript, they rested on the words his pencil had just written:

'It is often to those very persons who think that the truth would ruin them, that it is simply salvation.'

Mr. Rhys had two very distinctive manners of speaking. When he dwelt on the ancient glories of Wales, or on the pages of an ancient illumination, he would be discursive, eloquent—full in his speech, but also slow. When, on the contrary, he was in action he spoke few, but curt and decisive words, such as habits of command abroad had given him. It was thus he now spoke to the curate, after they had shaken hands silently; and Daniel Lloyd could see that he scarcely remembered, as he went on, what was due to him whom he addressed.

'You have seen my wife lately ? '

'Yes.'

'Will you be good enough to tell me what passed ? '

'I do not know that I can do that.'

'Indeed ! '

'Candidly, Mr. Rhys, I would have been very glad to have seen you here on any other business.'

'We may agree in that, Mr. Lloyd.'

The curate paused a moment, with eyes bent on the ground as if in reflection, then began, bluntly, and with effort—

'The Sunday before your return, Mrs. Rhys came to our English service. Only two or three other persons were present, one of them my old pupil. After the service she went out ; but while I was unrobing she came back in deep agitation, and shutting the doors, came towards me with a cry of anguish and fell down at my feet.

'Astonished, I endeavoured to raise her ; and failing that— for she clung to my knees—I strove to quiet her, and induce her to speak.

'When she did so, it was in broken murmurs, reminding me of the next Sunday's communion I had announced, and of the words in the Prayer Book, authorising those who need it, to seek counsel beforehand.

'She did need it, she said ; and at last I drew from her that there was some one hovering about in the neighbourhood to see her, whom, to use her own words, it was not for her soul's health she should see.

'Shocked as I was, I could not but see how wisely she had resolved, by making this appeal, and I assured her of my fullest help and sympathy.

'Did she tell you who ? '

'No,' said the curate; 'nor would she tell me, in spite of

my strong reproof. But she promised me solemnly, that if he
compelled the meeting, I should be not far off, to protect her,
her name, and yours. He did compel that meeting—I too
went—and I never lost sight of them till they separated.
That is substantially all I know. And I believe he yielded
to her resolve, and left her in peace.'

'And you—a minister of Christ—did not think it necessary
or right to inform me?'

'What good could I have hoped for in doing so?' demanded
the curate. 'What could I have said but that which I now
say—deal tenderly with your wife. She has erred, I doubt
not; but not too far to be readily forgiven. As I am Christ's
minister, I say to you, one such sinner who repents is, or ought
to be, dearer than a thousand who have not known her temptations, and would have sunk irretrievably if they had.'

Mr. Rhys listened in gloomy silence, and walked two or
three times with the curate to and fro on the grassy avenue,
then abruptly took his leave with the words:

'I thank you. Perhaps I have been harsh. You confirm,
then, my wife's statement, that you knew of her meeting with
—with—before it took place?'

'I do most emphatically.'

'Can you tell me anything more about him, Mr. Lloyd?'

'Nothing.'

'Good-morning, Mr. Lloyd.'

'Stay—if you please, one moment. Your wife sought me
first. You seek now. I did not seek her. I do not seek you.
But you are here. Pardon me, then, if I ask you what benefit
can accrue from your discovery of this man, whoever he be, if
it is clear your wife and he no longer hold any kind of communion?'

There was a kind of smile, and a raising of the eyebrows, and
a dreamy, vacant look in Mr. Rhys' face, as he listened to this;
but now, as elsewhere, through the brief interview, he did not
trouble himself with what Daniel Lloyd thought, but what
Daniel Lloyd could tell. For that alone he had evidently
come, and looked baffled that he got no other answer.

'Beware! my dear sir, I entreat you,' said the curate,
earnestly. 'Beware how you reject the wife that turns to you
in time. If I understand her rightly, she must need you now
more than ever she did in her life before need you, your respect,
your love, your returning confidence—'

'Thanks!' said Mr. Rhys, interrupting him. He put out

his hand, which the curate clasped and held, looking wistfully in the hard face, but seeing nothing there, was fain to let the hand go.

As Mr. Rhys walked away, the curate looked after him, remembering he had not told him all ; for he had not told him how earnestly he had striven to persuade Mrs. Rhys to speak to her husband, or to let him (Lloyd) speak to him. Neither did he tell Mr. Rhys that he had only consented to be silent at his wife's appeal, or receiving her solemn and voluntary promise never again to see this stranger, unless in case of absolute necessity ; and then that he, the curate, should know.

He looked after the tall menacing form, and sighed heavily as he turned to go back to his damp little study. The sunny clean-swept yard had lost its charm for him.

CHAPTER XXII.

HUGH'S LAST HOURS AT HOME.

THEY were too busy at Bod Elian to give way to much grief at the thoughts of the approaching separation, for Kezia's furniture had arrived, and Dr. Robarts having been and seen Mr. Rymer, and given orders that he should be removed, as soon as possible, to a livelier room, they were all assisting in fitting up the two new parlours for his use.

By tea-time this was accomplished, and the invalid was helped downstairs by Elias, and led into a bright little bower, the existence of which, in such a place, he could scarcely understand. As he lay back on the little sofa, looking round the room, he felt that it was charming, but in what its charm lay he could not conceive.

The new paper on the wall was false in design, and gaudy in colour ; the carpet almost threadbare, the furniture black and worm-eaten. Yet everything seemed harmonious and pleasant. The darkness of the furniture perhaps sent the eye gratefully to the bright roses on the wall, though they might be out of drawing ; and their brightness, again, made the dingy carpet pleasant to rest on. White full curtains at the two little windows threw an air of dainty elegance over all. A fire was burning in the bright new grate. Kezia's old time-piece, with its white face and black frame, ticked on the mantel-shelf. A plate of African marigolds stood in each window, and filled the room with rich aromatic odour ; and a few branches of mountain-ash berries, and a pale China rose, were set in a vase on the table among the tiny tea-service, every piece of which had been wrapped up separately and packed away for years in a box of Kezia's mother's.

The sofa was so placed that he could see, through the window, the wildest side of Moel Mawr, where furze-fires were flaming up fitfully in the twilight. He could see through the door, too, which he had begged might remain open, into the passage, along which some one or other would be constantly passing; and now and then a door on the other side was left open, and he could see into the great kitchen where Hugh was spending his last few hours, regarding grudgingly every little duty which took either his brother, or Hirell, or Kezia, during one of those precious moments, from his sight.

Rymer saw that tea was spread there also, and that the brothers, unlike their usual custom, were sitting side by side at the table—their faces towards him. Hugh very often had to get up and leave Elias to go and speak to some one who came to the outer door to wish him farewell.

Such visitors were frequent, and Rymer fancied that the lad's voice was less and less cheery and strong every time he answered their adieus and good wishes.

Rymer knew when the time for the parting had come, for Elias rose and said something to Hugh, who got up also, and followed him out of the room. Hirell and Kezia lingered a little while, then they too went out.

The brothers had gone into the old parlour, which was generally called Elias's room, because his bureau was in it, and he sat here at his accounts a good part of every afternoon.

When Elias had shut the door, he turned to Hugh and said :

'I can only give you money enough for your journey, and to keep you for one week.'

Hugh nodded sadly, and Elias knew his sadness was not at having so little to take with him, but at having to take it at all.

'Look here, Hugh,' said Elias; and he lifted up the lid of the bureau.

Hugh looked, and saw just what he knew he should see—little packets of bills and letters in perfect order—the old account-book lying open, and the Bible beside it. Hugh saw that the last entry was his brother's gift to him, and that there was left in hand—nothing.

Hugh stood looking at the figures gloomily, and thinking that Elias might have spared him the sight.

'How can I take it, Elias ? ' he asked, almost reproachfully; ' what will you do ? '

' Hugh,' answered Elias, ' I did not show you this to prove how poor I am after this poor gift to you. I wished to tell you the comfort I have found in order and accuracy. I have been rich, and I have been poor, and I have come to believe that in poverty alone can a man rulo his soul and his fortunes with something of that divine order of which the mighty possessions of God are ruled. Here are two books ; ' and he gave him two like those that laid in his bureau : ' in one, let God see written in honest figures the exact state of your fortune, day by day ; in the other, find words to tell Him the condition of your soul, and He shall cast up both for you with the eye of a father and master. Though the column where the sum of your possessions should be written is a blank ; leave the blank there cheerfully, for God's eye to see ; pray for your daily bread, and go forth to your work.'

He closed the bureau, just as Hirell and Kezia came to the door. Hugh started, as he heard the handle turned, and glanced at Elias. The elder brother guessed by his look that he wished to remain alone with him a minute or two longer, and as Hirell appeared in the doorway, raised his hand to warn her back. She nodded, and went away with Kezia.

Elias then looked inquiringly at Hugh, and was surprised to see him with a suddenly heightened colour, as he stood looking at the money in his hand. Elias sighed, for he thought that some other unavoidable expense must have occurred to perplex him.

' What is the matter, Hugh ? ' he asked.

Hugh sat down in a chair near him at the table on which he laid the money, and began to move one coin after another, as if counting it slowly.

' Well, Hugh ? '

' Perhaps,' said Hugh, ' I had better not say it now ; perhaps I'd better write to you, Elias.'

' If you have anything you wish to relieve your mind of, why not do it at once, Hugh ? Are you sure it is something you wish me to know ? '

' I do, I do, Elias. I wish you knew. I know you ought to know.'

' **Then** tell it me simply, lad.'

' Oh, Elias ! perhaps you guess it.   Sometimes I think you do.'

' I never guess,' answered Elias ; ' I have enough to do to understand and cope with what I know.'

' But you must have thought sometimes—'

' What about ? '

' Kezia,' said Hugh ; ' that I care for her ; that I love her.'

Hugh was accustomed to long silences, on his brother's part, in time of surprise or excitement, but no silence had ever seemed so long or so oppressive as this which followed his own agitated, hastily-uttered confession.

Elias was standing at the window, with his back towards him. He had not been standing so when Hugh began to speak.

Suddenly he turned round.

' Have you told her ? Does she know ? ' he asked.

' I never said anything to her till last night.'

' And it was after you spoke,' asked Elias, in a slow measured tone, ' that she wished to come home ? '

' Yes ; but I don't know if it was through my speaking.   I do not know if she even understood me,' said Hugh.

' Do you wish to speak to her now, before you go ? '

' I think not.   I think I could not, Elias—going out of this place as she knows I go—a beggar.   No ; I'll wait till I have done something to give her faith in me, and to give you faith in me, Elias.'

And Hugh rose, with a light in his face that seemed to say he meant that something to be very great and decisive, but his brother's glance did not respond to it.

At this minute Hirell and Kezia came again to the door to say that the car which was to take Hugh to Aber was waiting. Kezia, in her quiet, subdued way, went straight up to Hugh to say something about his things.

Elias watched her with a strange, wistful scrutiny.

' Here is a list of the things I have not marked, Hugh,' said Kezia, slipping a little piece of paper in his hand ; ' pray don't forget to get the ink, and mark them as you promised.'

Elias watched her glance at Hugh's troubled face, and then turn away gently, as feeling she should have no place in his thoughts or sight at such a time. *Did* she feel this ? he wondered.

Kezia let them all go before her into the hall, and stood

waiting, feeling a pleasant confidence in soon hearing the young man's footsteps come in her direction.

She waited, listening to the boxes being lifted into the car, and to the confusion of footsteps in the hall.

'Now he must be coming,' she thought, and a gentle, motherly yearning came into her eyes. The next minute, those soft eyes of Kezia looked startled and grieved, for the wheels of the car were heard cutting sharply through the moist gravel.

Surely it was not possible Hugh had gone without wishing her good-bye! Then she heard Hirell go back into the kitchen to speak to Nanny. Then Elias came towards the stairs before which Kezia stood.

'Oh, Elias!' she cried out in a pained voice, 'did he forget me?'

Elias looked at her sharply, and passed by her, and went upstairs without a word.

Kezia stood still, pursing her mouth and bridling her neck a little, and the tears rose to her eyes; but after a little while she wiped them meekly away, saying to herself:

'They have too much upon them to think of me;' and then she went about her work as cheerfully as ever.

In about an hour she had so quieted her mind as to be able to sing one of the hymns she had heard at Aber Chapel the previous evening. Her soft voice penetrated one of the upper rooms, the door of which had been closed and locked since Hugh's departure. As Kezia's voice came softly stealing up, the door was opened, and Elias stood on the staircase looking down and listening.

It was a dove-like, soothing voice, neither very sweet nor very powerful, but soft and winning, and full of peace. It was not a voice to excite any powerful emotion; yet, as Elias listened, his chest heaved; and he said in a low, deep voice:

'Lord, I thank thee that she can sing in my service, though he is gone.'

There were other ears that also found the voice of Kezia pleasant. Mr. Rymer, in his little quaint parlour, with its mixture of age and newness, listened to it in a great sense of peace. It had been a strange day for him altogether. A soft, continuous flow of fresh, healthful visions and sounds had pressed back old thoughts with a strange, sweet pertinacity that even habit and sickness could resist.

When ho first woke in the morning, he remembered that the previous day had not gone by exactly as the days had done for so long—the night closing on him like an additional prison door, none the less gloomy and hopeless to him if nailed with stars. What had made it different? He looked at a sunbeam lying across the splintery floor, and that reminded him of a name which made him smile as he said it to himself. A soft lowing of cattle drew his eyes to the field before his window, and what he saw made him say the name again. He had looked at the flowers when he came into the room where he sat now, and they too brought tho name to his thoughts and lips.

As he sat listening to Kezia's singing, he was also listening for a step to return—a step that had gone away a few minutes since. He had listened to it all day, as it fell along the passages, upon the stairs; it seemed to have a music—a meaning different from all other footsteps.

Soon he heard it going past his window, and then he heard another footstep join it, and knew that Elias and his daughter were walking up and down on the little raised path on which the window of the bedroom opened. The one footstep sounded heavy and despairing, the other light and blithe.

Rymer went to the window and sat down behind the curtain. He saw the two standing still there—Hirell looking at the stars that were crowding out everywhere, Elias looking at her with his slow, wondering gaze.

'What are you thinking of, Hirell?' Rymer heard him ask, when they had stood so for some time. He spoke in a wistful pathetic voice, as if wearying for some of the light that he saw on her face.

'I was thinking, father,' answered Hirell, 'while this our world is growing dark, how many, many worlds grow bright.'

Then Kezia called Hirell, and Rymer saw Elias standing looking at the stars alone and bareheaded.

CHAPTER XXIII.

THE VIRGIN MARTYR.

ABOUT half an hour later, coming from his bedroom into his little parlour adjoining it, he saw Hirell and Nanny, who had just brought in his supper, holding up something between them, and looking at it in a passion of admiration.

He stood a moment without disturbing them, listening to their exclamations, of which the tone only was comprehensible to him.

They were holding, carefully spread out, an artist's proof of an engraving of the Virgin Martyr. He had that evening taken it from his portmanteau, where it had lain rolled up since he left London, and had opened it out on the table.

There was no mistaking the poise of Nanny's rough head, nor the parted lips and dilating eyes of Hirell, as the two girls held it up between them.

Suddenly the door, opening between this and his bedroom, creaked.

Hirell started and cried imperatively to Nanny to let go.

Nanny glanced carelessly towards the door, and seeing no one there—for Rymer was just behind her—retained her hold on the picture, answering Hirell's entreaty by a rude refusal, and continued to feast her eyes upon it.

Hirell implored, commanded, and, thinking Nanny would yield, tried to draw it from her. Nanny gave it a rough pull, and tore it right across the centre.

Hirell dropped it and burst into tears. She had never seen a picture anything like it before, and vaguely estimated its value as something immense.

Rymer approached, making the aghast and contrite Nanny jump as she saw him so close to her.

'I hope,' said he to Hirell, as he touched the torn picture, 'it isn't this little accident that's distressing you? The thing is of no value whatever.'

Hirell lifted her tearful eyes in timid amazement to his; and then Nanny and she looked at each other as two penniless wayfarers might do, hearing a prince declare the same after having his watch and diamond ring stolen from him. How rich he must be to call this worthless!

'Indeed, sir, I am truly sorry and ashamed, I am, indeed,' Hirell said with such a sweet and utterly humble look of sorrow that he was at once amused—charmed—yet quite grieved that she should take the trifling accident so much to heart.

'I assure you it doesn't matter in the least. You seemed pleased with the picture,' he said, looking at it carelessly as it lay torn on the table.

'Oh, sir, it is the most wonderful thing I ever saw in my life ; and to think—'

And she dropped her wet, flushed face and went slowly from the room, murmuring :

'I must go and tell father about it, and see what is to be done.'

Rymer followed her after a minute's perplexity, and found that Elias was not in the kitchen, but out in the front field. It was yet early, and Kezia was setting off to Dolgarrog to make some purchases for the lodger.

Seeing this, he went back to his room and waited with some impatience for her invariable visit to him before such an expedition, and the usual timid enquiry as to whether she could do anything for him at the town. He was not supposed to know she went there purposely for him.

This evening when she came, instead of the surly 'No, thank you,' she was intrusted with a delicate little commission which put her into a sad state of nervousness.

She was repaid, however, on her return, by the perfect satisfaction and polite thanks of Mr. Rymer, who immediately after opening the little parcels she brought him, set to work with paste, pasteboard, and little tacks, with gum, camel's-hair pencil, and dark paints, to the great surprise and curiosity of Nanny. Just before prayer-time, when Elias was taking his good night look into the stable and cow-houses, and Hirell and Kezia were knitting in the kitchen, Mr. Rymer issued from his room with something in his hands.

He approached Hirell and held it before her with a smile.

It was the torn picture wonderfully mended, mounted and framed in a plain, bright gilt frame.

'Is it worth being hung up in your room now? I am afraid not,' he said, meeting her wondering eyes with a strange thrill of delight.

'My room, sir!' echoed Hirell faintly.

'Or anywhere you like. I have put it together for you as well as I could, as you liked it so much.'

Hirell rose, putting her little hands timidly on the frame, but so tremulously that he thought if he let go it would fall.

Again she looked full into his eyes, her own strangely bright —her cheeks a shade paler than usual—it seemed, he thought, if not too absurd to believe—with emotion.

'You have done this for—me ? You give it to me ?' she said.

'No, perhaps not ; it's not worth having, is it ?' said he, pretending to draw it away.

Then her fingers took firmer hold on it.

Once having it out of his hands, the joy of possession made her forget herself.

'Kezia!' she cried in a voice of sweet childish triumph, 'look—it is mine—my very own!'

'But you have never thanked Mr. Rymer, Hirell,' said Kezia reprovingly.

'No, and I never can,' she replied, turning to him suddenly, with swimming eyes, 'only when I look at it—only then to myself.'

'Nonsense, child,' said Kezia in Welsh, 'you can say thank you.'

'Yes, I can say—thank you.' And she looked over her picture at him, and uttered the two words with a mixture of delight, despair of being able to express her delight, and of entreaty to him to believe in her gratitude.

The look and voice haunted him all night. Several times he found himself shaken by a tender laughter as he thought of Hirell and Nanny over the torn picture ; and constantly, when he hardly suspected himself of thinking about her, his lips twitched with some such exclamation as—

'Quaint little creature !'

'Solemn, delicious gratitude.'

'Sweet, holy little face !'

CHAPTER XXIV

AFTERNOON AT DOLA' HUDOL.

On his return from the Abbey Farm, Mr. Rhys went into his library, where such pleasant hours had been spent that morning, and, after standing hesitatingly a minute before the bell-rope, rang.

'Ask your mistress to be kind enough to come to me here,' he said to the servant, and then sat down in the throne-like chair, took a pen and sheet of note-paper, and began to write a letter.

Before five minutes had passed his wife came in. He did not look up or take any notice, but her keen eye saw that he was conscious of her presence. She put on no assumption of carelessness or annoyance, but walked straight up to the window, and stood by the table where he was writing, and looked gravely out on to the lawn.

His hand trembled a little at feeling her so near. It was hard to sit unmoved while she stood there in her sweet, pale, morning colours, fresh as the new-blown bells of the convolvulus, that waved against the window—hard to know how the living gold of her hair was glittering in the sun, nor dare to lift his eyes to it—hard to know the sweet rose on her cheek was deepening in colour at his silence, yet remain mute—to feel the kindling fire of her blue, averted eye, and keep his own cold—to know how her breast was heaving with the misery of her young, passionate heart, and not fall down a cringing lover at her feet, and sue for it once more.

But a little quiver of the hand, and the passion was subdued; he wrote on; his wife waited at the window, and whenever she glanced at him his profile was cold as that of his bust on the bookcase.

At last he felt she was beginning to be impatient—to lose her self-command. Perhaps he needed this to begin his task at all.

She walked once or twice to the door. Suddenly she turned upon him.

'Owen!' she said, in a rich, half-laughing voice, while her eyes looked at him gravely enough, 'if ever I commit suicide, it will be while I am waiting for you to speak. For God's sake, say what you have to say. Your words may kill me, but your silence maddens me, and I'd rather be killed than sent mad. If I am what I am sane, God knows what I should be as a lunatic.'

He paused in his writing, looked up at her, laid down his pen, and said with the old courtesy:

'Pardon me, I forgot; I hoped to have finished this before speaking to you. I am writing to your uncle.'

'To my uncle!' Was it merely the fire-light he saw suddenly reflected in his wife's eyes, or was it—but he did not choose to pause to answer himself.

'Owen, beware! I can bear much. You may easily degrade me in my own eyes, almost as much as I see I am already degraded in your eyes;—but—but—he loves me; is the one being that thinks me not altogether worthless. You would not—oh, you would not ruin me with him—my last friend!'

'I desire, Catherine, to spare you every pain that your own

behaviour has left it in my power to spare you ; but as regards your uncle—'

'As regards him,' she interrupted, 'if you are wise you will be silent.   He will believe me, if I must speak.   In Heaven's name, Owen, let us both spare the old man.   You, like myself, have had much kindness from him.'

'You are too quick—too impetuous.   I beg you to be calm. You are young, and can bear, perhaps, these exhausting emotions ; I am old, and cannot.   You have discovered, Catherine, though somewhat late, that I am old ; pray, then, let age have its needful immunities.'

'Oh, my husband !   What madness possesses you that you fling your words at me like those poisoned weapons that you once told me about as in use among barbarous nations ?   Why do you use these cruel sarcasms ?   When did I ever show you by look, or word, or act, that your age is—'

'What ! do you reject the one excuse that even I can find for you—ay, in my very heart ?   Shall I, because I played the fool once in marrying you, never again cease to play the fool ?   You are wrong, unreasonable, unjust to yourself. You have taught me much ! '

He ceased ; and taking no heed of the bitter distress that she could no longer hide, turned away, and again went on with his letter.

It would   seem   that   Catherine   had   come   into   the   room possessed by some secret desire or determination that enabled her to bear up against the terrible severity of his words.

Again she interrupted him :

'Have you seen Mr. Lloyd ? '

'Yes.'

'Does he confirm my statement to you ? '

He was silent.

'I know he does,' she said, 'and, Owen, I know not whether it is God that prompts me, in spite of myself, to do now what is so hopeless ; but see—my husband—I kneel to you, and ask you, perhaps for the last time in life, to listen to me.'

'Do not mock me,' he answered, 'any more by idle appeals. If you will be good enough to be silent for a few minutes—'

'No, Owen, I will not be silent.   I do not know what new outrage on me you are meditating.'

·' You shall know, soon!' he said, with a quietude of tone that only made the listener more and more desperate.

'Owen, you have hitherto seen in me a woman conscious of error, deeply repentant for it, making all restitution in her power, stopping in time; see here, in the presence of God and the dear Saviour of mankind, I swear to you I stopped in time, and with the strongest resolution and desire to be to you once more an honest wife. But you believe nothing; you thrust me back upon my miserable self, even when my heart goes out towards you; you are blind to all that ought to satisfy you—my own isolation here, Mr. Lloyd's testimony, your own letter—'

She paused as she thought of that letter, lest once more grief should conquer the rising anger which she now wished to call forth.

'What letter?' he demanded, not looking up nor removing his pen or eye from the paper.

'That one you wrote me from the Continent, so noble in its language, so confiding. Ah! do you not know, have you never yet suspected, that it was that that suddenly changed me? Owen, do you not know that?'

He made no answer, but remained in his bent position, as if he could not trust himself to speak.

'I cannot, I will not, live in this fearful, this wretched state! I demand now, then, that you speak plainly out— here, if you please, and now—else before my uncle, to whom I myself will go, and before him challenge you to impeach my innocence!'

'Catherine, while I try incessantly to narrow the ground between us, you make it wider at every step. I want to think of you as well as I can. I want to take things as they are. I am too old to dream. The days of romance are gone for me. Would they had never been revived, as they have been, to tell me what I have lost. Why, then, are you not content?'

'Content! To be suspected of I know not what! Watched at every turn! Unable to say one truthful word, without finding it come back to me stamped, like a base coin, with fraud. No; I will bear this no longer. Say then, plainly, what you have to say; and I will defend myself, with God's help, as I best can.'

He gazed at her with surprise, wonder, almost admiration,

for a single moment, then pushed aside his writing-desk, and rose to his feet ; and then, as if beginning at last to share her own agitation, he walked once from end to end of the room ; then returned, again sat and gazed once more in silence upon her anguished, burning face.

'So be it,' at last he said, and he spoke with extreme deliberation as one might suppose a just judge to speak when compelled, by some unhappy combination of circumstances, to give judgment in a matter affecting most deeply his own most sacred interests.

'Do you know that handwriting?' he asked, placing before her a short and merely complimentary note, professing to be written from London, on some unimportant matter, from Mr. Cunliff to herself, on the very day of her meeting with him at the Maiden's Lake. This bore the London post-mark of the day after—had come by the morning mail—and been delivered the same afternoon.

Scarcely knowing what to say or to do, and naturally truthful, she faintly responded,

'Yes.'

'Read it,' said her husband. 'I received it and opened it the day after that of *my* meeting with you *and his.*'

When she had done so, and noticed the date, she understood, in a moment, its intention, and was lost in wonder to know how the thing had been done.

Cunliff, as he reached Dolgarrog on that memorable evening, was in one of those moods when the most desperate thing seems the most prudent. He sat down, wrote a few words with forced slowness and care, put them into an envelope with a few words addressed to his housekeeper, got out a saddled horse, which he occasionally hired, and, riding at an almost incredible pace, reached a place eighteen miles distant before the mail-cart, that had started more than half-an-hour before; there found the night-mail train, and a passenger who undertook to deliver the letter immediately the mail arrived in London. He had done so soon after daybreak ; the housekeeper, obeying the order inclosed, drove off to St. Martin's le Grand, and posted the letter, which returned to Wales by the day-mail, and was delivered the same afternoon at Dola' Hudol. All this Cunliff did, besides getting back the same night so as to cause no remark from Chamberlayne, in the mere hope that he might thus help Mrs. Rhys to convince her

husband (if necessary) that he, Cunliff, was in London when
that letter was written.

'And you opened this?' said Mrs. Rhys, after a prolonged
pause.

'I did—when I found you still silent as to the meeting I
had interrupted. You wonder at me, Catherine, I know.
Well, I confess I wonder at myself; the change was sudden
from faith to incredulity. But consider that seemingly
courteous and most innocent letter. Do you believe it?'

'Had you asked me at the time I could have replied to
you,' said Mrs. Rhys, with a touch of the sex's skill in answering difficult questions by a retort on the questioner.

'I read this, and of course ought to have believed that this
Mr. Cunliff was in London, when he seemed, to my imperfect
vision, to be much nearer to me and you. What I did was to
write to a friend, who learned for me that Mr. Cunliff had
left London before the date of that letter, and had not returned since. That, then, Catherine, is one of your friends—
a trickster, who, no doubt for excellent reasons, finds it
necessary to lie in this fashion. Do you desire me to go
farther? It is my turn, wife, to ask you to spare me. I
have loved my wife—honoured her—and the contrast is too
painful.'

'Do you make me responsible for Mr. Cunliff's doings?'

'Yes; while you stand at his side, and dishonestly shelter
him, and refuse to say, "That is the villain!"'

'Owen, Cunliff is no villain!'

'Ah, indeed! Come. Try me. I can listen, if you please,
to all his virtues. I should like, indeed, to be sure that it is
a noble victim who—'

He stopped, and evidently with the manner of one who
goes farther than he intended.

'Goes to the sacrifice!—is that what you were about to
say?'

'Look to yourself, woman. I will deal with him.'

She was about to reply, but checked herself as she noted
the unerring sign that was for an instant visible on his face.
Yes, she could read there vengeance, and an unsleeping energy
of purpose.

A sudden calmness came over her, for him. For him—Cunliff—she suddenly found the power she had failed to evoke
for herself; for he was in danger beyond all question. Yet
how? To what extent? Had her husband already seen him?

'You bid me, Owen, look to myself. That is what I seek to do, now that you drive me to extremities. Is this, then, all you have to lay to my charge in explanation of your recent behaviour to me? Is this all, that Mr. Cunliff has written me such a letter?'

He looked at her with surprise, as if thinking of her audacity, and almost he seemed to feel the pity of it—that he must go on.

'If I understand you, Catherine, rightly—I mean as to what you wish me to think about you—your understanding with Mr. Lloyd was that you were never more to hold any kind of communication with the stranger that it was possible to avoid. Do you wish me to believe that you have kept that engagement?'

Her slow speech gave her, so it seemed, a few extra seconds of time in which to think of the answer to this dreadful question.

If she acknowledged the last interview, she felt there would be no limit to the severity of his judgments, because no longer would he listen to anything but his own absolute certainty of her guilt.

'I do wish you so to believe,' she said in a hard, but firm tone.

'Liar!' he cried, 'do I convict you at last!'

He went to the handle of the bell, to pull it, in awful silence.

'What would you do?' she asked.

'Call the servant, who has seen him and you exchange communications—O shameless woman—within this very week!'

'Owen, Owen; stop; hear me. I—I am innocent of aught but the despair you force into my soul—innocent—in—'

She had fainted; and Mr. Rhys was for some time unable to complete the business on which he had set his heart. When she revived, slowly, silently, the courage of despair began to strengthen the unhappy woman, and so feeling, she said to him when an hour or more had passed and he had finished his letter—

'Please to express your will, and let me go.'

'Can you listen to the letter I have written to your uncle?'

'I will try,' she said, with a sweet and most cruel smile, that almost repaid to him the pain he had inflicted on her.

He began to read it, thus :

'DEAR SIR,—I write to ask from you a personal favour. It is that you will receive Catherine for a time, the duration of which it is now impossible to fix, in your house ; and with the understanding that she receives no visitors but your visitors, and never leaves your house and grounds without your express permission.

'How much is involved in these requests, I, alas ! of all men, have the saddest reason to know. Nor should I put them to you—how could I ?—for myself; but I do put them and urge them for her.

'She has deeply wronged me, but to what extent I leave her to explain. I am willing to hope for the best. I demand that for a time, at least, she keeps aloof from society; and I in return will do my best to hold her reputation safe before the world, so long, at least, as she will let me.

'I grieve to see that I am not writing as I intended to write. The bitterness of the heart, I feel, is infecting my every word, and making me unjust.

'I do think she is personally innocent. I do think, for one so young, so beautiful, so inexpressibly lovely in that loveliness of the spirit which is as heaven to earth compared with the body's attractions—I do think, I repeat, that all these things, with my own age and rigidity of character, may excuse her in your eyes. Ah! I would to God that they might in mine too. You do not know—she does not—how I worshipped her.

'I dreamed again I was of the kind capable of loving and being loved. All the chivalry of the past seemed to be revived—all the romance of my youth, and I said, my life may be of little worth to her, but it cannot but be glorified in such light, and whatever I am, or have, or may be, all is hers.

'What my state is now, it is worse than useless to speak of, if she be lost to me.

'Ah, sir ! will you try to win her back to me ?

'Hear her story. Keep her by your side. Win her confidence. Then—though not too soon—write to me. If you can then say in solemn truthfulness of soul, "Take back your wife; she is no longer unworthy of the love of an honest man,"—then, indeed, will I give her, what now I cannot, my trust.

'Dare I still think this may yet be so ? My life cannot be

prolonged to any great extent, but whatever it be, then it shall be devoted once more to her, to smooth over the past, to struggle for a future—one where I may indeed feel peace—and so feeling, may show to her an old man's boundless gratitude.'

She had never once interrupted him, except by the occasional half-stifled cry of despair his words wrung from her; but when he had finished, she rose hastily, wiped away the moisture off her face, and said with sudden animation:

'Owen, I accept this—I do—indeed I do; and now will you let us part, as we should part. Oh! my husband—my heart still beats for you—and your happiness—if—if—'

He could no longer resist. Before he was himself conscious of what he was doing, he opened his arms, and she flung herself upon his breast, and wept there a long time.

After a time she whispered—

'When do you wish me to go?'

'To-morrow. We will ride together to the station, then part—your groom and maid going with you.'

'Very well.'

'Do you, Catherine, now see why I have done this?'

'No.'

'Because I feel I am no fit judge of my own case. My heart seems to harden against you—while—while—'

'I understand. This, then, is our farewell?'

'Yes—substantially.'

'Then, O my husband, will you not—not—even—say—God bless you?'

She knelt down, with bowed head.

His trembling hands were upon her—his murmured words floated in her ear—unrecognised, yet fully understood.

'And pardon?'

'Do you deserve that, Catherine?'

She looked up at him. He had not spoken severely, she saw.

'I do! as God is my other Judge, I do!'

'Take it, then—and let us both hope all the barriers are removed that lie between us and a future.'

'One word more. You spoke as if desiring vengeance—'

She could go no farther—so terrible was the look that came upon his face.

She would not be warned. Cunliff was in danger—that was all she could think of. She prayed in her inmost soul not to be obliged to see him or write to him ever again.   But she could not allow him to—

'Owen, you have forgiven me—you must also forgive him.'

'Catherine, I will not be tempted.   There has been enough, and too much, of violence.   Leave him to God!'

'Will you do so?'

He went away without answering her question.

Catherine had said before that his silence had maddened her, but never had it been to her so terrible as now.

In the night she made a resolution, reckless of consequences, and in the morning she carried it out as recklessly.

CHAPTER XXV.

THE MOUNTAIN ORCHARD.

Mrs. RHYS rode over to Capel Illtyd before breaakfst next morning.   When she reached the gate of the lowest field of Bod Elian, she got down from her horse, and told her groom she was going to walk up to see the people at the farm.

She had a vague hope of meeting Cunliff rambling about before she reached the house; but her determination to warn him was so fixed, and her fears as concerned her own safety so slight, that she scarcely paused once to think how or where the interview she wished for was to take place.

In this manner, defying more and more the danger that became more and more apparent to her as she went on, Mrs. Rhys reached the flat field in front of Bod Elian.

The doors were open—the house seemed empty, and indeed it was just the time when Nanny was away with the cows, and Elias had ridden out to set the men to their day's work.

Standing hesitatingly a minute at the open door, Mrs. Rhys thought she heard voices somewhere behind the house, and gathering up the skirt of her habit, walked quickly round towards the garden trees.

In the wall that inclosed those trees, she saw a broken door swinging back on its hinges; she entered by this, and found herself in a garden.   On her right was a long path, sloping downward; on her left a flight of uneven steps, with moss and ferns growing out of them.   The instant that she reached that spot she heard Cunliff's voice—not so as to

understand a word he was saying—but only in a murmur,
audible enough for her to know it was his voice. It came
from somewhere above. She looked up, and saw that the
steps led to a little orchard, whose trees bore scarcely anything but moss upon their branches, which were all bent one
way by the sea wind that came along the valley on the other
side.

Mrs. Rhys mounted the steps in that same spirit of impetuous courage and generosity that had let her dare so much
already in coming to Bod Elian on such an errand.

She followed the only path she saw in the weird little
orchard, and it took her straight to the other side, where the
valley, with its walls of mountains, its glittering little thread
of a river, and the great flashing line of sea at the end, burst
suddenly upon her view.

But the beautiful valley, in all the glory of the morning
sun, was only a background to the picture by which the eyes
of Catherine Rhys, in their brave, reckless search, were suddenly riveted. Just before where she stood a part of the
loose stone wall had fallen long ago; and the stones, all
thickly cushioned with moss, were scattered for some way
down a little green hill, at one side of which a waterfall
dashed down with a force and noise as if it had all the sea in
its flow.

On one of these stones sat the man for whose sake her
heart was so full of misery—her eyes so dim with midnight
tears that she could scarcely bear the morning sun which lit
the picture. There he sat, looking in tender, smiling interest,
at a girl, whom apparently some question of his had plunged
in a fit of sweet, thoughtful embarrassment. She was very
lovely. Catherine Rhys felt her loveliness through all her
heart, which seemed to drink it in like poisoned honey—the
dewy hazed eyes, full of fresh fancy and tender wildness—the
smiling lips—the fresh, natural grace of the form, which the
poor dark clothes suited as the foliage of the young willow
suits the tree—the pretty, childish fingers twining round the
great horn of the cow against which she leaned, with her feet
crossed, and her other hand stretched down caressingly to a
little calf, that rubbed its blind, soft head, against her knee
—nothing was lost to Catherine's eyes, which looked upon the
picture till it and they seemed both to turn to fire, and she
pressed her hands over her face, but only to snatch them
down and gaze once more.

CHAPTER XXVI.

MR. CUNLIFF AGAIN VISITS DOLA' HUDOL.

KEZIA WILLIAMS was standing near the kitchen window kneading a dark mass of dough, when she saw a stranger come into the yard and look about him. One of the farm boys passing, the man stopped him, and asked him some questions which, as the boy did not answer, Kezia concluded must have been spoken in English. The man was dressed as a groom, and she thought he had, perhaps, come with an order from some large house. Muffling her hands in her apron and raising the window, she asked in English—

'What is your business, please?'

The man turned sulkily, like one who has had his patience rather sorely tried.

'Do you know if my mistress is ready?' he said.

Kezia looked perplexed.

'Whose servant are you?' she asked.

'Mr. Rhys's at Dola' Hudol. Mrs. Rhys came up here about an hour ago—she ain't gone, is she?'

Kezia was quite amazed and flustered at the idea of such a visitor, but she answered quietly—

'I have not heard of her being here, but I will see and let you know if she is ready.'

She rubbed the dough from her hands and went out into the passage calling Hirell. She thought she might have met the lady of Dola' Hudol and taken her into the parlour—but that was empty, and so seemed all the house beside.

Kezia took her hat and went round towards the garden. Then she heard, as Mrs. Rhys had done, voices above in the little orchard. She went lightly up the steps, seeing no one till she came upon the same picture—the bit of broken wall, the cow, Hirell leaning against it, the little blind calf rubbing against her knees, Mr. Rymer sitting on the stone—his pale face all brightness and animation.

'Hirell!' cried Kezia with the faintest tone of reproach in her voice.

'Yes, Kezia. Do you want me?'

Rymer rose laughing, and looking, Kezia thought, a little confused.

'Have you seen Mrs. Rhys, of Dola' Hudol?'

'No, indeed—why, Kezia, is she here?' asked Hirell.

'Yes, it seems she is here—her groom is waiting; he came round to the kitchen window and asked me if she was ready. Do put up your hair, Hirell, and see about it.'

Hirell obediently raised her hands to twine up a long twisted roll that had escaped from the little brown felt hat. While she was doing so she glanced towards Rymer, and the thought struck her that she had never seen him so pale; but the idea of the distinguished visitor whom she had to seek, the beautiful wife of Hugh's patron, had such complete possession of her mind that everything else was forgotten as she sprang over the fallen stones and passed under the light foliage of the orchard.

Kezia went back into the house, to see that it was fit for the expected guest.

When they were both gone, Rymer turned and looked up after them with a face full of intense and sad alarm.

He rose, feeling half stunned with the sense of some senseless calamity. Catherine here! what could have brought her? What but something worse than he dared think of?

All at once a cry reached his ears, and made his feet bound towards the spot it came from—up past the scattered stones, in under the trees.

He saw Hirell standing looking down upon the ground, and knew by her face it was she who had uttered the cry.

Before her at her feet a beautiful form lay prostrate, its hands clasped over its head, its face crushed flatly to the damp earth beside a little spring. In the long riding-habit, it looked, as it lay, of peculiarly noble stature, and as still as death.

While Hirell stood pale and amazed, she saw Mr. Rymer lay his hands on the lady's shoulders and try to lift her face from the ground, and heard him whisper in a hoarse voice—

'Catherine!'

At that time a shudder shook the form and the hands unlocked. A face stained with earth was lifted suddenly. It was so shocking to see its youth, its beauty, its convulsive passion, its stains as from a grave, that Hirell burst out sobbing at the first sight of it.

Mr. Rymer looked up at her keenly—entreatingly—

'Be her friend—and mine,' he besought her; 'some water —here, wet me this handkerchief.'

He tore it from the grasp of the little gauntleted hand. Hirell dipped it in the basin of the spring and brought it to him, and watched him touch the face with it very gently, though his hand might have been palsied to tremble as it did.

In a little while Hirell saw the lady make a sudden movement with her hand, as if to push back Mr. Rymer's, and he looked at her with a deep sorrow and tenderness, and said—

'Catherine—Catherine—what made you do this?'

'She smiled at him—such a smile as Hirell had never seen before, cold, mysterious, cruel—she could not help gazing at Mr. Rymer's face to see how he received it, and she saw him turn yet a shade paler.

In another minute Mrs. Rhys was standing. She walked a few steps slowly, supporting herself by the trees—then more firmly and quickly, and without support, she went down the orchard steps, Rymer following her in silence.

Hirell found her hat upon the ground and went after them with it.

The groom was waiting at the door of the house with the two horses. Mrs. Rhys mounted with his assistance. Cunliff took her hat from Hirell and gave it to her, and she received it with the same peculiar smile.

Before her servant had mounted she had gone—leapt the field gate, and was galloping down the steep road at a fearful speed. Hirell looked at the groom and at Rymer, and with difficulty restrained from crying out.

Without a word Rymer seized the rein from the man's hand, leaped on his horse and followed.

Hirell ran to that part of the field from which she could see farther down the Dolgarrog road, and soon she saw the two horses abreast of each other, galloping towards Dola' Hudol.

Kezia saw her from the window, and came out.

'Did you see Mrs. Rhys, Hirell?' she asked. 'Has she gone without coming in?'

'She has gone. She came to see Mr. Rymer, and he has gone back with her.'

'Surely! how strange he knew them and has never been to Dola' Hudol before!' And Kezia went back to her bread-making puzzled, and Hirell went to work proud, secretly proud, of her sagacity in understanding from a certain tone in Rymer's voice, when he said, 'Be her friend and mine,' that he wished this strange event to be kept a secret among those who had witnessed it.

Mr. Rhys was standing in the hall when he heard the horses coming up the park. He looked, wondering who such early visitors could be, and was greatly amazed to see his wife, whom he thought to be still in her own room. As she reined in sharply before him he looked at the gentleman who had ridden up with her to the door, and something in his pale, excited face riveted his eyes.

Cunliff saw Mrs. Rhys look from one to the other, and fall forward with a deadly sickness in her face; and motioning Rhys, exclaimed passionately, 'Quick, quick, help her; she is ill.'

Rhys answered the appeal with a glance full of meaning, took his wife in his arms and lifted her gently to the ground.

As he turned he saw Cunliff dismounted standing before him, and bowing with deep respect, hat in hand.

'I must ask your pardon for this intrusion,' said he, in a clear, unfaltering voice. 'I have had the pleasure of meeting Mrs. Rhys in London, and finding her this morning too unwell to be riding alone or in the charge of a servant, have ventured to accompany her home.'

'I thank you,' said Mr. Rhys; 'may I know to whom I am so deeply obliged?'

'My name is Cunliff.'

The question was asked and answered as they stood face to face. Cunliff, with one foot on the step, and the groom's thick, short whip in his hand; Rhys, with his arm round his wife, as she leaned half fainting against him.

She seemed to feel the look with which the two men were regarding each other, for she shuddered, and slowly turned her face towards Cunliff. Then she turned it away with a sharp spasm of pain on her own, and looking at her husband, said—

'Owen, as Mr. Cunliff does not seem inclined, even in self-defence, to tell the story of my humiliation—I—must tell it myself.'

'Catherine,' said Mr. Rhys sternly, 'quiet yourself; go to your room. I will take care that Mr. Cunliff shall explain all.'

'That he will never do,' answered she.

'That he shall do before he leaves this house,' said Mr. Rhys, with extreme calmness.

'Owen,' cried Catherine, turning upon him suddenly, ' do you know what you would hear of your wife ?—hear it from her own lips at least—would you have *him* tell you how I have been mistaken all this time—that I alone have been guilty in all this scandal—this misery ? '

'You are excited, Catherine; you do not know what you are saying. Let me take you in. Come.'

'Do I not know what I am saying ? Look at me, Owen—look into my face and see if you think I feel it a truth or not when I tell you that man does not love me.'

She had laid her hand on her husband's arm, and was looking up at him with a despair so deep and wild, it fascinated him. He gazed down at her with a great anguish, almost forgetting Cunliff's presence. He knew she spoke the truth, and he saw what the truth cost her.

'Do you believe me ? ' she cried again, in a voiceless whisper. ' He does not love me.'

Still her husband gazed at her, and did not speak.

'He does not love me,' said Catherine ; 'it is not for my sake he is staying here. I went to warn him this morning of your anger, and saw who it is he is staying for, and learnt what I tell you, that he does not love me. I saw the one that he does love—I saw him with her. I saw him light-hearted and happy—while I—the sight nearly killed me—I fell down where I stood—and when I came to myself my mouth was full of earth, as if my teeth had tried to gnaw an opening to my grave. They found me, and tended, and were kind to me. I broke from them, and rode away madly in hopes some accident might happen to me before I reached you ; but you see *he* followed, and cherished and guarded me. Oh, thank him —thank him for the precious life he has saved. Oh, Owen, thank him ! '

He felt the little hand relinquishing its hold upon his arm— he knew the sudden rush of strength was failing—and he had scarcely time to seize both hands, before she sank at his feet white and still as if in death.

He looked across her at Cunliff.

His look was simply one of dismissal—pathetic and stern. There was no fury in it—no hatred. The sword of vengeance

which had been sharpened by one sorrow, was blunted by
another.

Cunliff saw this—received the look with deep respect—
bowed low and turned away.

CHAPTER XXVII.

HUGH'S FIRST LETTER HOME.

HIRELL did not mention to anyone the scene which she had
witnessed in the orchard. Cunliff discovered this soon, and
wondered at her silence upon the subject.

The next day Kezia came home from a visit to Dolgarrog,
and brought the news that Dola' Hudol was deserted
again—that Mr. Rhys had gone on a foreign tour, and that
his wife had returned to her uncle's house. Hirell looked at
Cunliff when Kezia had told them of this, and their eyes met,
and were withdrawn in much embarrassment. In the evening,
happening to meet her as he was crossing the orchard, he said
to her—

'How can I thank you for your kind considerate silence as
to what took place here yesterday?'

Hirell was standing by the little spring near which Mrs.
Rhys had lain ; she had been thinking of the lovely stained
face as Cunliff came towards her, and of his low passionate
cry of 'Catherine!' and she seemed to hear it still in the
murmur of the water.

'I shall never speak of it,' she said quietly.

'You are very kind. I thank you much.' He held out his
hand. To have taken it, Hirell must have extended hers over
the very spot where Mrs. Rhys had fallen. Perhaps she had
been standing in the dusk and listening to the water till she
had grown superstitious ; for as Cunliff held out his hand she
hesitated, looked down on the ground, and then up at him,
with eyes sweet, sad, and questioning.

'Is it worth thanks to be silent on such a matter?' she
said gently.

'The best thanks of my heart.'

She did not take his hand, and he drew it back and went
away from her in silence, and not without some humiliation.

Elias had been absent at the cattle fair of Dolgarrog all

day, and his return was being looked for most anxiously by Hirell and Kezia, for on the dresser in a conspicuous place—that their eyes might be gladdened by the sight of it all day—was Hugh's first letter.

Even when Elias returned, it was not taken down from its place till the meal was over, and the fireside prepared as for an honoured guest, and then Elias got up and took the letter, and, returning to his place, read it aloud to Hirell and Kezia.

London, ——

'DEAR BROTHER,—I hope you will all forgive me for not writing before; I have so little time to myself, but I will manage differently in future. I will write as you wished me, regularly, and conceal nothing from you. In the first place, then, to do this I am afraid I must shock you, as I have already done Ephraim Jones, by declaring that I like, admire, and almost reverence London.'

Elias paused, and read the passage to himself again slowly, while Kezia and Hirell looked at him thoughtfully. He made no comment, however, but went on.

'Life here *is* life indeed. Since I came I have seemed hardly to want food or sleep.'

'Then surely he isn't well,' said Kezia, anxiously; 'but I beg your pardon, Elias;' and Elias continued—

'I am at the office by nine, but between that time and the time I rise I have generally seen more than I have done in the whole course of my life at home. Then when I leave the office my real day begins. I wish I could describe to you the feeling of hope and confidence I have as I roam about by myself—as I stand on the bridges, looking at the reflection of the lamps in the river and thinking of home—of what temptations I have to do something with this restless strength which the rich life of this place and its infinite possibilities give me. I have already some good news for you. It was only yesterday that I summoned up courage to go to Mr. ——, with the letter of introduction—recommendation, perhaps I should call it—from Mr. Rhys. I found him very stiff before he read the letter, and very kind afterwards. When we had talked a little while, chiefly about the Eisteddfod, he took me into the study, where his harp, a present from the Queen, was, and he asked me to let him hear me play. I did so. I was prepared for any roughness, any condemnation—for great musicians are proverbially eccentric—and I said to myself, if I have made a mistake, or if Mr. Rhys is mistaken in me, I shall hear it now without ceremony. I was prepared to see him laugh, sneer, anything but come to me in the simple manner he did, and tell me that his friend Owen Rhys was quite right, that my talent was very extraordinary. His extreme gentleness and quietness made me quiet while with him, but no sooner was I out of the house than it seemed as if my happiness would choke me. I whistled, hummed, walked, ran, but my excitement only increased as it grew later, and I approached nearer home. To put my finger under the door, find my latch-key, and go up to my room, seemed an impossibility. I wandered on past the house to the end of the street. It was a moonlight night, and I heard something like music. I found it was a wretched tinkling when I came to the public-house at the corner of a low street, where three fellows were playing on a fiddle, flageolet, and—O Cambria! —a harp. It was a wretched thing, but not so bad as the poor old chap who played it would have made us believe. His fingers trembled as if he had the palsy. His poor, thin face was turned over his shoulder, as if sick of his own music. Of his two companions, one looked an idiot and the other a rogue, on whose face appeared to me stamped all sorts of vilainy.

'When I saw the poor creatures creeping out of the gin-shop, and out of the wretched houses down the street, and approaching to listen to this trio, I watched them to observe whether they derived from the music the comfort, or pleasure, or excitement they seemed to expect. The air, which made itself apparent to me through the discord, had a certain low, smart cunning in its turns that I cannot describe to you, but that seemed to gratify the listeners vastly and to awaken in them emotions which, judging from the expressions of their faces, the antics of their hands and feet, must have been at once ugly, wicked, and, in spite of a gleam of devilish mirth, most miserable. Elias, you will be annoyed at what I did, but you must remember how excited I was with Mr. ——'s praise, and the bright hopes that had been kindled by it; and when I saw these poor souls being played to by disease, idiotcy, and vice, each of which infused its own peculiar spirit into the music and was reflected on the listeners' faces, I felt as if something most holy, most divine, were being desecrated, and made to lie to those who had the sorest need of its truth, its sweetness, and comfort. Music was beating, burning at my fingers' ends. Almost before I knew what I was doing, I had gently taken my place between the poor old fellow and his harp, and the ill-treated chords and I understood each other. You will laugh at my egotism, but I never enjoyed the possession of such power as I did at that moment. It was as though the spirit of all the music that had been murdered on those strings revived and sang under my hands. I played the "March of the Men of Harlech." With increasing power, excitement and delight, I watched slouching limbs straighten slowly, and eyes lose their gin-fevered light, as if a breath of our own mountain air, borne on the music, had blown it out. They hurried, more and more of them, up the street—they crowded round me. The march to which I was calling them became to me as a march of souls—the battle as a battle against poverty, misery, and infamy.

'Oh Elias! no Cambrian chivalry ever answered to the call more readily than they. Up they came from street and alley, in rags, dirt, half nakedness, and tinsel. At any other time I should have seen such a crowd with horror, for I had never realised the existence of such beings as I saw about me. But what could I do? whither could I lead them, now that they had come? I asked myself, as I played on. My heart seemed to dissolve at the thought that they must go away no richer than they came. I stopped the march, and played our sweet "Ar hyd y nos," as tenderly as I could, trying, like a modern David, to tame and comfort this wild and many-headed Saul.

'Suddenly a heavy hand fell on my shoulder, I was forced to let go the harp, and thrust unceremoniously through the crowd, and in a few minutes found myself at the door of the house where I lodge, struggling and laughing in the grasp of Ephraim Jones.

'I must stop now. It is nearly three o'clock, and while I am at that place—which something prophesies will not be for long—I must keep its hours; so now for bed. If Ephraim Jones goes down to Dolgarrog next month, about this new prayer society, I shall send you some powder for destroying

rats. It is advertised everywhere here. Give my love to
Hirell, and tell her not to laugh at my first bardic exploit ; and
please to give Kezia my most respectful regards, and believe
me, Elias, your affectionate brother,

' HUGH MORGAN.

' N.B.—In Kezia's last letter she tells me of every one but
herself. Let her know that I have noticed this.'

Kezia looked up and coloured faintly at the idea of being so
remembered by one whom she and Hirell were regarding as
the greatest hero in London. Both pairs of eyes that Elias
met as he finished Hugh's letter were so full of pride and
tenderness, that he was for the moment half ashamed of the
anxiety in his own.

Hugh had not said one word about his work at Tidman's
office, the real business of his life, except in the hint about not
long keeping to it, a hint which filled Elias with alarm.

Seeing them so proud and happy over the letter, Elias could
not bear to damp their pleasure by showing them this, but
took it to himself as another cross to bear in secret.

─────────

CHAPTER XXVIII.

DOES HE STAY OR GO?

THE intentions of his lodger concerning his winter home
became a theme of anxious speculation to Elias Morgan.
Would he stay with them till the spring, or would he suddenly
make up his mind to go ? As far as Elias could tell, he was in
a strange state of indecision. One day he would talk of sending
him a certain farming book if he should be in London next
month, and the next would express his intention of ascending
Criba Ban in mid-winter, or visiting certain waterfalls in Febru-
ary. He did not know what hopes, fears, and grave consultations
every word of this kind caused Elias and Kezia, or he would,
perhaps, have been more careful.

As Mr. Rymer paid well for his rooms, it would have been
a great comfort to Elias could he have been certain of his continuing with them through the winter. But the lodger seemed
resolved on not letting them enjoy any certainty on the subject.

Weeks passed and still he did not go, neither did he state or hint at any intention of staying.

When the long, cold evenings had set in and made all the little household draw closer together round the chimney-place, Mr. Rymer was still there to draw his chair in with the rest.

When the first fall of snow lay on the mountains, still there he was to delight them by his admiration of the soft and lovely outlines.

When the Christmas waits came round, he was still there. They heard his window open to let in the wild music, and his silver ring down merrily on the frosty ground.

On Christmas day, when all at Bod Elian rose up before six and went by starlight and lantern light to early service at the little chapel, Mr. Rymer was among them.

When one morning, after the winds had been for many days blowing soft and sweet, Hirell ran into the house and called all to come and see a snowy, shivering, little creature, the first lamb of the new year, bleating piteously behind the back shed door, she called Mr. Rymer with the rest, for he had not gone.

When the almost perpendicular field in front of Bod Elian, to which Elias's chief care had been given, shone like an emerald shield on the breast of Moel Mawr, and began to be silvered over with daisies, he praised it with the rest, for yet he had not gone.

When the ethereal garden trees put on their faint white and green, he was still there to think how much more than ever like the apparition of a garden it looked upon the black hillside.

When the carnival of solitude had begun, and a sweet life and tumult pervaded the secret places of the hills; when the primroses gleamed like lamps along the way, and the dog-violets like little blue-hooded peasants came thronging up the mountain sides, his wandering footsteps crushed them oftener than any other—lingering still.

They lingered and seemed likely to linger; yet never at the beginning of the much-dreaded winter had Elias Morgan wished his lodger to stay half as earnestly as he now longed for his departure.

Kezia had discovered—and shown to Elias—certain cards bearing the name of Mr. John R. Cunliff.

' Kezia,' he said one evening, entering the kitchen and looking at the young woman with a sharp anxious glance, ' Where is Hirell ? '

' She is gone with her work to Judy Griffith's,' answered Kezia.

' I thought so,' said Elias, a gloom overspreading his face. ' Mr. Rymer is standing at the door talking to some one.'

Judy Griffiths was the bedridden mother of one of Elias's labourers, and lived in a hovel above Bod Elian.

Kezia said nothing in answer to Elias's last statement, but bent over her knitting with a tender concern and perplexity in her eyes. Elias sat down just as he had come in from work, in his soiled clothes and wet boots. He laid his tall-crowned beaver hat on the table, and with his elbow on its wide brim leaned his head on his hand.

' Kezia,' he said, ' you are right. Wherever Hirell goes he follows her ; and she—have you noticed her? have you watched her ? does it seem to you as it does to me, that she is not herself when he is away ? Yesterday when he went to Aber, do you recollect how dull and tired she seemed all the afternoon—and then in the evening did you notice her, Kezia ? '

The question was asked in a voice yearning for a denial of the thing it intimated, but Kezia's eyes looked into his, as they always did, with perfect truthfulness. Her looks at this moment sorrowfully confirmed his fears, while meekly claiming to share them.

' I know she thinks a great deal of him, Elias. I used to think it was his book-learning only at first that made her brighten so when he spoke—but I'm afraid now,' and Kezia finished by shaking her head gently.

' He must go,' said Elias. ' He must go, Kezia. I must tell him so.'

Elias on saying this rose and went out, as he generally did when he came to any important decision ; for, though seldom overruled by any of his family, he judged it best not to allow himself to be tempted by listening to their arguments.

That night Mr. Rymer received notice to leave.

CHAPTER XXIX.

A FRIENDLY LETTER.

WHILE yet the annoyance of Elias's notice to leave was upon Mr. Rymer's mind, and before he had even attempted to think out the many embarrassing questions involved, he had another surprise in the shape of a letter brought by the postman, addressed—Mr. John Rymer, Dolgarrog, but with a note appended in brackets [Inquire in the neighbourhood of the gold mines].

' 'Tis from Arnold! How on earth has he found me out ? '

Found me out! The words seemed to mock him with their double meaning. His cheek reddened as he remembered their last interview, and the falsehood he had told his friend about Mrs. Rhys. It was with no pleasure he began the perusal of the lengthy document.

'House of Commons, 186–.

' My DEAR RYMER,—You will wonder to see yourself thus addressed : but your wonder will hardly be greater than mine in having so to write. Thus it happens : Our friend, Lord Bullyblow (to stick to the old name), has just been touring it through North Wales ; and he tells me that one day he came somewhat abruptly on a gentleman lying on the sward and seemingly in a deep reverie, who started at the intrusion, and looked disturbed as he turned away. Our noble friend apologised—received a polite bow in acknowledgment—and saw nothing more of the musing solitary, except his back as he walked off. Bullyblow is great in the knowledge of backs. He swears he can tell any man whom he has once known, no matter how different or disguising the address, by the look of his back. And thus he declares the owner of *that* back was Mr. John Cunliff.

' He thought he would ask a question about the stranger at the toll-gate near ; and learned he was a gentleman who looked after speculations in gold mines—his name Rymer.

' He said nothing till he saw me—then swore that Rymer was Cunliff ; and wanted to set me talking as to the possible meaning of such an incident.

' I told him what you had told me : that you were going to the Continent ; that I had never known you lie, no matter what the temptation, even if one of women, and *therefore* he must be mistaken. He hemmed and laughed, and so the matter passed off.

' And now, old fellow, if this notion of his be true, you must let me speak my mind.

' It is already known that something serious has occurred in the R—— family. R—— has again gone abroad. Mrs.

R—— has gone to reside with her gouty uncle; and all this happens just after the former had returned full of honours and of years to enjoy what of life might remain in the solace of home, and the affection of one of the most charming of women.

'And now Bullyblow seems to complete for me the story!

'I may now also tell you that when we talked before I was in deep concern about this matter. I had heard more than I cared to repeat to you. I thought the abrupt hint I gave you, taken in connection with the new career I tried to open to you, might suffice to turn the tempter away. I have no notion of men preaching to one another, and so I hoped even my slight touch, as from a friend, might benefit.

'Nor shall I preach now. I only want to say to you—and now I talk to Mr. Rymer—that if you have irremediably injured this hapless lady, you are—. Well, I won't put the word in—fill the place up yourself; but, by the Lord, you can't put in one too black, too terrible, too *branding*. But no, Cunliff, I cannot—*can* NOT think you so great a scoundrel! So for the present let me preserve my old faith in Cunliff, while I abuse the, I hope, imaginary villain Rymer to my heart's content.

'There, old fellow, I have said what I felt I *must* say—and now for a different tune.

'Do you remember observing to me, in our last memorable talk before your departure, that politics didn't interest you, and your bidding me wait till the close of the American war. " If," said you," the North wins, there'll be a tremendous shaking of the dry bones all over the world sooner or later—*and then perhaps*—"

'The war is over, substantially. Lee is a prisoner. The North *has* won. Already in England the dry bones *do* shake, and so we get to the highly suggestive *perhaps*.

'Jesting apart—Cunliff—*has not the time come?* Is not the era of *laissez faire*, and of expediency, and of government by ear tickling, dying or dead at last? Look around you and answer. Look at your own university, Oxford. Try, if you can, to conceive the magnitude of the change there. The boldest democratic and religious theories springing from the place that was once the very citadel of aristocratic belief, and prejudice, and routine—alike in religion and politics. In ordinary times it is through our young men all great changes come. Their as yet unspoiled faith and instinct give the

necessary strength and momentum to the movements which
their elders have thought out, waited, yearned, and struggled
for.

'The young men of Oxford are, I hear on all sides, growing
up in the light of new thought, in the warmth of new desires.
Of course you know the sort of men I mean. Not the empty-
headed fox-hunting country squires, and game-preserving
justices of the peace, in embryo, who make up so large a nu-
merical proportion of the whole—but the men of mark, of
ability, our future statesmen, bishops, law lords, philosophers,
doctors, authors, and musicians. The men from whom these
come—our mental aristocracy—are feeling the ground-swell,
and being carried off their feet, intellectually speaking;
though knowing not yet in what direction to go, or to which
men they should look as men who can guide.

'Do you feel nothing responsive as I tell you this?

'Listen, then; I am going to speak to you of something
that interested me, and perhaps may interest you, particularly if that bird of evil omen, Rymer, is not just now at your
elbow.

'A dozen or so of us have been lately meeting together almost nightly, since we began to see, or fancy we saw, our
time coming. All sorts of discussions have taken place, all
sorts of theories have been ventilated, most comprehensive
tables of statistics duly set forth with scientific and laborious
accuracy; the phenomena of life, society, government, inter-
national relations, in the gross and in detail, glanced at—and
all to what end? Why simply to muddle those of us that
really did believe in and desire to see some way through
so much intricate ground; and to confirm the obstinacy of the
others, who stick to the old liberal formulas, and think all
that is wanted is to perfect the structure by wider suffrage,
and the ballot, etc., etc., and then to improve the end sought,
the general well-being of society, by a few measures of
practical importance in the interest of the great bulk of the
people. But no reorganizing, no revolutionizing—only safe
and steady progress. In fact, doing as we have done—
perhaps a little better, perhaps a little worse, but substantially
the same.

'This last party was about to triumph, when lo, a new
actor appeared in the field, and changed the fortunes of the
campaign:

' Mr. Sillman, a brother M.P., whom you must know as the most cruel torturer of an Admiralty that ever a Providence, whom we must still think to be benevolent, inflicted on a first lord, this gentleman, who had listened, according to his wont, in silence, except when figures were in question, and then dominated alike us and them—he now produced from his pockets, in his usual quiet, penetrating, undemonstrative way, a paper, which he said had been put into his hands, and which he thought it might be worth while for us all to read.

'We happened to be just then in the mood to snatch at anything. Sheer despair of ourselves made us ready to welcome any interference, however unlikely, that still had the audacity to promise.

' Mr. Sillman accordingly, at our request, read the paper, of which I shall give you briefly the substance, stripped of the very striking garb it wore. In truth, Cunliff, it was wonderfully eloquent without being rhetorical. It impressed you, at every sentence, with the idea that the author was himself so deeply smitten with the force, beauty, and significance of his own faith, as to be afraid to compromise it by the least taint of literary display or affectation.

' Speaking from memory, I cannot if I would give you any notion of the real power it exhibited, notwithstanding this restraint, and I would not if I could; because I want you to see the bottom of the thing at once, and then judge. I have seen enough of pretty-looking theories. So now, however much I admire the original shapes, I invariably *gut* them, and *then* I *can* say something about their insides.

' The leading point, then, is this—that a profound vice lies at the root of our method of government, and that hence flows its failure to compass the ends of government for any but a small portion of the people, even if—which the author doubts—that portion does get the benefit it thinks it gets.

' This vice is, he says, the making government a thing for aggregate society rather than a thing for individual man.'

' Hollo! What the devil's this!' exclaimed Mr. Cunliff, stopping in his perusal of his friend's letter, staring at it, turning the leaves over to the last page with an odd mixture of surprise, incredulity, and amusement in his face; then settling himself with quickened interest and curiosity once more to the letter.

'Let a man ask what is good for society, and who shall answer him?   But let him ask what is good for man, and the answer comes precise, clear, and full.   The whole then comes under law.

'What is society but a mere framework for the inclusion of so many individual men and women as compose it?   If each of these is born under good conditions of health, is properly trained and educated, is secured in due time the enjoyment of natural rights and privileges, such as the power to labour for adequate reward in a suitable occupation, the power to marry, to become a citizen, and to share in what then becomes the one principal business of legislation—the securing that his children shall have like or still greater advantages; if, he says, all these obviously necessary conditions are substantially guaranteed by wise, prudent and beneficent legislation, who afterwards needs to trouble himself about the fate of society?

'Does anybody fear that a universal state of well-being, a state freed from the cruel lotteries of life, but enriched with infinite aspirations and infinite possibilities of realizing them, will prevent by force of law, "good society" from its meetings, scandal, gossip; or interfere in any way with those public operations which are for the public good, except to improve them?

'But reverse the question.   Forget the individual and take care of society, and what do you see?   Why, just that which is the disgrace of every so-called civilized government—devotion of the strength and resources of the whole people to the comfort and interests of a part—at the top of the social edifice—and neglect of the seething, miserable mass of people at the bottom—ignorant, dwelling in pigsties, living a life of unrequited labour while they can labour, then passed on to a workhouse, which, under pretence of being a place of shelter for the poor, is in fact a place for their punishment for the crime of becoming a burden to society, the logic being as exquisite as the humanity.

'No doubt that even on the existing theory it is intended to go gradually downward from the care of society as a whole, to care of its parts, but unluckily the way is so long to humanity and justice at the bottom that they are never reached.

Ask society whether it wants more schools, better systems of education, better houses or higher wages for working-men, freer opportunities for the poor to rise, and it answers by

plunging into a bottomless pit of averages, as though John-
son was cheered by knowing there ought to be a good school
for his boy according to the figures; and as if Smith were
able to keep off the ravages of hunger by having it clearly explained to him there was an exact average of two quartern
loaves a day somewhere expended on him and others according to the figures.

'This was the leading point of the paper; the next was the
necessity of a clean sweep among our officials. Pension them
if you like to their heart's content, but remove them, or improvement is hopeless. No system of doing can be carried
out by men who have lived on the system of not-doing. It is
not merely their intellectual unfitness, or lack of enterprise,
but that the not-doing system corrupts the men engaged in it.
Perpetually the evils that exist come face to face with the
men who ought to deal with them—they do not—and then
are driven to deny, to equivocate, and, if necessary, to attack
all who see through them.

'The third and last prominent feature was the making all
governments consist of an exact series of operations, where
there was always, with every mechanical duty to be fulfilled,
an ideal aim also to be attained through the mechanism; and
lastly, a man responsible for the results. *For example :*

'Can you so govern that poor-law union that the poor shall
feel it is for them a real home when needed, and yet not want
to stay any longer than they are obliged?

'Can you employ the people in it so that each shall make
some sensible use of such faculties as he or she has got, so as
at once to lighten the burden of expense, and improve rather
than deteriorate the unfortunate inmates?

'Can you distinguish between the sensitive, the ordinary,
and the brutal; and that with such success in after-manage-
ment, that while all complaints shall be honestly heard, few or
no complaints shall need to be made?

'Can you realize to yourself the idea of a true poor-law, as
intended to guard humanity at its lowest level; to be always
striving to raise that level, conscious that even the most
benevolent of men may feel some satisfaction when he can say:
" We take in all; none can sink below this; then if we take
care of these—firmly uphold these at all times and in all circumstances—the body and heart of the nation must be sound,
and ready to be raised by a thousand different agencies, such

as our illimitable wealth, and skill, and knowledge can enable
us to set going ? "

' Such are the questions our author would ask of the future
governors of our workhouses, while saying to them, " You will
have time, counsel, generous help, but you will succeed, or—
be displaced ! "

' So with our prisons, hospitals, asylums, and schools; so
with our army and navy; so with our organizers of emigra-
tion, co-operation, and of whatever other methods may be
found most potent for the lifting of the toiling poor to a
state of comparative comfort and culture, when they will only
be too glad to take care of themselves.

' And the man who is over all these subordinate or local
governors must be under similar conditions. He cannot prevent mismanagement, but he must be responsible for speedy
and certain discovery of the mismanagement when it does
occur, and for decisive remedies.

' The law and philosophy of the whole being—the strong to
take care of themselves, but the weak to be cared for with all
the skill and might of the state, so that they or their children
shall also grow strong.

' Of course this opens a vast field for labour, expense, skill,
courage, faith, patriotism, but promises to reward them all by
the spectacle of such a people as only the eyes of a man like
John Milton has ever seen. Caring for the individual is hard
but noble, and wonderfully fruitful; caring for society very
easy—almost as easy as the effort is contemptible and impotent.

' Such, Cunliff, was the spirit of the paper, which branched
out into and dealt with all the great departments of public
life and duty.

' And who was the author, think you ?

' I read with my own eyes the name at the end, and
was certainly " dazed," as some old poet says.

' That name was " John Cunliff, aged twenty-one, under-
graduate of St. John's, Oxford ! "

' Have you forgotten all this ?   I hope so, for how else is one
to believe you sane, staying where you now are, for such ends ?

' Cunliff, we want you.   Come forth out of the Slough of
Despond.   We want you.   I want you.   I have some courage
—some small talent—some bull-dog tenacity in holding on
when I see aught to grab at; but I and all the men I know

need what you only possess—the statesman's imagination. A quality as vital to him as to the poet or to the natural philosopher. What are the laws, or the worlds, that a Newton's mental eye can imagine before discovering them (and without which power of imagination he never would have discovered them), to the human laws, and to the human world, which wait the discovery of the statesman?

 "The time is ripe. England's material supremacy is passing away. A greater England is rising into competition across the Atlantic, and attracting the eyes of every nation on the globe. The praters cry, " Don't Americanize your institutions! Don't follow in the wake of the United States!" But we cannot help ourselves, *while they are in advance of us*, because in all essential respects the genius as well as the blood of both nations is the same.

 'But let us boldly step out. Think as they do—for one's self—and think grandly. And then where would we be? Side by side with America, at least. But I too am English, and want—Englishman-like—more than equality of national fame and influence. Will any man dare to tell me that a nation, merely because she is big, and has got an unlimited supply of land, is *therefore* great? No. America is materially rich and comfortable through her land, but her grandeur springs from the grandeur of her aims. Let it be so with us. Let ours be the grandeur of our ideal life. Let us make a reality of the old delusion about teaching the nations how to live. With our glorious history, our centuries of culture, our long line of illustrious men, and our possession of the wealth, skill, and material agencies requisite to develop the sublimest national career that poet or patriot ever dreamed of, let us so act that it is the Americans who shall have to croak—" Do not, for God's sake—do *not* Anglicize our precious institutions!"

 'Cunliff, come to us. Enter Parliament, and I promise you in three years such a success—if you are not yet quite lost in indulgence—as will repay you a thousand times over whatever sacrifices you may have to make of habit or aught else.

 'I fear you have dipped deeply into your future income ; if so, I have a thousand or two at your service. Don't be ashamed—for yourself—or troubled for me. The cotton-mills are going merrily, to the tune of a clear fifteen thousand pounds profit this year, so the beggar can afford to bleed, you see.

 'Now will you come? If not—may the devil take you— as he will. Yours ever,   'FRANCIS ARNOLD.'

It so happened, that the close of the letter—as thus far shown—occurred on the first page of the last sheet of note-paper used, and there was no indication given of any writing beyond. Cunliff therefore remained in entire ignorance for some little time of a somewhat important communication which was annexed. But turning the leaves over with a kind of restless impatience, as a man will who receives an important communication, one suggestive of grave cause for doubt and anxiety, he saw a postscript overleaf, which not a little startled him.

' N.B.—I reopen this to tell you I have just seen Sir George. He is strangely altered for the worse, and is certainly breaking fast. He is conscious of the fact, and spoke of you with a kind of irritable affection, that moved me to attempt a half apology for your long absence from his house ; but he became angry and seriously ill, and quite silenced me when he spoke again, by saying, " Oh, he'll turn up, no doubt, in his own time ! Depend upon him to pay his *last* respects to me. Haven't I got what he wants, and which he knows I can't keep from him,—the title and the estates ? " I think you must now take this further fact with you, that you will soon have to emerge, not merely from the Mr. Rymer, but also from the Mr. Cunliff state, and stand forth as an English baronet of great wealth, and greater responsibilities.'

In deep silence, Cunliff, after a pause, put the letter into his pocket and went forth into the cool air to think.

An hour later he wrote to Arnold, saying he should come— that he was just able to say nothing did as yet prevent him —and now that *nothing should.*

<hr>

CHAPTER XXX.

EWYN Y RHAIADR.

In the evening of the same day on which Mr. Rymer had been requested to quit Bod Elian, and had received Arnold's letter, he heard, as he sat in his little parlour, Hirell receiving in-structions concerning an errand she was to undertake for Elias on the following morning.

She was to purchase some cloth at a little clothmill

situated in a spot so famous for its beauty that few tourists go to Dolgarrog without visiting it. Mr. Rymer had not yet done so; and when he heard them talking of it, he told himself it was a great omission to have made, and he had half a mind to go and see it yet before his departure.

He had heard them arrange that Hirell was to start early in the morning; and, taking some oat-cake and apples in her pocket, was to eat her dinner by the waterfalls, and to treat the day altogether as a holiday.

While they were doing this, Mr. Rymer rose, paced quietly up and down, and asked himself two questions which took him all the rest of the evening and late into the night to answer to his satisfaction.

They were these: Should he meet Hirell at Ewyn y Rhaiadr to have the understanding which he must have before leaving Wales? And what was that understanding to be?

What was he to say to her?

Pausing once near the door when her sweet voice was speaking, the answer came to him almost so as to overpower him. He felt the water in his eyes; his hands locked, while the answer was put to him in this fashion:

Say to her! What should he say to her but that he loved her—that he owed to her his deliverance out of a misery and despair too deep and dark for his own thought to look back into without growing dizzy. That he loved her, and that his love had been founded on—had grown with—all true and noble influences, radiating from her as from her centre, even when not all her own.

Ah—yes! and were there no such things as ambition, or 'good society,' through which even the noblest ambition finds itself compelled and humiliated to pass—then Hirell was for him his life's one and only want—his most perfect ideal realized.

Yes, if he could now renounce all aims beyond those of a simple country gentleman, no scheme of happiness mortal man ever fashioned could be more full of the certainty of fruition.

Can he do that?

Strictly examining himself, he sees and honestly confesses that he cannot. He cannot make such a sacrifice, for if he did it would fail. Whenever he does finally extricate himself from the indulgences of the past, it can only be under new temptations of a better kind, such as a career of vigorous public life may probably afford.

Arnold's letter, and its extraordinary effect upon him, brings all to a point—to a single alternative. Hirell and a private career, or Hirell abandoned honourably for public duty.

Yet how is he to explain to her his motives?

Can she think it enough for him to tell her he expects to be a baronet, and the possessor of great estates?

Or that he is ambitious, not only as before from inclination, but now also from duty and position?

Or that he sees in Elias and her family influences from which he can never hope to extricate her, and with which it is impossible for him to enter into intimate communion?

Or lastly, can he allege Hirell's ignorance of the world, and lack of educational culture, never thought of before?

So John Cunliff reviews his position; and finds unhappily that, just as he begins most strongly to convince himself he must go, does he also see the extreme improbability of Hirell's mind and heart being equally open to the same conclusion from the same arguments.

'Well, what must be, must be,' he cries, irritably. Thus does the Englishman cut the knot which he has busied himself, in so seemingly exemplary a manner, by trying to untie. And then comes the satisfying salvo:

'If I suffered in such a marriage and regretted it, she must suffer and regret too. Have I not seen in my own painful experience the danger of ill-assorted unions? Let Mrs. Rhys's fate warn me, and save Hirell. I may hurt her for a while by leaving her, but the hurt of an unhappy marriage could end only with death.'

Nothing was said to Hirell that night as to the notice which had been given Mr. Rymer. A strange feeling kept Elias silent on the subject; and Kezia waited for him first to break the news to Hirell before she herself made any mention of it to her. So Hirell went upstairs to bed without knowing anything about it, and slept untroubled by any of the doubts and misgivings which long kept sleep from the eyes of her father and Cunliff.

The next morning was very fine and bright, and Hirell was out earlier than usual that she might get her work done by breakfast time, and set forth on her little journey immediately afterwards.

She was in the little outhouse arranging for the comfort of her lambs, when above the noise of their bleating she heard a voice say,

' Hirell ! '

She turned quickly towards the little window, whence it came, and saw there Mr. Rymer's face, which startled her by the extreme gravity and sadness of its look.

He smiled as he met her direct questioning glance, and said,

' Hirell, I should like to talk with you a little this morning. I shall wait on the lawn of the burnt house below Ewyn y Rhaiadr ; will you look for me as you pass ? '

Hirell bowed her head, and said ' yes ' in a low voice, and then he went quickly from the window.

Seeing that he was gone, she rose from her stooping attitude, and sat down on a bundle of straw with a great change in her face. It was very pale and profoundly thoughtful. Her hands trembled as she clasped them in her lap, and her eyes had a strange light and anguish in them.

Had Cunliff stayed and watched her he would have thought that some foreshadowing of the truth had come before her— some sad foreboding caught from his own face. But he would have conjectured falsely, for nothing of this was in Hirell's thoughts. What she gathered from his face, and his manner of putting his request to her, was simply a confirmation of what had long been her secret belief, that this gentleman, so much above her in station, culture, and worldly advantages, loved her, and wished to make her his wife. He had chosen this day to tell her so. This, and only this, was what she drew from his face and voice when he had looked in and spoken to her through the outhouse window.

Sitting looking down upon her lambs and her sordid work, Hirell looked less like an agitated Griselda than an inspired Joan of Arc in one of her visionary trances. Her hands stroked each other as if to still their trembling ; and her eyes, full of tears, were raised to the black roof with a saintly light, but a sharp human anguish in them.

Could Cunliff have known her thoughts as to his intentions concerning her, could he have seen the prospect which she fully believed he was about to offer her, as his wife, he would have expected she should indeed be overcome by happiness, for he was not without a belief that she loved him, and the contrast of the life she lived at Bod Elian and that which she would live as his wife was thoroughly appreciated by him. He could not have believed that the idea of a marriage with him could have been regarded by Hirell as otherwise than a great honour under any circumstances, a great happiness if she loved him as he believed she did.

He had little idea that marriage with him in his present state would be looked on by Hirell and Hirell's family as almost a crime, and therefore an impossibility. But so it was with her and them. No Capulot was ever more implacable against a Montague than Elias was prepared to be against this creedless mysterious stranger bearing a false name, should he think of such a thing as marriage with his daughter—that pure, regenerate child of God, that saint whose birth to him he regarded as the surest sign of grace his God had ever shown him. When his doubt of his own worth, his own regeneracy, was strongest he had but to look at Hirell's beauty, and bethink himself of her great merits, to be filled again with faith—to feel that such a flower could not have proceeded from a tree meant only to be ' hewn down and cast into the fire.'

Hirell, on her part, regarded the religion in which she had grown up as a sanctuary in which everything was beautiful and perfect to those whose hearts were like Elias's strong, or like Kezia's calm and humble ; and when she found the windows dark and the air oppressive, she blamed her own restlessness, and want of peace, and humility, and steadfastness. But she loved it too well, and believed it too entirely, to think that she could live away from it. She had yearnings towards the great world beyond; and for the poor wounded wanderer that had fallen in her way she felt much pity, and a strong desire that he might be ' raised and gathered into the fold of the elect.' She tried to be better for his sake, as an inspired chorister, seeing an infidel at a cathedral door, might sing the sweeter in hopes to lure his wavering steps into the sacred place.

She saw, and with a deep delight and reverence, the many gifts he possessed with which she had never before seen any creature gifted. 'If he has all this in his dark state,' she thought, ' what would he be, enlightened with grace like ourselves ? How infinitely above me, and such as me ! '

Cunliff, perhaps unconsciously, used all his powers to make her see the largeness and grandeur of *his* views as compared

with hers, but succeeded only in making her see and love the
mind that held them—the soul that she thought would be lost
through them. Hirell tried every hour of her life so to live
as to make her religion beautiful and holy in his eyes, but
succeeded only in inspiring him with a sense of her own
beauty and holiness.

But now if what she expected was coming did indeed come,
if he should ask her to be his wife, there must be an end to
this hovering towards each other across the threshold of her
faith; either he must enter ere she can depart with him, or
he must be sent away and the door of redemption closed on
him. She knew well he would expect her to depart with him,
that his people might be her people, his God her God; and
this is what she was trying to arm her soul against. She
thought that the temptation would be strong; and remembered how sweet the tempter's voice was to her—how piteous
it would be to cast away the soul for whose salvation she had
thought it her peculiar mission to make hers shine.

As her lambs came bleating round her asking for their bed,
which was the straw on which she sat, she stooped and fondled
them, looking upwards the while as if she would remind her
Maker she was, without His help, as weak as these.

At this moment came Kezia calling her to breakfast. So
she rose and shook down the straw, and the little creatures
lay in pretty attitudes shivering upon it, for the early
morning was cold, though fine, and giving promise of a warm,
bright day.

Hirell then went in to breakfast, and affecting haste, that
her want of appetite might not be perceived, soon left the
table, dressed herself, and taking leave of her father and
Kezia, set out upon her journey.

During her long walk her spirit underwent many changes.
At first the beauty and exhilarating freshness of the morning,
as well as a sense of liberty in being abroad and having a
holiday before her, made her joyous and full of hope in spite
of herself. But by degrees, as the distance between her and
the burnt house at Ewyn y Rhaiadr lessened, and she remembered how soon she should be face to face with Mr. Rymer,
she felt her courage die within her. She imagined, with
suspended breath and tears starting to her eyes, the face, the
voice, the speech she so revered and loved using their powers

to press upon her an honour so dearly and so richly esteemed by her. She looked down at her old clothes, which just then seemed but as a type of the poverty and narrowness of all her life, and said to herself—'Me, so poor in all things, to presume to—and he knows everything, and will think me mad.' And then her poverty and ignorance, looked at as with his eyes, became very contemptible to her, almost shameful and hateful. A vision of her home swam drearily before her eyes ; but in one of the fields there happened to be a single figure toiling, and her mind's eye saw the face turn and look at her. It was the face of Elias, and its patience, its vigilance, strength, and faith, which, in Hirell's imagination, were truly pourtrayed, sent all her shame away ; her step grew firm again, her eyes filled with the old saintly peace and security. She reminded herself how often she had wished for some opportunity for exercising for her creed that zeal and devotion so much commended in her ; and told herself that the hour of trial was now before her, that to-day she must either become the means of adding to the elect a great and noble soul, or by its loss, and the loss of all her earthly hopes, become a martyr whose martyrdom must be unseen by any eye but God's.

At the foot of Ewyn y Rhaiadr was a deserted house, that had been partially destroyed by fire, and stood in rich grounds ; where past culture, neglect, and nature, had made strange and picturesque work of trees, paths, parterres, and lawn.

Hirell stopped near this, and sat down on a rustic seat left before a half-circle of magnificent evergreens, growing so wild and thick as to almost hide the little walks between them. A beautiful lawn stretched away before her, towards the mountains across the valley ; some clusters of daffodils by the brim of a sheet of water, shallow and broad and clear, kept a light and sparkle in the place.

She had hardly seated herself, and begun to glance nervously about her, when suddenly she heard a step in a little path near ; and turning her head, saw Mr. Rymer coming towards her.

She sat still, but the best blood of her heart, and the best light of her soul, flew to her cheeks and eyes in acknowledgment of his presence. That form had become for her the one form, whose absence made all places alike dull. She looked at the lawn, the water, the daffodils, and thought that something must have been lifted from them at this instant—so bright, so full of exquisite meaning their beauty had become.

Yet, delicious as the change was, a sharp pain came with it. If all the beauty of the world was no longer free to her, but all locked up, and the key with him, what would life be—if—

She dared think no more at that instant, for he stood before her holding out his hand.

She gave hers rather coldly, and he saw tears in her eyes.

It struck him that he might have brought blame upon her from Elias, for having made this appointment.

'I hope it has not caused you annoyance, my having asked you to let me meet you here?' he said.

'No, it has caused me no annoyance, Mr. Rymer.'

'I was afraid it had, Hirell—I thought you seemed sad.'

She made no answer, and again he wondered if it were possible she had some foreboding of the truth. Perhaps she had heard he was going to leave Bod Elian.

As they rose and went off the lawn, he said—

'Has your father told you of some talk we had yesterday, Hirell?'

'No,' answered Hirell, 'he has not said anything to me about it.'

So her sadness was still inexplicable to him, and he was much puzzled by it as he walked beside her out of the grounds of the ruined house.

He did not feel at all inclined to begin his task, nor did he think there was need for much haste. They had the day before them, and it was very sweet and lovely, and why should they not enjoy as much of its sweetness and beauty as they could, and let its hours, falling away one by one, like rose-leaves that conceal a thorn, bring them to its sorrow by degrees?

They were now walking by the bed of the torrent.

'And is this Ewyn y Rhaiadr?' asked Cunliff.

'Yes, this is it,' said Hirell; 'it means "foam of the water-fall," and was named from the great circles of foam that are almost always to be found on it, and that you will see higher up.'

They were ascending a sort of magnificent natural staircase, through whose centre rushed a stream of clear water—broken into all kinds of wild and beautiful shapes by the rocks and stones that intercepted its headlong course. It was walled—

and in some places roofed over—by slender trees, growing in
infinite profusion the whole way up; and often bearing on
their highest branches little patches of moss, from which grew
ferns in great luxuriance and beauty. The old, dark, cast-off
garments of the trees still lay mouldering at their feet,
making the fair green in which they were now dressed appear
yet more faint and fair ; and the wild flowers and roots that
here and there pricked through the rotten leaves looked like
bits and scraps let fall by the tree in their attiring. The
stream was the presiding genius of the place. To it the trees
were bent, and the fairest primroses sacrificed, growing on
mid-water stones, where nothing but its spray, which kept
them so fresh and luminous, could ever reach them.

Through the pale net-work of new leaves the sunshine
glanced quiveringly, making the water and the green glitter
as with golden lightning.

Cunliff was charmed at all he saw.

'I shall not soon forget my first walk with you, Hirell,' he
said, as he held out his hand to assist her up a more steep and
stony bit of ground than they had before passed. 'I have
seen nothing so exquisite yet as this Ewyn y Rhaiadr.'

Hirell looked round her with less delight, though perhaps
not with less appreciation, than Cunliff. To her, indeed, the
place was beautiful ; but its beauty became to her as a solemn,
almost an awful thing, as she felt that it was perhaps the rob-
bing and decorating of the altar where she was to sacrifice—
Abraham-like—the Isaac of her heart.

Cunliff's exclamations of delight added strangely to her
sadness, and she could only answer them by bowing her head
gently, and turning away her eyes that he might not see the
tears in them.

They came to the rustic bridge, one side of which was the
little cloth-mill where Hirell was to buy cloth for Elias, and
on the other a little saw-mill for cutting up the slender trees,
that grew so abundantly on the sides of Ewyn y Rhaiadr.
The saw-mill was deserted, its owner having gone to his dinner at Dolgarrog. The cloth-mill consisted of one room,
where one man was at work, and singing ; and as they passed
on—for Hirell decided on delaying her visit till their return
homeward—the increasing force of the torrent drowning his
voice, the trees hid the smoke of his little chimney, and the
solitude of Ewyn y Rhaiadr but seemed the more profound
for this passing glimpse of primitive life and business.

For some little time they had both remained silent. They had never before been so thoroughly alone together, and both felt an embarrassment which made it seem impossible for them to talk on any trifling subject that might present itself. In spite of this, and in spite of Hirell's melancholy, Cunliff was inexpressibly happy. Perhaps a less selfish man would have found it impossible to be otherwise than miserable with the prospect of giving another such disappointment as he expected he would give to Hirell, when he should make known to her his intention never to see her more. But there was in Cunliff a strange power of snatching at passing gleams of happiness. He would live a gnat-like life of pleasure in a moment of sunshine, that would scarcely be perceived by senses less acute. He saw that if he had no sacrifice to make, if he were here to tell Hirell that he loved her, and to learn what he was certain he might learn if he liked, that she loved him, he saw that then this place and hour might indeed contain a joy greater and more exquisite than he had ever before known; that under such influence his vision would become clear, so that he could see the errors of his life, and be able to resolve upon a new one, great and true and possible. He felt that were it but thus, he should find on this sweet fresh day of April that all nature was charged with a divine message to him ; that each lovely form of a tree, or cascade, or glistening leaf, or bright flower, were characters in a language which truth used to woo him to her again ; to bid him cast off the stains and shackles of the world, and receive from her once more the old pure and high aspirations revived again by Hirell's unconscious touch.

Seeing that such good would certainly result from this meeting were it not for the sacrifice he had to make, and liking goodness as his purity of taste made him like most beautiful things, he allowed himself to put from his mind as much as possible all thoughts of that sacrifice ; and to enjoy Hirell's presence and the beauty of the place, and the influence of both as much as if he intended no sacrifice at all.

Hirell, when she found he still delayed speaking in that manner in which she had all along been expecting to hear him speak, and when she saw how his face was full of happiness, began to ask herself whether he felt already assured of her love and of her acceptance, and this made her still more sad, and anxious for him to know all that was in her mind.

'Mr. Rymer,' she said, turning to him with heightened

colour and eyes turned to the ground, ' I am waiting anxiously to hear what it is you wished to talk to me about that made you come to meet me.'

It had caused her much effort to say this, as she believed it to be an invitation for a confession of love. She stood trembling when it was said, and her blush died away and left her very pale.

As she spoke they were stopping beside a large stone on the bank, thickly cushioned in the moss; and such a seat for beauty, elastic softness, and luxury, as kings might covet for a throne. Cunliff was touching it with his stick as she turned upon him and spoke so suddenly.

He remained stooping over it. She had taken him by surprise ; he had not meant to speak yet. It had become so sweet to imagine that all was going to be well between them —that he need not say that which he knew he must say, and of which she reminded him—that he began to wish earnestly he had not to say it. He had played with what was good and true till goodness and truth began really to influence him.

For some time it had seemed to him that he was not only mounting by Hirell's side to where the air was purer, the foliage fresher, the rushing water more musical, strong, and bright, but to be attaining also heights where existence itself was larger and more joyous. It even occurred to him that in thus yielding to the influence of this love, of which neither had yet spoken, and which appeared the more wonderful for making itself so manifest in its dumbness, it even occurred to him that he was in spirit retracing steps which he had once taken in blindness and recklessness. For in those days when he had tried to persuade himself it was his fate to love Catherine Rhys, and to win her love, he had known, though he had not paused to think of it, that all life was but a descent, reckless and headlong, in which the mind had grown more and more confused and dizzy—just as now, reversing the process, it became clearer and purer with the ascent.

As he stood probing the moss with his stick, he was tempted by everything noble within him to look up and answer Hirell's question by saying that he had asked her here in order to offer for her acceptance a husband, fortune, and position, in every way unworthy of her, but that by her all might be one day made more worthy.

Caution, however, was one of Cunliff's habits, and often

clung to him when he would have been much better without
it; for his rapid, instinctive impulses were, after all, the best
part of his character, and against these caution was always
busily at work, waylaying and destroying. It waylaid and
held back the words he would have said to Hirell then, and
suggested that to begin more guardedly would save him from
committing himself one way or the other. So he answered,
as he still held his stick plunged deep in the cushion of moss,
and tried to shake it gently—

'You would not blame me for this delay, Hirell, if you knew
how unhappy it makes me even to think of what I have to tell
you!'

Hirell looked puzzled. Unhappy! What could he have to
say to her that made him unhappy? Was it possible he had
already spoken to her father, and been answered as she knew
he would be answered were it so. Her lips quivered, and she
felt ready to cry at the thought of this, for she was woman
enough to think things impossible to her father might be possible for her.

'Pray tell me, Mr. Rymer,' she asked falteringly, 'pray tell
me at once.'

He paused a moment, then looking up at her as he stooped
over the stone, said—

'Hirell, I received a letter yesterday which shows me that
I must go away immediately.'

Hirell heard this without much surprise. It had often been
a matter of wonder to her that no business, private or public,
had called him away before. She did not understand from
what he said that he was going for more than a few days or
weeks; and if he loved her—if he desired to ask her that
which she was prepared to hear, she thought it natural he
should do so before such an absence. While, therefore, she
waited for him to go on with what he had to say, she tried
hard to strengthen in her heart those resolutions she had
formed as she sat in the outhouse, with the little lambs bleating round her, before she started on her journey. The effort
and the inward prayer, with which she did this, gave to her
face and form so noble and tender a grace, that Cunliff asked
himself if this could indeed be her whose unfitness to share his
exalted fortunes he had decided upon, and was about to prove
to her. He was, too, surprised and a little saddened at the
quiet way in which she had received the news of his intended

departure, for it did not occur to him she regarded his absence from Bod Elian as only a temporary thing. His task was, he felt, much to his reluctance, now fairly begun, and must be proceeded with.

'Hirell,' said he, 'I think there is enough friendship betwixt you and me for us to have made some surmise by this time as to the hopes and aims of each other's lives. It often seems to me that, strange as I am to you in all that concerns my past life and affairs, you are possessed by a kind of prophetic instinct that my rightful and true duty does not lie here. Tell me, Hirell, have you not felt this?'

'Oh, Mr. Rymer,' answered Hirell, 'how could I—I, so ignorant as you know I am, how could I? No, I have never thought you wrong in any one thing, but—'

'But—Hirell!'

'But the greatest thing of all—' she added, in a trembling voice.

'My abominable idleness?'

'No, no, no. Oh, I think you—I think, as you must know, so much—oh, so much too highly of you, to judge you in anything; and I can but honour, while I mourn, the rare self-doubt, the proud humility, which—which—'

In her earnestness her tears had risen so fast as to make it hard for her to speak—

'Which makes you,' she went on, with indescribable mournfulness and tenderness, 'keep so long from its place among the elect of God a soul so surely, so plainly showing itself by its great gifts to have been predestinated to enjoy all the glory and love of His chosen ones.'

Though he was very much moved by her earnestness—its simplicity, and strength, and sweetness—and by the beauty of her face in its emotion, he could not help smiling at that favourite word of her creed, 'predestinated.'

Now that she had begun to talk about religion, Cunliff suddenly became conscious of her childishness, and ignorance, and his own superiority.

'You must not trouble about my soul, Hirell,' he said, trying to hide some of his amused contempt. 'I cannot give you any comfort concerning that. If, as your people believe, all the world is given over to everlasting wrath, save those few you call the elect, depend upon it I am among the damned.'

'Mr. Rymer, I entreat you not to talk so. You do not know what it is to me, you cannot.'

'Well, well, Hirell! go back upon your elect, and forget me. Your father, at all events, does not want me among the chosen few.'

'I do not understand you, Mr. Rymer; how strangely you speak.'

'I will speak more plainly, Hirell. God knows I feel in no mood to jest. I am leaving you to-day; your father thinks it better for us all; perhaps he is right; for myself, as I told you, I fear my duty does indeed lie elsewhere. I fear, too. I should forget that if I stayed here much longer.'

'Then you asked me to meet you here to—'

'To bid you good-bye, Hirell, for ever.'

They had continued their ascent, while the rush of water had become fiercer and fiercer, and now they had reached that spot where the falls were at their grandest; where, as one of the poets of the country had described it—

> Foaming and frothing from mountainous height,
>   Roaring like thunder the Rhaiadr falls;
> Though its silvery splendour the eye may delight,
>   Its fury the heart of the bravest appals; [1]

while below one great ring of the foam which gave the place its name, perfectly round, flat, and compact, and measuring five or six feet across, was swinging about in the current.

There was a seat opposite the falls. Hirell sat down upon it, and Cunliff stood watching her. Her eyes were half closed, her lips very white. She had come prepared for martyrdom, but not of this kind. This was too hard, too bitter; there was no glory in it, nothing but shame. She had almost confessed her love to him, in her certainty that she had his. Where was the sacrifice she was to have made? What had she to sacrifice? She thought she could bring this man into the sanctuary of her creed, or be compelled, for the honour of that creed, to send him from her broken-hearted. And now, after having been cherished in sickness, and his soul watched for and prayed for so long and unceasingly, he could talk coolly of going away—for ever.

As she exerted all her energies to look up, to try and answer his farewell calmly, she found her two hands suddenly taken and held in a tender passionate grasp.

'I *did* come to bid you an eternal farewell, Hirell, but I cannot—I will not. Duty! Oh Hirell, how can I fail in that, if

---

[1] Borrow's translation.

you will give your love, if you will be the wife of a man
unworthy of you in all respects save one—his love, his reverence for you—my darling, my sweet saint!'

In the Morgan family sudden changes of purpose were so
little known, that Hirell, for a moment or two after Mr. Rymer
had asked her to become his wife, felt her mind much confused
between that fact and the statement he had made a few
minutes before, as to the necessity for their final parting.

Alarm for him, and at the thought of what he might be forgetting in his love for her, mingled with her rising joy and
relief from humiliation.

Pressing his hands that held hers, and trying to look with
some calmness in his face, which was just then very eloquent
and nobly impassioned, she said gently—

'Wait, wait, dear friend! You speak too hastily, too generously; wait, and let us talk of this when—when we are
calmer.'

That she could keep an unselfish and tender consideration
for him in the midst of her emotion, which he saw was little
less than his own, filled Cunliff with amazement. He was
determined to be no less generous. He would not think; he
would not wait and reason calmly, as she begged him to do;
he would so bind himself that he could not retrace, if he should
ever find himself base enough to wish to do so.

'Let me hear you say you love me, Hirell; nothing else
in the world matters now'

He had seated himself beside her, and had put his arm
round her as he spoke, as if he would fain take her and her
confessions, for which he asked, together to his heart.

She rose and stood before him.

'If I loved you, Mr. Rymer, should I not remember these
words you spoke before—a little while ago: you said your
duty called you elsewhere, that it was best for you to leave me,
and to see me no more. If I loved you, and loved you much,
should I not do better to remind you of those words, than to
confess my love to you?'

He looked up at her.

'My dearest Hirell, by all that is most true, I tell you that
to give me your love, and this dear hand, will do more to accomplish my welfare here and hereafter than anything else in
all the world.'

'And this you say as God is your judge?'

'As He is my judge.'

'Then, then,' said Hirell, with her face full of intense joy and hope, and stepping back from him, and standing in an attitude in which a sculptor might have carved a rapt and worshipping angel in the divine presence, 'Will you come to us? Here into the light in which we live? The blessed haven of the true faith? Oh, will you learn of my father and our ministers the way to be saved? Will you let them lead your soul to its appointed place among the safe and happy ones? You desire our lives should join; then, dear sir, will you come to us? will you join our faith?'

Cunliff was too much moved by the loveliness of Hirell's face in its enthusiasm not to take the hands outstretched to him, and kiss them with deep reverence and emotion.

'I take your faith, Hirell, so far as God permits me,' said he. 'Hirell, you have won me.'

'Ah! am I so happy—so honoured?'

'I take your faith, my innocent and beautiful, so far as I can, with my dim eyes, see its truth. All in it that makes my darling so sweet and true above all others, I desire to share, find it in what manner of creed I may.'

'Oh, sir; it is but the one that could have inspired me with courage to speak to you as I have spoken.'

Cunliff had not intended the slightest untruth when he said those words which made Hirell feel herself the most joyful and privileged among women. Neither had he the smallest intention of becoming a Calvinistic Methodist. He had, he told himself, spoken broadly; and when those wonderful brown eyes, suffused with tears and fired with triumph, rested on his face, he was too jealous of his own present happiness, and hers, to undeceive her. Of course he would undeceive her; but he must not let such a trifling matter as her religious scruples stand in the way of their happiness when he was willing to make such great sacrifices for it.

Hirell was so accustomed to hear such questions treated with the most sacred truth and solemnity, that she could not doubt his words, though she had heard them with astonishment and trembling joy. He had spoken, too, with a reverence that she had not thought of being inspired by herself; and she attributed his earnest manner entirely to his sense of the solemnity of the charge he was accepting.

She stood looking on him with wondering, almost adoring

eyes, as on one newly anointed by her God, and trembled with delight to think it was herself who had been the means of his conversion.

'And yet, Hirell,' said Cunliff, taking her hands, and looking deep into her eyes, as his jealous passion tried to penetrate beyond the unselfish tears and light that filled them, 'you have not told me; do you love me? Hirell, do you love me?'

'Do I love you?' Her gathered tears ran over, her lips whitened, as if with despair at their powerlessness to express what her heart, now unrestrained, would commit to them. Each word she spoke came to him so clothed in low, delicious, clinging music, that their sense would have been missed by other ears than his, 'I should have loved you, lost or saved. I should not have turned from my people, from my faith, for your sake, because it is to me as a safe chamber set apart by God for His elect, out of which I dare not go. If you had left me I should have staid there, but I should have found it as a place hung with black, and its lights gone, and the stone hard where I must kneel, but now you are with me! I hold your hand, and instead of its being hard to me to pray, as sometimes it has been, my thoughts spring up in prayer as if they'd known no other way. Oh! when I say I love you—I love you—do you not feel in my voice something that is not speaking to you; a joy that cries out even in those very words to my Lord, whom your love lifts me near, so near I already feel I can defy death? Yes, gladly, gladly die!'

A tender thrill, too vague to be called fear, made Cunliff hold her closer to his heart, and say, pleading passionately he knew not against what—

'My life—my life!'

Besides its beauty and its perfume, the rose has another power which perhaps shares not a little in its charm. It is the thought of its evanescence which gives that inexpressible tenderness to the delight with which we regard the bloom and odour—the thought of death's hand on the stem as well as the glowing flower that holds our gaze.

Cunliff, drawing Hirell to the seat, gazed into her face. Did that hand grasp the flower of *her* beauty? Would it be snatched away out of the world? Was her youth so radiant because death was feeding it with wasteful hand from the light of years to come? No; it could not be. This sweet colour on the cheek was not the hectic flush of a day drawing near its close; but the fresh brightness of the morning sky. The wonderful hazel eyes surely had in them none of the fatal fire of too rapidly-consuming life, but were full of the dewy light of health. He thought, too, of her hardy life, and wondered how the idea of the loss of her could have entered his mind. Why had he felt it as a sort of prophecy of evil? Could anything but death take her from him, or change the heart so full of love for him?

'Do not let them reason you against me, my Hirell,' he said, with the same vague dread in his soul that had been there ever since she showed him her great love, and he felt its priceless value to him. 'Don't let them persuade you that because I have lived in the world, and you out of it, we cannot make each other happy.'

'Do you think that might be so?'

She raised her head and looked into his eyes with a half startled look in her own.

'It might cause us trouble, Hirell, if we loved each other less.'

Her face was very thoughtful as her head leaned lightly against his shoulder. He looked down into it. Again the bright eyes glanced up with a shade of melancholy in them.

'Suppose you do love me less than you think?'

'How can I do that when every minute I am with my darling I love her more? Why do you speak so, Hirell—can you doubt me?'

'I should doubt myself—my power of making you at all happy, if you left off loving me.'

'And you think that possible, Hirell?'

She was silent. She was thinking of Mrs. Rhys—of the stained, death-smitten face by the little spring in the orchard. She had thought of her very often, but always remained silent about her. The story seemed to Hirell an easy one to guess. This lady had loved Mr. Rymer before her marriage with Hugh's patron, and he had loved her; then he had changed, and she married another, and had been unhappy, keeping in her heart her first love still. She had come to Bod Elian, and seen Mr. Rymer unexpectedly, after all these changes, and had seen him with one so unworthy to take her place in his heart; and the surprise and anguish had stricken her as they had found her. From the reports that had reached them at Bod Elian concerning the life of the gay and fashionable mistress of Dola' Hudol, the Morgans had tacitly regarded her as one of the light daughters of Zion—with stretched-forth necks and wanton eyes ' walking and mincing as they go, and making a tinkling with their feet;' therefore Hirell exonerated Cunliff from blame; and the doubt that crossed her mind was not a serious one. *That* love could not have been blessed by God, as surely this was.

'No,' she said, with her wet lashes rising quiveringly from her cheek, ' I do not believe it possible that either of us can cease to love the other.'

'No earthly consideration shall part us,' asserted Cunliff, as if reasoning with some real and pertinacious antagonist. 'Let nothing, let no one persuade you that the differences of our previous lives shall interfere with our happiness.'

'I suppose you mean that they will try to persuade me that I shall disgrace you,' said Hirell, lifting her head, and looking with a sweet, half pensive thoughtfulness on the ground. 'But they cannot do that, Mr. Rymer.'

'It would be strange, indeed, if they could, Hirell.'

'And I would never have you doubt me until you doubt your own love for me.'

'Doubt you? In what, my Hirell?'

'Doubt my power of fitting myself to the duties that will come to me as your wife.'

'Have I shown any such doubt?'

'You have seen me,' she interrupted him with a sweet, strong confidence in her eyes and rich tremulous voice, ' you have seen me at all kinds of hard work, Mr. Rymer. It is likely you should doubt my fitness for a life so different; but '—she rose, and stood before him with the grace of a queen—' I ask you not to doubt me. I know such doubts may come. I dread them. I am not given to overrate my powers, but I do assure you that I believe with all my heart and soul that this hand that has known no other defilement than labour—that has never been a day unlifted to its Maker, can serve you faithfully in your own sight, and in the Lord's. By the world I do not desire to be judged.'

Again Cunliff kissed the little hand most tenderly, most reverentially, answering her by a look more eloquent than any words he could have spoken. He then drew her once more closely to him, and kissed her, and felt that the betrothal was now indeed final, sacred, indissoluble.

Their happiness was deep and perfect. They sat silently, looking at the torrent, whose voice sounded thick with whispers of the great eternal joy of the new world love had opened to them.

There are times when everything near us seems to take up the story of our great happiness or sorrow, and to bear it for evermore; meeting us with it at strange times, and in strange places. The eye that wet with joy or anguish falls on any little common flower, finds, after no matter what years, what changes, the passion of that moment in the flower still, rise up where it may. There are memories in which the pale sweet gleam of the primrose casts too cruel a light to be looked at without tears. There are eyes to which the edges of the fresh spring daisy seem to have been crimsoned in the very blood of a lost love. There are ears for which the hare-bell rings with a subtle, creeping music that will not be shut out. It is as if the soul in moments of great joy escaped from its prison, and became a part of all beautiful and living things, shining in the sun, and breathing in the flower, and never gathering itself completely in its prison again; so that it often appears to us to be a more real, living, passionate self we find in these tokens of the past, than exists in the weary frame bent over them.

Hirell and Cunliff knew that the joy of these moments was being stamped on all things—sky, trees, water, flowers—never to be erased while memory lived. When the clouds in after years should look a little as they looked now, it would bring it all before them again. When the sunshine of later Aprils should fall again through tender, pale foliage, it would make the same writing on the moss that their happy eyes read now; the water would fall, and the flowers glow with and breathe the same story as when they sat there, young and true, feeling their spirits to be as a part of the joy and light, the tenderness and the passion of the spring time.

They rose, and wandered about the place; and Hirell's holiday sped on as fast as sunny, delicious April hours could bear it.

The time came at last— and all too quickly—when they must part; for Cunliff had, he told her, decided on leaving Dolgarrog for Llansaintfraid that very night, that he might be in time for the first train in the morning. Matters of great importance—about which they must talk, but not now—demanded his presence in London. He had too long neglected them. She spoke of her father, and how she should break the news to him. At the mention of this, Cunliff's eyes lost some of their joyous light and became coldly thoughtful. He told her he would like the matter to be left in his hands. Let him tell Elias when he returned after these pressing matters of business were settled. Hirell was not surprised or grieved at the request, but pleaded against it sweetly and earnestly, and won at last a reluctant permission to tell him all.

'But don't make too much of my conversion, Hirell,' he added, when he gave it.

The words did not trouble her then, because as he spoke them he was taking her hands in the parting clasp, and a strange dizziness and pain she had never known before took all her strength to struggle against it.

'Only a few weeks, Hirell—a month at most,' he promised her; but Hirell shook her head, and begged that nothing he had to attend to might be hurried for her sake.

'With your love to think of at home, and your soul to rejoice over in the house of God, have I not happiness to content me long, long?' she said.

They had returned to the seat opposite the falls, as Cunliff was going to the town that way, and Hirell home through the grounds of the deserted house; and when he had left her she sat there still for some minutes. Looking back, he saw the checkered sunlight quivering on her closed eyes and pale face. It was so pale that he had half a mind to return to her—but, as he hesitated, he saw her slip from the seat to her knees in that devout rigid attitude which he had noticed as peculiar to the congregation of Morgan's Chapel, and the ecstatic look upon her face made him—knowing as he did whom she rejoiced over—turn quickly and silently from the spot.

CHAPTER XXXI.

HARD QUESTIONS.

HIRELL reached home just as the twilight was disguising the familiar shapes of the fields round Bod Elian, and making the tops of the mountains indistinguishable.

She knew she was much later than her father and Kezia had expected her to be, and as she drew nigh a vague **fear** crossed her mind; but her whole being was too full of light to let its shadow rest, and it went flitting instantly like the shade of a filmy cloud over a field of buttercups. Hirell had no half-guilty, trembling happiness, nor did she feel in the least abashed or shame-faced at the thought of the news she had to tell Elias. She longed to meet him; not to hang down her head before him, and make tearful and blushing confession of her love, but to look into his grave eyes and make them glad with the story of the grace that had been shown her. She found him sitting with Kezia in the kitchen, and saw the moment she entered that his face was more than usually careworn, and that Kezia's eyes as she looked up were a little red. Still Hirell felt no self-reproach. She advanced towards them, her face beaming with happiness, till the voice of Elias startled her—

'So the man who calls himself John Rymer has been with you to-day.'

She turned pale, and recoiled like one who had been stung. Elias sat looking at her, evidently holding great control over himself.

'Did you think to deceive me, my daughter?' he asked.

'Indeed, Hirell, this is not like you,' murmured Kezia, not with any wish to reproach, but from an instinct that if another besides himself blamed Hirell, Elias might be moved to make his own blame less stern.

'Oh Kezia! Oh father!' cried Hirell, 'why are you angry with me? what have I done?'

'Hush, dear Hirell,' said Kezia, 'you must know it was not right.'

'I know that all which has happened me to-day has been right and holy and blessed in the sight of God,' Hirell said with streaming eyes, 'and, father, the man of whom you speak so sternly is now rejoiced over by the angels of heaven. He is saved—he comes to us—he will be your son by marriage, and in the Lord he will learn of you and our minis-ters. Ah, put no trouble in my heart this night, for it is so glad! Like Hannah and like Mary, my soul exults to think how its lowliness has been regarded.'

There was something so sweet and thrilling in her voice that Elias and Kezia simultaneously raised their eyes to look at her; and beheld on her face an expression so tender, so seraphic, that they withdrew their gaze quickly lest their looks of reproach should be changed to adoration.

Elias, putting his hand before his eyes, so as not to be moved by the sight of her, said in as calm and hard a voice as he could command—

'Give me simple and true explanations, Hirell. Does this man wish you to marry him?'

'I know, father,' she answered, 'it is hard for you to believe that this gentleman has so honoured me; yet it is true, and is the least of the miracles that have been shown me this day.'

'Then,' said Elias, 'John Rymer *so-called*,' he added sternly, has agreed to become a member of the Calvinistic Methodist Church.'

'And through me your unworthy—your—' Her sweet voice became choked, she bent her head meekly, and let her emotion find vent in an unrestrained rush of tears.

'Why does he not come back with you, to ask for you at my hands? Why keep away like a backslider and deceiver?' asked Elias, rising.

'Oh Kezia,' cried Hirell, falling upon her neck, 'tell him he is coming—tell him he is true and honourable as any man living.'

'Is he coming to-night?' demanded her father, sternly.

'No; he was compelled to leave to-day, but in a few weeks he will be here.'

'Why did he steal from my house like a thief, letting none know the time of his going?'

'He had letters, he told me; his business was sudden.'

'And of more importance than the consecration of the soul he has, you say, newly given to God; or, than his marriage with you?'

'Indeed, Kezia, my father should understand he is not as other men—he has great matters on his mind.'

'So has Satan,' groaned Elias internally; but aloud he said —'Why did he sojourn with us under a feigned name?'

Hirell raised her head from Kezia's shoulder, and looked at her father with parted lip and dilated eyes.

'Feigned! *his* name! Oh father!'

'I have said it,' answered Elias coldly, returning her look.

'May I ask how?—what makes you believe this?'

'Kezia knows—let her say.'

'I found in his room, Hirell, cards with the names he bears, and another added—John R. Cunliff,' answered Kezia, kissing the pale cheek turned attentively towards her.

'Is that all?—that may be the name of a relative.'

'Can you so easily deceive yourself, Hirell?' asked Elias.

'Could he so cruelly deceive me? No. I tell you, father, no. Be careful, dear father, and Kezia, what is true must be known and—and—borne—but—oh! oh!'

She broke from Kezia and stood alone, her arms crossed tightly on her breast, her form swaying like a slender mountain tree in a cruel tempest, and then, laying one hand on her father's wrist and the other on Kezia's, she said—

'But oh, it would be more charitable in both of you to desire to see my death—my death—than the breaking of my trust in this man.'

Alarmed at her passionate manner, so unusual, so strange to her, Kezia gently stroked the hand that burned and trembled on her wrist. Elias looked down helplessly at that which lay on his, and dropping it, said:

'Has it then gone so deep with you, Hirell?'

'Deep as life.'

'And you desire to walk with your eyes blindfolded?'

'No, only to walk in faith. I love him. What is love without faith? I will trust him. When the words of his own lips defile him, then only will I doubt. Let me believe till then—*then*, which means always.'

She said the last words with a smile breaking round her lips, and in a tone at once strong and tremulous with happy trust.

'Go then,' said Elias, not unkindly, 'I will not reason with you more to-night. Go to your room, Hirell, subdue passion, pray for wisdom, "commune with your own heart and be still."'

'Good-night, my father.'

'Good-night.'

'Good-night, Kezia,' she said, and the embrace she dared not give to her stern-eyed father she pressed with unwonted tenderness on the gentle housekeeper—holding her in her arms, and clinging to her as a child to a mother.

'Dear—God bless you,' whispered Kezia, and gave her a candle, and Hirell took it and went out.

Turning towards Elias, Kezia saw he was watching his daughter from the room with eyes in which was a mixture of great tenderness and anger.

'Bright spirit!' he said, still looking at the door by which she had gone out, his hard voice broken, 'if this man prove false, may her purity and faith be made the fire by which his God shall scathe him. As to my wrath—God deal with it, God deal with it!'

CHAPTER XXXII.

KEZIA TURNS PERVERSE.

THOUGH Elias had been suffering all that day a most tormenting anxiety concerning Hirell, after hearing that his lodger had been seen to take the road to Ewyn y Rhaiadr about half an hour before she started, it was to cares of another kind that the clouded looks on his face, and the red eyes of Kezia noticed by Hirell when she came in, were due.

It was now about six months since Hugh Morgan had entrusted to Elias the secret of his love for Kezia. The confidence reposed in him, as well as the absence and poverty of the young man, made Elias regard it as his sacred duty to influence Kezia in his favour as much as he possibly could. During this six months Hugh had not fulfilled his promise about writing home regularly and acquainting his family with all that happened him.

His letters were few and arrived irregularly—were sometimes utterly despairing, sometimes wildly sanguine. At first they generally contained half tender, half bantering messages to Kezia, and Elias invariably read them to her, she listening with the simple affectionate pleasure of one unexpectedly remembered.

In the last three or four, however, Elias had come upon certain passages which he had felt obliged to evade reading aloud. Hugh complained of never hearing anything about Kezia; she must speak of him sometimes; surely Elias might give him more comfort than he did concerning her; or if she had no regard for him at all, would it not be kinder in his brother to tell him the truth at once? Then perhaps the next letter would contain a passionate avowal of his incapability of living without hope of her acceptance; and so the elder brother was loaded by more and more perplexities and care.

He thought the time had now come for him to acquaint Kezia with the truth, and learn the state of her mind towards Hugh. He had been kept from doing this before, partly by the wish his brother had expressed on leaving home that she should not be told till he had done something to give her faith in him ; and partly because Elias was haunted by the fear that Kezia would not receive the announcement as Hugh expected she would.

Hirell's absence seemed to offer a good opportunity for Elias to speak to her ; and as soon as the most pressing business of the morning was seen to, he came home with the intention of requesting her presence in the little parlour, where all interviews or consultations of any importance in the family were invariably held.

It revealed a strange perversity in the mind of Elias Morgan, that though he saw Kezia alone in the kitchen, and everything most favourable to his purpose, he turned away from the door, and came back to it no less than three times, before he spoke the words he intended to say.

The first time he paused on the threshold, as if in reluctance to sully the floor with his muddy boots, for the kitchen was in a state of cold, polished cleanliness. The beam hooks, once so plentifully stored, were now almost empty ; the fire had been let out till the time for cooking the men's dinner ; the gaunt chairs were drawn up to their places, and on one of them near the open window, looking small in the great brown chamber, and solitary, and primitive, was Kezia. She wore a print gown which had once been a bright puce colour, but which age and frequent washing had faded to the pretty faint hue of the dog-violets on the mountains. On the fresh scoured table before her was the scant stock of linen she had just been gathering from the hedges where it had been spread to dry, and which she was now mending. The place smelt sweetly of it, and of the little spray of cherry blossom she had brought in with it and placed on the open leaves of her hymn-book that lay before her. The side of her face was towards the door, and the line of her hair as it went from the centre of her low forehead, and over her small fair ear, to the thick plaits behind, undulated in pretty waves, which gave her profile a richness that almost turned its simplicity into beauty. Her eyes bent over her work and her lips apart, as she sang in the low somewhat monotonous tone of a person having no faith in her own vocal powers, but who sings from an overflow of peace and contentment.

She looked up as the footsteps of Elias crossed the hall and came to the door, but seeing that he only stood looking on the floor in a sternly contemplative manner, went on with her work, taking no further notice of his presence. He then, after pausing a moment or two, went upstairs to his own room, and presently re-appeared on the threshold of the kitchen in the clothes he usually put on when his hard, out-of-door work was over.

This time he fixed his eyes on the clock, as if he had come there merely to consult that. Then he went away as far as the house-door, and Kezia thought he was going out; but the next moment his form again stood in the doorway of the kitchen.

'Kezia!'

The soft, peaceful eyes look up inquiringly.

'Will you come into my room? There is a matter on which I have to speak with you.'

'Surely, Elias.'

She rose and followed him.

Elias went to his bureau, and took out the well-known packet of Hugh's letters. From these he selected four.

'Sit down, Kezia, and read those.'

She thought his voice and manner peculiar, and, looking at him anxiously as she received the letters, said—

'There's nothing wrong with the lad, Elias, is there?'

He sat down, holding the packet in both his hands, and answered gently—

'Read, Kezia.'

She began to read the letters in the order they were given to her.

The first one was written when Hugh's enthusiasm for London had experienced a sudden revulsion. All was now as poor, mean, and hopeless as before all had been rich, alluring, infinite. His musical friend, having raised his hopes by the very highest of praise, considered his duty towards him done, and left him to his own resources. Thus his happiness was made to depend solely on the manner in which he performed his business at Tidman's and on his office companions, both of which he described as becoming more and more distasteful to him.

'You ask me, Elias,' he wrote, 'if I have made any friends among my fellow-clerks yet. Lonely as I am, I am thankful to answer " no " to that. I wonder what you would think of them—their views—their conversation—the intense meanness of their lives and aims—the way they speak of women— as if they had never known a mother or sister, or any but the wretchedly artificial fast-looking creatures I meet them with at theatres and some of the concerts. Elias, how inexpressibly dear and angelic the image that is always with me grows by such a contrast. Sometimes I wish she knew. You might say more about her than you have done lately. I am afraid you are not able to give me much hope, as you carefully avoid saying anything about her whenever you can.'

Here the letter finished with the usual messages to each. Kezia had heard it all before, except this last passage. Folding the letter, and handing it to Elias, she asked, with deepening colour—

' Who is it he means, Elias—the image that is always with him ? I do not understand.'

' Take the next—perhaps you will understand that better,' was the answer—and Kezia took up the next with a trembling hand.

This one she remembered well. It had touched them all deeply, for in it Hugh told—with a generous regret for his former hasty judgment—of the great goodness that in many instances lay behind the outward vulgarity and disagreeableness of his fellow-clerks. He told them how one whom he had laughed at for his effeminacy—who had a nervous horror of thieves, cattle, dogs, and draughts, was, by his persistent labours to support a wife and seven children, in spite of the encroachments of a deadly and painful disease, proving himself a miracle of courage and heroic strength. He told them how another, whom he had before described as utterly selfish, was capable of an act of such self-abnegation as breaking off his engagement to the woman he loved, in order to devote himself to the support of his newly-widowed mother and young sisters. ' Let them appear as commonplace, vulgar, apathetic, cowardly as they please,' Hugh wrote, ' they cannot deceive me longer, or incite me to self-glorification. I know there is in this office as much delicate sentiment, refined sense of honour, and chivalrous bravery, as ever existed in the olden times, among the same number of men. What becomes of all the old ledgers, I wonder, when they are full, and done with ? It seems to me there are histories in those long lines of figures which should be read and treasured when "The House," whose accounts they contained, is no more.

'You must all have thought me very rambling and unsuccessful since I came here ; but, strange to say, something has been growing in my mind which my very mistakes have helped to enrich. It is a new adaptation of Kezia's favourite air, one I find quite unknown here—it is wonderful to me how it has "come to me "—or, as Ephraim Jones would say, "been borne in upon me." I find myself able to work at it really, steadily, and progressively. You may be sure that I find my work all the pleasanter for remembering who used to sing it. Oh, Elias, if I could but come home and see her—how it would refresh me after all I have passed through here ! Tell her—but no, I cannot send the usual message. Let her think I have forgotten to mention her in this, and tell me what she says. Love to Hirell. Your affectionate brother,

'HUGH MORGAN.'

Kezia kept the letter in her fingers a minute after she had read it.

Elias took it from her, and gently placed another in her hand.

This was the most eventful one that had been received from Hugh since his departure. It contained the joyful news that his song was accepted by a well-known publisher, who thought it would have a great success, but he wanted words to it. Hugh knew that his brother's lodger was the author of several anonymous poems of some power and grace. Did Elias think he would write a song of the character of the enclosed description ? From some conversation Hugh had had with him during their brief acquaintance, Hugh thought it likely Mr. Rymer might be pleased with the idea he suggested for the poem. And now,' he wrote, 'if, Elias, you think as I do, that this is the foundation of a great prosperity and success, you may tell Kezia how long and how deeply I have loved her ; but if you still doubt me, I am willing to wait till I have still stronger evidence to convince you I am worthy to be trusted with one so dear to us all.'

Kezia laid this letter down, and rose with wet eyes and burning cheeks.

'I understand what you would have me know, Elias Morgan,' she said, 'need I read more ? '

'Yes, Kezia, read that;' and he gave her the fourth and last of the letters he had selected from the packet.

This was written after the brilliant success of his song, to which the desired verses had been written by Rymer.

'Of course I have thrown up my situation at Tidman's; it would be sheer nonsense to stay there. My plans are not yet quite settled. I shall write again in a day or two. I was certainly surprised you did not speak to Kezia as I wished, upon receiving my last. I shall begin to think, Elias, if you still show such reluctance to let her know the truth, that I am but a poor, miserable fellow, with all my success—I mean that you feel there is no hope for me. It would certainly be better for me to know the worst.'

This was the last letter Elias had received from him, and a month had elapsed since its arrival.

Kezia had read it standing.

'Oh what a pity this is, Elias; what a great, great pity,' she said in a trembling voice, without looking up from the letter.

'You will be his wife, Kezia—you will make him happy;' said Elias, in a tone half entreating, half authoritative.

He heard her tears pattering on the letter, but her head was unusually erect, her cheek very bright and hot.

He walked to the other end of the room and back, then said to her again,

'You will be his wife, Kezia? You will let me write to-day and set his heart at rest?'

The letter rustled in her hands, then fluttered to the floor, and she turned slowly, holding the edge of the table.

'Elias Morgan, do not ask me that again. I am sorry—no one could be more sorry—but never ask me again!'

They stood looking in each other's faces, and there was a strange light in the eyes of Elias that might have been taken for a gleam of intense joy, but that, as he spoke, his voice was so harsh and measured.

'And do you know, Kezia, that he looks to me to win you for him—to give you to him?'

'That you cannot do.'

'You say it, Kezia, I cannot;' he said, with a strange passion in his voice and eyes. 'If you will not, how can I force you? Had I, like the patriarchs of old, full power over all my house, I would command you to marry him—the Lord be my witness, I would command you to marry him!'

'And it would be the first command of yours, Elias, that—'

She had gone to the door, and now, without finishing her sentence, glided out gently.

They did not meet again till evening, and then not a word was said till Hirell's return.

When Kezia, some time after Hirell, went up to bed, she took from an old box of hers a little packet, and sat down with it in her lap before her bare, blindless window, which showed, through its small square panes, the April stars and moon. Kezia opened the paper with trembling fingers. Soon there glittered in them a plain gold ring; and where it had lain, words were traced—too faintly for her to see by the moonlight but that she knew them as well as she knew her own name.

'I leave this, my wedding-ring, to Kezia Williams, my death-bed comforter and friend, whom I earnestly desire one day to take my place as my husband's wife and my daughter's mother, with the blessing of her who shall have gone before to dwell with her Saviour.'

Kezia looked at the faint lines, and laid back the ring, saying softly—

'Mary, Mary! it is over!'

CHAPTER XXXIII.

THE REVEREND EPHRAIM JONES SENDS EVIL NEWS.

THE next morning Elias received the following letter from the Reverend Ephraim Jones:—

'DEAR FRIEND,—Your brother has given great dissatisfaction at Tidman's by his negligence during the last few weeks of his being there, and by his leaving suddenly without any reasonable warning. He seems, by his manner of dress and living, to be prosperous; but I warn you he is among evil companions. You will do wisely to order him home at any cost.   'Yours truly,

'EPHRAIM JONES.'

Elias never thought of questioning the advisability of carrying out his old friend's advice. He wrote commanding Hugh to come home instantly.

His trouble seemed indeed thickening round him. The spring days lengthened in care for him, as well as in light and beauty.

Kezia was cold and timid, and had ceased to sing over her work. Hirell loved to spend the fine sweet days out of doors, roaming alone in a wild, bird-like joyousness that made the fearful heart of Elias tremble for her. Could the man who caused her happiness be honest, when he had never yet even written to him ?

From morning till night he waited in unutterable anxiety for Hugh, or for some news of him. Days, weeks passed, and neither came.

And now another began to turn her eyes down the road with him, and to watch and long as he watched and longed.

Hirell told no one that the time of her lover's absence was longer, much longer than he had said it should be ; but her father and Kezia knew it, and watched her with increasing pain.

Unable to endure any longer the suspense about his brother, Elias wrote again to the minister entreating him to seek Hugh, and learn why he did not come home or answer his letter.

The reply came the third day after the letter had been dispatched.

'DEAR FRIEND,—I have news that will need all your fortitude. Hugh has left his lodgings, and gone none seem to know where. He stole from the house in the night—being deeply in debt there and in the neighbourhood.

'Yours in tribulation,

'EPHRAIM JONES.'

The women sobbed aloud. Elias remained in a stupor for a few minutes, then rose and began making preparation for a journey.

Hirell went after him.

'Oh father, what shall you do ? '

'Sell the horse, and go to London to seek him,' answered Elias.

CHAPTER XXXIV.

THE IRONY OF FORTUNE.

CUNLIFF again sits in his London room overlooking the park—a water-colour drawing of Welsh scenery, just purchased, occupies the place which the Raphael photograph occupied when first he was introduced in this story—outwardly all things else remain the same—the pictures, furniture, writing-desk, the conservatory, newly-furnished, and bright with the floral brightness of May—all look so like what they did last September, that it is difficult to believe that the owner has passed through so much mental and other experience; even his very look, gestures, and attitude, at times seem to recall the hesitation and conflict he felt on that momentous and evil day when he wrote his letter to Mrs. Rhys, and waited for her answer.

Yet, in spite of the exterior resemblances, it is impossible to study him with attention, and not see that he, at least, is changed. The brightness and perfume of the conservatory—which only seems to concentrate the brightness and sweetness of the lovely morning outside into a focus—seem also to have entered into Cunliff. His step is springy, in spite of a certain sedate and compelled gravity; his grey eye glances to and fro with a quick suddenness of apprehension and with a sort of eager joyous light; his head is thrown back proudly and haughtily, if for the moment unpleasant recollections cross his mental vision; and in his work—for he is very busy—there is none of that obvious concentration upon a single secret thought and aim, which so characterised him on the day that began for him events and influences, the end of which is not yet. Whatever secret thought may now perplex him, it certainly does not injure his activity in dealing with all sorts of affairs.

By his side lies the rough draft of an address to the electors of ——. Through Arnold's influence, a very old member of the House of Commons has delayed till now an intended resignation, in order that Cunliff might step in, as he stepped out. The writ for a new election will be issued to-morrow. The old member's printed address, not yet made public, hangs on the back of a chair; and Cunliff glances at it now and then while reading and correcting his own composition, which at last pleases him sufficiently to be dismissed. He folds it up, sends it, with a genial letter of thanks, to the aged M.P., and as he drops it into the letter-box, thinks—

' The farther one sees—and the deeper one hopes to go down to the root of things for social and political remedies—the more necessary is it to give the silly world the notion that your fault is over-timidity; your defect, unwillingness to acknowledge the necessity for changes too soon. Establish the right character, and then you may lead the world—to the devil—or a good long way in the opposite direction. I wonder whether my cautious speaking will bother Arnold? No, I think not; though he adopts the very opposite course, and is so frank and generous that he seems always ready to go anywhere and with anybody, till the push comes, and then uses his character to moderate, and do only just what he likes. Still, a fine fellow, and as little of a self-seeker as any of us are likely to be.'

This business over, was in a minute utterly forgotten. Drafts of leases were brought forth, with accompanying lawyers' letters, and read with such scrupulous care, that one might have fancied the reader's daily bread depended on his judgment and accuracy. Then a few words were written on the back, which told exactly the state of the landlord's mind, which agents and tenants already knew was a mind that changed not.

These things dealt with, a batch of the letters of the morning were answered—some by a contemptuous ' pish! ' some by a silent thoughtful drop into the waste-paper basket, and some by a few kindly and generous written words, including, in two instances, a cheque in each letter. The batch was what may vulgarly be called begging-letters, though Cunliff himself had so much of the generosity of the gentleman in him, that he would not for the world have applied that epithet to some of the many he had gone through.

Between all this hard work, Cunliff frequently paused, in an inexplicable manner, as though suddenly forgetting the very sentence he had been reading or writing, and stared fixedly right opposite at the wall for perhaps half a minute, his face grave, almost sad; and before resuming work, he invariably, though with no sort of consciousness, allowed his eyes to rest on that water-colour in front of his desk, which represented a bit of wild Welsh scenery—one that he had never seen, but which seemed to him to be as familiar in all its characteristics as if he had lived in it from a boy.

A double tap at the door roused him from one of those odd reveries, which began to recur more and more frequently as the long array of work began visibly to lessen.

'Come in!' he said, with an uninterested voice and manner.

The door opened, and closed again behind Cunliff—and there was silence, and then forgetfulness, and the busy and busier thoughts moved on with renewed impetus, till a low and very respectful cough made Cunliff suddenly turn round, chair and all, when he saw his agent, Mr. Jarman, bowing more obsequiously than ever, even while still allowing some sort of half-grown spirit of independence to assert itself by his look.

'Jarman, my good fellow, what on earth made you stand there, as if suddenly stricken with palsy? I thought it was the servant who knocked, and I forgot all about him.'

He stretched out his hand, and shook the agent's cordially —and then the two set to work together in a somewhat remarkable fashion. Cunliff handed paper after paper—lease after lease—document after document—one at a time—in solemn silence to Jarman; who looked at the remarks written on the back, gravely inclined his head, took possession, and held out his hand for the next; only twice stopping to put now a query and now an objection—the objection was recognised, and the endorsement altered; the query answered to Mr. Jarman's entire satisfaction—and so no more. When the whole of the pending matters were thus disposed of—and some of them involved matters of life or death, pecuniarily speaking, to tenants and others—Cunliff said.

'Have we done?'

'Yes, Sir John, I—I think so.'

Cunliff noticed the hesitation, and a certain darkening of the agent's face; and, moved by some secret misgiving, hesitated to do as he ordinarily did—dash at it, and demand to know its meaning—but said:

'Because after you have done—*after*, I say, you have quite done—I want to speak to you about one or two matters demanding your instant and most careful attention.'

Mr. Jarman's eyes that had scanned boldly enough his employer's face, now bent down towards his feet; and there was a moment of awkward delay, from which the agent suddenly extricated himself by saying in a low perturbed tone—

'She's dead!'

'She? Who? Good God! who can you mean? Don't keep me in suspense. Not—'

Hirell—he was about to say—till the full force of the revelation contained in the mere utterance of the name struck him, and he was silent—gazing sternly yet anxiously on Jarman's face.

'The wife of that man, Sir John, who was so long ill in the cottage at—'

Cunliff waved his hand impatiently—he needed to know no more. He remembered only too vividly that incident of his mad pursuit of Mrs. Rhys—when the man with his dirty hooked fingers hung on to the window of the railway carriage, talking to the doctor and threatening Jarman.

Cunliff rose, and with an impassive face, observed—

'I have forgotten something,' and left the apartment.

He returned in a minute or two, with a paper in his hand.

'That, I think, was your plan for the repair or rebuilding of those cottages. Put the matter in hand at once, and let me hear they are done within the shortest possible time.'

Mr. Jarman bowed, but, to Cunliff's discomfort, would say something more.

'I think, Sir John, you ought to know that a coroner's inquest has sat—'

Cunliff glared at his agent—but the agent went on—

'And it came out that the woman had heart-disease; and—and—the jury attributed her death to that; and—that's all, Sir John.'

There was a moment or two of significant silence, during which Cunliff could not but reflect on that irony of Fortune which here and now should have brought to his recollection the warning he had previously received in the same place and from the same lips.

Then he turned, and with a genial, almost friendly look, that was full of meaning, he said in low tones:

'Mr. Jarman, I thank you.'

They had a glass or two of wine together, and the agent fancied it was not only in compliment to him, but that **Sir**

John himself felt the energy of his will shaken for the moment, and wisely enough paused for recovery.

'Jarman,' and he now spoke as friend might speak to friend, while the gray, bright, piercing eyes glanced again at the water-colour, 'I want to ask you a favour—to do some things for me, not in the formal spirit of business, but—'

'I understand, Sir John,' said Mr. Jarman, with a sort of grateful smile lighting up his whole countenance, and reddening his complexion to the very roots of his hair, 'and feel myself more honoured than I can easily express.'

Cunliff then, in a few words, and without any sort of preliminary or accompanying explanation, told the story which Robert Chamberlayne had told to him on their first meeting of the Morgans' supposed fortune; and then of the bursting of the bubble, and its consequences to the 'Morgans,' who were permitted to be known to the agent only through the individuality of Elias.

'It's a cruel position. He is in debt which he cannot pay, except through long years of exhausting labour and anxiety. But he will take nothing from my friend Chamberlayne, therefore I, a stranger, cannot hope he will take anything from me. A sort of fanatic of independence, goodness, and piety; but, after all, a good sort of fellow enough at the bottom. I *can* aid him, if only you will undertake for the way. My notion is that some debtor of the bankruptcy concern in years gone by, who has since grown rich, may by accident hear of the Morgans' misfortune, and offer to send a sum of money, on the understanding that it is to be devoted exclusively to the use of the family. I see the difficulties, and improbabilities, but I want it done.'

'Exactly, Sir John!' said the agent thoughtfully.

'And it'll be no good unless it's so well done that no one can get behind the pretences to see the real actors.'

'I will do my best.'

'Don't say that, or I must give the thing up. Say you *will* do it, and I'll leave the whole in your hands—sure of your tact, skill, and secrecy.'

'I will do it, Sir John. Already I see how to improve on your idea. I *think* I can make the offer to Elias seem *bonâ fide*—a something due; and I am *sure* I can keep off all suspicion from you or me, by acting through my own solicitors, who will then act through other solicitors, on whom we may all rely.'

'Very good. Mind, it is not now done, therefore I cannot now know it is done. When it is done, I wish to hear nothing about it; therefore I shall still know nothing. You understand?'

'Perfectly, Sir John.'

'This to me is serious—I mean for the family's sake.'

'And to what extent?'

'Just so far as you can go without exciting suspicion.'

'Would a capital realising an income of a hundred a year be—?'

'No! Too much to be believed. Five hundred in all would set Elias on his legs, and enable him to take a larger farm. And let it be in the funds, so that if the acceptance be once got over, the recipient will be sure of the value of what he gets. If I know Elias rightly—'

'You do know him, then, Sir John?' thoughtlessly interrupted Mr. Jarman.

Cunliff's reply was only by a look; one, however, that considerably disturbed the agent, who felt he had been an ass to let out such a womanish bit of gossip or curiosity.

'If I know Elias Morgan rightly,' Cunliff repeated, 'he will never use the bulk of the money, but keep it as a safeguard for—for the future. I wish you a very good morning, Mr. Jarman.'

'Good morning, Sir John.'

They shook hands, and Cunliff accompanied his agent with unusual ceremony downstairs to the very door leading to the street. There he said,

'Can you go to-day about this business?'

'Instantly! Nor will I let it alone till it is quite accomplished.'

He descended the steps, bowed, and turned.

'Jarman!' was called after him.

'I thought there was something else. Can you manage within a week from this time to be at my late uncle's place?'

'Certainly, Sir John.'

'Say this day week—Monday.'

'Yes.'

'I have an odd fancy to walk through the place alone, or possibly with a friend; could you'—here some person passed by, and Cunliff whispered low into the agent's ear a few words, which, to make sure of their being exactly understood, he repeated.

Mr. Jarman bowed, did not again look in his employer's face, but said,

'Everything shall be, Sir John, as you wish.'

And then they separated.

Cunliff returned to his desk, but, strange to say, all his old self-dissatisfaction seemed to have suddenly returned upon him, and with it all his old irritability.

He could no longer work, but paced to and fro in gloomy reverie, uttering now and then an angry or impatient exclamation, and making as if he would renew his labours, but after two or three ineffectual efforts he gave up the attempt, saying to himself,

'No, no; the matter must be fought out now once for all. Delay will only deepen the difficulty, till it becomes insurmountable. Fool that I was, and am! What on earth must she be thinking about my prolonged absence and silence?

'And, Arnold! He must put a new ingredient into this devil's broth which Fate a second time, with her infernal irony, seems to commend to my lips.'

He took up a letter that had been laid aside from the others after a first hasty perusal, and read a second time a certain passage in it. He read it slowly—very slowly, as if to give himself time to branch out in thought in any direction he liked as he read.

'Shall I tell you something that almost exposes me to a charge of breach of faith, and against one of the most charming of women—my cousin, Miss Harrington? She was asked her opinion of you, not by me, trust me, but by one who had a right to say what he pleased to her—her grandfather. I was present. "Sir John Cunliff," she said—but, no, on further consideration, I will not tell you. You are already one of the vainest of men, and my telling you may spoil her telling you when you ask her, as I hope you will. Cunliff, my friend, one serious word with you. No man ever really settles to any worthy labours after a life like yours, till he marries. When a man like you does marry, his whole future is to a large extent in the hands of his wife. You must not only love your wife's person and heart, but you must honour her intellect

and character. There must be sympathy between you.
Cunliff, I will tell you what I have never before spoken of
to mortal man. That I am what I am, I owe to my wife.
Spare your sarcasm, it is out of place. I know God gave me
little of original personal gift, but she has helped me to make
the best of what he did give; and in no spirit of vanity or
conceit do I say I am satisfied as regards myself; I am happy
as a reasonable man expects to be, and grateful alike to God
and to her. You are too shrewd not to understand what all
this means. If you like Miss Harrington, as I fancy you do,
pray attend to her a bit, study her, and, my life on it, you
will thank me for the hint. I shall not for a moment use my
privilege as a cousin, or my knowledge of her thus obtained,
to extol her virtue, her talent, beauty, or accomplishments,
because you of all men are the one to take nothing in trust,
but to judge from your own independent point of view. Still
less do I feel inclined to speak of mere worldly advantages, or
the powerful political influence her relatives could and would
exercise in behalf of one they esteemed worthy of her. But
this slight remark may be ventured, I hope, without offence.
Were you to marry my cousin, and take your position as one
of England's future statesmen, I know no woman in all my
circle of acquaintances who would be so fit as she to grace
your every conquest or smooth over your every difficulty, by
her exquisite tact, and perfect knowledge and estimate of all
those social influences which play so large though unacknow-
ledged a part in our public life. Forgive this plain speaking;
if it offend you, I shall never certainly repeat the offence.'

The letter was laid down with a sort of tender and respectful care; and the man to whom it was addressed sat with
it before him on the desk, his head supported on his elbows,
till a sudden and seemingly accidental resemblance, suggested,
perhaps, by the water-colour, made him start as if stung, rise,
turn, and lay the water-colour flat on the table, and then
again pace about the room in deep, brooding anxiety.

Yes, John Cunliff was feeling deeply now the cruel irony of
fortune, which brought him a second time, in the same place,
without a single admonitory warning beforehand, to deliberate
on certain matters, while even now the deliberation itself was
a something so disgraceful he could not courageously face it,
or truthfully and frankly characterise it.

'At least, whatever I do, she shall see I do not fear to meet her. I think I can trust myself. The world—my best compliments to it!—has in a few weeks once more taught me, I think, the lesson I have been so near forgetting—to take care of myself.

'And will she too take care of herself? It is calumny to doubt it. From her spiritual elevation—it is childish to pursue the thought. It is I who have to fear; and my safety must come out of my full knowledge of that fact beforehand. Yes, I plunge, and hesitate no more.'

Again retracing the old ground, past Shrewsbury ; past the spot where Chamberlayne jumped in so unceremoniously; past his own bare-looking fields, which the young farmer had so condemned ; past the station where that tenant of his had hung on to the window ; past the precise spot—how well he knew it—where he had looked out of the other window while Robert Chamberlayne was wanting to know the name of the landlord who then dealt out, for a weekly rent, disease, misery, and since then, death ; all this he now vividly remembered, but somehow found his chief consolation in the fact that it was he who had faced doctor and querist, and silenced them by his answer—'Cunliff.'

When he arrived at Dolgarrog, and made arrangements to stay the night at the new hotel, his old recollection and perplexity returned upon him, and he sat brooding over the fire in the coffee-room hour after hour, as if he had come to Wales with no other purpose. At last his friend and landlord of the Council House, having heard of his arrival, came in to him full of Elias Morgan's trouble, and his journey to town in search of Hugh.

Cunliff's hesitation was now at an end. He immediately gave orders for a car to be made ready for him at half-past five o'clock the next morning to take him to Capel Illtyd.

Before it was announced he had already breakfasted, and for many minutes paced restlessly up and down the room, to the great annoyance of some gentlemen belonging to the gold mines, who, with sundry white papers of yellow dust and peculiar-looking stones beside them, were making calculations over their coffee at the same untimely hour.

Cunliff left the car waiting at the toll-gate, and began to ascend the familiar fields of Bod Elian with a quick, springing step.

CHAPTER XXXV

KEZIA PROVES AN UNFAITHFUL STEWARD.

THE absence of the master made little difference in the aspect of things at Bod Elian. Knowing so well as everyone there did what he would desire and expect to be done, and the relentless manner with which he would regard any neglect, his absence became almost as impressive as his presence. Kezia felt that it gave a sacred responsibility to her; and she went about the house with a firmer step, a more erect bearing, and a greater seriousness and earnestness in her watchful eyes. Hirell, seeing that she considered her her chief and most anxious charge, showed a gentle, childlike submission as sweet to Kezia as it was unexpected; for Hirell's will was not generally very yielding to any but Elias, who in his house made all wills bend to his, not by tyranny, but by the force of his own example in obeying that Will to which he tried to shape his whole life.

The farm labourers were as punctual to their hours as when he was at home; the very sheep-dog seemed to assume a look of graver responsibility than was his wont, and to rush up the mountain at the appointed time, and drive his charge down, and trot round them as he brought them home, with more than usual zeal. The yard-dog was perhaps low-spirited at missing his master's firm step and short salutation, for he had been captious all day and restless all night, barking loudly when light appeared in any window on his side of the house, and even when the moonbeams glided across the yard, or when the deepening silence of all other things made the torrents sound loud and grand—worthy of the mighty hills whose silver tongues they are.

'Hirell,' said Kezia, as they sat at work together earlier than usual on the morning when Cunliff, who knew, of course, their early habits, was making his way towards Bod Elian, 'is it well, dear, to give yourself so much time for thinking when it only makes you sad?'

Kezia was sitting at the hall door, Hirell just outside, on the ancient stone which was used in olden times to assist the portly dames of Bod Elian to mount their horses when they rode to church or fair; and above her head hung by a rusty chain the little cow-horn bugle by which the guests of those days announced themselves.

When Kezia spoke to her she was looking away far down the field-path by the ravine where she had stood and listened to Robert Chamberlayne's footsteps, on that quiet autumnal night when she felt he was leaving Bod Elian never to return. The ravine was now one long tangled wilderness of fresh May beauty ; and it did not remind her of that night, or of Robert Chamberlayne, but of the day at Ewyn y Rhaiadr, and of the hard words Elias had spoken to her on her return. As Kezia spoke she broke off her reverie, and gently took up a piece of homely work on which Kezia was engaged, saying,

' Wise or foolish, Kezia, it certainly is not kind while you have so much to do. As to its making me sad to think, I must not mind that, if it brings to me things that I ought to know.'

' What things, Hirell ? '

' Don't ask me, Kezia ; miserable things.'

' Yet you told me you could not help being happy, even in spite of poor Hugh.'

' And I told you the truth. I am happy.'

' Then what have you to do with these miserable thoughts you speak of ? '

' Ah, what have I to do with them ? ' said Hirell, dropping her work, and playing with the rusty chain above her head, which she leaned against the wall, to hide from Kezia the tears that came into her eyes. ' What have I to do with them, Kezia ? why, when I am happiest, are they sent down before me, like the unclean creatures in Peter's vision ? Like him, Kezia, I sicken and cry, " *Not so, Lord !* " but again and again they come.'

' I don't know how it is, Hirell, but you never had such thoughts as these before,' said Kezia.

' Do not say so, Kezia ! I know whom you blame for it.'

So saying, she roused herself, and again took up her work, smiling and shaking her head.

' I blame no one, dear,' Kezia protested, ' but I can see it is with you as with so many others—these strong earthly affections bring with them so much pain, restlessness, anxiety, and—'

She stopped, and something in her voice made Hirell look at her with a shrewd and loving glance.

'And yet we must believe it to be a gift from heaven,' added Kezia.

' The greatest of heaven's wonders,' Hirell said ; 'which I suppose we mortals scarcely know what to do with, better than we should know what to do with any of the lesser wonders— the moon or the stars—were they given to us. Ah! Kezia, look, look ! '

Kezia glanced inquiringly at her, not knowing where she meant her to look, for Hirell's eyes were bent upon her work. There was on her face a strongly subdued joy, the meaning of which Kezia did not for the moment understand ; but soon she heard a step, and the next instant her hand was in Mr. Rymer's, and he was speaking *to* her with very hearty friend- liness ; and then a few moments later she was away in the house alone, feeling glad she had had presence of mind enough to gather up her work and come in quickly, leaving the two by themselves.

The quiet, deep joy and tenderness of Hirell's look as he stood before her, made Cunliff forget everything but her and his own pleasure at their meeting again.

Joy chooses its own seasons for coming to us, and as often as not makes its way to our hearts over sorrow's writhing form. Hirell thought of this as, in a voice of self-reproach, she mur- mured—taking her hands from Cunliff—

'Ah poor, poor Hugh ! '

'I know, I have heard all, Hirell,' said Cunliff. ' I will help your father to discover where he is, I will do all I can for him, all that they will let me when he is found. But Hirell, I have come to ask you to spend this day with me as we spent one memorable day together. I have things to say to you that I cannot talk of hurriedly, and I have business which takes me from here again instantly.'

'Away again ! Instantly,' repeated Hirell.

'Yes, instantly. I must within a few hours be in the neighbourhood of Shrewsbury to see the agent of some great man's property there. I need only spend a few minutes with him, then all the day, this exquisite May-day, with you, Hirell, if you will come with me. You will like to look over the castle and grounds. You shall be back here at night. Can you refuse me ? The first time I ever asked you to trust me.'

'It cannot, cannot be, Mr. Rymer. My father would never

forgive me. Ah! he was so hurt when he heard how it was with us. He thought we had practised deception towards him. He never used such words to me before, and to hear *you* spoken of so harshly, that is what I cannot bear. And, Kezia! I am under a solemn promise to my father to be guided by her in all things while he is away, and I know she would never, never consent to my going away—so far too—oh no, Mr. Rymer, ask me no more.'

'Hirell, I do not ask you again, as you have no faith in me —but now *I* shall go and speak to Kezia myself.'

Then leaving Hirell agitated by a great longing to go— dread of acting wrongly to her father in his absence, and a yet more tender fear of offending Mr. Rymer, in whom she had such perfect reliance, he went into the house, found Kezia, and pleaded his cause before her.

She was terribly startled when she first understood what his request was; but he made the excuses for it so unanswerable, spoke so well of the engrossing nature of his affairs, the shortness of the time at his command, the necessity for Hirell and himself (and here he spoke with a grave seriousness) arranging their plans definitely for the future, and settling how he could best move with regard to Hugh, gave such sacred promises as a gentleman and a man of honour as to the care he would take of Hirell, and the hour at which he would bring her safely back to Bod Elian; in short, so impressed and overpowered the timid Kezia, that she was already half inclined to yield, when Hirell came in, and added her entreaties to her lover's.

She assured Kezia she would not for the world consent to this, still less urge it, if, after thought and prayer, it seemed to her wrong. But she had thought and had asked counsel, and felt sure no warning against it had entered her heart. She asked Kezia if her conduct since her father's departure had given her cause to doubt or trust her; and at that question the sweetness of her humility and submission came to Kezia's heart, and moved her lips to a trembling consent.

Mr. Rymer gallantly kissed her hand, and Hirell's sweet eyes looked their thanks. In less than a quarter of an hour they were gone, and Kezia sitting alone, her heart full of misgivings.

Suppose Elias should return before the day was out. What would he say to her? What an unfaithful steward would he think her! How slowly the time went in her loneliness! When would the day and her anxiety be over?

It was yet early in the afternoon when she was sitting with her work on the old mountain-stone, and her eyes most unreasonably beginning already to look for the return of her charge, when she heard a step, the sound of which turned all her vague anxiety to very painful and certain fear.

She rose and turned. Elias was toiling up the path, his face and attitude eloquent of failure, fatigue, hopelessness.

CHAPTER XXXVI.

HIRELL'S JOURNEY.

CUNLIFF felt himself possessed by a wild joyousness, unlike the calm, deep happiness he had had in Hirell's society at Ewyn y Rhaiadr. His step was quick and elastic, his glance restless, his very voice irrepressible; and Hirell smiled to hear him several times singing a snatch of some sweet air she had never heard, and which, as soon as she was interested in it, would be stopped and another begun.

Hirell's mood was very different. She was silent, and her steps were slow and measured.

As they were descending the little path between the ravine and the field, Cunliff looked round at her quickly.

'This is the first time, Hirell, I've seen you walk down here,' said he. 'At other times you have always come bounding down with the speed of a born mountaineer as you are. The chamois itself could hardly have so certain, vigorous, or delicate a foothold. Do you come so slowly to-day, as a wholesome check on my impatience, or why?'

Hirell looked into his half-laughing, half-jealous eyes, and smiled with an affection so deep and tender, that his doubting was changed to delight.

'How bright and merry of heart you can be,' she said. 'I envy you, Mr. Rymer, and yet I don't know for why. I believe my happiness is at least as great as your own.'

'Yet till I reminded you—you are coming along blithely now—you walked at that funereal pace.'

'When I see Nanny rushing down the hill,' said Hirell, 'and her pails swinging lightly in her hands, Kezia and I look cross at one another, for we know she has little or nothing in them—but when she comes slowly and sedately down, looking slyly out of the corners of her eyes into the pails, I clap my hands and run to meet and help her; for I know then her burden is very precious and bounteous. And if you won't think it *very* rustic and milk-maidish, Mr. Rymer, I should say a full heart, like a full milk-pail, must be carried quietly, soberly, or it will overflow—as—look, you have made mine.'

For great tears were rolling down her cheeks, even while her laughter rang gaily in his ears.

They found the carriage close by, waiting for them under a little avenue of trees; and the driver looking with sharp curiosity to see who it was the English gentleman had come to fetch at so unlikely an hour from Bod Elian.

The horses were striking the ground impatiently, thinking they had been there long enough, and the driver was standing at their head quieting them with his hand and voice, while his glances were turned towards the coming lady.

'Oh, Hirell Morgan, is that you?' he exclaimed, as she came up to him. He spoke with an air of familiarity not at all disrespectful, but intensely annoying to Cunliff.

'Now, my man, mount! I'll see to the rest,' he said irritably.

'Yes, David,' answered Hirell with a smile, and the faintest possible indication of increased colour. She knew David, he was one of their congregation, and her first thought was how she should like to run back and comfort Kezia by telling her that David Roberts was the driver; and that both going and returning she would be for a considerable time under his care.

For one single moment she looked back, but the next she saw how foolish it would be to keep her lover and the carriage waiting, without being able to give an intelligible reason; for she would not even seem to Mr. Rymer to have confidence in any but him; so with glad trust she dismissed the thought and entered the carriage. Cunliff followed, fastened the door after him, and away went the horses at a great pace, in obedience to Cunliff's hint of—

'Fast as you can!'

Cunliff had done well to strike a kind of mirthful keynote by his buoyant vivacity at the moment of departure, if his aim were simply and honestly to banish from Hirell's loving and filial heart all fear of her father's displeasure: there was something so genial, so pure, so unlike aught that suggests danger or doubt, in his behaviour, that Hirell would as soon have questioned the beneficence of heaven, as her lover's truth on this sweet May morning.

Hirell wore her chapel dress, a very different one from that which had made so sweet a glow of colour in the market-place of Dolgarrog on the Sunday when Mr. Rymer first saw her.

Even if Elias had permitted her to keep one of the fine dresses of that time, she would not dare to be seen in it by a congregation among whom she was one of the poorest. But the experiences of that bright and busy time had made Hirell so cunning in the management of the poor clothes remaining to her, that she had been able to unite the prettiest fashion of the day with the austere simplicity demanded by her sect, in the common, coarse linsey which she now wore. Its colour reminded Cunliff of her own native mountains when the heather was in bloom—a kind of misty violet, not bright, but soft and rich. A 'train' in the chapel would have been thought almost as great a defilement to the stones as the cloven foot itself; therefore Hirell's dress was short, and looped up at each side over a snowy crimped frill which was Kezia's pride to keep, as she said, 'like the snow when it lies on the ribbed sands at Aber.' A little cape the same as her dress fitted closely to her figure. Her hat was also home-made. It was tuscan, of a rich, old-fashioned plait, and was made out of some ancient bonnet that had been left to the family with the effects of a rich grand-aunt of Elias Morgan's. Hirell had undone the straws and made them up again into as charming a little round hat as Cunliff had ever seen at picnic or croquet. As he looked he was again changing his opinion, and going back with fresh zest to his first impressions. And now he could not but notice that Hirell wore new and delicate kid gloves. It had been a matter of some consideration with Hirell, as she stood looking at them in her bedroom, whether she should or should not take them from the long resting-place for Cunliff's sake. There was something sacred about them as a lost friend's last gift. When Robert Chamberlayne was Mr. Lloyd's pupil, he had once taken Hirell into the chief shop of Dolgarrog on her birthday, and told her to choose whatever she liked best for a present. She had chosen a pair of bright, delicately coloured kid gloves, never having had such things on her hands before. And ever since, as the

birthday came round, a pair of gloves from Robert had arrived
with it. Her latest birthday was in the week following
Robert Chamberlayne's last visit; and thinking that visit
would be a long one, he had brought his offering with him,
daintily fresh and perfumed. Then when he found how
things were between him and Elias and Hirell, he gave them
into Kezia's charge. 'Ask her to accept the old present for
the last time, Kezia,' he said; and added with a tone of unusual despondency, 'Who knows, Kezia, but what she may
give her little hand away to some other fellow in that very
glove? Somehow I feel she will.'

'It's a shame, Robert,' Hirell had said to herself as she put
them on, while Cunliff was impatiently calling to her at the
foot of the stairs that morning; 'but,' she said, touching the
soft, scented surface with her lips, 'they shall not be defiled
by the touch of any hand less honest and true than your own,
Robert.'

Of these thoughts Cunliff knew nothing, nor needed to
know. As he finished his examination of her, he said to
himself:

'Whence comes this wondrous instinct of woman for self-
adornment? By heaven, she is artistically perfect, and I was
a most conventionally-minded ass to doubt it!'

On the bridge, over which they went at a walking pace,
they met the postman who delivered letters along the road
beyond Dolgarrog, and whose beat included Bod Elian.

Hirell looked wistfully towards him, then suddenly lowered
the window, and putting her head out, said to the man:

'Any letters for us, Richard Pugh?'

'Eh! Miss Morgan, that you? Yes, there is one.'

'Indeed! I am so glad I stopped you,' said Hirell, continuing to talk in order to cover her anxiety while he
ransacked his bag. 'I am so anxious about Hugh and my
father,' she said, turning to Cunliff as half apologizing for the
delay, for he had immediately called to the driver to stop, on
understanding her wish.

A rather bulky-looking letter was at last discovered and
given to Hirell, who looked at it with obvious surprise; and
after a moment or two of hesitation put it in her pocket, and
begged Cunliff to tell the driver to go on.

Cunliff wondered, and did as he was bid; then wondered
why he had wondered, and answered himself by the mental

comment that he had seen the address, that it was not from Elias, that it was from some one who wrote a formal, but handsome and manly-looking hand.

Who could be the writer ?

Hirell on her part did not seem in the least conscious he was or might be putting such questions to himself; and there was some thing so naïve, simple, and frank in her behaviour under these, as Cunliff thought them, peculiar circumstances, that he could not help giving her for the first time credit for some little taint of the wisdom of the serpent in modification of the innocence of his dove.

'Your letter, Hirell; pray don't mind me,' he said, after a brief pause.

'Oh, I had forgotten it already,' said Hirell, with a look that Cunliff thought conscious of guilt; and he was the more satisfied of this when he observed she made no movement to correct the omission.

The sight of the people iu the market-place, gathering for some holiday excursion, stopped for a moment further questioning.

As they passed through Dolgarrog, Cunliff drew back into the obscurity of his corner as far as possible, and in doing so noticed that Hirell did the same. But the charming tint that her secret thought had raised on her cheek had, he felt, no response on his; and the fact once more began to make him very thoughtful.

For a moment or two only. He had come into this day's work with a determination not to think, not at least until the inevitable hour when all must be made known.

'Now, Hirell, hey for England!' said Cunliff, gaily, as they cleared the town of Dolgarrog, and began the long and picturesque ascent round the shoulder of Criba Ban.

'For England!' exclaimed Hirell, with eyes dilating, and a momentary spasm of fear, which passed away in a sweet shame as she saw his enjoyment of her surprise. 'I have never been there.'

'Is it possible ? Never in England!'

'Never! But oh, Mr. Rymer, how can we do that, and be home again to-night?'

'Easily,' was the answer. 'We do just advance a little way into England beyond the Welsh border, that is all.'

'Ah, well! I am so glad. It is something to say one has been there at last.'

Somehow this little incident set Cunliff thinking in silence to himself as to many things about Hirell which he fancied so secluded and inexperienced a life must involve ; but suddenly he began to explain the course of their journey, as including two or three hours of the present conveyance, then rail for a like space, then again some vehicle for half an hour to reach their destination, the great house where Mr. Rymer was to meet his friend, the steward of the estate, and where—

And there ' Mr. Rymer ' as the sweet musical lips continued to call him, stopped ; with the abrupt reflection that, however she might receive what he then proposed to say to her, it would be cruel to risk telling her while so much of the bright, happy day remained, and which his words might—

A kind of thrill ran through him as he thought and thought of what lay before them, and especially as he pictured the having to travel together homeward.

He felt for her, no doubt ; while obeying the prudent philosophy of his and our teachers—felt as much as it was in his nature to do. Cunliff unhappily shared—but as a victim rather than as an originater—in the heartlessness of intellect which is one of the most deplorable phenomena of our time ; and which seems to be chiefly due to the egotism of the national character when not restrained by noble aims, and a vigorous activity of life in the effort to realise them ; but when rather—as with us now—it is fostered by the itch for and habit of ceaseless criticism. We are all of us nothing if we are not critical. The trader who has not an idea beyond his ledger, the woman whose one thought is fashion, the boy and girl with their eyes just opening on life, the rich and poor, the idle and industrious, are each and all as critical as the cultured teacher who steps forth from his studies prepared to show the hollowness of everything that old-fashioned men have been accustomed to revere ; or as the practised statesmen so called, who, originating nothing, stand ever on the watch to attack with their destructive criticism those who attempt to build in the light of faith, and with the results of the knowledge of the past. And all the while they seem to have no idea—these insatiable critics—that their process is one that may or may not achieve what they expect from it, but is sure to destroy the best part of themselves. One can hardly help asking if this

be not the modern way of selling souls to the Evil One; who
was the first—and remains the most powerful—of critics; and
who—with creation for his theme—works out his principles of
criticism to their natural end.

The credulity that can believe in the value of a perpetual
system of cynical analysis, is only one step removed from the
credulity that teaches the analyser he or she is too superior a
being to be obliged to recognise ordinary laws of humanity;
which accordingly they lose faith in, and so themselves become what they imagine others to be. A false atmosphere
hangs about them, distorting all natural objects—an atmosphere in which no good or great thing can possibly grow.
Charity becomes an economical blunder; sentiment, 'senti-
mentality;' philanthropy, 'mawkishness;' patriotism, when it
rises to heroic proportions and world-wide scope, 'brainless;'
and the only philosophy worth acceptation is the philosophy of
brute force, impregnated with the delicate flavour of a touch
of fraud. These be thy heroes, O modern Israel!

And so, having criticised away all the sweet courtesies of
life which ought to regulate, and might regulate, if Christianity be a truth, the relations of the whole human family;
having taught everyone to expect nothing by rendering
nothing; made faith, earnestness, chivalrous feeling, self abnegation in our everyday lives, things of banter and ridicule;
made men and women generally ashamed to avow a desire for
a better state of things, or an intention to try to help it on
by their own life and teaching—having accomplished all this,
they explain away religion, and put back God into His place:
leaving—what?—Themselves.

Ah, but do they not admire themselves, and have they not
reason? Is not the object they see when they happen to look
that way worthy of a Brahmin's devoutest self-contempla-
tion? Can they help but fancy they see a kind of magnified
image of themselves influencing men, manners, and nations,
correcting the past, photographing the present, shaping the
future?—a figure as grand-looking and potential as that
stately old Etrurian king who sat through unnumbered centuries in his tomb in his habit as he lived, unassailable by
Time or any other enemy, so it seemed, till an unlucky spectator opened a crevice to look through, and while gazing in
great awe of soul on the spectacle, let in unconsciously a breath
of fresh air, just a single puff, but full of its own true natural

elements, and lo ! there was a shimmer, a shiver, the fall as of
a scarcely perceptible veil, and king and state and all were
gone, leaving only a handful of gray ashes on the pavement.

Some such speculations were in Cunliff's mind this bright
jocund May morning, as he thought of the pain he might
have to inflict, of his own feelings during the process, and of
the influences that must have been upon him the last few
years to make the meditated business possible to him. Such
men are often fond of analysing themselves, and can do it
with a certain skill and accuracy, though also with a tender
touch for sore or dangerous places ; and they take at times a
morbid pleasure in it, in believing in its virtue, and in calling it
' philosophy ;' which very probably it may be in the modern
acceptation of the word, seeing it never leads to anything,
never leads to action, except, indeed, to paralyse action when
ideas, sentiments, threaten to become dangerous to ease and
self-love. We are fast becoming a nation of Hamlets, with all
that is most valuable in the character of Hamlet—his faith,
imagination, and deep tenderness for humanity—omitted by
particular desire.

But if Cunliff, like all his kind, felt once in a way he had
a heart, and the presence of a worm at the core, it was quickly
forgotten in the stream of the world. He and men like him
have so profound a faith in themselves as to think that, in
spite of a vicious and purely self-solacing life, they are quite
as open as ever to receive the purest, and deepest, and most
abiding impressions from things worthy of creating them.

But he and they are alike deceived. They have after such
experience no more of the natural strength to flower and fruit
virtuously and nobly than trees have that are constantly trans-
planted ; which have no tap-root of conscience ; no spreading
network of moral fibre ; and so are easily displaced, or torn
up, by any strong wind of circumstance.

Cunliff, as he sat by Hirell, and luxuriated in the delight of
her society, thought only of his present state, and was well
satisfied with himself and state ; and did not therefore care to
dwell on how all had been with him during the many weeks of
his absence ; did not recall how Hirell's image had grown
each day more and more dim ; how soon he had practically
forgotten Wales, and the many deep and tender glimpses of
spiritual beauty he had there enjoyed with her, in the scenery
and among her people ; with what zest rank and fortune had

come upon him; how he and the world had again smiled
upon each other; and how at last he had come only to think
of Hirell as one whom in a moment of folly he had committed
himself to marry; thus leaving him quite prepared to reflect
on the beauty and salvation to be found in a prudent life and
wiser marriage, if they were still practicable.

But with Hirell again by his side all this is forgotten, so far
as his habits of mental introspection are concerned. The old
thirst for pleasure is on him once more; and happily, or unhappily, it is on the present occasion pleasure of the purest
kind—so he persuades himself—that he desires to drink
deeply of, for how much need may he not yet have of it, if—

To do Cunliff justice even while also thereby committing
him to a deeper condemnation, one of the most real things
about him, and at all times and under all circumstances, was
his ideal desire for, and earnest love of, excellence in woman.
That excellence, which is the soul's beauty, was in truth at
least as precious to him, ideally, as any mere physical beauty
could be.

In Hirell this abounds—he is with her, the world forgotten,
the moment is very sweet, again he worships in the spirit of a
devotee.

He thought of Mrs. Rhys—not to ask where she was, how
enduring the life-long martyrdom to which in all probability
he had condemned her, but to refresh himself with the recollection of the fact that it was because she had been to his imagination, more even than to his eyes, the most lovely woman
he had known, that he had cared for her, and only in heart
and in aim left her when Hirell came and raised and glorified
his standard.

Had society developed heart as well as head in John Cunliff, he would now need but to gaze on this latest object of
passion, receive her glance in return, and at once decide,
beyond possibility or desire of recall, to take so sweet and
precious a gift as God seemed now Himself to offer with out-
stretched hands.

Being as he is, what is he doing, or about to do? Perhaps
he could not answer the latter part of the question with absolute precision, if he would; but as to the former, he is continually reviewing his position, his promise to her, her future if
he rejects her, his past evil life, which he cannot but feel has
through some inscrutable process been chiefly changed, and

for ever changed, through contact with her and her family.
All this he considers, looks at in every possible way, and ends
the doubts that oppress him by plunging once more into conversation with his future wife—or victim.   Soon to go back to
his solitary ponderings.

Three things abide with him through all the secret chaos of
thought and feeling :

He had told her before his declaration of love that he had
meant to leave her : surely an important fact !

He had also beforehand pledged himself to Arnold to take a
course which for most weighty reasons decided his judgment
—his calm, cool, earnest judgment—against a marriage with
Hirell.

Certainly since then he had been weak, though that was
due to the unexpected strength of her beauty ; but not the less
was it clear that nothing of his former belief had changed, or
been met with reasons for change, while his public career, his
new rank, his large fortune, suggested a thousand additional
arguments for remaining *true to himself*, to those really un-
biassed convictions of his.

All this was intellectually very clear ; but when the question came of reducing all to practice, the way was not so easy
—when it was Hirell that had to be dealt with—Hirell with
her delicate, fresh beauty of person, which yet seemed not
itself to be so much an independent power as the mould
formed from within by the growth of one of the sweetest,
purest, and most religious of souls.   With all Cunliff's delight
of eye and heart in mere external beauty, he always found
himself forgetting, with Hirell, the eye, in thinking of what it
expressed—the lip, in sympathising with the thought that
issued from it—the form, in the wondrous grace of her individuality of character, as shown by her every gesture, as well
as by her most eloquent silences.

Hirell did not for some time notice the gathering gloom in
her lover's countenance, so instantaneously did it lighten at
her look, or smile, or word—so prompt was he to reply to her
innocent questionings, which were incessant, and dealt with
all sorts of matters.

' I have always wanted to know so many things—things
that people could not or would not tell me about.   Now, when
I ask you, everything becomes clear—so clear ! '

Thus spake Hirell during a certain pause, when she became

conscious how inquisitive she had been, and with a sort of sweet shame rising on her features that he was noticing it.

'Ah, Hirell, I wish to God somebody could and would do as much for me!' responded Cunliff, with a half laugh, that did not conceal some dark gulf of doubt or remorse below.

'Dear Mr. Rymer, out of your own true and good words are you convicted. "You wish to God," you said. Ah—if indeed you do that! But you do! You will!'

'We'll see. But I am not going to discuss religious matters with you to-day.'

The slow but certain shadow he saw overcasting Hirell's face warned him to speak further, so he promptly added—

'Not, I mean, till we have our great talk by-and-by. "Sufficient for the day is the *good* thereof," I would say, with an alteration of the phrase that I hope may be forgiven me.'

Hirell smiled again, but the smile was a thoughtful one; and Cunliff, to change the current of her thought, stopped the carriage and leaped out.

He went to a hedge, and cut with his knife a branch, and brought it back to Hirell, who saw one of the most lovely of natural garlands, a long, flexible branch of the wild white hawthorn, oozing, as it were, with blossom at every joint and pore, the first significant sign of the coming season that Hirell had yet seen.

'Do you know what I am going to do with this?' he asked, as he called out to the driver to push on, and then began paring away the thorns with extreme care, that none might be left, interjecting an exclamation now and then, as the thorns retaliated on their enemy by piercing his hands to the quick.

'N—o,' said Hirell, with a half-consciousness of a fib, and a more than half-consciousness that he must see that it was a fib, exhibiting itself on her rosy temples by way of anticipation.

'I am going to put the finest of earthly coronets on the most lovely of all women,' and so saying, he, with tender care and respect, wound the beautiful spray round the beautiful head, which shyly advanced a little to facilitate the operation, and when that was over, was held by him for just a few seconds, while he gazed at her—in the spirit of an artist, as he said; but even while he gazed, he saw bright tears begin to ooze, and deep emotions to flicker over the face; he felt an irresistible desire to kiss her—he did so—and then their eyes met—hers so full of love and boundless faith, that he could no longer bear it, but seemed struck to the heart as by a spasm, and turned so deadly pale that Hirell was alarmed, and somehow from that moment the day lost for her—what, she knew not—but something of which there was no return, then or thereafter.

'Hirell,' said he, 'I am curious to know how you—a woman—have so lost all curiosity?'

'I—I really don't understand,' and she certainly did look puzzled; then suddenly her face flushed, and flushed again as she thought to herself he meant why she did not ask about his name, his condition, vocation, &c.

Cunliff saw the flushes, and attributed them to the letter, which he was determined to have forth, or know something about.

'I mean that *I* could not exercise so much self-denial as to keep a letter in my pocket, unopened.'

'Oh, I know who it is from!' and as Hirell said this her cheek undoubtedly did colour a little, though instantly there followed a kind of tender severity of expression.

'Indeed!' said Cunliff, in a tone so significant, that Hirell found it impossible to pass it without notice.

'It is—it is,' she said, with an ingenuous smile breaking forth over her face, 'it is from my relative—Robert Chamberlayne.'

'Indeed!' again commented Cunliff, and the tone and look said plainly, 'Why did you not say so before?'

He saw Hirell grew more and more uncomfortable, and at last he drew from her the whole story of Robert Chamberlayne's devotion, offer, and rejection, which the present lover listened to with chequered feelings. He could not but admire Chamberlayne : could not but acknowledge there was something more than mere sunny pleasantness of character in the man who had so behaved; but for that very reason he was only the more annoyed that Hirell should have been so mysterious about the letter.

The incident suggested to him quite a new field of speculation, and apparently it was a very unpleasant prospect he thought he saw.

Hirell, meanwhile, had drawn forth the letter from her pocket, and began to read it; Cunliff turned a little away, but not so far but he could see, under his half-closed lids, her every movement, look, or thought, as he fancied.

As she went on with the perusal, her face became very serious for a time, then full of strange light; and as she ended there was a rapt look heavenward, such as Cunliff remembered in an old print of one of Bellini's saints.

'Read, dear friend, read! Oh, God is with us still. My father! My dear father! If now we could only find Hugh!'

Cunliff took the letter, and also read it with deep interest—for reasons perhaps little guessed by Hirell.

'MY DEAR HIRELL,—A curious thing has happened, which I think it best for you and your father to judge of, without my interference in the matter any farther than I am compelled.

'But I must first tell you that had the letter—of which the below is a copy—reached me only a day sooner, your father would have had it, for he has been here seeking poor Hugh. Unfortunately I could only say I had never seen him—never heard from him since his removal to London.

'The letter itself I have sent after your father to an address he gave me, for he could not even then give up the idea that Hugh would sooner or later find his way to me, but I have made a copy of it first for you, which I shall here transcribe:

'"SIR,—Mr. James Morgan, a partner in the late firm of Morgan & Garnet, of Bermondsey, in which you were, we understand, largely interested, and by whose failure you were a great sufferer, has, since the bankruptcy, and the receipt of his certificate, come into some little property; and in consequence is desirous—for special reasons, which he would rather explain personally than by letter—to make you, a countryman of his own, some compensation for the heavy loss you endured, preparatory to his paying the whole of the debts at some future day, should fortune favour him.

'" We may, from ourselves, hint that our client feels very deeply the deception practised in dividing profits, while trading at a loss, but is confident you would exonerate *him* if you knew the whole truth.

'" For the present, suffice it to say he has lodged five hundred pounds in our hands to be paid to you, as a part of your own,—morally, *not legally*, due to you, and it is accompanied only by this condition, that nothing be said to the other creditors, till such time as he himself may be prepared to deal with them.

' "He makes an exception in your case first, because he knows, he says, of certain facts which you are not acquainted with, which makes your position a peculiarly hard one, as regards the firm ; secondly, because he hears of your debts, and how cruelly the disappointment fell on you; and lastly, because the sum that alone he could spare would, if divided among all the creditors, produce but slight benefit or satisfaction at present, and lead possibly to unreasonable expectations and annoyance as regards the future. We are, sir, your obedient servants, ' " MAXWELL & DODD."

' Such, dear Hirell, was the letter which was sent first to the solicitors I before employed, and by them forwarded to me, when they were made aware of the contents; they thinking, I suppose, that I had managed so wonderfully well before, it would not do to employ anybody but me now—confound them !

' Of course I went to my lawyers and asked them whether the thing wasn't mere humbug.

' They replied that the five hundred pounds were ready to be paid to them at a moment's notice, on receiving Elias Morgan's authority, and left me to judge whether *that* was humbug.

' Greatly puzzled, I went then to Maxwell and Dodd, strongly inclined to ask them to let me see and handle the said five hundred.

' The upshot is, the money is there—so *they* say ; and that your father—so *they* say—can get it either personally, or by getting a Dolgarrog attorney to prepare and send up a proper document.

'So *they* say, mind—not I.

' If you ask me whether I believe they mean what they say, I reply, "Yes, but will be responsible to your father for nothing, after what happened before."

' But now, my dear Hirell, I want to speak to you. I have not been a very exacting relative, companion, or friend, I think, and if you think so too, I want to get some benefit from some such a character.

Your father, when I saw him, seemed to me under such a

strain as no man can long stand.　Either he or that must give way.　Hugh, too, whom I love as a brother, and in whom I have still full faith—what is to be done with him in your father's present poverty ?

'Well, then, I want you to accept from me, as an advance out of this new and most fortunate acquisition, a hundred pounds, to be used as you and Kezia shall see fit, saying nothing to your father till he has received and is quite satisfied about the five hundred pounds.

'Should he reject the proffer—as he certainly will, if he can find any loophole or crevice through which a moral doubt may pass, and take possession—then let me be Kezia's creditor only, if you are too proud, or too unkind, to give me this one single pleasure that might be given.

'I entreat you for your father's sake to accept this—and for Hugh's.

'I will not ask you to be sure I shall never seek *any kind of return*, for you are quite incapable of thinking so ill of me as the words might imply.

'Unluckily I am not likely to remain your and Kezia's creditor long enough even to believe in my own merits, so no more from your true friend,　　　'ROBERT CHAMBERLAYNE.'

Cunliff smiled once in reading this—a very curious smile, which Hirell saw; but before she could ponder on its meaning, it was gone—never to return, and she forgot it almost as soon.

No wonder he did give one brief smile at the ingenuity of Mr. Jarman in obeying the instructions he—Cunliff—had given; and which seemed to leave the business—however seemingly improbable in the abstract—quite beyond cavil practically.

But Chamberlayne again ! He saw tears in Hirell's eyes, and was foolish enough, while divining their meaning, to obtain confirmation from her own lips.

Yes, it was Chamberlayne's behaviour, she owned, that had drawn forth those sweet tears.　She confessed it, while calling on him to say whether he did not share with her in the general emotion she felt.

'Yes,' he said aloud, and then to himself he added—'D—n him !'

With a cry of surprise, Hirell now took a cheque from the envelope, that had not before been noticed.

'See, Mr. Rymer, see; he has sent the money without even saying so. That is so like him, is it not?'

'You will send it back of course?' said Cunliff.

'I think not,' said Hirell, thoughtfully; yet with a kind of decision in the tone that struck Cunliff as new—or at least new towards him.

'You must! you must indeed! I will do instead what he proposes.'

'Are you so rich?' asked Hirell, wistfully.

'Will you oblige me, Hirell?'

'Dear friend, do you not see, I could not so offend my own relative and old companion, neither could I take from you—'

Hirell stopped in quite a fit of distress, that she could not make her lover understand without words, how indelicate she would have felt it, to take money from him, to say nothing of her father's thoughts.

Cunliff was silent and moody, but her next words restored peace.

'I would not take it even from Robert Chamberlayne, but I know—that he knows—that—'

Cunliff finished the broken sentence by another kiss, as if to show her he understood and perfectly appreciated the distinction between a friend who was and a friend who was not a lover.

But the thought of Chamberlayne, and the tears and smiles and high glow of colour that his name, character, and letter had brought into Hirell's face, continued not merely to trouble and perplex Cunliff, but to give a certain hardening and crystallizing character to purposes that before swayed to and fro in a state of flux.

CHAPTER XXXVII.

WERGE CASTLE.

IT was a great effort that Cunliff had to make to keep up the flow of talk, and yet avoid the topics that were pressing constantly upon his mind with ever-increasing urgency. He concealed the efforts from Hirell, but only at the cost of feeling his own burden the more heavily.

The railway was reached, passed over, and again they were driving in a hired vehicle, which soon set them down within the distance of half an hour's walk of the place where Mr. Rymer was to meet his friend the steward.

They got out, the driver was told to stay till they returned, and Hirell gazed curiously about over the broad undulating scenery.

Her eyes fell upon a grand-looking old tower that seemed to issue from among the trees at some distance.

'Is that a church?' asked Hirell.

'That is the old keep of Werge Castle, the place to which we are bound. Come.'

'And to whom does it belong?'

'It did belong to one who lately died; who the heir is I am not prepared to say. You see the flagstaff on the keep?'

'Yes.'

'There would be a flag flying from its top if the owner were at home, so we are not likely to be prevented seeing the place.'

The winding road they were pursuing—a private one—was so constructed, so veiled in parts, so opened out in other parts, that at every turn some new view of the castle presented itself; and Hirell could not but exclaim with delight at the continued changes, and the growing developments of the picture as they went on.

They are now stopping to gaze at the first view they have been able to get of any considerable portion of the pile. They see water of some breadth, a bridge across the water, an entrance gateway consisting of two strong towers, and a portcullis gate between; the whole, with the keep in perfect preservation towering beyond, presenting the aspect of a noble mediæval fortress, standing within its own moat.

Presently that view is hidden, and a new one gradually comes into play. It is a long castellated front, some of the high arched windows showing the sunlight through their ruined state, but the whole wonderfully picturesque from the beauty of the architecture, and the ivy that clothes it.

Again, as they move on, the trees shut out the pile, till they come to a spot where the entire structure comes into the line of vision; but where the barbican towers, the embattled and ruinous front, and the keep over all, are softened and in part hidden by the modern front which here challenges attention; not only by its own stately beauty, but by the happy art with which the new architecture seems artistically to echo the old, without losing any of the characteristics required for modern ideas and habits.

But it is hardly these features which impress Hirell the most; she sees their magnificence, but it is, as it were, afar off; there is something nearer her heart in that which lies between her and the gracious stateliness of the new façade.

She and her lover stand on a little hillock, looking down into one of the most perfect gardens that poet or painter ever conceived as a part of a real work-a-day place of recreation for men and women—one where dreams must be realisable to be of any value. It was not the beauty of the lawns, the colours of the flowers, exquisitely as they were arranged, the individual forms of solitary trees remarkable for their elegance of foliage and rarity, the broad lake and its islands, but the consummate art with which you were led on from one kind of beauty to another; from the unpremeditated wildness, as it seemed, of the glades behind where the lovers stood, surrounded by magnificent forest-trees of almost preternatural height and size, and where the scenery around was almost too grand and primeval-looking to be called park—it was, we repeat, the art with which you were led on, step by step, the wildness decreasing, the culture increasing, till you rested at last on the parterres and lawns about the castle base; and felt that the refinement without must be intimately allied with the refinement within; the one a kind of repetition of the other—God's work in the flowers and gardens, becoming a standard and guide for man's work in the saloons and chambers; the same life inside and outside: life in luxury, redeemed by consummate taste and poetic refinement, that gave nameless charm to everything.

Hirell's joy became almost pain. She sat down on the grass, forgot Rymer, Elias, Hugh—forgot everything in gazing on the picture before her, which was too brilliant, too rich, too full of parts, and altogether too baffling in its witchery, for her to understand one bit of the details, or to guess even what skill, time, money, and devotion must have combined, before Werge Castle and the gardens, as she now saw them, became possible. Amid the dazzling glory of the whole, there were only three things she could fix on—a little pond full of water-lilies in bloom, a long bank of scarlet rhododendrons that formed the boundary in a particular direction at the edge of a precipitous hill, and an arcade of rose-trees.

'Come, Hirell, we have little time to spare,' said Cunliff,

who watched her unceasingly, and took now a malicious pleasure in breaking in upon her reverie.

She turned and looked at him for a moment, as if she did not see him through the golden haze that affected her mental eyesight; then became conscious, smiled, rose hastily, and again stopped, and said with a profound sigh—

'I do not think it would be good for me to stay long here.'

'Why?' demanded her lover.

He watched her while she stood considering her answer, as she nearly always did consider her answers to him; sometimes taking so long about it that he perceived the current of her thought was quite changed during her consideration. It was so now. He knew that if she had replied to him quickly, she would have spoken of the hard contrast between this place and Bod Elian. In those moments of silence, however, that thought and its sadness was swept away from Hirell's mind; and lifting her eyes to Rymer's, she said in a voice very sweet and tremulous—

' I had forgotten. What contrast can hurt me now?'

And the great dilating eyes, almost divine in their pure truthfulness, let Cunliff read in them how he had become much more to Hirell Morgan than home and kin, than the scenes so loved from infancy, than the little chapel so venerated, the much-reverenced ministers, the sweetest, most holy recollections of the past, than all these he was dearer—her eyes filled with tears of tender shame as they confessed how much, how very much dearer.

But they did confess it; and whether he felt, as many a better man might have felt, a sense of his own unworthiness; or as many a worse man might have felt, exalted and purified by the confession, he could not answer her in words or by looks, but could only lift and touch her hand with his lips, and hold it almost timidly as they walked on in silence.

They were passing down an incline between banks, and under an arch, from which they emerged into a bit of wild, rocky scenery; a very small but very perfect imitation of those little rifts or ravines one finds so often running down the slopes of Welsh mountains, water running along the bottom, the banks on each side falling back a little, but reaching across to each other by means of tree-branches, and long shoots of shrubby spray, the home generally of some of the most beautiful of ferns.

It was a fernery Hirell looked on, and there was something in it that affected her strangely. Her eyes gleamed.

'Ah!' she said, 'this *is* sweet. There is a place quite near our house just like it. I know where every one of these ferns can be found in it.'

Two or three minutes brought them to some outlying but connected portion of the castle. Cunliff knocked gently, the door opened, and a gentleman stood before them, who immediately and very warmly welcomed them.

Hirell could not but notice with a secret thrill of pleasure the deep, almost profound respect Mr. Jarman showed in look, tone, and gesture, to her lover, in spite of the familiar tone of equality that marked his words. It was the first opportunity she had enjoyed of estimating how the world looked upon the man who was so dear to her, and it was decisive.

Mr. Jarman led the way to a banqueting-room, where the walls were decorated with pictures of great size, which instantly attracted Hirell's gaze, though she scarcely dared to venture to ask questions about them. Her heart was already full, too full for her to preserve the equanimity she desired; and now her head began to turn dizzy with the novelty of all about her, for she had never seen anything of the kind before.

Refreshments were on the table ready. No servants appeared, for none were needed; and the viands were so various, so full of delicacies for the appetite, and all so strange, that she felt she should be able to eat nothing, and began to wish for a quiet meal after the fashion of Bod Elian.

But Cunliff understood in part her difficulty; and in tending her, conveyed in an unobtrusive manner to her sufficient knowledge of the things offered to enable her to enjoy herself and satisfy her hunger, for she soon began to discover she was hungry.

Mr. Jarman and Cunliff withdrew for a few minutes, to deal, as the latter said, with the business that had brought them together, and she was left alone.

The solitude was an immense relief. She rose, moved a few steps, as if to realise the feeling she was for the time once more free, then in a calmer mood began to study the pictures on the wall.

Cunliff returned alone, and said Mr. Jarman had given him *carte blanche* to take the young lady over the house without the annoyance of a companion.

'He seems a dear, charming person,' said Hirell wistfully, as if hoping Cunliff would speak of their relations; for she wanted now to know what she thought others must know of the goodness and nobleness of Mr. John Rymer.

Cunliff laughed, and said,

'Oh yes, he's very well, as men go;' but there was something that jarred upon Hirell; it seemed to show so little response to the good steward's own feelings towards his friend.

They now went together into the place; Cunliff directing her attention only to those things which a man of his own culture cared to speak of—the Roman mosaic let into the centre of the pavement of the entrance-hall, and which had been found on the estate; the rare armour, ranged along the walls of the inner saloon; the marquetry, the rare china, bronzes, and articles of *vertù* in the splendid suite of reception-rooms; the pictures in the chambers, some of which he, in the innate delicacy that still survived in him when in presence of womanly purity, took care that she should not see; the frescoes in the billiard-room, the ball-room, and the music saloon, or theatre; but Hirell, while listening with all possible attention, rapt at times in his words when some fine thought dropped from him unconsciously, found her eyes drawn in spite of herself to the more visible and material splendours of the place.

She was trying to realize the life of the mistress of such a place, the liveried servants, the reception of the guests, the dresses, the jewels, the beauty, the youth, the distinction of the bright and happy ones assembled in that exquisite drawing-room and alcove she had passed through, the government of so many people, the order required in so magnificent a home; and the result was that one bright vision after another kept pressing on through her eager and yearning brain, but leaving nothing clear or definite behind, except the sense of a lovely chaos.

One natural bit of pleasure, one quiet, pure bit of enjoyment stood out ever after to her as a remembrance of the eventful day. It was Cunliff's pause in the business of teaching, and explaining, and suggesting, when he discovered, to his amusement, that Hirell wanted him to show her how to play the game he said was so fascinating—billiards. He did so. They spent perhaps ten minutes there together, laughing at every unlucky plunge of the cue from Hirell's charming hands, till the cloth was cut, and the bit of sunny, pleasant life ended— for ever, as far as these two were concerned.

The picture gallery delayed them some time, not in order that Hirell might receive her first lesson in the glories of art, here gloriously represented, but that after they had walked through the entire length of the gallery she might return to look at a small sketch that Cunliff had drawn her attention to, with the remark,

'Look well at that. I will tell you some story about it by and-by.'

She had done so, and once gazing needed no other incentive, and he had some difficulty in drawing her away.

To this she now returned.

It was a woman's face, very lovely and tender, but its beauty did not strike Hirell as being more remarkable than that of many faces in the paintings she had already seen on the gallery walls. Like them it bore signs of rank and wealth. There was the rich circlet of jewels on the brow, the queenly carriage of the head, the gracious smile, yet though so like, how far different it was from all the others! Under the circlet the artist had drawn on the gentle young forehead a little line, strange to see there. Under the cheerful, commanding eyes, a deep shade, that should have surely been only under eyes that were more used to tears than these could be; and the long, raised lashes seemed almost to quiver, as if, in spite of the eyes' bright courage, they must presently fall in deathly weariness upon the pale cheek, and rest there never to rise more. The smiling lips had something very faint and ethereal about them, like those clouds that the sun in rising touches with rose-colour, and leaves fading; and the slender throat was so cunningly portrayed, that, stately and noble as was its bearing, a subtle touch, showing the tension of a vein or nerve, gave to it a tragic meaning—a patience most heroic —a pathetic weariness that seemed to show how in an instant, if it could have liberty from that stern, brave will that supported it, it would, like a broken flower, hang down its head and die.

' You said I was not curious some hours ago ; now you have quite cured me of that fault, so please tell me about this picture, of the lady whose face haunts me and saddens me.'

'Presently—presently—presently,' said Cunliff, with a half laugh, as he took her away to the outside of the mansion, thence across a croquet-ground, to the base of the great keep,

which now stood before them revealed in its full and grand
proportions, and in all the sad expression of a great age.

Many—many times had Hirell wondered to herself what
had become of the servants. The strange solitude, amid the
extreme freshness, and perfection of state, of all she had seen,
was very striking,—almost, at times, to Hirell, mournful—
without her exactly knowing why.

No servant even here was visible. Cunliff seemed to know
and be prepared for everything. He took a great key from
his pocket, opened a door high up, to which they ascended by
a sloping platform (probably removed in time of war or siege),
and taking Hirell's hand, led her in, reclosed the door, and
they were in complete darkness.

'Are you frightened?' asked Cunliff, after a moment's
pause, during which he felt her fingers tremble and her
breath come and go in short, stifled gasps.

'No,' she said simply.

He made no response, except to re-open the door; then he
lifted a trapdoor on the ground, and bade her look down.

She did so shudderingly, as he said—

' A pretty piece of business was done down there, long ago,
but by no ancestor of m— of my friend's master; the castle
then belonged to a boy, who lived here in the care of a relative, to whom he was ward, and by whom he was—so says
tradition—pitilessly murdered in the depths here below.'

'Oh, shut it down—cover it up! I cannot bear to be near
such places. Dear Mr. Rymer, this tower is horrible to me.
Let us go!'

'Presently, Hirell. But I want you to see the prospect
from the top. Strangers come here merely to see it. Mr.
Jarman would never forgive our want of taste if—come.'

He took her hand, and led her by a winding stair, up and
up, story above story, to the top, where in a moment Hirell
felt repaid for all.

It was a scene to make an Englishman's heart exult in
the beauty and serenity of his country—the serenity meaning
so much of peace, law, freedom, culture, that the beauty itself
seemed almost to flow from them, rather than from the
natural features of the landscape.

Hirell gazed for some time without speaking, on woods and
rising meadows, and leas and lanes, all blooming and lustrous
in the sunshine of May.

'How wonderful,' she said soon, 'that I should see it just at this most perfect time of all the year!'

Then she began in a low voice repeating some lines of poetry in her own language, her eyes full of tender joy and admiration as they still looked far over the large, fair prospect, her hand under his, on the little wall, trembling.

'What a pity I can't understand that!' said Cunliff.

'Oh, I can say it in English too,' answered Hirell, a little proud for once of her learning: and then, with a deeper glow on her cheek, she repeated to him a translation of some lines from Davydd ab Gwilym's poem to the summer—

> Thou Summer! father of delight,
>   With thy dense spray and thickets deep;
> Gemmed monarch, with thy rapt'rous light
>   Rousing thy subject glens from sleep;
> Proud has thy march of triumph been,
> Thou prophet prince of forest green!
> Artificer of wood and tree,
>   Thou painter of unrivalled skill,
> Who ever scattered gems like thee,
>   And gorgeous webs on park and hill,
> Till vale and hill, with radiant dyes,
> Become another paradise!

For some minutes longer the hands on the little wall remained clasped in silence, very happy silence to Hirell.

'How many counties do you think can be seen from here?' asked Cunliff.

'I cannot guess; are there—four!' said Hirell.

'Eleven.'

'And those mountains—'

'Well, yes;—true Welshwoman to fasten on them first! they are the Berwyn mountains.'

Hirell gazed on them as if she felt her soul had wings to fly to them, and was poising itself to start, when her lover called her attention again.

'Do you see that wood far away on the slope of a great hill?'

'Yes.'

'Do you see to the right of it—still at a great distance—the gleam of water?'

'Yes.'

'Turn still farther to the right. Do you now see the church spire and village—they are very faint?'

'Oh, but I see them.'

'Now finally turn in this direction, and you will have looked east, west, north and south; and you see the viaduct, with its long series of arches, over which a railway passes?'

'Yes: that is very plain.'

'Within those limits, then, behold the possessions of the master of this place!'

'What all those villages?—and farms?—and innumerable fields—and woods—and—'

'All!'

'And is he happy?'

There was a pause—a deep silence—then Cunliff said—

'I cannot answer that. He may be too great a fool to benefit by all that fortune has given or offers.'

'Is he married?'

'I—I believe not.'

'Well, that is a pity. I cannot fancy any one living single in a place like this. Can you? I should feel if I were the single gentleman among a crowd of servants in all this empty and roomy splendour, that fortune was laughing at me.'

'You never heard of the irony of fortune, I suppose?'

'No: what does it mean?'

Cunliff did not speak for a few seconds, and then seemed to have forgotten the question.

'The wind blows cold here, so we must go down, else I had intended—'

He stopped, took her hand to guide her down the winding staircase, and in doing so their looks met.

All the way down those seemingly interminable steps, did Hirell ponder over that look, but ponder vainly.

They went back, but entered at another door; and to Hirell's astonishment they stood in a Gothic chapel; small, but of the most elegant proportions, and of the most delicately beautiful architecture.

Hirell stood as one ravished, gazing at the altar end, where above the altar-stone was the one window of the place, of stained glass, now literally blazing and burning with molten colour, and sparkling gem-like effects, through the vividness of the sun outside.

'Come, Hirell,' said Cunliff, with grave voice and pre-occupied air, no longer thinking of her thoughts.

'Oh, but is it not good to be here? Let me stay here while you—you tell me what you said you would.'

'The place strikes chill; you will feel it soon.'

'Oh no—no! See!' and she sat herself down on a step, that formed a kind of daïs for the altar. 'It is so pleasant. Let me be here. You do not, cannot think how happy I was to see what place you had brought me to last of all—last of all!'

She spoke with mournful sweetness, then suddenly remembering the very different interpretation Mr. Rymer might give to her words, rose hastily, and with a hot blush on her cheek, which she mainly strove to master, said—

' Perhaps it will be better to—'

'No; since you wish it, let it be so.'

He made her sit down again, and sat by her side.

' You liked that picture—I mean the face of the lady ?'

'Ah, yes, surely ; it has a history ?'

'Did you ever hear the story of the Lady of Burleigh ?'

'No !'

' Not in Tennyson ? '

'Who is Tennyson ?'

Cunliff looked at her a moment, as if in astonishment, but immediately glossed over the incident, and said,

'Well that is a kind of impromptu painting, made from recollection only, of the lady in question by another lady who knew her, admired her, loved her, and lamented her—so at least I was told when a boy, and that is all I know about the picture. I cannot from my own, or any other trustworthy knowledge, even say whether it does or does not truly represent, or was intended to represent the Lady of Burleigh. But the face is *the* face to me—and ever will be—that I have believed in. I think you will say so too when you hear the story.'

He was holding her hand as he began to speak ; his eyes fixed now on her eyes, just for one single moment, then turning away, with a kind of affectation of carefulness, to remember accurately the facts he had to recount.

'A young painter—an artist, as supposed—came to a certain village, and lodged in a certain house, where the daughter was a maiden of surpassing beauty. I often wonder, Hirell, whether or no surpassing yours.'

'That I am sure is no part of the story,' said Hirell

'Is it not ? I thought—Hirell, you confuse me when you look at me as if you saw right into my very soul.'

' Forgive me if—'

'Pooh, darling; I do but jest, though God knows I have little of mirth-material in me just now. Where was I?'

'At the lady's beauty—'

'No, Hirell, at yours—if truth *is* above the world, as you Welsh people are always dinning into one. Hearken:

'The painter was a quiet, unobtrusive, gentlemanly sort of person, and the affair took the usual course, and there was another pair of fools in the world.'

'Ah, what do you deserve, to speak so to me?' asked Hirell

'Give me, then, that which I deserve. What is it? A kiss? Come, life is full of surprises. What if it were the last you were ever to give me?'

'Mr. Rymer!'

'Let us only imagine it the last for the moment. We might be killed by lightning, you know, like the lovers of which our story book tells us. Come, one kiss; as if it were to be the last.'

There was such a mingling of the passionate, the tender, the stern, and the pathetic in his look and words, that Hirell, bewildered, knew not for the moment what to do.

'I will be bribed,' said he, ' or I tell no story.'

The kiss was given by a trembling lip, cold as ice—and a lip full of fire and determined purpose.

Hirell drew off a little from him, hardly knowing that she did so; but he noticed it, and went on at once with his story, with new vivacity.

'The young lady accepted the artist's love, of course, even while he told her he had little of the world's goods. They were married; he took her away to go to their own future home. As they went, he had a fancy to show her one of the grand mansions of the country—the seat of an English noble. They went, just as we have gone to-day, only I am no English noble.'

'God forbid!' ejaculated Hirell—and so softly, that she must have fancied she spoke only to herself—but he heard.

'He took her through the gardens—showed her the environing woods—the armorial bearings on the gate—took her through the stately reception-rooms and galleries—but—'

'But what?' said Hirell, in a tone that seemed to be intended to be playful, but was obviously under some inexplicable constraint.

'The young wife, the beautiful maiden, could see none of these things, for something else that she saw.'

Again he stopped, as if wilfully.

'And that was?' suggested Hirell, softly.

'That her painter-husband was lost to her in a single moment—as by the glance of her eye—which saw forms bending humbly on every side before him; and when she turned in trembling wonder and affright to ask what all this meant, he simply said to her—

' " All this is thine!" '

'Oh how sweet! How beautiful!'

'Very. But beauty is apt to be short-lived—even this beauty was so. The lady was much shaken by the news. No wonder. The life she had lived, and the life she was to live, were divided by an awful gulf. Do you not think so?'

'Yes,' said Hirell, sadly. 'Poor lady!'

'What would you have done, Hirell?'

'Asked my husband to let me trust everything to his love and to God, and asked both to forgive me when I should fail.'

'He did not wait for her to ask.'

'Ah, no. One like him would not!'

'He cheered her, quieted her, brought peace back into her soul. She accepted her duties gallantly, fulfilled them charmingly, bore him children, won everybody's love, and then—'

His voice ceased. The mournfulness of the tone of his last words remained like an echo in Hirell's heart, and she too was silent.

She could not tell what passed during the next few minutes, as she looked around, as she thought of the behaviour and looks of the man by her side, as she thought of herself, and the resemblance—could it be accidental?—between the story just told and her own story, so far as she knew of it, even to the journey and to such a place as this.

A little thrill or shiver ran through her, and she said in a piteous voice,

'I am cold!' and was about to rise. But Cunliff said to her,

'Do you not wish to hear the end?'

Strange to say, Hirell's absorbing interest in the story of the Lady of Burleigh could not prevent her forgetting all about it during those few eventful moments which passed after Cunliff had suspended his narrative. But now brought back to it, she said simply—

'If you please!'

'Borne down by her secret sense of her unfitness, she sickened, and died within a very few years—three or four, I believe—in spite of all that the tenderest love could do for her. That is the story of the picture.'

'And of nothing more?' demanded Hirell, a change passing over her face.

'What more can there be?'

'I ask you that.'

Again there was the little shiver; and then the eyes shut for a moment, then again opened and dilated as she went on, and said—

'Are you John Rymer—and such as I have thought you?'

'I was John Rymer Cunliff, a plain English gentleman; I am Sir John Cunliff, and this place is *mine!* and all I have shown you.'

Did he purposely use words that Hirell could not but instantly contrast with those other words, 'All this is *thine*' —or was it accidental? Whatever it was, it did its work.

'Hirell,' he began, 'I am here to-day with you to tell you the truth that it concerns us both to know. Listen to me, I entreat. I have done wrong. Shall I remedy that by more wrong? I have led an evil, indulgent life; that you have cured for me. Never forget that your God, whether He be my God or no, will reward you—He must. My rank, my tastes, my education, my duties, all now impel me to a public career. What that involves for my wife, in all sorts of ways—'

'We shall be late, Mr. Rymer,' said Hirell, rising hurriedly.

'Pardon me, I will but detain you for a very brief space. In this place—look round you—nay look! and believe that I feel something at least of the religious awe you feel—here then, in the eye and ear of God, I swear to you that I love you dearly, that in my soul I believe I never can cease to love you, and that I would take you, if you were a beggar in the street—if being what you are, you could also be that which—'

'Yes, yes. I understand. Spare me—now—if—'

She caught his hand convulsively, and he, mistaking the cause—for she was, she thought, about to swoon and fall, cried out passionately, 'Darling!'

But the word, the tone, and the look revived her in time; and she, without heat, almost for the moment without agitation, removed his hands from her, and said in a kind of hollow whisper,

'We shall be late! Think how far we have to go. We shall be late. Oh!'

Nature could bear no more. She sat down again to avert the danger of his touch or a fall, and bending herself all of a heap, gave way to all the frenzies and agony of her young soul.

'Hirell, I am pledged to marry you. If I cannot redeem the pledge itself, you must let me do the best I can. I shall settle on you an independent fortune.'

A cry, followed by a light, hysteric laugh, rang through the chapel, but was stopped in a minute or so; and the bending form was again still as death.

'Hirell, I do not expect you to agree with me to-day. I only want you to listen. Your father! Think of his poverty. Hugh—think of his genius, difficulties, and future career. Think of yourself—mistress of yourself—free to move as you please—live as you please—where you please. Come, dearest, do not believe the day is to set in eternal gloom because the clouds are heavy for a little while. What am I? A man burdened with many follies, and, I fear, some vices. Can we not still be friends? Not just now;—but when the first bitterness shall have passed off? Consider! How much of all that our marriage might have given you might yet be yours—ah, how much you need still!'

He stopped—Sir John Cunliff stopped, as if aware of the abyss on the very edge of which he stood, and looked down.

Hirell saw that abyss too—he was sure of it.

But she, like himself, was silent! And it is possible he drew auguries, evil as they were vague, of a possible future from the silence.

At last she lifted her head, and in doing so Cunliff saw the ruin he had wrought already only too plainly there visible. And before he could speak to assuage the anguish he had created, he saw Hirell's face confronting his own, fearless, proud, as he had never before seen her; her eyes searching through his with a kind of scornful light that seemed to burn them; then in deep silence she rose, her strength apparently recovered, and was about to leave the place alone.

'Hirell!' and Cunliff laid his hand upon her arm.

'Sir!' she said, turning coldly, while every limb shook as with ague.

'You shall not leave me thus—by Heaven you shall not!'

'What—what do you now wish?' she said in great fear, and every word spoken with difficulty, as though her nervous system was suddenly paralysed.

'That you try to think over in a calm and kindly spirit, what I have said to you.'

'I will!'

'Thanks. I will then say no more to you now; we must both try to think no more now, or how shall we get over the journey back?'

'I shall go alone.'

'Not while I live to prevent you. Hirell, this is not the way to deal with me. I love you and honour you, wish to do all that man can do to extricate us both from a false position: but if you begin to contend—to fight—to—'

'No—no—no. You will take me home, and by the time?'

'I will, on my soul.'

'And—and—let me—let me, do—yes—what you said—try to forget all this—till we—I—reach home!'

'I will. And, if you wish it, will ride outside in both the vehicles, so that you shall not again be alone with me. Oh, Hirell! can you not trust me?'

'Yes.'

The journey was, in effect, spent throughont in the deepest silence. Cunliff forgot his offer to ride outside, and Hirell's instinct warned her to shun every kind of antagonism. Cunliff spoke only when a favourable opportunity offered, and Hirell invariably replied to him either by a single word, or 'yes' or 'no,' or by a slight bend of the head. She had neither heart nor inclination to play a part—to seem to throw off the humiliation put upon her; all she desired was to draw herself shrinkingly into the corner as far as possible from her companion, and to be allowed to keep silent, so that when she wept he might not know of it, nor she be again made to weep by him when the tears were awhile driven back upon their source.

He often saw her lips moving, and tortured himself by fancies of what the words might be.

They were for the most part little other than—

'Father! Father! Kezia! Kezia! when shall I reach you? When?—when?'

Bod Elian was reached at last.

She let him ascend the hill with her, though her whole frame quivered at the thought of her father seeing him.

But she again promised him to think over all he had said, and then, as if moved by some strong revulsion of feeling that she could not control, she tried to say a few kindly parting words, then broke down, when Cunliff said, as his last words—

'When all this is over, I shall again see you to ask and earn your forgiveness;' but when he made as he would kiss her, she put him aside, and said—

'Good-night!' and disappeared in the darkness.

Was it fancy that made him think he heard a cry that curdled his blood, only a minute or two afterwards? It was low, penetrating, but full of such concentrated essence of all mortal suffering—at least, so his conscience received it—that it rang in his ears, in his heart, in his brain, all the way to the hotel, and through the live-long night, which for him passed without a moment of sleep.

CHAPTER XXXVIII.

HIRELL'S RETURN.

Elias had indeed returned in an anxious and despairing state of mind. The efforts which the Reverend Ephraim Jones and himself had made to discover Hugh, had been as unavailing as they had been injurious to his home affairs and to his purse. To continue the search longer would have been simply ruinous to him. He had parted from the minister with a despair on his face so settled and deep, that Ephraim Jones had considered it his duty to rebuke him; but broke down ignominiously in the attempt, at the mildness with which Elias received his lecture. The accounts he heard of Hugh's manner of living from the people to whom he owed money, and therefore probably exaggerated accounts, were such as to fill one so inexperienced in town life, and so austere in his own, with dismay and deep anger.

On reaching Bod Elian, and hearing from Kezia of Hirell's absence, he sat like one overtaken by a storm, and not knowing which way to turn for shelter. He did not reproach Kezia in words, but looked at her in a manner that filled her heart with remorse and foreboding.

These two sat waiting for Hirell through the long hours of the May afternoon, never speaking to each other, but going in

turn to the door to look for her.   Elias made no attempt to
work, his whole soul was in expectancy ; he knew he could
not work ; he would not pretend ; he knew, too, perhaps, how
great a punishment it was to Kezia to see him thus doing
nothing, but sitting, apparently unconscious of his great
fatigue, grimly waiting.

Kezia was the first to hear the footsteps coming, and
watched Elias growing gradually conscious of them too.
They were the footsteps of a single person, and were familiar
to them.

Elias rises and goes to the door, opens it, and sees his
daughter's form alone at the door, while another form is dimly
revealed in the moonlight retreating along the wall.

' Hirell Morgan,' he says to her, ' is this how you employ
your time while I am away ? '

She stands still without attempting to enter, and he hears
her sigh heavily.

' It is coming back to such a home, no doubt,' thinks Elias.
Then he says aloud and very sternly—

' So the man avoids me, Hirell ? '

' No, father,' answers she in a languid, faint voice, ' he
would have seen you and spoken to you if he had heard you
had come back ; but I—I saw no good in such a meeting.'

He pauses a minute, perplexed and troubled greatly at the
strangeness of her voice, then moves back as a sign to her to
come in.

She walks slowly across the kitchen, bringing with her
fresh odours of the spring evening, and stands by the fire
holding her hand towards it and shivering.   The two look at
her in some bewilderment at seeing her show no fear of her
father's anger, and they see that her face is very pale, her
eyes look large, bright, and very sadly thoughtful.

Suddenly while they are looking at her she turns to her
father.

' Father, any news of Hugh ? '

' None, Hirell,' returned Elias, ' it seems that *he* is lost
to us.'

' No, father, I think not,' says Hirell ; then looking down
deeper and deeper into the fire she says—' Do you remember
my once asking you to let me go away from home, father ?
Do you remember how much we always wished—poor Hugh
and I—to see the world, to see what it was like, and what life

was like away from here? I have not been very many miles to-day, father; but—but—'

She sobbed out, and Elias approached her in alarm.

'Hirell!'

'But my journey has been too much for me; I—I am weary; I want to see and hear no more of anything—of any one away from here. Yes, and to forget what I have seen.'

'Hirell,' said Elias, 'I desire to hear where you have spent this day, and how you have spent it.'

'Mr. Rymer came here this morning, the gentleman we have known as Mr. Rymer,' answered Hirell, speaking in a quiet but strained voice, 'Kezia has told you what he wanted—have you not done so, Kezia? I went with him, thinking that when I came back I should tell you the time for our marriage was arranged, and that if father returned with good news of Hugh, we should all be very joyful together.'

Elias looked at her searchingly; Hirell returned his look with steady eyes.

'We looked over a beautiful estate,' said Hirell, 'we talked a great deal of the owner, Mr. Rymer showed me how great a man he must be, and then how much responsibility and care would fall to the wife of such a man, and how no one but a lady born and bred should aspire to such an honour. He made me to agree with him, and then at last it came out that Rymer himself was the great man—owner of the place—that he is Sir John Cunliff.'

Kezia could scarcely take in so much romance as this all at once. She sat gazing in fixed astonishment at Hirell. Elias went to his daughter, and took her hand.

'Go on, Hirell, tell me all,' he said.

'He convinced me of the truth of what he said. Oh, yes, he convinced me!' answered Hirell.

'Why has he chosen so strange and unstraightforward a plan for doing this?'

They still looked into each other's eyes. At last Hirell's filled and overflowed, and her lips quivered.

'My father,' said she, 'does this matter to us, who are parted from him for ever? Is it not between him and his God?'

'Have we done with him for ever, Hirell?'

'When I say my prayers to-night, father, I shall try to say "I have done with this man," with the same calmness and resignation with which good Christians at their death-bed say, " I have done with life," though mine—mine—mine are the harder words, and in saying them I think I say the others too.'

'Kezia, she is faint,' said Elias, 'help her to her room. I will see you, my child, before I go to bed myself.'

They went out together; and Elias sat himself down alone, and life was more bitter and mysterious to him than ever.

CHAPTER XXXIX.

GONE.

THE next evening Sir John Cunliff received the following letter :—

'SIR,—You desired me to think over our interview calmly before answering you. Not calmly, but in as peaceful and forgiving a spirit as after long prayer God gives me, I have thought of your actions on this dreadful day just past; and now, in the night—not calmly as you requested—but not I trust with unchristian passion—I sit down to write to you. I wish first to inform you that I have not made known to my father or any one the whole truth of this day. I feel no need to do so—I feel no need of being protected from you more than you have protected me by showing me that which you really are; so believe me, sir, and be thankful for it, this poor, labouring household of God's elect, of which I am so unworthy a member, shall never know how cruelly, how treacherously its peace and honour have been struck at through me. Thank God, they sleep, and I, only I am awake, bearing my sorrow by myself as best I may.

'My answer, sir, is only this—I will never of my own will see you more in this world. I need to take no oath, to bind myself by no vow; the resolve that comes from humble prayer and conquered passion is sufficient in God's eyes. Oh! let it be in yours, and do not try me. Farewell, Mr. Rymer, I use the name I loved once more. May God forgive and bless you, and guide you to His kingdom, where, if we meet, humble will be my place compared to yours. Your servant,
　　　　　　　　　　　　　　'HIRELL MORGAN.'

On the day after he had received the letter, Cunliff was at Capel Illtyd. Here he heard news which kept him from continuing his journey to Bod Elian.

Hirell was away from home.

Her father had taken her away, no one knew whither.

Hugh had not been heard of. Special prayer had been offered at the chapel for Elias.

Cunliff in a few hours was once more at Llansaintfraid, and there took his place in the night train for London.

CHAPTER XL.

NEWS OF THE PRODIGAL.

HIRELL had been absent some days, and Elias back at Bod Elian, when he received the following letter from the Reverend Ephraim Jones :—

'DEAR FRIEND,—The prodigal is found. Fain would he arise and go to you, who are to him as his earthly father, but that severe sickness holds him to his bed, from whence it is doubtful whether he will ever arise. The physician and death are in combat for his body, and myself and Satan for his soul. The manner in which I discovered him you shall hear of another time. His spirit is full of despair; his bones are almost through his skin. This night will perhaps decide his fate. Wait till you hear again, to-morrow. Yours in commiseration, 'EPHRAIM JONES.'

Elias rose up from the reading dry-eyed and silent. He went out to his work, but found no comfort in it. The emerald fields—the flowery coppices of May—the skylark letting down from the impenetrable blue distance a faint pathway of song that seemed thronged, like Jacob's ladder, with heavenly company—the rich-voiced thrush, whose breast has become dyed as with the rich flickering shade and sunshine that plays over it through the dancing leaves of her home tree —the tiny, thrilling linnet—all seem to Elias this morning to be singing the songs of Hugh. He strides through the furrows, his hard hands to the plough, and as he reaches a corner where a cluster of young fruit-trees drop their blossoms on to the brown mould, his eyes rest upon a long, broken bough that

lies across his path. Its bright leaves and fresh white blossoms
are drooping and dying. He turns his plough sharply, as if
his eyes had found in the sight an emblem of Hugh's fate.

The minister's words, ' the prodigal is found,' are constantly
before him. Found! and what has Elias to welcome him
with ?—neither rich garments to put on him, nor fatted calf to
kill. He must do his meanest labourers' work to win him
common bread. Prodigal! of what has he been prodigal?
Did not Elias send him portionless from his father's house?
In his toilsome progress he again comes to the bough with its
withering blossoms, and the word ' broken—broken ' issues
from his stern, compressed lips.

' I knew he was less strong than Hirell, yet I sent him out,
and kept my own—and kept my own.'

All day he toiled in the sun, and in the evening was somewhat comforted to look back on the stony field, and see that
he had done the work of two men. The birds were singing
as he came home, but Elias found nothing but sadness in their
burden. He thought of how Hugh whistled or sang as he
came home at his side, and how their singing and all the
sounds of the evening used to seem to become a part of his
song.

Would he never walk by him again across these fields in
the sunset, lifting his rich, sweet voice, which the echoes sent
back, as if proud to repeat such music? The sunset was as
beautiful as on those last-year summer evenings, when the
brothers returned together from their labour. There was a
silent cry in the heart of Elias, to which the birds seemed to
give voice, till he forgot it was from himself, and could almost
fancy they really sang them to him reproachfully as he went
along; instead of which, it was his heart that gave words to
their voices, which seemed to cry—' Elias, Elias, what hast
thou done with him ? Where is the sweet musician ? '

In the evening, several times his head was turned sharply
towards the door, at slight noises. If Hugh were to die,
could the moment of his death be to Elias as all other moments ?—would he not be allowed to know it by any sign or
warning ?

In the night, when he was asleep, his rest was troubled by
sounds of music, piercingly sweet. He dreamed he saw his
father beside his bed, and that he asked him what they were,
and he answered him with a stern voice—' Turn to your sleep,

Elias; the burden that I left you is removed. The music you now hear is your brother playing in God's choir.'

Elias went out early to his ploughing, feeling very lonely in the glory of sunrise, as he thought he might be the only one of his father's house left for it to shine upon. He came in his laborious turns upon the broken bough, and found all its blossoms withered.

A few minutes before the letters arrived, he stood in the little post-office garden, looking down the winding road. When he saw the postman's white horse galloping across the bridge, he gazed at him as if he expected to see some sign about him of the kind of news he brought. He came close; one of his bags whirled through the air and fell in the midst of the cabbage-bed in the post-office garden, and the white horse dashed on.

Some miners were waiting for their letters, and Elias watched them as the bag was sorted—almost passionately envious of those who received what they had come for, and full of pity for such as turned away empty-handed.

'Elias Morgan!' called the postmaster.

Elias took the packet held out to him, and turning quickly from all inquisitive looks, went homeward with his prize.

It was from the minister, and these were the contents, which Elias, as usual, read aloud to Kezia :—

'DEAR FRIEND,—My hearty supplications, and the prayers which I know you have offered up for him at Bod Elian, have prevailed with the Lord, who has given your brother back into my hands out of the valley of the shadow of death. He is not yet safe; he lies, as it were, upon the slippery bank; but as strongly as one mortal may hold another, will I hold him for you, Elias. I will now tell you how it came to pass that I was permitted thus to find and succour him even at the eleventh hour. My mission for the last week has been to preach in the place of a well-meaning, but feeble brother, at ——Street, a crowded, poor, and sinful neighbourhood, as doubtless you may have heard. Large bills, certifying my intent and the subjects of my discourse, had been displayed for some days previous to my arrival in the locality; and I make no doubt but that the unfortunate lad saw my name on them, and was moved, not by its associations with the Master I serve, but by its carnal associations with home and kindred,

to enter into the little tabernable, that he might see me and
hear my voice.   Probably he intended to depart as he came in,
unnoticed by me ; but even as the presence of the nightingale
is made known by her song, so was his betrayed to me by the
peculiar power given him by the only Giver of those gifts of
the spirit.

'The day of our meeting was Saturday, the busiest in the
week with the tradesmen of that tinsel and gingerbread
booth of vanity fair ; and, owing to this accident, it transpired
that the young organist, a shoemaker's apprentice, was not at
the chapel.   When, therefore, having grown warm with my
discourse, and wishing to take rest, I called for a hymn, no
response was made to me, till presently one of the congregation whispered to me the state of the case, whereat I was
vexed in spirit, for melody is as healthful to the soul as dew
to your fields.   "Brethren," said I, "is there not amongst
you one whose hands have cunning to do our missing brother's
duty ?   Can no one play upon this instrument ?"

'So long a silence ensued, that I was about to tell them to
sing without accompaniment, when a slight movement took
place among those near to the door, and in a few moments,
without seeing the person who had just seated himself before
it, the sounds of the organ rose, and rolled with a vast power
and most melting sweetness ; and over our heads there began,
as it were, a mighty converse—in which human and divine
voices seemed mingled.   It was to me as if a band of angels
had come rushing down to meet and to embrace the ascending but still chained souls; and that the spirits of earth and
the spirits of Heaven did for the time hold passionate communion with each other, uttering piercing complaint, and
profound and tender comfort—deep-voiced despair, and clear,
thrilling whispers of hope—which seemed to be all rending
the air at once, in a harmony so grand, so tumultuous, I could
but think thus at the Judgment-Day men and spirits shall
meet.

'The music ceased, and I bethought me of the master-hand
to whom we were indebted for moments of such exalted
emotion.

' "We thank thee, brother," I said, looking at the curtains
that concealed the lower part of the organ ; and not unwilling
to take advantage of the incident, according to my wont, to
stimulate the attention and keep alive the curiosity of the very

rough congregation that these special services call together. "Who art thou? For fain would I know the name and calling of one so gifted by the Lord."

'Without answer, without a look towards me, a form rose up and went down the steps leading from the organ. The form so slim and slight, and now so thin; the motion of the arm, the pale downcast face—Elias, I knew it—I knew him. I understood the power of the music—it was that lost, misguided youth, thy brother. I saw him hastening towards the chapel door, and was moved to call out his name in a loud voice. He only hastened the more—I was determined he should not escape me.

'"Brethren," I said, "I have much to say to you. My evening's mission is not fulfilled, but stopped midway by another. What man of you having an hundred sheep, if he lose one of them doth not leave the ninety and nine in the wilderness, and go after that which is lost until he find it? Such a one I go to seek. Brother Robert will pray with you the while. I may return presently."

'I left the chapel, and went in search. I was in time to see his form again, before he turned the street corner, and hastened after him. Before I reached within a few yards of him he had heard my hurrying and somewhat heavy footstep and turned. Seeing me, he fled; but speed was given me to bear him yet in sight, which I did for the length of several small streets. At last I saw him stop and enter a house, and then saw him no more, and neither could I remember with any certainty when I came to the spot which house in the row it was that he had gone into. I therefore took note of the name and position of the buildings, went back to the chapel, and brought our meeting to a more decent conclusion.

'Early in the morning I went again to the place to seek him. I enquired at three houses, without discovering that any such person as I described lodged there. At a fourth I obtained tidings of the wanderer, and sad tidings, too, friend Elias. A woman, as dark of aspect and almost as loud-voiced as a thunder-cloud, began to rail at him as soon as I pronounced his name. "Lodge here?" quoth she; "a wheedling young swindler! I reckon he lodges at the bottom of the Thames by this time—anything with some folks to cheat honest, hard-working people of their due." She then bade me come up to her young lodger's room, and witness for myself

whether it was not left by one who was bidding farewell to
life as well as to it. And truly the sight of letters in your
handwriting, my friend, in small pieces on the floor, and sheets
of written music torn as by a passionate hand that wildly
seeks to silence life itself, as it silences these evidences of life—
gave me the gloomiest forebodings.

' I picked up some of the scraps of paper, thinking to find a
clue to his trouble, but was as prompt to put them down
again as if they had been covered with plague-spots. My
very hands felt blistered. My cheeks grew hot. Then my
heart was moved within me to a transport of indignation
against the iniquity of our time and state, that allows iniquity
to sow broadcast its seed through our streets and waysides,
so that our young and undefiled country children, when they
come up full of hope and belief of great things in store
for them—pure, simple-hearted, unsuspicious children—find
harlotry in silks and satins, vice no longer shame-faced but
triumphant, and systematically fed by a thousand different
agencies. What wonder then if they cannot see and understand the hideous truth beneath, till it is too late to profit by
the knowledge ? Oh for the days of our puritan forefathers !
But they will yet come again ; and then, God willing, we will
make one clean sweep of the whole, and breathe once more
the pure air of an uncorrupted dwelling—this dear old England,
which has been and shall again be the abode and dowry of
the saints. In God's time ! Yea, in God's own time !

' I made the woman promise to send me word instantly by
a private messenger, should her lodger return. But I could
not sleep, Elias, that night, for thinking of the lad and thee ;
and so I got up and walked the streets for some hours, obeying first this thought, then that, but had to return empty-
handed to my poor, lonely, bereaved wife ; who by this time
had, I verily believe, transferred all the hidden away love of
her heart for the child we lost to thy brother, and lamented
my every failure as if Hugh were indeed our son. "Woman,"
I said to her once, "am I this lad's keeper ? " for she began
almost to persuade me the guilt and misery lay all at my door,
that I had not more and better looked after him.

' Next day I went again to the lodging ; the same the day
after ; and yet again on the third day, when I was later than
I had intended, and so evening had come. As I approached I
heard the high-pitched voice of the woman sounding angrily

from above; a word or two reached me, and they seemed sweeter than the songs of angels. I ascended the stairs as quickly and as lightly as my heaviness of body permitted, and stood outside the half-open door to listen, glad of the rest, for I was somewhat out of breath.

'"And if you ain't come to pay me, what are you come for?" the woman screamed out.

'Elias, I will not tell you what the lad said, or was trying to say, but I understood partly then, and the rest afterwards. He had resisted suicide—had fled from the tempter-devil's last fitting blandishment—had thought of you, Kezia, Hirell, me; and so in his extremity had run, literally run through the darkening streets in the fear that his better mood might pass away; and thus he had come back like a poor hunted hare to his form, knowing not where else to get even a crust of bread.

'Every bit of clothing beyond what bare decency required he had pawned and sold, and the lad was literally starving; yet he would fain have filled his belly with the husks that the swine did eat, and no man gave unto him, or was willing to give.

'I went in, pushed aside the brawling virago, and went to Hugh, who was supporting himself, while confronting her, against the corner of a table; his head drooping in spite of a certain rigidity and uprightness of his frame; his face shrivelled and ghastly, full of misery and despair; and yet, Elias there was a kind of mocking smile upon it fearful to behold, as though he rather looked on like a bystander, amused at the pretence of a struggle betwixt life and death, between God and Satan, and waited in a strange patience the issue.

'But I sent that damnable smile out of his face pretty soon, I can tell you. This was, as well as I can remember, our first salutations, when I sent the woman out and locked the door:

'"Hugh!"

'"Well."

'"Is it well? Dare you say it is well, with that friend at your elbow?"

'He turned hastily, and seeing no one, said—

'"What friend? I see no friend."

'I did not choose to notice the touch of bitterness in the last few words, and the low, half-stifled sigh that accompanied them.

' "Look again, young man," said I, and in no gentle accents. "He is there, whispering even now in your ear, and bidding you keep his whisperings from me. Oh, your friend and I have had many a tussle. The devil, Hugh, is behind you; and I bid you kneel with me now, and let us try which of us, he or I, has the best right to you!"

' He stared, and seemed half inclined to laugh.

' "Down on your knees—down before God Ask Him pardon, while I, too, offer my soul in prayer!"

' I said no more, but knelt.

' He stood still; stiff, silent, and gloomy.

' I prayed aloud: first to God on my own account, that He would forgive whatever of remissness I had shown in not watching more closely the youth given to my charge. Then I asked for power to speak, that this unhappy sinner by my side should understand that he was yet precious in his Father's sight: and then I poured forth all I felt of the beauty of the life thou hadst taught him, of the wondrous gift I myself was witness to; of the temptations to which I supposed his young spirit had given way; of the chastisement he had received and was then enduring—but for what? why, that he might yearn once more for innocence, pardon, and peace; and I was about to conclude with words of promise, when he stopped me.

' I had known for some time that he was beginning to be moved by my words, or rather by God's Holy Spirit that moved me, and 1 felt as though I could have struggled then, and successfully, for a soul ten thousand million times more evil than his; but as I was about to finish, as I said, with words of divine promise, he gasped out hoarsely rather than spake the word "Stop!"—came to my side in a terrible silence, knelt down as one possessed might do, while I, though I said nothing, marvelled greatly, and looked at him for perhaps a full quarter of a minute or so.

' "My son!" I said, at last, feeling truly as though he were bone of my bone, and flesh of my flesh.

' And my voice, I suppose, getting somewhat shaky, the lad could bear no more, but fell into my arms as I opened them, and cried on my breast like a child.

' He would not let me stir, even to get food, till he had told me his whole story, which I am sure he told me truly, excusing nothing—concealing nothing, except the shame that I saw overpowered every other emotion, and at times threatened to affect his very wits.

'That story I do not propose to tell thee, Elias, unless thou expressly wishest it. It will be a great comfort to him, if thou canst forgive, and take him to thee unknowing the particulars. I advise thy doing so.

'Friend Elias, the lad greatly needs comfort. His very life depends upon it. So let me say this : he has done nothing to prevent him from yet going forth again into the world, with a renewed heart and strengthened frame, and becoming a true and shining light.

'He is now at home with us; but I see he must remain no longer than is indispensably necessary, or the poor wife will complain she loses a second son when he goes. Expect us, therefore, soon. Ever thy friend, 'EPHRAIM JONES.'

CHAPTER XLI.

BROCKHURST.

ROBERT CHAMBERLAYNE lived in the village of Nytimber, in Kent.

A three-cornered pound stands where the roads meet at the entrance of the village, which seems to have been almost deserted at this end, for there is seldom anything in the pound but the stones thrown by the Nytimber boys at unfortunate strays in the times when it was kept in better use. Tramps are fond of resting on its low wall to eat their bread and cheese while spelling out and digesting the meanings of the names on the finger-post, and deciding their further progress.

On Sundays some lazy reprobate from the village will come and smoke his pipe there, to be out of the way of the church-goers in the morning; or if sent out by his wife to take the children for a walk, is glad to impound them there while paying a visit to the "Hop Pole," kept by John Clutterbuck, whose sign swings at the bottom of the long narrow garden, before a crumbling house a little beyond.

Opposite this, a pond lies stagnant, trying to draw over its dead water a decent covering of duckweed, which the dipping of a willow bough disturbs; lifting it as an inconsolable mourner lifts the shroud to kiss the cold face of the dead.

No more signs of the village appear for some twenty yards or so, when the little church comes in view, and the old parish stocks just outside the graveyard wall, in passing which the gaitered legs of certain elders of Nytimber may still be seen to twitch a little as they go by with their gaily-dressed, unconcerned sons and daughters.

Cottage gardens walled right in, and approached by steps over the wall, come next, with their flowers and vegetables, their luxuriance, poverty, order, and untidiness. After these the road narrows, and on each side of it the hay-ricks stand so thickly together that the beholder trembles at the thought of the conflagration that would ensue if a lighted match were dropped among them. The air begins to smell of farmyards. Grunting snouts appear under large wooden gates, bits of yellow hay stick to the hedges, the wagon ruts in the muddy road cross and recross just here, like lines at a railway junction; for the two huge barnyards on either side are the head-quarters of two farms—Brockhurst and the Rookery Farm.

If one watches the fowls of either farm just here, it will be seen that they are not particular as to which of the two yards they run into, out of the way of the brisk mail-cart or lumbering wagon. The great, placid, heavy-maned horses, too, unharnessed from the plough, will, with great content-ment, turn into whichever gate chances to stand open; and the dogs, who were the last to allow of such neighbourly freedoms, are now deriving more advantages from the alliance of Brockhurst and the Rookery than any other animals on the two estates; and are constantly trotting across the road, giving and receiving each other's experience and advice concerning the barn rats and other important matters of business.

Brockhurst farmhouse stands with its back to the road, a stone's throw from the great gates, covered from basement to chimneys with ivy cut sharply all round the windows, and looking simply very warm and comfortable and well kept from here; but over the wall one catches a glimpse of something more than warmth and comfort—of vine-houses and conserva-tory; of great bow-windows shining through a well-trained luxuriance of fresh green beginning to cluster in coloured buds; of nearly covered trellises, archways, green mounds, lilac-tree tops dark with buds, quaint summer-house, roof dovecotes, white guelder roses, beehives—all these are to be seen over the rich old wall of the garden at Brockhurst.

The Rookery farmhouse is down an avenue, farther along the road. It has a rich moated-grange air about the ancient windows, every one of which has a thatched projection over it like a hood. The rooms are dark; near the house the trees have been allowed to grow too tall and bushy—the whole place wants the brightness and loving cultivation of Brockhurst. Yet it is at the old hooded Rookery-house that the master of the two farms had resided for the last month, and there he had made arrangements to stay for the rest of the summer. Till his mother's death Brockhurst would not really be his own; and he had taken the Rookery Farm on lease, intending to go on with certain experiments which the careful old-world agriculturist, who was his mother's foreman, looked grave over when being tried on her property. So the young man took up his residence at the hooded house down the avenue, and went to work as if he had all his fortune to make.

As the two houses were so near, this was much wondered at in Nytimber; and another reason besides anxiety about his new farm was hinted at, by certain wiseacres, for his having left the comforts of Brockhurst and his invalid mother for the damp old Rookery place. It was reported that Mrs. Chamberlayne had had a poor relation thrown suddenly upon her—a very pretty girl—but so humble and so poor, so beneath Mr. Robert in every respect, that his mother, who knew there had once been a foolish fancy for her in his mind, had judged it best to encourage him in his whim of living at his new tenancy.

The pretty, smart maids, whose pleasant faces and bright ribbons made the passages of oak and the many ivied doorways of Brockhurst more lively and homely still, were constantly flitting to and from the hooded house with little notes and messages to Mrs. Payne, the old woman who lived there, concerning Mr. Robert's comforts. Every morning there was something to be sent over—his garden lounging chair—a new magazine, a bunch of lilac for the hall, or a dish of young peas, at each of which attentions Mrs. Payne murmured inwardly. Had she not kept house for old Farmer Stubbes, who held the farm before Mr. Robert? Had she no peas and lilacs in the Rookery garden? What need, then, for such litter from Brockhurst? And as for cooking, she thought it time enough when Mr. Robert complained for his mother to interfere, sending those 'tossed-off jades' over every hour of the day to hinder all the men about the place. It was all their tale-bearing, Mrs. Payne declared, that made the lady of Brockhurst so over-anxious. If she could have got over to the Rookery herself she could have seen how comfortable things really were for her son; but, of course, poor thing, that was impossible.

It was impossible—not on account of Mrs. Chamberlayne's age, for she was but nineteen years older than her son; and looking at them together, it was hard to believe even that that difference existed between them; but she had been for some years confined by a hopeless spinal complaint to the two rooms on the ground-floor, with the great bow-window opening into the garden, into which she was carried on her sofa when the weather was warm and fine.

The old garden parlour at Brockhurst was one of those rooms possessing a mysterious richness and comfort—a charm which the upholsterer's art has little share in imparting. Every bit of furniture seemed to have worn, as it were, to its place. It was mellow and rich with the love and attendance of several generations. There was a patriarchal largeness and suggestiveness about it. One felt that grandfathers and grandmothers, young men and maidens and little children, had all made merry together here; and there was a cheeriness in the ticking of the ebony timepiece, and a sort of jovial expectancy about the large easy-chairs, and in the grotesque faces in the great Chinese vases, whose light mosaic colours contrasted so well with the oak wainscoting and sideboards, that seemed to prophesy a return of those good old times.

The position of that brown leather arm-chair just out of the draught and of the way of careless feet, has been studied by more than one of the old Kentish patriarchs, whose names are written in the great square Bible on the sideboard. The hanging of the ancient little oval mirrors with candlesticks before them, has been seen to by eyes who knew well in what light their own was best reflected. For so many years so much had been added to it—so little taken away—hand after hand had been laid upon it with so much tenderness for those hands which had done their work there and been folded away in rest—that it could but grow rich and beautiful, gathering from time a peculiar tenderness of its own, as the little church of Nytimber had gathered the moss about its dull red roof.

Here, on a crimson sofa that was worn to a very comfortable dulness, Mrs. Chamberlayne spent her days. She was a tall woman, with a full, fair face, blue-eyed, and of that transparent complexion which usually accompanies red hair —and Mrs. Chamberlayne's was red—not auburn or golden brown, but uncompromisingly red. She wore a dainty bit of white lace she called a cap over it, that gave much grace and softness to the rich bright waves that crowned a forehead broad and placid. She was a prisoner, probably for life, but her prison was one of the pleasantest spots of the earth, and she rested in it with much tranquillity and lively contentment. She was neither languid nor idle. The good books—old and new—and the fresh magazines and newspapers on her low table were well read ; the pretty wool or silk embroidery had generally gained another flower or leaf for the vicar's wife to admire at each of her frequent visits. But the invalid's thoughts and fingers were most busy over her little writing case. She was an indefatigable letter-writer. Her old school girl friends had been retained in spite of her great seclusion, simply by the constancy of her correspondence. Romantic, girlish attachments had become deep, strong friendships with many of those to whom her letters—staid, sweet, sensible— came as, perhaps, the only tokens of what life had once been, for they were still full of the warmth and heartiness of a girl's affection ; while the deepening wisdom of a woman who studied attentively and humbly the experiences of others as well as her own, made them inexpressibly precious to many a heart wavering between wrong and right, or sinking in despair.

In the atmosphere of her garden, her flowers, her books, her calm and sunny household, she received and considered the stories of her friends' troubles and anxieties, thinking out for them counsel which might well be sweet, since she came by much of it as bees come by their honey, in communion with flowers, pure air, bright sunshine, and softened shade, for these were the chief pleasures of her life and her untiring companions.

It was to this person that Elias Morgan, in the helplessness of his poverty and sorrow, brought his daughter, after discovering that an aged relative with whom he had thought to place her had gone to that narrow home in which none can receive guests.

'Charlotte Chamberlayne,' he had said, standing by her

sofa and looking down at her, 'I little thought, after your son Robert's betrayal of me, to ask anything of you or yours, but I am pressed sorely. There are other friends who would perhaps help me, but blood is thicker than water ; I choose to come to you. My child is beset by the snares of the wicked. The doors of the poor are weak ; will you guard her for me ? '

The two travellers, their clothes covered with dust, and their faces pale and drawn, and almost haggard with intense mental suffering, seemed to have risen up like spectres before Mrs. Chamberlayne's astonished eyes. Her first movement was to glide her trembling hand under her lace shawl and lay it on her heart, which, unused to sudden agitations, had begun to beat so violently as to alarm her. Her kinsman's tale of sharp suffering, told more plainly by his voice than in his words, had come like a bitter wintry blast on the calm, sweet summer of her life. She held her hand against her side, and, closing her eyes, struggled to regain the calmness without which she was so unused to act.

Elias, who regarded Mrs. Chamberlayne in her luxurious surroundings as a kind of domestic Queen of Sheba, mistook the meaning of her rather prolonged silence and stillness, and after gazing upon her a few moments with great anguish and proud humiliation, he turned aud drew Hirell towards the door, pausing before it to say,

'When my child, like Lazarus shall lie upon the bosom of her father Abraham, if you, like Dives, shall call to her for help, then may she have power to serve you, Charlotte.'

Elias was punished for his haste. His name was gently called, and, turning, he saw his afflicted kinswoman, who had been prostrate so many years, standing erect. There was a certain majesty in her form as she stood upright but helpless, reminding Elias of some newly descended angel, whose unaccustomed feet doubted the earth's vile contact. The mingled command and entreaty of the attitude was not to be resisted. Elias approached her in some fear for her, and indeed no sooner had she seen her relatives returning, than she sank back on her sofa and fainted.

Her kind-hearted, quick-handed maids were soon about her, and had her completely restored ; and in half an hour Elias was sipping his tea with a sort of sad, stern peace at his heart concerning Hirell, whom Mrs. Chamberlayne had promised to cherish as a daughter so long as he should think fit to let her remain at Brockhurst.

If Robert Chamberlayne felt much surprise, when he came in to his tea, at the sight of his mother's visitors, he did not allow his surprise to embarrass himself or them very long; but began to talk about his own affairs, his worry and disappointment about the new farm, and other home matters, with unusual volubility; the whole drift of his discourse being to show his mother the urgent necessity for him to take up his quarters for a time at the hooded house. This unsympathetic and selfish conduct of Robert's, instead of disgusting, seemed to please both his mother and Elias; his other listener being too much prostrated by sadness and exhaustion to notice anything that was said or done. She sat like a tired child whose mind was incapable of understanding the things that the others talked of.

Elias had left Brockhurst the next morning, and it was not till after his departure that Mrs. Chamberlayne began to feel some misgivings as to the charge she had undertaken.

When the door closed upon her father, Hirell, who was sitting on a chair near it, rose, stretched out her hand as if to re-open it, but refrained, and again sat down. Her gesture had been so impetuous, so passionate, Mrs. Chamberlayne thought to hear a childish exclamation of grief or sudden burst of tears, but she was mistaken; Hirell was quite still and mute. It was then Mrs. Chamberlayne felt a keen regret at not being able to rise and go to her. Calling her to her side was such a different thing. She felt very kindly towards her, and was grieved to see how much a stranger Hirell evidently felt her to be.

Like some wild mountain-bird, whose broken wing had let it fall into a rich garden, she looked with startled eyes, bewildered and stupefied, on the strange things about her. Her sad heart, more passionately loyal in its sadness than ever to the old home, the old mountains, the old customs, turned against all she saw. In her mind she was certainly grateful for the kindnesses shown her, but she regarded them as the listless eye of a dying bird regards the dainties which children hold to the wires of its cage to bribe it back to life and song. They had no power to comfort or to arouse her.

Day after day she went, in obedience to Mrs. Chamberlayne's wish, to walk about the garden, every yard of which, above and below, began to be a revelation of fresh beauty— such beauty as was not to be found in her wild mountain home, while the thick trees hid fuller choirs of birds than she had ever heard before, singing the prologue of the summer. She looked most often to the clouds, that best imitated her own hills. Mrs. Chamberlayne used to watch her looking up at them, and think how strange a fancy it was for such young eyes to seek so wistfully through blossoms and fresh green and sunshine for the clouds whose shadows dim their beauty.

When the minister's letter about Hugh reached her it increased her depression, and seemed to make her more than ever sick of the world.

The soft, rich beauty of the budding Kentish summer was too exquisite not to be apparent to her—not to be a pain or a delight. It was a pain—it touched her to the quick—moving, yet sickening her spirit, like the passionate pleading of an unwelcome wooer.

Mrs. Chamberlayne watched and waited for improvement, but she watched and waited vainly. Perfectly tractable and gentle as her charge was in all her outward conduct, she felt her heart was yet as unapproachable and untamable in its pain as the wildest creature's in creation.

One morning she missed her. The poor bird was not, as usual, fluttering wearily about her sunny cage. She lay still in a corner of it, with dull, heavy eye, and dry, beating throat.

Mrs. Chamberlayne made her servants carry her on her light garden couch into Hirell's room, which was on the same floor as her own, and she found her in her bed too ill to move, moaning quietly, and murmuring piteously, 'Father,' and ' Kezia,' and other old home names.

After that Mrs. Chamberlayne's doctor from Reculcester, whose handsome brougham used to stop twice a week regularly outside the ivied house, became a daily visitor at Brockhurst. Every evening, at dusk, Mr. Robert used to cross the lawn and sit in the American chair outside his mother's window, and they would talk together in low voices.

At one time the smart, lively servant-maids went about the house on tip-toe, with faces and voices very much subdued. Mrs. Chamberlayne became pale, and worn-looking. Mr. Robert paid brief visits to her window many times in the day. Straw was laid down on the roadside of the house to deaden the rumbling of the carts and wagons.

CHAPTER XLII.

THE REFUGE DISCOVERED.

BUT the dark time passed over; the patient's youth and fine constitution brought her safely through all the dangers by which she had been so fiercely beset. The straw was gathered away, the wagons rumbled by as heavily as before, the servants knocked with their brooms, and sang, and gossiped, and slammed doors. Mrs. Chamberlayne's faint colour returned to her cheek, her charge was still safe in her keeping.

One June morning this young kinswoman of Mrs. Chamberlayne's woke from a refreshing sleep, and looked with an affectionate and grateful gaze about her room. It was the look of a person whose life for many weeks had been as one dark night. She had a sweet and bright morning for her awakening. Its light came through the striped dimity curtain that met across the open window, which admitted the scents of hay and lilac-time.

'Thy servant liveth—thy sun is sweet,' she said, and the tears stole softly and peacefully down the wasted cheeks.

The maid came in with her trim breakfast-tray; the arrangement of which Mrs. Chamberlayne had superintended, looking at it, before she let it go, with her head on one side, as lovingly as any would-be R.A. parting with his first picture.

A picture Hirell found it, with its old silver service, pretty pale pink china, delicate white loaf, so different from the coarse, almost black bread of Bod Elian, its pat of butter impressed with the prettiest of all the little wooden stamps kept for the purpose in the Brockhurst dairy, the freshly-gathered flowers on its snowy cloth, the magazine just come by post, the little pearl paper-knife beside it—all these Hirell's soft, grateful eye took note of as the servant placed the tray upon her bed, and covered her shoulders, and told her she looked so much better and 'more nat'ral,' and didn't she smell the hay? They were making it in the crosspath field, and were going to mow the Star meadow to-morrow, and cook's hands ached with drawing the ale, and she, Susan herself, must go and help, but would be back soon, to see how she got on with her breakfast.

Then Hirell—when she was gone—felt her heart beginning to stir a little, like something that had been numbed and is quickening. The sick bird began to lift up its head and warm itself in the sunshine from which it had shrank before ; but even as it did so it again cowered and shivered, as if it had suddenly seen rising once more the head of the serpent that had wounded it.

Hirell drew back a little from the tray, pale and faint, and looking down on the flowers in fear and anguish.

To make the tray still more inviting to the invalid, Mrs. Chamberlayne had laid a letter that had come for her charge among the flowers she had gathered for her.

'What,' said Hirell to herself, 'not over yet—not over yet! Oh, I cannot bear much! What can he be cruel enough to say to me now ? '

She drew the letter from where it lay, under a long green leaf holding a lily of the valley, and tore it open with fingers that trembled so she could scarcely keep the paper still enough to see to read it.

And this was her letter :

'My dear Hirell,—It was but at eight o'clock last night, while I was dining with some friends at my new town-house in Eaton Square, that I heard for the first time of your place of abode and illness. I now write this from a village ale-house only a couple of miles from you ; where I mean to stay till I see you, and renew the conversation so abruptly broken at Werge Castle, by causes that originated at least in my over-prudent anxiety for you as well as for myself.

'Before daybreak I was beneath your window, which I soon discovered by signs that I thought could not mislead me ; and while I listened, I heard your window opened, saw your nurse look out, and report to you on the beauty of the morning—heard you answer her. How I refrained from then speaking to you, from then demanding instant admittance to you, surely the recording angel will note to my credit, knowing I did it only as fearing to startle and injure you. You know not how I have sought you. Since our ill-omened parting at Bod Elian, I have had neither rest of body nor peace of mind. This is a third attempt in search of you here,

I came before your arrival, and—I went away deceived. Then I sent our friend, Mr. Jarman, and he went to the other farm. Now again I come, and find you, never again to lose sight of you. Be sure of that.

'Hirell, I cannot live without you. I have tried—yes, I *have* tried—and failed. Will you now punish me for this honest confession, or forgive me because of its honesty? Ah, yes. Love, true love, rich as life and profound as death— this is your need and mine. We have gone too far to retreat: so, darling, *trust* me henceforward as you would trust your own soul. I see clearly at last my wants and my duty: both bring me here.

'Hirell, dearest, I cannot bear to say to you in this cold-blooded fashion things that ought to be said, and must be said, when we are face to face. Then, when the old world— that is to say, whatever of sweet savour the world contains— is concentrated, essenced in you, and I need only to look at you, listen to you, then, indeed, may I speak to you out of the fulness of my own yearning, passionate belief and worship that which shall not be unworthy for you to hear.

'I have wronged you in many things that you know of, but there is one wrong of which you do not know—you are too unselfish to have discovered it, too deeply engrossed for others when you care for them to have found me out in this. Enough, I have found myself out, and now play the informer, not without secret hope of reward, I have defrauded you! Do not look startled—do not disbelieve. I have not taken of your worldly goods; no, but I have, in my delectable egotism, in my calm consciousness of superiority of sex, social position, age, experience, and what not, defrauded you of love's sweetest and most precious offerings, the outpourings of a worshipping heart. Can you help turning away in disgust if I tell you that I have discovered, since your absence has com-pelled me to look more sharply into things, and above all, into myself, that it is you who have played the lover, and I who have condescended to be so loved! Am I not judged now— judged, sentenced, and given over to swift execution?

'Laugh at me—that is my true punishment. I laugh at myself, but with a bitterness of scorn that heaven forefend you should ever feel towards the humblest thing that breathes, much less towards me. Laugh at me—if you can —but when you have done so, remember God loves mercy as well as justice.   Above all, forget not I am now a suppliant at your feet.   I descend from the throne, place my beautiful one there instead, and henceforth take my seat on the steps, and on the level of her footstool.

'Hirell, I begin to understand myself and you better, much better.   Is it fortunate or unfortunate, that you in the process improve on acquaintance while I horribly deteriorate?   But then do you not see that goodness like yours, so pure, sweet, exalted, boundless, could not possibly have been given by God for your own personal gratification alone?   And therefore, sinner that I am, unregenerate even in my regeneration, I cannot but conclude that the excess on your side is meant to balance the defect in mine; and that the two have but to coalesce to become both perfect for this life—which *is* earth, remember, not heaven.

'In deep sincerity of heart, Hirell, I ask you to pardon— that which I can never again speak of while I live, never again think of without shame, and which I will not deny, even though I might with some show of truth do so.   It would not be true truth—I own that; you saw to the depth of my guilty soul; and then I saw too; and now bend before you humbly, and in a contrite spirit, as the prayer-books say, to ask your full forgiveness.

'To assure me of that, I need only one little line from those dear gentle fingers, that even hard work could not spoil, and that I have so often kissed in wonder and reverence of soul— one little line only, saying to me—" Sinner, come."

'All else (and how much *that* includes you cannot, I am sure, conceive) I will then tell you; and if I do not satisfy you, I will ask no more, but go my way and demand of myself, if enough sense remains to me to answer the question —" Can it be that thou hast won this priceless treasure and lost her?"

' But I will *not* lose her.   No, thank God, she is not lost. She will get better, and there is a vain belief in my heart that I can help her, not only to get better still, but well, quite well, and with rapid steps, when she once more admits me to her society, the only society that John Cunliff, baronet as he is, M.P. as he is, and worldly to the heart's core as he begins to fear he has long been, now finds he cares for.

' Hirell, only one little line to bid the truant " come! "

'If you are unfit to talk, let me only look on you, rest with you but a few minutes, and I will leave you in boundless content and gratitude. Ever yours, and yours only,

'JOHN CUNLIFF.'

This letter did Hirell some good as well as harm. It had re-opened her heart's wound, but it had poured balm into it. When Susan came to take away her breakfast she begged for a pencil and paper, and wrote her answer.

'DEAR SIR,—I pray you not to think too much about my illness. I am getting better. God has raised up for me in my need friends whom only He can thank. They have saved me not only from death, but from something much worse than death—my own heart's despair and base ingratitude. I shudder as I look back upon the way I have come, but there is light near me and above me, and I am trusting that in time peace may come again.

'I am grieved that you have written to me, yet inexpressibly thankful for much you say in your good and kind letter. I wish I knew how to make you understand what I feel. I do so want—and now more than ever that you have given me so great a relief—that you shall think of me as kindly as I must think of you. Dear sir, all else is at an end between us —do believe that, for it is so!

'You ask my forgiveness. I do give it to you, I do indeed, with all my heart, and soul, and strength, and humbly as becomes one so much beneath you.

'I find I can write no more. Dear Mrs. Chamberlayne will be angry with me for sitting up so long to do this, for I write very slow and painfully, and I hope you will excuse any mistake, for there is a sort of mist that comes over my eyes at times that frightens me.

'So now, dear sir, with many wishes and prayers for your happiness, in this world and in the next, I am your humble servant, 'HIRELL MORGAN.

'P.S.—I can *now* say, without one pang at my heart, that I believe you were right in thinking the position of your wife unfit for me. If at times thoughts of me make you impatient with yourself, think of that too—and that my last words to you were to ask you to do so.'

When her letter was finished and given to Susan to post,

Hirell laid down and slept for some hours ; and in the afternoon, though quiet and peaceful, was too ill to bear the blind up, or to see any of the hay-making in the Cross-path fields.

She passed a good night, and found no letter among her flowers to disturb her at her breakfast. She read a chapter in her little Bible without much pain to her eyes, for the first time for many days. She lay half sleeping, with a smile on her lips, and the book open in her feeble hands, when her nurse came in with a letter, which she said Clutterbuck's boy from the 'Hop Pole' had just brought, and to which answer was to be waited for. It bore the writing she expected, but sorrowed to see.

'HIRELL,—I will not receive this from you. Rather than destroy the paper on which your fingers have traced your thoughts, I would tear my own flesh off my body, but I *have* torn up that which you have now sent me. When shall I see you ? Choose your own time. I can wait.

'JOHN CUNLIFF.'

When Mrs. Chamberlayne was brought in to pay her usual morning visit, she found, to her surprise, Hirell sitting up, pale as her night-dress, and with bright, excited eyes, writing a letter.

'Hirell, this is very wrong—really it is wilful,' she said.

'Please forgive me,' answered Hirell, 'but I am doing that which I must not leave undone. I will rest and do all you wish me, but do not hinder me—my head is strange, and I *must* finish.'

'Don't distress yourself, my child. I will leave you, but exert yourself no more than you are positively obliged.'

Left to herself, she wrote on—her old dangerous fever-red creeping back into her cheek, and making the tears scorch her, as now and then in the pauses of her thoughts they stole slowly down.

'SIR,' she wrote, 'again and again in the darkness of my long black night, when a little space of sense came to me, I felt such bitterness of sorrow that I was glad to go back again even to that shelter—if only to forget.

'Always it was the same—the cry of my heart against you, sir, which I could not help but begin to pour out, till my own thoughts stifled me, and there was a blank once more.

'You will not, you say, heed the one last dear wish of my soul, that we should part in peace. O God forgive you for the wrong you do, for the suffering you inflict!

'What I was when you found me, you know. Sad often, when I dreamed of that great world without, and compared it with my own narrow gloomy home, but happy in the love of my father, and all in my house; and if I was too conscious how they exalted me, I never forgot that it was they, not myself, to whom my seeming elevation was due.

'There you found me. You were in great trouble, sir, and what woman's heart could help doing what mine did—trying to comfort you, even while I sought to keep such things unknown.

'There you saw me day by day, hour by hour—saw my father, and what I was to him—saw my ignorance, my every defect. You knew me—I dare to say it—as truly as it was in your nature to know me, had the years we passed together been more in number than the weeks of our real acquaintance.

'You loved me, you said. How I trusted you in return I need not speak of. But I would have given you more, a thousand-thousand times more, had that been possible, than I did give. How often have I not prayed to God to enrich my heart, to enlighten my soul, to make me worthy of being given to one so full of all that stamps honour and nobleness on the name of man! I do not think any poor creature ever knelt in secret with more boundless, swelling gratitude, or with more sense of the glory of life and of the world than I did, for the wondrous chance of knowing and being loved by you. It was a secret I knew not how sufficiently to keep. I have cried often when, unawares, words, looks, or accidents of any kind, made me think I had been unmaidenly in not concealing both the delight and pride I felt.

' And once loving you, from that time I could have borne any disappointment, however bitter, if only it did not come from you.

'You told me at Ewyn y Rhaiadr you had intended to leave me, and then made me confess my love. I thought of it afterwards, and while my heart was in its joyfulness and pride, found great pleasure in the remembrance. I thought of it on the evening of that dreadful day, and felt I could have been reconciled by the remembrance to the worst, could have forgiven your thoughtlessness in committing me to such a hopeless future, had you simply told me in a fitting manner you could not marry me.

'I tremble and shiver when I think of myself on that day, and of what might have been had not a higher hand protected me—overwhelmed in darkness from which there seemed no escaping but by a cry to you, who watched and waited, seeking if there were but one spot in the poor soul through which evil powers might steal, with you to follow them in triumph.

'Oh, sir! Oh, sir! you have wrung this from me, as you might by a like inhuman violence squeeze the blood out of this weak body. I wanted to spare you this. I yearned to be permitted to think you would be sorry for all this when we had separated, and that then I, like so many more, might watch your good works, and desire all else to be forgotten. This, too, is only another dream. Well, I shall dream never, never more!

'I am ill—very ill. If you try me much more you will kill me.

'I do forgive, in spite of all I have said—only, let me rest. I entreat you, let me rest, and may the peace that passeth all understanding be yours is still the prayer of

'HIRELL MORGAN.'

CHAPTER XLIII.

DARK DAYS.

HIRELL continued to recover slowly, but Mrs. Chamberlayne was not mistaken in saying that the excitement of her correspondence with Sir John Cunliff had taken all the spring from her recovery. She became well enough to join her aunt in the pleasant old parlour, to change the flowers in the Chinese vases for her, to go on with her lessons in Welsh stocking-knitting; but Mrs Chamberlayne saw, under the true eagerness to please, an apathy and a listlessness that the girl spent all her little strength in trying to conceal.

'Do you think you can *never* like Nytimber, Hirell, dear?' she asked once, as she saw her grand-niece standing in the window and looking as usual, not down along the alleys of the garden, but up at the white clouds.

Hirell could not answer—her throat seemed to tighten.

She still looked up at the sky as long as she could see for the upwelling tears, and that moment felt a loathing for the bright blooming country about her, that smothered the gentle and grateful reply she would fain have given. She thought of her own home as of something cold and soulless, out of which all the life and joy had passed for ever; but it was as a mother thinks of her dead child—feeling it to be far dearer in its coldness and soullessness than any strange one, however beautiful.

The lovely yellow laburnums were all in their glory, shining here and there among the old trees of the garden like sunshine, that both bloomed and burned. And Hirell was conscious of them as a bereaved mother is of the tossing golden locks of some strange fair child. She withdrew her eyes, and answered her aunt with an inward shiver:

'It is very pretty.'

Mrs. Chamberlayne did not try to draw from her a more direct answer to her question, but in her own mind began to fear the understanding and healing of this strange, suffering heart was beyond her skill.

She was better—yes—she could move about, only feeling a little tired; but she began to think she should never have her old health and light-heartedness again, she should never *care* for life any more. Living would be like climbing a toilsome hill to look upon a prospect that she had seen, by some magician's aid, to be barren and dreary; it would be like watching the unfolding of a rose at whose heart she knew a canker to be lying. It was in vain she told herself that health and happiness would come again; the most alarming thing to her was the certainty, the sharp reality, of her heart's suffering and despair. When Mrs. Chamberlayne prepared little surprises for her, which she often did—a new dress, or bonnet, or something that she thought would please her—Hirell would thank her with expressions of pleasure and gratitude which she thought must be sincere, till a choking feeling at her throat and a hot mist at her eyes made her say to herself, 'Miserable hypocrite, you know you have no more gratitude than a stone for these things.'

When she prayed, a half-smiling, half-cynical face came between her and the glory and power she had once been used to feel through her inmost soul, when she knelt at Bod Elian, in the chapel of her people. It seemed to waylay her most

passionate sentences of prayer, and smile over and reason
with her about them—half in mirth and half in earnestness
and wisdom. She knew it was the recollection of things
Cunliff had said at different times, in the same bantering
manner in which this haunting voice spoke to her.

Her own fate was a great mystery to her. Why should it
have come upon her ?—this peculiar trouble. Why should
her peace have been broken in upon, and her faith in life, and
the world, and heaven itself, been so cruelly shaken. She
asked things of her own heart and in her prayers piteously,
but not impatiently, though day after day dragged on and
left her unenlightened, and her weariness and hopelessness
increased.

Late one evening Mrs. Chamberlayne was carried to her
room, and in her gentle way gave her unwelcome news. She
brought her another letter. She did not wish to give it, she
told Hirell, knowing how much she had been disturbed by
others from the same writer; but Robert had given his word
to Sir John Cunliff, who had appealed to him, that it should
be placed in Hirell's hands that night.

When her aunt had left her, Hirell held her hands clasped
in her lap a moment, looking at the letter as it lay on the
table before her, with something of her father's sternness in
her eyes.

It remained there when she opened it, and while she read it
through.

'Hirell, your letter is horrible—but I do not wonder at it.
As soon as I can forget the smart, I shall only see in it new
evidence of what you are. That I already know,

'This is sent to say that if ever man was ashamed, I am.

'What can you need more ?

'I must, in spite of all, keep some self-respect, or be worthless alike to myself and others. Do not ask further abase-
ment.

'This is a black spot in my life, which I will wash out.

'I have again read your painful letter—inexpressibly painful ! I have brought myself to receive it, as I am sure it was in
your own secret, tender, and loving soul meant to be received,
as the inevitable overflow of a wronged love towards its
wronger. I lay it to my heart. I will read it again and
again, till I have drawn out of it, if possible, every bit of

virtue it contains for the healing of distempered minds. Hirell, I have wept over it, for the first time since manhood.

'Are you now content? It is idle to talk of my going away. I shall never go away without you!

'But you are ill. Oh, my sweet darling, if I might but be by you, to nurse you, to amuse you, to lighten your load of depression!

'You want mirth, not medicine—hope, not anodynes—the one who loves you, and whom you love—have you not said so? —and not troops of bewailing friends.

'But you think to teach me patience, perhaps. So be it. Hirell, there is nothing I will not learn, if only you say it will please you, and make you grow strong.

'Shall I tell you what I have been dreaming about of late? Yes. Because I want to know what you think of the dream.

'Hirell, I often wonder whether you are like the clerk of Oxenford, of whom our first great national poet, Chaucer speaks, when he says—

> And gladly would he learn, and gladly teach.

Hirell, tell me frankly, would you gladly learn?

'Do you wonder why I ask? Listen. I am going to propose something that I see beforehand will be very dangerous to me, and perhaps very foolish, into the bargain.

'What subject ever asks his despotic queen to put on attributes that shall give her greater power than before over him? Yet that is what I am about to do, either because I can't help myself, or because I have such unbounded faith in my own particular despot.

'What if you were a queen—suddenly transformed as regards blood, descent, and position—but in all other respects just such as you are; a queen who *must* reign, say at the risk of war and bloodshed, and social convulsion—what would be your first desire, the immediate and overpowering cry of your soul?

'Would it not be, "O God, make me fit! make me fit!"

'And what, Hirell, would you make fit? Is the vista of difficulty so appalling in detail, so interminable in apparent length, that you cannot readily grasp the whole, and say to yourself, "Can I, or can I not do this thing?"

'You might say "No" at once, in your sweet modesty, humility, and inexperience—when these are placed side by side with an idea apparently so formidable as this, of turning a poor simple maiden, fresh from tending her sheep on the Welsh mountains, into a woman capable of queening it in the eyes of a critical world.

'But can you say "No" to the actual truth, as I shall now put it before you? I think not.

'Hirell, you need one, two, perhaps three years (for I will rather exaggerate than diminish the sacrifice I am about to ask from you) of that particular kind of education that shall best supplement the education given you by your father (a truly admirable one, for how else could you be that which you are?); of an education that shall qualify you to converse in any circle on the topics that are always current there, and in the tone peculiar to the best-bred women. Hirell, my ear even now seems to listen entranced to the music of *your* voice, than which nothing can be more full of fascination, sweet and pure, trained as it might be, and to your own enjoyment. I care little for mere accomplishments, but I do not think you would find the French language any difficulty. Do you remember the lesson I once gave you, and in which you really delighted me by your progress, only it was impossible to get you farther, for your mocking laughter and unseasonable merriment?

'As to music, you ought to sing and play to perfection. Hugh has impregnated your whole being with the love of sweet sounds; and music is to me, when good, a supreme enjoyment. Still I should wish no more than this—that you bent your mind steadily to it for a sufficient time; then if you were not satisfied, I would cheerfully say, "Let it go."

'How do you like the first half of my sermon? Is it very hard to accept? You laugh! Well you may! They are indeed trifles.

'But there is another limb to the homily. I am a rich man, a man of rank, a politician, likely to be a minister some day, if my ambition and my industry hold. What *ought* these things to involve for my wife? More, much more, I take leave to say, than the wives of men like myself generally give to their husbands. I shall mention in few words one point as suggestive of all the rest. I should not like my wife to become a furious fanatic in politics, but I should like her to take a real living interest in the subject, if only for my sake.

'Can you, Hirell, *for my sake*, do such things? They

demand work, perseverance, devotion, but success is assured, and the reward great. The very best masters England can give would be at your service.

'Dare I even dream that I deserve to have such a wife as mine would be, if to her present self these externals and improvements were added?

'I will not answer that. I only know how I need her.

'Once more I plead for the line, the one little line, "Sinner, come to me!"

'I will come. I will, indeed, whether you say it or no; but not yet, nor without your permission, if I can get it, or see hope of getting it within any endurable time.

'Believe me I suffer in your suffering, and dare not do aught rashly to endanger or retard even for an hour your recovery, for which I will this night try to pray to God, where, I'm ashamed to say, I have not knelt, even in thought, for many many years, in the solitude of my chamber. Yes, I will try to pray to Him to make your restoration as swift and entire as your best friend could wish, among whom henceforward I claim the first place.

'Did I say claim? Strike out the word for me. I can only plead—but I do it with a passionate something gnawing at my heart, which you alone can remove.

'I will read nothing more—I swear it—from you till I see the words—

' "Sinner, come, for pardon and peace, first; then for—"

'I will not conclude my sentence, in the hope you will do it for me. Ever yours sincerely, 'JOHN R. CUNLIFF.

'P.S.—You have been in haste to answer my previous letters, and in your haste have been most cruel. In answering this—a repentant and true heart's last appeal to you—take time, and I will wait, trusting to God your leisure may be more merciful than your haste. 'J. R. C.'

The letter read and laid down, Hirell leaned back in her soft little chintz-covered chair, and, turning her face against it, shed some bitter tears over its bright roses.

But in a little while her father's strong, stern spirit seemed again to enter her heart, and rouse and strengthen it, and she got up to fetch her writing things, and began her answer immediately.

'SIR,—I reply to your letter at once. I have so few words to say that I find it quite unnecessary to take time to choose them as you suggest. Sir John Cunliff, believe me, as one to whom you know truth is dear, there is nothing now that you can write or speak that would make me change my determination never to become your wife. I entreat you, therefore, not to pain me by so humiliating that which I in my own mind had set up higher than all things but God. For you do humiliate your-self by using your powers in pleadings to one who can never more have faith in you. Though I cannot read your words of repentance without tears, I do not believe in them. Oh, sir, you are not repentant of more than having lost what you wished for by setting too low a price on it. No, it is the simple truth that I do not believe in your repentance or your sorrow. Indeed, sir, in your kindly-expressed intentions with regard to my better instruction, and in your generous com-pliments to myself, I could fancy you almost gay, or at least in a state of mind little in keeping with the broken spirit you profess to plead with, and so movingly as to cause me many tears, notwithstanding my doubt of it.

'If you persist in taking advantage of the kindness of my aunt and Robert, I must trouble my father in the matter, which I shall be loath to do, as he has enough to bear. Your humble servant,   'HIRELL MORGAN.'

CHAPTER XLIV.

EVENING VOICES.

THE next afternoon another letter was brought to Hirell, as she sat in the garden by Mrs. Chamberlayne's couch.

'This is the last I shall read from him, aunt,' she said, as she opened it. 'If he sends any more I shall send them to father to answer.'

'MY DEAREST HIRELL,' wrote Cunliff, 'still dearest, in spite of all your harsh words, so you do not believe in my repent-ance and sorrow—well, you shall at least believe in my patience and my love. I bear all that you say to me in a spirit as meek as even you could desire a sinner to take his punishment—a sufferer to kiss the rod. I have been most unwise, most cruel,

in troubling you just now, while you are so ill, and so overwhelmed by anxiety about your family. I have written to my
friend Kezia, for information as to poor Hugh's health, and
am so truly rejoiced to hear he is recovering. In his next
start in the world I trust to be allowed to be of some assistance
to him. And now I must tell you a most annoying thing has
happened, which compels me to go instantly to London. A
great debate is coming on in the House of Commons; the
result may influence the fate of the ministry; every vote is
important; and, in a word, honour and every consideration of
duty and character demand my presence. I am obliged to
own I must go.

'Can you not in this feel for me ?

'I write hurriedly, for I have already delayed too long.

'Hirell, dearest, I will make a compact with you, one I
little thought of a few hours ago. I will promise you on my
sacred honour to leave you alone henceforward, not only till
Parliament is over, but for some little time beyond, only entreating you to take no step in the meantime that will make
our union impossible,

'I won't deny I have my own objects to serve in this. I
want to be free when I do again place myself at your feet; so
I will stay patiently in London—that, to me, hideous wen—
till Parliament adjourns, then dispatch arrears of indispensable
private business, and be with you immediately after.

'How I shall exist till then I know not. Still I exact no
new promise, no fresh bonds, but offer you liberty for so long
a period, trusting that your sense of justice (even if there be
no more tender a thing pleading for me in your heart) may
keep you from doing anything to make my voluntary absence
a cruel mockery. By the time this reaches you I shall have
left Kent. Yours ever truly,

'JOHN R. CUNLIFF.'

All day Hirell could not think of the letter without a certain
vague alarm at the idea of seeming to give Cunliff permission
to hope, by being silent. But she saw no good in writing;
and, on the whole, felt it better to let her last words stand as
a final answer. Then, too, his absence was an inexpressible
relief to her.

She seemed able to breathe more freely—to hear sounds
about the house without starting and trembling—her slim

X

form when she sat down looked more restful—her very voice had more peace and sweetness in it.

When Hirell went to bed it was still daylight, and she stood a minute or two at her window, listening to the gradually subsiding hum of the village—that pleasantest sound of all the long summer's day—when mothers are calling home their children from their daisy-gathering in the roadside meadows, and neighbours gossip across fragrant garden hedges, and bird-boys, and ploughboys, just home from work, are shouting over their mysterious games, with mouths full of bread and butter—and the blacksmith is putting out his fire, and pot-house politicians are waxing warm in the little corner garden, where pewter mugs are turned down upon the dahlia-sticks. They are doubtless politicians of most narrow, illogical, and coarsely-expressed opinions; the blacksmith very likely breaks some promise concerning the shoeing of somebody's horse, in putting out his fire so early; the boys at play probably cheat in the laws of their games; the neighbours gossiping over the sweet-peas are perhaps virulent scandal-mongers; the mothers calling home their children may be harsh-voiced and ungentle, bringing the little ones in trembling haste from out the long flowered grass, which has been to them as a wonderful fairy forest where they could fight their way easily with their soft little hands, and lose and find each other at will. And how strange that out of such discords should flow a sound so sweet and full of mysterious happiness, so redolent of home and comfort, and the poetry of labour and of rest, as that which floats softly to Hirell's window, with the odours of the little Nytimber gardens. It is as if the earth in the beauty of its fading summer day and coming summer night has been attuned to yield nothing but music, even to the bitter and complaining breath of humanity.

Hirell stood and listened to this homely and pleasant murmur, which, in the full, large voice of nature, rich with the chirpings of callow blackbirds in the elms, and the jovial whirring of gnats, and tinkling of sheep-bells, was small and dreamy, like an infant's crying overpowered by its mother's lullaby. As Hirell listened it sounded to her as the happy murmur of a world from which her sorrow parted her. She felt very lonely, and almost sadder than when her trouble had been new. Then her spirit had been content to lie crushed, but now that it tried to rise it felt bitterly how much it had been wounded and enfeebled.

The stars that were golden in the waning daylight grew brilliant and silvery as the evening deepened; the nightingale began to sing in the screen of trees dividing the two long fields dotted with little hillocks of hay. The village hum came to her softly and sweetly, and moved her heart with a great tenderness for the world of which it seemed to speak so pleasantly. Her thoughts, as she looked up at the stars, fell into a silent entreaty for comfort, and a reconciliation of her soul with life, and life's duties and pleasures. From that sorrow in which she felt she had been placed as in an ark of safety when sinking in dangerous waters, she sent a prayer, as Noah sent the dove, entreating God that if one green leaf of hope were left for her on the waste of her grief-invaded life, He would let some messenger bring it to her for her sad heart's comfort.

CHAPTER XLV.

AT THE HOODED HOUSE.

Sir John Cunliff had left Kent very well pleased with Robert Chamberlayne.

On the morning of the same day on which Hirell had received his farewell letter he had called on Robert at the Hooded House. It was the first time he had done this, though he had twice waylaid the young farmer in his fields, and found him tolerably genial and willing to assist him in getting his letters conveyed to Hirell.

It is true he might not have found him so kind a friend in this respect, had he not managed, and without saying anything positively untrue, to make Robert believe it was solely on her father's account that she was now refusing him; after, as Sir John assured him, there had been a solemn engagement between them.

Robert certainly thought the baronet hardly treated, and said as much.

'It's their religion,' he muttered; 'it's always making them do some unheard-of thing.'

Robert had sat in the little Nytimber church till its doctrines had become bone of his bone, and flesh of his flesh. He was not bigoted—he believed in some men being able to see farther than he saw in such matters—even farther than the portly old Vicar of Nytimber himself could see—but in his own heart Robert had a calm deep-rooted content in the old state of things that had agreed so well with the Chamberlaynes and their land time out of mind. He had a great respect for Elias and his stern, high principles, and for the sweet, fearless transparency of Hirell's nature; but, do as he would, Robert could not help seeing in their constant trouble and poverty of their land, a sort of judgment on them for departing from the more orthodox and comfortable state of things.

When Sir John called upon him, Robert was sitting down to a one o'clock dinner in the unfurnished dining-room of the Hooded House; and it did not take his visitor many minutes to discover that Robert's self-banishment from Brockhurst was attended by not a few inconveniences, and sacrifices of domestic comfort.

The easy-chair and one or two favourite pictures—the pretty little davenport, with its stand of books—the bouquet of roses, and other luxuries and ornamentations sent over by Mrs. Chamberlayne, looked almost absurd in the great unfurnished room, the ceiling of which was not entirely free from cobwebs.

Sir John's quick eye also noted that the simple dinner was ill cooked and ill served, and that Robert seemed afraid of uttering his remonstrances loud enough for Mrs. Payne, who was very deaf, to hear. He evidently had as great a horror of rousing her temper, as of rousing a kenneled mastiff; and indeed his visitor saw it was not without some reason; for when Robert asked for another plate and glass for Sir John, she informed him flatly that she had not agreed to cook for all the parish, or all the strangers that liked to come after him, ' ringing the bells as if a body had no ears.'

When Sir John had praised the views from the hooded windows, and had had the politeness to discover that he was fond of home-made bread and cheese, the only thing on the table that Robert ventured to recommend him, Hirell was spoken of, and Sir John's intentions concerning her made known to Robert.

Robert thought the plan of leaving Hirell alone, till she should be sufficiently strong to hear Sir John plead his own cause personally, a good one, and said so.

Then Cunliff thanked him for having befriended him thus

far, and asked him bluntly if he might go in the hope that he would still continue to further his cause as much as lay in his power, both with Hirell and her family.

When the question was put to him, Robert was standing by the window, and for a moment or two afterwards he remained silent, looking out on scenes that were too familiar to him not to speak now as eloquent witnesses of his own past hopes.

But thinking of those hopes now did not injure Sir John's cause; for the strongest among them had been the hope of making Hirell's sad life happier. And from all that Robert had learnt of her state, from the words she had uttered during her illness, from his knowledge of the fascination she would find in a man of Cunliff's tastes and accomplishments—from all these Robert had gathered the firm belief, that Hirell Morgan's happiness now depended on her marriage with the man who was asking him to stand his friend.

Cunliff studied Robert's face that moment or two furtively and shrewdly, and the study gave him additional respect for the friend he wanted to take up his cause. He saw a man who was not ashamed or too much afraid of his own weakness to think over unflinchingly before another man the tenderest secrets of his heart. Sir John would not have cared for Hirell to have seen Robert as he stood there weighing the worth of his love for her, to have seen his face just a little stung, perhaps, by Sir John's request, but otherwise full of tenderness, bold, honest, strong, unabashed, unveiled by any show of indifference.

'Well,' he said suddenly, 'I want to see her happy, if there's any possibility of persuading her people to let her be so. I suppose you know—you have heard from her how I have failed as regards myself?'

'Hirell has told me all,' answered Cunliff, 'and of your admirable consideration.'

'Well,' interrupted Robert bluntly, 'if you know that I failed on my own account, don't expect me to do very brilliant things on yours—that's all I wanted to say. What I can do with Hirell and her father in the matter I will do.'

And he held out his hand, which Sir John grasped gratefully, though he *did* observe that the rest of Robert's form held rather proudly and rebelliously aloof, reminding Sir John of Ephraim Jones's favourite saying, 'The spirit is willing, but the flesh is weak.'

They walked up the village together, and parted at the cross-roads.

Sir John, on the whole, was well pleased with the advocate he had left behind him, He knew that while Hirell had never been in the least degree in love with him, she yet had what Sir John thought an absurdly high opinion of his judgment and general character. He had certainly a little modified his own estimate of Robert since he had been in Kent, and had so many opportunities for observing how greatly he was respected.

It was not long before he discovered that Robert had the good fortune to be wonderfully popular without making any kind of sacrifice to obtain his popularity. His independence in his dealings with men above himself in social position was shown in so simple, natural, and quiet a manner, as not to offend, though it might occasionally surprise, the squires, magistrates, and other rural magnates with whom he came in contact. It was not easy to frown down a man who paid his labourers higher wages than any one in the country; and whose love of justice and of honesty in its purest and most primitive sense was a byword of the neighbourhood.

In spite of his being constantly seen in his own fields and farmyards hard at work, he was admitted into good society at Reculcester, though not into the 'bishop's set.' He had a fine voice, and sang well, and gave faded gaslight pleasures a dash of freshness and hearty reality.

And it was no mere jealousy made Cunliff decide that Robert Chamberlayne was very handsome.

Those Kentish autumns that had ripened twenty-six harvests in his life had put their spells about him, as they had put them about his corn-fields and his orchards—the spells of their burning noontides and their still, breathless nights, and had given his form a supple strength and grace, and his face a perpetual sunshine.

The young ladies of that limited circle of Reculcester society into which Robert was allowed, declared him to be far more handsome than striking. His face wanted expression; its unchanging good humour was very pleasant and refreshing to see—very lovable—but also very tantalising, when the sad, soul-smitten glance was being watched for. In fact, Robert had the behaviour of a man who already loved, and was contented and happy in his love.

CHAPTER XLVI.

CARRYING THE HAY IN THE STAR MEADOW.

THE next morning—though by that time she had lost her yearning towards life—a messenger of hope did come to Hirell.

It was about eight o'clock, an hour before Mrs. Chamberlayne's breakfast-time, that, having dressed herself, Hirell sat down near her window and began some needlework; stitching rapidly, as if she could keep off dangerous thoughts with the point of her needle; and to show the tears that always came pressing at this hour when body and soul felt weakest, that there was no time for their falling. The curtains of her window were open only just wide enough for her to see a green tree, whose leaves had come later than those of its neighbours, and were fresher and paler. The sun was shining on them, and they were very bright—quite luminous, as with a light of their own.

Suddenly she heard a rush of swift small wings, and, looking up, saw that a little brown bird had perched at the end of a twig of the bright tree, and was swinging vehemently to and fro.

Something about the bird made Hirell lay down her work and look at it. It was a sparrow, very sleek and small, his little bead-like eye glittering in the sun. Surfeited with the summer's sweets, his breast throbbing as though it would burst, he had come there wild for solitude, to embower and hide himself from all his mates, and to swing and to rock himself alone, balancing his happy little heart. He turned his head from side to side, and chirruped sharply. And still he rocked and swung, and his shadow was on one of the leaves as they waved about him, bright as with the light of that mysterious world from which they had so lately come. Sometimes he would lift his tiny wings, spreading them out to the breeze and stroking them with his beak, as if even his little feathers were cloyed with happiness.

After he had been there a while he flew away refreshed by his brief solitude, and Hirell felt as if the tiny shadow that had left the leaf staid and quivered over her heart still.

The overflow of the little creature's joy went to her grief

and swelled it till its bitter waters found passage from her eyes.

Where was this sweetness and this joy with which her small guest was so sated and overburdened? Was there such wealth at a little sparrow's service, and none for a starving human heart?

She draws back her curtain and looks out with a yearning and hungry look for the first time since she has been in Kent, *desiring* to see. She does see : and soon her eyes begin to lose their haggard hopelessness, and to grow soft and absorbed. She leans her head on her hand, and a tenderness comes over her face, and a peace that is almost gladness.

The road that lies between Hirell and the two long meadows is unusually silent and deserted ; for the hay-fields form the centre of attraction. Under the long hedge on the stubble are seated in a row such little girls from the village as are spared the discipline of the Nytimber school on account of the babies, whose calico sun-bonnets, which reveal nothing of their owners but a rattle or a buttercup-grasping fist, dot the field in considerable numbers, like some strange fungi peculiar to hay-time. That half of the Star meadow which lies nearest the road is cleared of the fragrant heaps that in orderly profusion still lie on the farthest half, right to where the hedge divides it from a cornfield of lustrous young green ; and beyond the cornfield wave the grasses of another meadow in all their glory of sorrel, and flower, and seed. Here the mowers are at work, driving the sharp line of tall, blooming grass farther and farther away.

This field shelves suddenly down, so that Hirell sees the wagon, which is in the middle of the meadow, nearest her, standing against the sky with its rich yellow load ; on the top of which a man, with careless hardihood, is standing, holding a hayfork, receiving and packing down the fresh contributions to the russet load that the others are tossing up to him. On the right is a hill covered with a little forest of hopsticks, whose bare tops look strange enough ; for the tightly-clinging fresh young plants afford them as yet but a scant covering. On the left of the hayfields is the avenue and the Hooded House, the grounds of which are separated from the black, furrowed field where the plough is at work, by a great cluster of oaks ; whose leaves are now in their freshest gold-green beauty, and still retain that crisp crimp of the folds in which they have lain in the bud. A delicious gurgling of young throats and old ones comes from this copse ; and now and then an army of chattering specks, disorganised and uncertain, will rise from its midst, advance and hover over the cornfield, then, at the report of an unseen gun, wheel round and retreat in the blue distance, spreading and condensing, and again spreading and condensing, with a strange sort of disorderly method.

Early as it is indoors, the day appears to have attained its noon heat and mellowness. A sky of deep, burning blue spreads like a thing that can never change, over the full country ; the sun, a clear ball, pale with intensity, is high, smiting even lusty strength with languor ; the heavily-maned team-horses smoke as their great limbs strain over the furrows, while the ploughman takes mechanically his toilsome, plunging steps beside them, and the haymakers twirl their forks with a slow monotonous movement, a subdued strength that looks like sleepy indolence.

While every dog-rose on the hedges, and every bell of the little bindweed under the hedges, had its deepest secrets of tint and perfume, and golden floss laid bare to the burning sun, the flowers on the shady side of the garden, of which a small slip is visible from Hirell's window, still remain in their dewy stillness, like sleeping princesses in a guarded palace. The heavy, wet lilac plumes are drooping and still among their leaves ; the laburnum's gold tresses lie in tangled, dewy luxuriance on the wall top ; over which a great bee, tired of the field beauties, comes humming noisily into the quiet garden.

The wagon, with its russet load standing out against the sky, and making, by its hugeness, horses and men look small, is quite the centre-piece of the picture—set in a grand half-oval—by the hop-pole-covered hill on the right side, and the avenue trees and thatched gables of the hooded house on the left. Towards it stare the cows, as they lift their drowsy, dripping faces from the open pond near the road ; and the mowers, in the farthest field beyond the corn, always look that way when they pause to rest and spit upon their palms.

Hirell's gaze also constantly returns to it, for it is the figure standing on the piled-up load that imparts to these scenes the familiarity and homeliness they have suddenly assumed for her. She owes to him the vague sweet memories of them— memories that have been lost, but that come again and take away the strangeness the place has worn till now. The sight of him reminds her that what she sees should not be strange, but as the reading, in its original language, of a poem, of which she has once heard with delight a feeble translation—as the listening to a melody, of which the key-note was struck long years ago.

On the broken wall, at the back of Bod Elian, she has often sat with Robert, talking of these scenes, and he has kicked the fallen stones into rough models of the house, the church, and the stocks, the pound, and the fields, with their dividing hedges and rustic fences and gates, striving hard to prove to her that if her father could ever be prevailed upon to let her spend a week with his mother at Brockhurst, when Robert himself was at home for the holidays, that week would fall little short in its effects of seven days spent in paradise. Hirell, in the time of her childish doubts of, and secret rebellion against, the austere religion and life of her small prison-like world, had begun to long for a taste of the rich plenty and sunny freedom of Robert's home, the reality of which his mother's letters seemed to prove more than all his own eloquence.

But all such wishes vanished when Hirell found herself beginning to be regarded as one of the shining lights of her people; when she saw eyes, usually cold and condemnatory or stern and preoccupied, rest upon her with wonder and reverential tenderness, she began joyfully and tremulously to believe in her own saintliness, and to put from her mind all earthly, or, as her ministers would have said, 'carnal' subjects, and Robert and Kent were in the list. She declined his offer of a small hamper of Nytimber Nonsuch apples, and burnt the copies he had sent her for the improvement of her hand-writing, as they were all on the same topic,—'Kent, the garden of England,' or 'Nytimber, a Village in Kent,' traced in Robert's bold hand, in characters large enough to fill up the line. The birthday gloves she had not the heart to refuse, but requested they might always be black, a request which Robert contemptuously disregarded.

And now the picture which had been the richest thing in her childhood's imagination lay before her, glowing warmly, breathing sweetly.

She remembered how one day Robert, in a fit of sharp home-sickness, when Mr. Lloyd had been cross, and Mrs.

Lloyd severe on the subject of spilt ink, sat with her on the same spot on the broken wall, and heard from her that she likewise had endured indescribable persecutions from the village schoolmistress, on account of her stupidity at learning to turn the heel of her first knitted stocking—and they sat together, she crying, and he plunged in a gloomy reverie, with his hands in his pockets, and his foot on his Latin grammar. Almost as vividly as she sees the real Robert on the hay wagon, she sees the slim young student who sat beside her on the fallen wall, rather thin and pale, and dark under the eyes with rapid growth, and unaccustomed 'worry' of his studies. She remembers how those blue, darkly-circled eyes turned on her suddenly, wistfully, and how Robert, putting off all that assumption of manliness by which most boys so disguise themselves, said simply, as he drew away the half-knitted stocking with one hand, and laid the other on her shoulder—

'Oh, Hirie, don't you wish we could put this horrid stocking in my Euclid, and pitch 'em over Criba Ban, and tramp off to Kent, and have no more horrid worry all our lives? *Don't* you, Hirie, darling?'

She remembers how she fell into the fascination of his idea, and answered that she should like it very much, and that of course they must expect the journey to be like the Pilgrim's Progress, full of fearful dangers, so that Robert might display a valour unheard of in these days, and both a devotion and faith that should carry them safely past lions and demons and Giant Despair, and the Valleys of Death, and all sorts of things invented by Satan to shake their faith in each other —and at last reach the enchanted fields of Nytimber, where they were to rest as in a prefatory Heaven of unlimited duration.

So the charm of sweet old acquaintance steals over all the summer scenes before her, giving a deeper sunshine to the gold of the buttercups and laburnums, a fresher sweetness to the scent of the lilacs and the hay. So her trouble has brought her to this: the shipwreck of all the richer, dearer hope of her womanhood has still left her in the enjoyment of her childish dream.

Could she be as she was then, and forget all that had happened since? Here are the fields she has longed for —more beautiful and rich than even Robert had taught her to imagine them. And then the gentle, wise and generous ruling spirit of the whole—the good Samaritan, under whose hands her wounds are healing—at the thought of her, tears rise hot and fast, and hide the pleasant fields and dazzling sky.

Strange that the very one who made her love this place and long for it should be the means of destroying its charm whenever she thought of him, and of bringing back the fierce throbbing life into her half-conquered sorrow. She can think of the slim lad with his half-troubled, half-laughing eyes, and good-tempered despair as to his own educational progress— she can think of him always with affectionate pleasure. But when she turns to him who now stands on the wagon of hay, laughingly inviting his men to throw up more and more to the rich burden, the full-faced, blue-eyed, supple-framed, young farmer—how can she look at him and not see the form that stood by him near the bridge at Dolgarrog one Sunday; or the blank disappointment that he brought into her happy prosperous home the morning after that Sunday, or the way in which he assisted them in their poverty—the lodger that he brought?

Wonderfully unconscious of his crimes poor Robert looks as he shouts to Mrs. Chamberlayne's overseer, who has objected to his taking the management of the Star meadow hay, on the plea that he would not be up early enough to set the men to work, and who now comes to find three hours' work done, and to see the men trying to conceal a grin as Robert greets him in a laughing voice, round and mellow, and far sounding.

'So you've come in time for the beer, Wrigley?'

Mr. Wrigley, after scornfully surveying the amount of work done, as if remarking, mentally, it was not done in the style *he* would have had it, turns his wrath upon the babies; and the sun-bonnets go crawling off in hasty and confused retreat, only to advance again as soon as his back is turned, and take up their former ground as securely as ever.

Meanwhile Robert descends from his exalted position, and stands leaning against his favourite black Bess, his straw hat pushed back in a most ungentlemanly fashion, and his face looking stupid enough in that blinding sun.

By this time the great can of beer has arrived at the scene of action, under the care of the Brockhurst groom, in morning undress, and smart, pretty Susan, who guards her face from the sun, and admiring and grateful eyes, with a branch of lilac she has snatched off in coming through the garden.

Mr. Wrigley gives out the beer, offering the first draught

to Robert, who perhaps would scarcely show so lively an appreciation of its refreshing and invigorating powers, did he know that the brightest eyes of all the Welsh teetotallers were watching him.

As Mr. Wrigley's task of giving out the beer draws to a close in the Star meadow, it may be seen that the men turn and glance across the green corn to that distant field where the mowers are at work, with a look at once congratulatory and envious, as they think that the pleasure which for themselves is over has yet to be enjoyed by their companions with the scythes.

Robert goes to the stile, and gives a peculiar cry in a high-pitched ringing voice. One of the stooping figures looks half round over its shoulder—the young master holds up the can, and raps it musically with the pewter mug. Up go the gleaming scythes, moving agitatedly in the sunshine an instant, then down again, and then a row of stooping figures come moving with a sort of lively slowness along by the green corn.

They are oldish men, some of them so old that one cannot help thinking each moves his scythe with that slow, measured sweep in the fear that if he gives it too wide a swing in his backward stroke it may clash against another scythe of another silent reaper very close behind him. They have more respect for Robert than the younger labourers, and give him the complimentary title of 'squire,' because his grandfather was known to them as the Squire of Nytimber when they first came to the farm; and there is much wiping of brows and twitching of rolled-up shirt-sleeves as they approach the stile where he sits.

There is also some old-fashioned, flattering toast muttered by the owner of the tanned arm that first receives the frothing mug, as one may see by the brusque, good-humoured nod and wave of the hand that Robert gives, as if he would accept so much graciously, but decline more.

The mug has passed through all the tanned hands now, and the mowers go back again along by the young corn.

The poetry of the morning for them is past, the flowered grasses may be very beautiful to look at as the sun shines on them, and the butterflies flutter and dip among them, but Robert's old mowers have only to do with the tough stalks, and the hard stones, that occasionally turn the edges of their scythes and tempers.

After performing this duty, Robert indulges himself with a

lounge on the hay to the delight of the dogs, of which those
belonging to the farm engage him in a spirited sham-fight;
while such canine strangers as are in the field look on from a
distance wistfully, giving vent from time to time to their
stifled longings by low whines and starts, and quiverings of
their bodies.

The wagon, with its high load, now moves off towards the
gate, under the directions of Mr. Wrigley, to the general confusion and scattering of the sun-bonnets and their guardians.

Robert comes across the field towards Susan, who ceases
flirting with her lilac branch, and meets him demurely,
evidently feeling sure he is going to speak to her.

He does, it is easy to perceive, ask Susan some question,
and Susan, in answering it, glances towards Hirell's window,
and, as if involuntarily, Robert's glance turns in the same
direction. He sees the dark, drooping head, against the white
curtain.

His hat is lifted, and a wonderfully radiant face smiles
towards her. From that sense of embarrassment with which
we discover ourselves suddenly observed by the person we
have been rather secretly and closely watching, Hirell blushes
deeply, while nodding and returning Robert's look.

In this recognition—their first since the day of her coming
—the eyes of each had a flash of pure, deep pleasure in them,
which perhaps each would rather have concealed from the
other; but as Adam and Eve must have seen in each other's
eyes some light of the lost Eden, Hirell could not look at
Robert, or Robert at Hirell, suddenly and without preparation, and not see some lingering glow and dew of a sweet
morning, whose tender promise they had shared together, and
which now might disappoint, but could never be banished from
their memories.

'We are old, old friends,' says Hirell, coming from the
window. Then in another minute she peeps again, and sees
the wagon staggering through the gate—Robert plodding
away towards the Hooded House, and Susan and the groom
coming home with the empty cans—she guarding her head
from the blows of the lilac branch, which he has captured from
her.

By-and-by comes a knock at Hirell's door. It is Susan,
settling her cap and apron, and saying that breakfast is ready.

Here is the garden parlour, as usual, all comfort and brightness, and the fair, rich, matronly face rising from its pillow to welcome her. There begins to be a little patient sort of despair in its morning smile to Hirell. This morning, however, Hirell is to give her a moment of gentle triumph and delight, such as she has not known for many years. She has bent over her sofa and given the usual respectful, but cold and timid greeting, when Mrs. Chamberlayne, instead of finding her hand set free, feels it held more and more tightly in warm and trembling fingers, and looking up at Hirell's eyes, finds them gazing at her with all the wildness and strangeness gone out of them.

' My darling child ! ' and she draws her gently down to kiss her again.

Hirell keeps back her face, with closed, full eyes and quivering lips ; but as she sinks on her knees by the sofa, a sob, and with it a broken word, bursts from her, with more passion than Mrs. Chamberlayne believed to be in her nature—

' Un-grate-ful ! '

CHAPTER XLVII.

ROBERT COMES TO TEA.

In the evening of that same day on which the hay in the Star meadow was carried, Robert came to Brockhurst to tea.

His visit was quite unexpected by his mother, who was even more surprised than Hirell to see him entering the parlour, with an almost impudent enjoyment of their astonished looks in his blue eyes.

' Robert,' said Mrs. Chamberlayne, laughing at the thought that it was so strange to see her son come uninvited into his own home, ' is anything the matter ? '

' Yes, I want a cup of tea,' he answered.

' Well, don't be so defiant about it,' said his mother. ' Susan, fetch another cup and saucer.'

He only said to Hirell, as he pressed her hand—

' I'm so glad you're better,' but he managed to make her feel that there *was* hearty gladness in his voice and in his hand's clasp, that made her ashamed of her own ingratitude for returning health.

He presently condescended to explain to Mrs. Chamberlayne

that he had been hard at work, hoping to clear the Star meadow before night, and it had occurred to him that he might as well save time by dropping in there for his tea instead of going all the way to the Rookery.

There was a low round table, before Mrs. Chamberlayne's sofa. Hirell was sitting at that side which was by the head of the sofa. Robert fetched one of the wicker chairs standing on the lawn, and seated himself on the other side of the table, half in and half out of the window.

It was an intensely hot evening, and tea was very pleasant to him in the old room again.

'This is nice,' he said, tilting back his chair, 'to sit at a window that hasn't a smothering straw-bonnet over it—full of cobwebs—and to have a cup of tea that's not quite black or quite white.'

'Now, Robert, it's of no use your trying to malign Mrs. Payne to me,' answered his mother; 'the very sight of you satisfies me as to her goodness and care. Could he dare, Hirell, to pass himself off as starved or neglected with that round full-moon of a face?'

The full-moon of a face looked comically at Hirell, whose thin, white cheek caught something of its brightness as she smiled faintly.

The heat and the scent of the syringa made her feel very languid; and her head began to ache with the thoughts that came crowding oppressively fast and thick through Robert's presence. There was his letter and its inclosure, which she had given into Kezia's care. He had never had any acknowledgment of it from her all this time. What must he think of *that* ingratitude? What must he think of her taste in allowing him to be the bearer of letters from Cunliff?

Of one thing she was very certain—and the fact was so far very satisfactory—Robert no longer loved her. Indeed, there was in his face so deep and tranquil a satisfaction—so sunny a calm, that she asked herself if a newer and deeper love had not come to him, and taught him to smile at the folly of the old. But sometimes even finding that a thing proves to be as we would have it, is a secret pain as well as a satisfaction to us, and Hirell began to think herself a poor unworthy creature, since one lover had so soon and so easily put her from his heart, and the other—oh! would there never, never come a day which the galling bitterness of that remembrance could not reach and overrun?

A little while ago she might have rather scorned Robert in spite of herself for his happy changeableness; but her respect for him had wonderfully increased since she had watched him among his men that morning. Robert had been so little in the habit of talking of his own work, that Hirell had not been quite sure whether he lived the life of an idle gentleman at Nytimber. She rather suspected when she had heard him talk of his mother's foreman that such was really the case.

'You must get out in the fields before they're all cleared, Hirell,' said Robert, helping himself to cream, which Hirell could only be brought to distribute as so much gold. 'If you promise to come to-morrow, I'll make them begin under the elms, so that you can sit in the shade, and have some shawls and lie down there.'

'Thank you, Robert! I shall be very glad to come—only don't take any trouble for me,' answered Hirell.

'As to that, I mean to take a good deal of trouble with you, Hirell,' Robert said, with a decision that rather astonished Mrs. Chamberlayne.

'You must come to church next Sunday, if it's only to see the difference between our comfortable old vicar and Ephraim Jones. Then I want you to let me drive you over to Reculcester to see the shops and the cathedral. And it's only eight miles to the Bay—we must go there, and have dinner at Uncle Stephen's.'

Mrs. Chamberlayne laughed.

'Why, Robert,' she said, 'whenever did you arrange all this round of dissipation for Hirell? you quite take our breath away.'

'Well, I don't mean to allow you the luxury of a companion invalid any longer, mother,' answered Robert. 'I'm under a pledge to get Hirell strong with the least possible delay; I shan't let her be moped up here any longer.'

When he had said this he looked up at Hirell to see if she guessed whom he had pledged himself to about her; and he saw a lovely faint flush spreading all over her pale face, and her lashes were trembling very low over her cheek.

He got up and took her hand.

'Good-night, Hirell,' he said, 'things will all be right soon. I know what your father is, where your happiness is concerned, better than you do; only keep up your spirits and get well.'

Y

Then he kissed his mother, and went out with a parting nod to Hirell.

He went the garden way, and had scarcely reached the lawn when he heard a quick step behind him.

Turning, he saw Hirell coming to him, and looking very pale and troubled.

'Robert,' said she, 'I want to speak to you before you go.'

Her hurry had made her breathless and wan-looking. Robert involuntarily made her take his arm, and walk very slowly up the lawn, whose trees were now all in commotion with the home-coming birds; who, by the chattering and quarrelling, seemed to have brought more trophies from the teeming summer fields than could be made room for.

'Robert,' said Hirell, trying to keep her voice calm, 'I didn't know quite what you meant just now. I understood about your wish to make me go out, and help me to get strong —and I feel very grateful, and you may be sure that I will try. I have tried, Robert, but I will try more than I have done. But, Robert, will you tell me, please, what you meant about—about father just now?'

'Oh, I mean he'll come round,' answered Robert rather confusedly.

'Come round to—to what, Robert?'

'He'll consent to your having Sir John Cunliff. Only let my mother and me do our best with him, and give him time, and I'm certain, Hirell, all will come right.'

'Robert!'

She had snatched her hand from his arm, and stood confronting him, looking at him with bright, angry eyes.

'Write to father, if you dare! Speak to me about marrying Sir John Cunliff again, if you dare! Understand, once for all, he's not what you or any of you think. Understand, Robert, if my father went on his knees to ask me to marry that man, I would not do it!'

Robert felt his senses so hopelessly confused by this outburst that he could at first do nothing but gaze on Hirell's face with a sort of stupor. Gradually, however, there came to him a sense of the deception that must have been practised upon him; and with it a kindling anger that began to burn more and more hotly, though he turned his eyes away that Hirell might not see it.

'Oh Robert' she said, her voice suddenly weak again and

gentle, ' how rude, how ill-tempered I am! What a return I
make for your kindness ! Forgive me—only, pray say no more
about this.'

'Then I'm to understand, Hirell, that your refusal of Sir
John Cunliff comes from yourself alone ? '

' It does, Robert, quite from myself. I have found he is
unworthy to be my father's son, and he shall not be. No, he
shall not be.'

'Then you have ceased to care for him, Hirell ? '

She looked up at Robert's face with a glance of kindly but
irrepressible contempt—as if she would ask him if he thought
her love were as easily disposed of as his own.

'No,' she said, ' I have *not* ceased to care for him—nor shall
I ever. Oh, Robert! we are not all made alike in this world.'

Robert smiled a very serious, short-lived sort of smile as he
thought how wide of its mark her little arrow had fallen.

He had been leading her back to the house, and by this time
they had reached the parlour window.

'Well, good night,' he said. ' I shall write the instant I get
home and retract my promise.'

And the letter was written and posted that night.

<hr>

CHAPTER XLVIII.

NEWS FROM HOME.

THE next morning, when Mrs. Chamberlayne was looking over
her letters, with her usual gentle excitement—it was her one
excitement of the day—she found among them the following
letter from Bod Elian for Hirell and handed it to her.

It was from Hugh—the first she had received from him since
the beginning of his troubles.

' Bod Elian.

'MY DEAR HIRELL,—I wonder which is the most truly selfish,
the ambition which makes us feel the world to be all ours, or
the tender grief for ourselves that comes after ambition's fall ;
when we realize that even the little chimney nook to which
that world is shrunk—that nook that once was ours is ours no
longer—that we have no sound right to it. And that is what
I feel now after my return.

' Forgive me—pray forgive me, that I have been too much

Y 2

engrossed, too much puffed up, and too much overwhelmed, to be able to write as I promised you. The collapse for the moment has been complete. My worst enemy could wish nothing worse for me than I feel, unless it were to come and sing some song of triumph under my windows.

‘Hirell, I feel something swell dangerously in my throat, when I contrast the tender mercies of our fellow-men outside with the loving-kindness of my brother, his considerateness, his boundless charity.

‘And I used to think him hard. God help me, it was the life that was hard—the life that he and all of us were condemned to.

‘When I returned—looking like a skeleton, Kezia, says—dreading the very sight of him, and picturing to myself the black, gloomy place destitute of common comforts, and made more destitute by the loss of the delusive hopes I had raised, while this was my state, I was carried into what seemed for the moment to my fancy a domestic paradise. The room was unusually light, there were flowers on the table ; everything, in a word, was as if for a feast. That big-boned, big-voiced Christian, with a still bigger heart, Ephraim Jones, I suspect had some hand in this. When I could speak, I told Elias that I thought it was only a more refined mode of punishment, and that he need not fear it was sufficient.

‘I had to go to bed, and from thence did not rise till yesterday week, and to-day I will write to you, I hope words of comfort.

‘Hirell, I live again. This first failure has humiliated but shall *not* destroy me. It is one of the dreams of the Saxon’s egotism that nobody but he is strong ; and in measuring strength he brutally mixes up all kinds of the most incongruous natures for comparison, and then judges them by his own narrow standard. My brief experience has taught me that however difficult the world is, however full of pitfalls, a man may still make way, if, with ambition, and the talent that justifies it, he has good sense and fixed principle ; and, to revert to myself, if he can tread down under his feet the artist’s deadliest enemy, Pleasure.

‘And now for a secret ; or rather for a whole nest of secrets. I am going away to-morrow. I am going away secretly. I am not going to please myself, for I would gladly have staid here a few weeks to feel that I and my mother-land were once again reconciled ; and yet I must go. And upon all these secrets comes another and greater one that explains them, and which you ought to know.

' Hirell, I have long and dearly loved Kezia.

' Elias knew of this long ago, and promised to speak for me. He has fulfilled that promise faithfully, but somehow my love by proxy did not get on; and he wrote to me when I was in the full of my mad holiday to say I had better come and see to the affair myself as soon as I *justly* could.

' In returning—broken alike in heart and fortune, as it seemed —I had secretly the faintest gleam of light still cheering me about Kezia. Her conduct when I did come was strange. It was tender, motherly, but accompanied with a certain restraint that I, exquisite coxcomb ! fancied was maidenly consciousness of love.

' It was no time for a pauper to talk, or dream ; and I was silent enough, though always thinking, one minute of Kezia, and the next of my second venture forth.

' Last night, or rather about half an hour after midnight, I felt very restless ; and got up with a strong inclination to see if my brother were awake, and would talk to me.

' Wishing not to disturb him if he were asleep, or Kezia, who would have fancied me ill, I trod as if my feet were shod with cotton wool ; went to his door, which as you know he often leaves ajar for air, pushed it open and went in. The room was in absolute darkness. I was instantly arrested by the sound of his voice. And to judge by the sound, he was kneeling, I think at the bedside ; and praying, according to his habit, aloud, that is to say, in a low, monotonous, but painfully earnest tone, which could not be heard by any one in the house less favourably situated than I was.

' I thought it would do me no harm to share in that which he was saying. Believe me, Hirell, I would not for the world have stayed to listen but in that spirit.

' His prayer lasted for some time, was too fine for me *now* to go into, but deeply interesting, without, however, any special application to myself, which I cannot say I desired.

' He had finished, or appeared to have done so by the pause, and I should have spoken, but that I knew he had not risen, and might therefore be still continuing, as I have often known him do, to pray in silence; as if there were subjects too holy, too mysterious, for the soiling of mortal words. Presently he broke out again, and the mere sound of the voice, so broken with trouble ; seemed to warn me instinctively of something I needed to hear. As nearly as I can repeat his words, they were these :

'" Lord, Thou knowest his heart and mine. Thou knowest his present affliction. Have I not asked Thee, besought Thee, wrestled with Thee, that Thou shouldest raise him up, and comfort him, and make him as one meet for Thy service? Have I not, O Lord, confessed that I know not whether these his aims are good, and left him with Thee and his own conscience? Thou gavest him his gifts. I am bound to believe Thou knowest well for what purpose. But now, O Lord, help me ; enlighten me about Thine handmaid. Thou canst look into the heart and judge it ; O Father, judge mine ! If it be the desire of the flesh, the pride of the eye, the delusions of the soul, that have moved me ; if I have been unfaithful to this my brother ; if I have turned her heart from him for my own gain, let me bend before Thee, and receive the chastisement due to me, even while I implore Thy pardon and mercy. O Lord ! the lad loves this Thine handmaiden. What must I do ? Can I, in his present low estate, tell him she inclines not to him ? That she is wounded if I plead for him ; that, in spite of Thy servant's unworthiness, she has thought to succeed in this Thy house to the love, and the duties, and holy responsibilities of that dear saint now in Thy bosom ? "

'Hirell, you will judge it was time for me to go out of that room, and I went. You will judge it is time for me to go out of that house, and I depart to-morrow. I have written to them both ; how I need not say. Their path henceforth is, I think, made clear. Another dream killed ! How many more murders of the innocents must there be ?

'Hirell, dearest friend, sister, write to me. I have no one but you to tell all this to, and expect some comforting words from in answer. I cannot express to you how I long to feel I have still the wise, kind, holy little sister I have always had in you. Sometimes I feel as if you must be indeed my sister and your father my father, for was ever brother to brother what he has been to me ? When I first came home and heard of your illness and unhappiness, and lay so ill myself in your little room, looking hour after hour at the " Virgin Martyr," and the texts on your walls, I used to think how we had both had our dearest wish, and got away from home, and then I used to wonder if we were only to come back to it to die of our experiences. But, thank God, we are not doomed to stand merely as sad remembrances to those who love us. We are to live, it seems, and work and suffer—ah, yes, to suffer for them.

Give my love to Bob, and ask him if he can manage to let me
see him in London. Dear Hirell, how I wish—how I know
they all wish you could have made him happy. He's one in a
thousand—one in a million, I should say. We only quarrelled
on one matter—Bob would never own whether he cared for the
harp or not, and used to be offended when I applied my
favourite verses to him. You know what I mean :

> The man to whom the harp is dear,
>   Who loves the sound of song and ode,
> Will cherish all that's cherished there
>   Where angels hold their blest abode.
>
> But he who loves not tune or strain,
>   Nature to him no love has given ;
> You'll see him, while his days remain,
>   Hateful at once to earth and Heaven.

'You can make Bob very angry by repeating this, if you like.
He always says it's mere Welsh poets' nonsense ; and that a
man may love music yet be a great rogue, or dislike music
and yet be a very good fellow ; a shocking notion of Bob's—
Saxon to the core. Root it out of him if you can.

'Good-bye, now, dear Hirell ; it is striking two ; by four I
must be beyond Dolgarrog.

'Ever affectionately yours,
'Hugh Morgan.'

CHAPTER XLIX.

OLD FRIENDS.

One morning, a week after Sir John Cunliff had left Kent,
when Mrs. Chamberlayne had had her couch moved into the
garden, Hirell came in through the window for something for
her workbasket, and to her surprise saw Robert leaning over
the table, his head buried in the sheets of a newspaper.

'Good-morning, Robert,' she said. 'Aunt's out under your
pear-tree. I suppose you wondered where we'd all gone ?'

Robert coughed—a little nervous cough quite unusual to him
—then looking up, half folded the paper, and came towards
her with it.

'This **was** sent to me by post this morning—of course it's
intended for you.'

He spoke quickly but gravely; and she saw that his face was very serious.   Looking at the paper as he had placed it in her hands, she saw in the corner Robert's name and address in Sir John Cunliff's writing.

'What is this, and why is it sent, Robert?' and she sat down in a chair by the table, her colour changing painfully.

'It's the "Times,"' answered Robert, dryly, 'and I suppose it's sent because it contains Sir John Cunliff's first speech in Parliament.'

Hirell did not feel capable of rising and going into the garden or to another room with it, as she much longed to do; and to sit there with the paper without looking at it must seem so strange to Robert.   She opened it—saw something that drew all her heart and mind away, miles away from Robert and Brockhurst.   She hardly seemed to read—she almost *heard* the voice, and saw the face speaking the words that were before her.

Robert had taken the 'Reculcester Guardian' in his hands, and had not looked at her once all the time she was reading. But hearing at last a little, quick, half-stifled gasp, he raised his face, and saw Hirell's, flushed with pride and triumph, looked smilingly at him.

'Have *you* read it?' she asked, with tears in her eyes, and a tremulous voice.

He looked at her face, and appeared to take no notice of what she said, startling her when he spoke by words unexpected and painful.

'Why don't you forgive the man and marry him?   You do love him.'

Hirell was silent for a minute with surprise and grief at the brusque, heartless manner in which it seemed to her Robert said this.   She turned pale, and her eyelids fell and quivered. When she lifted them slowly, and looked sadly and wonderingly at Robert, she met his looking up timidly and sorry.

'I'm sure,' she said, in an unsteady voice, 'you don't mean to be unkind, Robert, but you speak as if—as if you thought very hardly of me.'

He sat with his elbow thrown over the back of the chair, and his face turned aside from her, and did not answer when she waited for him to do so.

'This has not been much talked of between us before,' she went on, with effort, but much sweetness; 'you have been too good and kind to mention it, and I have been too ill—too cowardly—and so you have not had a word of my thanks, of my great, great gratitude—for your unlooked-for goodness to him. Oh! you were so good to him, when I—I had to be so cruel. It is remembered—it is treasured. God bless you for it, Robert.'

His eyes again met hers, as if against his will, and were withdrawn.

'I must tell you now, Robert, as this has come to be spoken of by us,' said Hirell, 'that everything which I have had to forgive in him has been long, long ago forgiven—so don't say anything to me again about forgiving him—it pains me for any one to think I have resentment against him. And I must tell you that I must not marry him, Robert, because—Robert, there are these reasons against it. The more I see of the world, the more I love my father—the more rare and beautiful the holiness of his life seems to me; and I think God means me to look to him as I always had done till—till *he* came. I think that I am to look to him, and find help for my weakness and faithfulness in the Daniel-like strength and faith of his spirit. I feel, Robert, that, utterly removed from him, I should be like that leaf rustling upon the carpet there, ready to be borne away by the first wind that blows. And *he*, Robert, *would* part us absolutely, entirely. I am sure of it—I am indeed—though perhaps he would not own it to himself. I know it would come to that—I have felt it al along—the "still small voice" has said all along to me, "Hirell, it will be so—you know it"—and, Robert, I do know it.'

She was silent, and Robert did not turn his head. He seemed to know that she had tears and sobs to struggle with, though she *was* silent. And soon he heard her voice again so low and so sweet, and chastened like birds' voices after a storm.

'Then another reason against my marrying him is, that if we were married, and anything made him impatient with me, and he should speak an unkind word to me, as of course in this life, where no voice can be always music to us, I must expect he will do, often, or sometimes—then, instead of being to me as it might to another, or *from* another—quickly forgotten and forgiven—there is something I should be reminded of by the lightest tone of harshness, the least word of impatience from his lips. Robert, there is something which I should remember—which would come back to me at such a moment, and make the hasty word, or tone, or look, full of such bitter terrible meaning—it would say to me, did he not warn me himself that I was not fit to—. I should tear the wedding-ring from my hand—I should die or I should become mad! Oh, it is so much better *as* it is. As it is, I can forgive and bless him. If I were married to him, I might learn *not* to forgive, and *not* to bless him.'

Robert struck the ' Reculeester Guardian ' which he held in one hand an impatient blow with the back of the other, but his averted face was very serious and sympathetic.

' Now that I have told you this, Robert, you won't think me obstinate, or resentful, or unkind,' said Hirell, ' in keeping to my resolution, will you ?—and you won't—oh, that pains me so much—you won't be always expecting me to change towards him ? I *have* resolved ; and you know that even when I was a little girl, when I made a solemn promise to myself I *did* keep it—you remember, don't you, Robert ?'

Robert did lift his eyes to hers now, with a long, gentle look that reminded Hirell of a certain childish promise which assuredly had *not* been unbroken; but she thought the re-membrance had come to her from herself, and not that Robert's eyes had anything to do with it, and it passed as quickly from her mind as the faint flush it had brought passed from her cheek.

That, however, returned again as Robert, after a short cough and another hit at the ' Guardian,' said,

' But you care for him still—you will only be miserable all your life.'

' I hope not, Robert,' she answered. ' I care for him, but I hope my life will not be miserable through caring for him. You must not think that, because the pleasure you have given me in bringing me this paper was a painful one, such news of him will not some day be a pleasure free from any pain. I feel that it will, but at present my loss is fresh to me. When I am strong and go back home, I shall try and work very hard for them. I shall work in the fields as you do, making my pleasure out of it—though neither I nor my fields will ever reflect the rich sunshine of God as you and yours do, Robert. It has been a great pleasure to me, seeing you so happy.'

'There are such things as fools' paradises,' answered Robert.

'I don't think *you* have to do with any such places, Robert. I think that the life you lead might have been planned by King Solomon in the very flower of his wisdom.'

Robert's hand that hung over the arm of his chair swung quickly to and fro as if beating an imaginary tambourine—but he said nothing.

'I think you are vexed with me, Robert,' Hirell said, looking at him anxiously. 'Is it about this paper being sent to you? Indeed it is far from being my wish that you should be troubled in this way.'

'No, I am not vexed—that's not the word for it,' Robert answered; 'that seems to mean some peevish sort of annoyance. You were agitated—you turned quite pale when I gave you that paper, because it was from some one you have loved a few months, and who loves you; but suppose'— and he turned his head, and looked full and steadily at her— 'suppose you had it from another woman who pretends to love him, and looks to you to give it to him—what should you feel then—especially if, instead of a few months, you had loved him for many years, as I have loved you?'

'Oh, Robert; that is past.'

'Is it? I have yet to learn that, Hirell.'

They looked at each other a moment, she scarcely believing him, and he wondering sadly how she could have doubted.

Then she bent her head, and pressed her hands together beneath the table in much distress.

'Oh, Robert! I hope I did not deceive you in any way when you spoke to me last September. Oh, I should be so grieved if—'

'You did not deceive me, Hirell. If deceived, I deceived myself. You know how much easier it is to me to look on the best side of things; and, as to your being grieved, rather than that—I would have let you go on, thinking my love no stronger and no more enduring than you evidently have thought it.'

Hirell put her thin little hands to her face, saying,

'This makes it worse and worse, Robert, my coming here, and being a burden to you, and a pain, through him—through those letters; but I didn't know; I didn't know. I never thought he would find out where I had gone, for one thing;

believe me, I could never have endured the thought of his coming to *your* house with letters and messages for me. And, when you spoke to me last year, I did not think for a moment that you were much disappointed by my answer; and the next hour I seemed to understand why you had spoken. I thought then that you did not love me at all, and it was only your generous wish to be in a position to give you the right of helping us that made you speak to me. Oh, I beg your pardon, Robert. You have much to forgive me for.'

'What have I to forgive you for, Hirell?' said Robert, in a voice that had in it a strange mingling of self-contempt and tender generosity; 'for being the means of keeping me to one ambition—that of making my home, and fortune, and my own life more worthy of you. Are they too good to you now, either of them, under their improvements? When I spoke to you it was altogether too sudden. I could not help myself. But I did not look on it as a fair answer from you. I hoped for a different one next time I should ask the same question. When I heard suddenly you were engaged to him whom I was fool enough to take to your house, of course I turned a nuisance to myself, and everybody else. When I heard that there was some trouble connected with the engagement, I supposed through your father, and you came here to us, you did me more good than anything else could have done. I thought if it is a brother and friend she wants, she shall have a right sound and faithful one. I went to your father to reason with him, and I often met Cunliff here, and told him not to be cast down. Yes, I offered *my* comfort, when he had *your* love. Oh, Hirell!'

'Robert!' cried Hirell, her face very white and streaming with tears, as she held out with a despairing gesture both her hands towards him; 'take the thanks, the poor poor thanks of one who has nothing else to offer you for all your goodness to her! Nothing, Robert, nothing; no love; no hope.'

'Then if *I* am satisfied with the poor poor thanks,' said Robert, laying the little hands together, and holding them very gently and reverentially in his own, 'will *you* be? or will you give me also the pain of seeing that you take your confidence from me, and look upon me as not to be trusted as your friend, because there happens to be in me more friendliness for you than you care to accept? Here is, certainly, much of it, Hirell; but only take what you want, and leave the rest. It will always be here for you.'

'Ah, yes, I *do* trust you, and I will always, Robert. But you must not mind me going home. I *must* go; indeed I must.'

'Then you shall go, and I will take you. When *must* you go?'

'This—no, to-morrow—I should *so* like to go to-morrow; but—but, indeed, I could go by myself.'

'Hirell,' said Robert, iu a tone of tender reproach.

'Then please take me.'

CHAPTER L.

ROBERT SETS HIS AFFAIRS IN ORDER.

ROBERT, when he went away from Brockhurst that morning, found a certain sense of relief in the fact that he would not have five minutes' time on his hands till the moment when he should depart with Hirell for Wales.

Nothing had been settled as to the exact train they were to go by, but in his own mind he fixed on one that started from Reculcester at about half-past nine in the morning. He knew that Hirell would look to him to arrange for her to go as soon as possible, yet he knew she would not wish to give his mother such surprise and uneasiness as going that same day would assuredly cause her. He got the exact time of the train from Wrigly, the foreman, and decided that he would go back to Brockhurst in the afternoon and have it settled.

He did not go to the hooded house for that formidable noon-day meal which Mrs. Payne made so much ado about; he felt very little inclined for the sight of it or her, but he persuaded himself it was want of time, not appetite, that kept him away.

So he busied himself in helping to move a light fence that was in the way of the mowers, and this taking him about two hours, brought him to the time when he knew Hirell and his mother would have taken their work and books, and settled themselves under the trees on the lawn. Then he went round to the garden-door, and came upon them in a hurried, business-like, matter-of-fact way, asking Hirell if the morning train would suit her.

'Very well indeed, Robert, thank you,' she answered; and

Robert seeing they had both been crying, became more in a hurry than ever.

'Then I'll be round with the trap at eight,' he said, and left them without another word.

And now that that duty was over, there was still the rest of the hot June afternoon and long June evening to get through. He must not go home till he was obliged—home to the dreary, unfurnished house, with its gloomy, darkened windows, and cobwebbed ceilings, and unnatural silence, broken only by the slipshod tread of Mrs. Payne on the stairs and in the great empty rooms. No, that must be put off as long as it possibly could be. Besides, had he not the new stands for the ricks to place, as well as the rick in the south yard to finish? And there was the mare, that had got slightly hurt with the pitchfork, to be taken over to the veterinary surgeon at Ninfield.

By four o'clock the new stands were ready, and were being admired by all who had assisted with them; and Robert had some hay brought to show how the foundations of the ricks were to be managed.

After this he went the round of the hay-fields, and had some tea brought out to him from Brockhurst kitchen. Then he finished in the south yard, and set off for Ninfield with the mare.

The surgeon advised that she should be left and sent for the next morning, so Robert had to walk home.

Ninfield is the nearest post town to Nytimber, which has no post-office of its own, and Robert, recollecting he would be gone before the letters reached home in the morning, thought he would call in for them as he passed the little shop. The postmaster left counting a pound of candles for a little girl, to attend to Robert; and when he had given him what letters he had for him, he asked, to Robert's great surprise, if Sir John Cunliff was staying at Nytimber.

'Certainly not,' said Robert, 'he's been gone above a week.'

Then the postmaster told him that some poor man had done nothing but tramp from here to Reculster, and back again from Reculster here, in search of Sir John the whole week.

Uneasy, wild ideas about Elias floated through Robert's mind as he went home. He soon dismissed them as he saw their absurdity. If Elias wanted Cunliff, he would certainly have gone to Nytimber first. Then he remembered some man had come making enquiries of Mrs. Payne about Cunliff, the day after his departure ; and Robert had taken no notice of it at the time, thinking the man was probably some public-house hanger-on, whom Cunliff had employed on some errand and forgotten to pay. In all probability this was the same man who had been so persistent in his enquiry at Ninfield, and as Robert remembered his appearance, he was able to dismiss all fears about Elias.

When he got home it was past nine, but still light, and though he was very tired, he nevertheless felt a great reluctance to go into the Hooded House. He had now seen to all that required his attention before a day's absence ; but there was upon him a strange fit of carefulness, an anxiety that nothing should be neglected, and a strong wish to leave all things in as much order as possible.

He had not the slightest idea of staying away an hour longer than he was obliged, yet he found himself arranging things so that work could go on a week or two without him.

He showed this so plainly by wanting things done which did not matter for some time to come, that his men were all of one mind as to his secret intention of making his absence longer than he said it would be.

Robert himself was not a little puzzled by the mood that was upon him. He had never experienced it before on the eve of a journey to Wales or anywhere else. He could not tell *why* he was so anxious about the padlock being put on the gate of the three-acre field, when the sheep were not to be turned into it for a fortnight ; he only felt that he *was* anxious, and should think and fidget about it if it were not done. Rather than neglect it, when he found he really had not courage to knock again at the door of Wrigley's cottage (he had already disturbed him three times since his return from Ninfield) he got a padlock and chain, and went himself to put it on the gate.

He did not return across the fields, but round by the road past the pound and the Hop Pole.

The moon had risen, and the hay-fields looked very pleasant under its soft light. There seemed an air of peace and order over all things that was soothing to Robert's restless mind, which grew quieter and more satisfied as he walked home along the silent road.

When he got past the Hop Pole he saw a figure approaching

from the opposite side, and quickly recognised it as belonging
to one whom he could not pass by.

'Sir John Cunliff!'

'I am glad to have found you at last, Mr. Chamberlayne; I
have been waiting more than an hour at your house. Is it not
rather strange that none of your people could find you?'

Sir John spoke in a half irritable, half satirical tone, that
astonished Robert even more than it annoyed him.

'Well, I don't know that it's very strange, Sir John,' he
answered, 'considering that my people—my only available people
at this hour—consist of poor rheumatic old Mrs. Payne, and
her little nephew.'

Robert had determined that he would not be the first to
hold out his hand after such a salutation from Sir John, but
he soon saw there was to be no hand-shaking for them that
night.

'No doubt you have been surprised at not seeing me down
before, Mr. Chamberlayne?'

'Not at all,' said Robert, 'I am only surprised at seeing you
here now.'

They had begun to walk slowly by the side of the churchyard wall: suddenly Cunliff stopped, and said almost
fiercely—

'Did you think I would receive such a letter as yours
without demanding an explanation?'

'Yes,' answered Robert, trying to keep down the bitterness
and contempt that seemed as if they would burst from him or
choke him; 'I did think you would be careful enough of what
self-respect you may have left to do so.'

'Then,' replied Cunliff growing more calm as Robert
became more excited, 'you are greatly mistaken. I do most
undoubtedly demand to hear your reasons for writing me such
a letter.'

'Very well, hear them, if you wish. Certain representations of yours caused me to undertake for another's sake a
most unwelcome office. When you had gone, I discovered
that those representations were false, and I wrote immediately
and told you that I withdrew my promise; there's your
explanation, Sir John!'

And Robert made as if he would continue his walk homeward, but Cunliff again stood in his path.

'Mr. Chamberlayne, you have most grossly misunderstood

either those representations of mine you mention, or the person who has made you believe them to be untrue I shall certainly require you to go, for my benefit, more fully into your motives for this sudden and not exactly honourable charge.'

Robert turned with the full intention of giving Sir John a very much plainer explanation than he had yet given—one that he should find it impossible to misunderstand; but as he turned, he saw a man standing watching them; apparently he had been there some little time, observing them with great interest.

When he saw he was noticed he came close to them, and looked with quiet, earnest scrutiny first at one and then the other.

Robert recognised him then as the stranger who had enquired after Sir John of the haymakers some days ago; and as the same, too, he had no doubt, who had so beset the postmaster at Ninfield all the week.

He was a short man with unusually broad shoulders, round back, and head projecting forward. The eyes that looked at Cunliff and Chamberlayne were large, of a greenish gray, and were bloodshot and heavy, as if with fatigue and want of sleep. Yet there was a restless, wild sort of light in them ; a fire that must long have destroyed sleep; that must have made the lids throb and ache, when they tried to keep closed. Dust, damp, and sun had dyed his clothes to the usual hue of the tramp's livery, mud colour. The sole and upper leather of one boot had come apart, and an inflamed, bleeding foot appeared between.

Chamberlayne felt an inward shrinking as the man looked at him, and thought to himself that if he had come with the lowest of tramps to the hop-picking, he should send him away with a shilling in his pocket rather than employ him.

Cunliff looked at him with less disgust and more curiosity, and a vague feeling of having seen him before.

When he had given that piercing look into the face of each, the man asked in a civil quiet voice, that seemed about as weary as the rest of him,—

' I ask pardon, gentlemen, but will you tell me which of you two might be Sir John Cunliff, Bart., the new member for the borough of—? '

He said ' Bart.' as if it were an indispensable part of the name.

'I am, my man; what do you want with me?' said Sir John.

The man went a step closer to him, and his eyes seemed to see nothing else now than Cunliff's face. When he spoke his voice was much deeper, much more laboured.

'Will you grant a poor man a few words with you in private, Sir John Cunliff, Bart.? I've come a long way, I've come from your own place, I've come a purpose for a few words with you.'

' Out with them, then,' said Cunliff, ' this is quite as private as needs be, my man. What is it you want to ask me?'

Robert had by no means any very friendly feelings towards Sir John just then, but he did not quite care to offer to leave him alone, at this deserted end of the village, with a character by whom he was so unpleasantly impressed. He leaned, half sitting, on the low churchyard wall, and watched the man closely.

He remained silent a moment or two after he saw that Sir John was not going to grant him a private interview, looked on the ground, then at Robert, then once more brought his bright, bloodshot gaze back to Cunliff's face, and said,

' I'm a tenant of yourn; I used to live at Prospect Cottages, about a mile from Werge Castle. Can you call 'em to mind—Prospect Cottages? P'raps you don't know you've got such things on the estate. P'raps if you've seen 'em you didn't know 'em from pigsties. A good many don't when they see 'em.'

Sir John began to feel hot and uncomfortable, and to wish Robert had not waited. These were the very cottages he had had such endless complaints about. He knew them well enough, though he answered the man's look with one proudly, almost insolently calm, when contrasted with the ungovernable passion of the other's face.

'P'raps you don't know 'em,' he went on; 'I hardly think myself as you do; but it lays between you and another, and I've come to you as a gentleman I can hear the truth from. I want to know whether you, or the devil in the shape o' that man Jarman, is responsible for the state o' them holes you call Prospect Cottages; and responsible for bullying and threatening the rent out of the poor wretches as tenants 'em, bullying and threatening it out penny by penny ? I don't say it's you, I don't believe it's you, but I want to *know*. I want to be able to give Jarman his lies back in his own throat if it's him, which he swears it isn't.'

' My man,' said Cunliff with sudden seriousness and decision, ' whatever you have to say—which I advise you to shorten as much as possible—say to me. I am alone entirely responsible for the things you mention. Jarman acts only under my orders. You would be a great coward as well as a fool to annoy him with your complaints.'

He paused a moment, intending to speak of contemplated, improvements and perhaps some compensation, but the prolonged and peculiar gaze of the man's eyes on his face stopped him, and made him say sharply :

'Come now, an end of this, if you please ! You've been seeking me to ask me for money, is that it ? Well, what is it you're in want of ? '

'What is it I'm in want of ? ' repeated the man without moving his eyes. ' Well, I'm very poor, sir. Now I think of it, I've nothing left but—but something as belongs to you.'

' To me ? well, what is that ? '

The man withdrew his eyes then, and, glancing furtively at Robert, began to feel in his pocket.

Then letting his hand remain there, he looked up at Cunliff again, and said—

' Well, you asked me—you kindly asked me—Sir John Cunliff, Bart., what money it is as I stand in need of. I have made my reckonings, I have considered what would make up to me for my wife's death, which between you and me and the Almighty—Sir John Cunliff Bart.—came of that stye we lived in ; of that and Jarman's d—d bullying tongue, and nothing else, let doctors put what cheating Latin name to it they like. I've reckoned her death, and the babby's at her stone cold breast, and my twin lads, born strong and hearty—so help me God, and my little eldest wench, the flower of the flock, the apple o' my eye ! All within a year o' their mother. Sir John Cunliff, Bart., I have made my reckonings, and I find nothing will pay me—no mortal money—nothing, Sir John Cunliff, Bart., but your cursed, lazy, profligate, murderous life ! '

His hand flew from the pocket wherein it had been hidden ; a pistol was levelled at Cunliff, who was quite off his guard, for he had not been able to follow the man in his thick, passionate speech, and had not the slightest idea of his danger till he saw the pistol, heard a cry from Robert, saw him rush to strike at the extended arm. But even Robert, watchful of the man and quick as he had been, was not in time—or at least was only in time to make the arm swerve and himself receive the shot.

He fell first to the wall, rested there an instant, then dropped heavily to the ground.

At that sight Cunliff leaped upon the man with the ferocity of a wild beast, and just prevented him firing a second time.

They struggled for some moments very fiercely. At first Cunliff had the best of it; but as soon as the man understood his antagonist, and in what way he was strongest or weakest, he began to have mastery over him. He seemed possessed by a kind of demoniac strength and spring. At last Cunliff feared he would really be able to get his hand free and fire; but at that moment they were so near Robert that the latter— helpless as he was—managed to seize the man's neck from behind, and hold his head down to the ground. Then Sir John got possession of the pistol, and struck the assassin a blow that partly stunned him.

He next ran to the 'Hop Pole' Inn, that was only a few yards off, and brought back the landlord and one or two of Robert's own men that were sitting in the general bar-room and kitchen.

When they reached the spot where Robert lay, they found the man standing up looking about him in a sort of stupor, and putting his hand to his bleeding forehead.

He made no sort of resistance when the landlord gave directions for him to be locked up in an outhouse, till the police at Ninfield could be sent to in the morning.

While this was being done Cunliff was on his knees examining Robert's wound. It was in the right shoulder, the ball having passed completely through.

Where was the nearest surgeon? Sir John demanded, with great agitation, as he looked up from the broad chest covered with blood. There was a surgeon living at Ninfield, but he was away on the Continent; so that none nearer than Mrs. Chamberlayne's own doctor at Recculeester could be thought of, and he never went out at night.

'What is his name? He shall come out to-night if he values his life,' said Sir John. Then he told one of Robert's men to get him Robert's black horse from the stables at the Hooded House.

Clutterbuck, the landlord of the 'Hop Pole,' had gone to unhook his long swing shutter to lay Robert on. Sir John bent over him, and whispered—

'I feel what a life has been risked in saving mine. Try and forgive me, Robert Chamberlayne.'

Robert's white lips smiled, and he gave Sir John's hand a very genial, but cold, weak grasp, and said—

'Let them fetch Wrigley. Let him go home first to tell— my mother.'

Wrigley, with whom Robert was always quarrelling, had already been called, and was standing close to him.

He was much touched by Robert's asking for him before anyone else, and hurried away without a word to fulfil his request. He knew the story he had to tell, that Mr. Robert had got hurt in saving Sir John Cunliff from a madman, who had tried to shoot him.

By the time he came back Sir John had gone off on Robert's horse for the surgeon, though not before he had helped to place him on the rude litter that had been prepared for him.

Robert did not lose consciousness: he saw, as one in a painful trance, the sights familiar from his childhood— the pound, the stocks, the church, the little cottages, the crowds of ricks, and the hay-fields. He noticed all as they bore him slowly down the village. He felt that he understood now his anxiety to set all his affairs in order. It was a strange foretaste of what was coming. He was glad now to think of all that he had done that day.

The rick in the south yard looked mellow and fair in the moonlight ; and it was pleasant to him, as his languid eyes rested on the soft undulating lines of raked hay in the fields, to think that the new stands were already for it, and it could all be managed so well without him. He was even pleased to think of the padlock and chain he had put on the gate of the three-acre field.

When the little procession stopped at Brockhurst, Robert's senses were a good deal confused by the lights, and by the figures standing in the hall.

He did not know whether they had carried him upstairs or not. He only knew that his mother and Hirell were standing or kneeling beside him, and that he tried to speak.

He did speak, but fainted away as soon as he had said to Hirell, with a smile—

'You must let me sleep at home to-night.'

CHAPTER LI.

LEAVE-TAKINGS AT BROCKHURST.

MRS. CHAMBERLAYNE behaved very bravely the first night, but the shock of Robert's accident, and the exertion it caused her to make, proved too much for her. The next day she was too ill to sit up, and her great anxiety to be at her son's bedside made her worse.

When Mrs. Payne of the Hooded House heard that a nurse for Robert was being sought, she came over with her little bundle, and entreated with tears to be allowed to take her place in his room. Knowing nothing of her shortcomings from Robert, they allowed her to do so, and she proved a miracle of patience and devotion.

Hirell's journey was indefinitely postponed. She could not leave Brockhurst while its master and mistress both lay ill, and unable to help each other.

It was a source of great bitterness to her that all this trouble had been brought upon the house through her, and she tried hard to do as much good and be as great a comfort to them as possible.

She managed all the house very cleverly and quietly. The doctor, and all who came to enquire after Robert, spoke of her with high praise.

One day a letter from her father enclosed the following from Cunliff:

'MY DEAR HIRELL,—Forgive me for troubling you at a time when you must unite with those around you in wishing you had never met me or heard my name. I wish, however, to give you a few particulars as to the end of this sad business, which has, I fear, lost me any lingering esteem you may have had left for me, and gained more than I dare think of for the brave saviour of my unworthy life. I know that both of you will feel far more with the outraged tenant than the outraged landlord, and that you will be glad to hear I have procured his discharge, and sent him off to Australia, with means that will give him a fair chance of beginning a new life. I arrived at Ninfield prison with his discharge, just in time to prevent the poor fellow from committing suicide. At first he cared little for his release, but when I had talked to him, confessing my own negligence, and showed him what sad and unlooked-for results had come of his vengeful resolution ; and when from my questions to him I discovered there was still one thing dear to him left in the world, and that he could benefit that thing by living and accepting my assistance, so much less than what I really owe him, he came round, listened to reason, yielded to reason. The 'one ewe lamb' proved to be a certain small deformed nephew, the superintendence of whose small outfit was the first thing that brought a gleam of interest on his uncle's face—whose small form he carried on board in his arms, and whose small hand waved me a friendly farewell as the vessel sailed away. Little peacemaker! May he live to outgrow bigger and better suits than the new corduroy ones that gave him so much pleasure !

'And now, Hirell, I must confess I have another motive for writing to you. I wish to tell you, as I have told your father in the letter that goes to him with this, that I shall seek you at his house on your return there, to receive your final answer. I claim such a meeting as due to me, even were my offences a thousand times greater than what they are. I entreat that you send me no answer to this, at least not that answer which, I fear, under present circumstances, would only be such a one as must destroy the hope that still lives in me, though perhaps it should long since have given up the ghost. But whilst I live, and whilst *you* live, Hirell, it never will. But even if you do send me such an answer I will not take it. No. I demand a meeting at your father's house. If you desire it to be a last one, you can make it so. Never will I molest you after that, if your heart remains hardened against me still.

'If Robert Chamberlayne will accept my hearty regards, give him them ; and remember, Hirell, it may some day be in your power to make us as warm friends as fate seems deter-mined we should be. Yours faithfully,   J. R. CUNLIFF.'

Hirell found on reading her father's letter that he had re-plied to Cunliff instantly, complying with his request, which he told his daughter was a natural and manly one, and that he would not have it refused.

So there would be fresh agitation waiting her in that home where she was so longing to go for rest and comfort.

But it did not make her wish to delay her return. It would, she felt, now be best to get back ; and have the meeting over and done with, and the old calm, pure, monotonous life be-ginning for her once more.

Hirell did not see Robert after the night they brought him home till the day she left. Mrs. Chamberlayne thought it best that it should be so. On the afternoon when Robert had come to them on the lawn, and found them with red eyes, they had opened their hearts to each other about him. Mrs. Chamberlayne had told Hirell how long, and with what patient hope Robert had loved her, but she had also sadly ac-cepted Hirell's passionate and despairing avowal of her love for the man whom she felt she could never consent to marry.

After that Mrs. Chamberlayne fully made up her mind that Hirell *would* sooner or later marry Sir John Cunliff. And when Robert lay ill, she jealously guarded him from one gleam of false hope. It would be so bitter to take it from him, if it grew into him with his new strength.

No one ever knew what suffering that one glimpse of Robert's white face had stamped on Hirell's heart ; or how for many days, as he lay between life and death, she was tor-mented by the horrible fear that he might never see his ripening harvest gathered in.

But Robert got better and began to regain his strength very soon, and as Mrs. Payne declared ' to eat like a wolf.'

Three weeks had elapsed since his accident, when it was decided that Mr. Wrigley was to take Hirell home.

Mrs. Chamberlayne, who was now well enough to be carried every day into her son's room, saw that Robert certainly would not be content without Hirell's coming to bid him farewell. So when she was dressed for her journey, Hirell had to go and tap at the sick-room door ; and was bidden to come in by Mrs. Chamberlayne, who was having a late breakfast at Robert's bedside

Hirell was determined not to disturb him by the sight of her own emotion. But when she saw him lying back on the bank of white pillows, his face almost as white, and thinner, and darker under the eyes than in his school-boy days, she felt something swelling in her throat that made her afraid to speak, as she took his hand, and returned his smile of greeting. Her eyes were full of tears, which ran over when Robert said,

'They will all miss you sadly, Hirie.'

That nearly made her burst out with passionate reproaches on herself, for ever having come and brought such misfortune upon them, but she controlled herself and only said,

'Oh, Robert, hush! Forgive me, but don't praise me, after all I have brought on you. Dear Robert, I cannot bear that!'

She sat down pressing her handkerchief to her eyes, and trying to grow calm.

'Will your father let me come down to Bod Elian, when I get out of Mrs. Payne's snuffy hands?' asked Robert; 'I shall need mountain air then if ever anyone did.'

'Oh yes, please, Robert, we shall all be so glad.'

'Well, I shall certainly come. How strange, if I am kept here till just about the same time that I was down last year!'

At that moment Susan knocked at the door, and told them Mr. Wrigley said the time was up, and was the young lady ready?

Hirell rose hastily, once more shook hands with Robert, then knelt down by Mrs. Chamberlayne, and the two clung to each other like mother and daughter.

When Hirell rose and was moving towards the door, she stood still and looked round, and saw that Robert had turned his face upon his arm. The morning sunshine was on his hand that used to be so brown, that now was white and thin. Her eyes followed the sunshine from it to the rich fields without, and a thrill went through her as she thought, what if that hand should never again be busy there with sickle or seed?

Mrs. Chamberlayne looked at her as if she would bid her to go without taking more notice of the invalid, but Hirell with an air of gentle defiance stood still a moment, then walked back to the bedside with something of the old sweet saintly gravity.

'May the Lord bless you and restore you, Robert!' she said solemnly, and kissed him.

She spoke the prayer while her lips were touching his forehead, so that the kiss was most holy, the prayer most sweet.

CHAPTER LII.

KEZIA.

Mr. WRIGLEY considered his time of far too much importance for him to think of staying an hour in Wales. Indeed he returned to Dolgarrog by the car in which he took Hirell up to Bod Elian.

Only Kezia was at home, Elias having gone to a cattle fair at Aber.

She was standing outside the kitchen door by the churn when Hirell came behind her. She had just left off her work to rest her arms, and was looking along the Aber road, visible from here for many miles.

'Kezia!' said Hirell, then burst out with a wild peal of laughter as Kezia started, and turned towards her. Kezia laughed a little, and cried a little, all in a tranquil way, very different from Hirell's. And then they went in and sat down, holding one another's hands by turns—asking and answering questions, and falling into fits of tearful or smiling silence.

'And father's well, Kezia—you're quite sure?'

'Yes, thank the Lord, he is well in health.'

'But is he very much troubled about things—about money, Kezia?'

'No, he says his affairs are coming more under his control.'

'Kezia, did he use Robert's money?'

'Oh dear, no! I never dared tell him. I sent it back to Robert, because the other money could be got. But somehow, your father did not think it all right; so he has not used any of it, but he will tell you what he thinks of it.'

'Kezia, it's not about *his* coming, is it, that father's troubled?'

'Oh no; he thinks that right and natural. You know he wrote to Sir John Cunliff yesterday, telling him you were coming home to-day.'

'Did he?' said Hirell, starting up, then sitting down again, and turning pale—'then he may be here any day—any minute,' she added with a shiver.

'Did your father tell you when he wrote,' asked Kezia, 'that Mr. Rhys had sent here to know whether Sir John was coming back, and if so, when we expected him?'

'No.'

'Then you don't know that they are back at Dola' Hudol, and that Mrs. Rhys is seriously ill?'

'No, indeed.'

'There has been a deal of talk about them since you've been away.'

Hirell looked at her with keen searching eyes.

That strange tragic little episode in the orchard last year had never quite left her mind; now it seemed to grow more vivid in it.

'Talk, Kezia,' she said, 'what kind of talk?'

'Sir John Cunliff is mixed up with it, Hirell. I should not tell you, but I think you might hear it directly in some extravagant way.'

'How is he mixed up in it, Kezia? Tell me all. You are right—I ought to know.'

'Oh, Hirell, they say Sir John Cunliff has broken her heart. They say they cared for each other too much, and when Mr. Rhys was away, kept meeting instead of avoiding each other. She led a wretched life when she came back here, through Mr. Rhys knowing about it; and now, though it's said he's forgiven her, and they are quite reconciled, her heart seems broken, and they say she's dying. But Hirell, *bach*, don't look so.'

'Go on, Kezia; is it known why they want *him?*'

'No, who can say? Hirell, Hirell! my sweet dear.'

Kezia put her arm round the poor drooping form, and drew it to the open door for air, and seating it there, fetched some water, which the white faint lips sipped gratefully.

After a long silence, Hirell roused herself, and said—

'Let us say no more about this, Kezia. Come, I'm longing to know all the news—*our* news—which, however sad and miserable, is never, never worse, never disgraceful. I think you mean father is troubled about something, if it isn't about money.'

There was a silence again, during which Kezia's light eyelashes grew wet.

'Dear Hirell, you know how Hugh left us. Your father has felt it very deeply.'

Another silence, and soon Kezia lays her hand on Hirell's, and says with a faint blush—

'I haven't thanked you yet, Hirell, for the dear note you wrote me after you had heard from Hugh.'

'And, Kezia, you haven't told me anything yet that you know I am longing to hear.'

'I'm afraid I have very, very little to tell you, dear.'

'But, Kezia, has nothing come, then, of those letters that Hugh told me he had left—one for you and one for father?'

Kezia shook her head, and smiled a sweet patient smile.

'Did Hugh tell you what he told me about—about father?' asked Hirell.

'Yes.'

'Kezia!' Hirell knelt down before her, and took hold of her arms, and looked searchingly into her timid serious blue eyes; 'tell me the truth, dear Kezia, do you after all care more for Hugh than father?'

The eyes looked back at her wonderingly, the head shook gently but emphatically.

'Then you do love father, Kezia?   Dearly?'

The fair puritan-looking little head wavered a moment, then fell forward on Hirell's shoulder.

'Oh Hirell! your mother joined our hands. She often told me how she dreaded leaving him—he was so stern to himself, she said, so severe and self-sacrificing, he needed some one to be always guarding him from himself. We had always been such friends—ever since I was a child. In her last moments, Hirell, she joined our hands, and asked him to let me take her place.   I have her written words about it; I will show it you, and her own wedding-ring. Well, dear Hirell, I thought—before Hugh wrote that letter—I thought I had never found favour in your father's sight; but though I thought so, I felt, dear, I'd rather be his servant all my days than another's wife.'

'But now, Kezia, that you know the truth?'

Kezia raised her head, and looked at Hirell with a gentle pride.

'And now that I know the truth, Hirell, what can *I* do?'

Then Hirell understood it all.   Hugh had been able to tell Kezia Elias's secret, but of Kezia's he had known nothing. Therefore Elias knew nothing of it either.   Hirell understood in a moment why her father had not been able to speak.   She knew his nature well enough to be sure of how he would doubt the possibility of Kezia's loving him.

She said nothing more, but kissed Kezia and went upstairs.

Kezia was the first to see Elias coming home, and she called Hirell to go and meet him.

She remained in the kitchen herself busily preparing supper.

Instead of coming in, Elias and Hirell when they reached the house remained, to Kezia's surprise, walking up and down in front of it.

At last they came in together, and Hirell took her father to his old seat. Kezia was busy at the fire warming buttermilk, to pour on the oat-cake she had been breaking into the basins on the supper-table.

To her amazement Hirell took hold of her hand, and drawing her to Elias put it into his hand, saying—

'Father, why don't you give me the mother that my own mother left me?'

And then she went out and left them alone.

It was not long before Elias opened the door and called—

'Hirell, my daughter, where are you?'

And when she came, he pointed with both his hands to Kezia as she stood with her head bent down weeping for joy, and said—

'See then—your mother. I go to give thanks where thanks are due.'

The evening was a very quiet and peaceful one. They talked chiefly of the great meeting there was to be at the opening of the chapel next month. Hirell had to hear how it had been arranged that there should be a great gathering of the English miners on Moel Mawr; and how they were to be addressed by the Reverend Ephraim Jones and other gifted friends.

CHAPTER LIII.

AN ARRIVAL AT BOD ELIAN.

A FORTNIGHT had passed since Hirell's return home, and yet Sir John had not made his appearance. His delay was, however, fully accounted for by the newspapers, which showed how importantly he was occupied—and which officious neighbours took care to bring or send in to the Morgans, although it was generally believed they had little reason to be pleased with him.

The Reverend Ephraim Jones, with whom Hugh now lodged, sent Elias several very favourable reports of him—though he owned himself he began to fear that his work at Messrs. Tidman's, to whose house he had been readmitted, was too hard for him, too exhausting, the minister owned—both to the spirit and the flesh.

A few days afterwards they had a letter from Hugh himself, in which he told them how, to his astonishment, and for the moment to his shame and humiliation, Sir John Cunliff had appeared one day at Tidman's, introduced himself to those gentlemen as a friend of Hugh's family, and begged to be permitted to take him away for a few hours, a request that was granted with a marked sense of the honour done in making it. Hugh said he could scarcely help laughing at the change that in an instant came over his employers' attitude towards him, as they looked at him and at the card on the table before them, bearing the words—'Sir John Cunliff, Bart., Werge Castle.'

Hugh told them he had spent a delightful day, and that his future prospects had been discussed as kindly by Sir John as if he had been his dearest friend for many years. When things were more settled, Hugh said he would tell them what Sir John had proposed to him.

It wanted three days to the first of the great prayer meetings, and Hirell and Kezia were sitting in the afternoon knitting near the open door, and practising the hymns in which they were to take the lead on the grand day, when they heard the sound of wheels coming sharply round the field road.

They were unmistakably the wheels of a Dolgarrog car. Hirell and Kezia both rose hastily, and went into the house.

'It is him at last,' said Hirell. 'Oh, Kezia, I wish father was at home.'

She had turned so pale and trembled so, Kezia thought her quite unfit to meet the visitor, and drew her gently into her father's room.

Then Kezia went herself to receive Sir John, as she had no doubt whatever the guest would prove to be.

Hirell heard her in another minute returning, a manly step accompanying hers.

Surely she would not bring him here, Hirell thought, rising and holding fast the edge of the open bureau.

The door opened—Kezia appeared, beaming—and behind her came Robert Chamberlayne,

Was it intense relief or bitter disappointment? Kezia wondered, that made Hirell burst into tears, and sob so violently that it was several minutes before she could quiet her.

Robert stood looking very serious and astonished.

'There,' said Kezia, when she had got her a little quiet, 'now see how well master Robert is looking ; I shouldn't have guessed he had been ill at all if I hadn't known all about it ; no, indeed ! '

'Robert ! ' said Hirell, smiling through her tears, and holding out her hand 'I couldn't help it—I think I never was so startled.'

'What, did you take me for my own ghost, Hirell ? ' asked Robert.

'I thought—I was afraid—you were to be as I left you a long time—much longer than this. And you came in looking as well as if nothing had happened. It is no wonder I was startled, Robert. When one has got used to everything being quite changed, it does startle one to see anybody looking so exactly the same as ever, as you did when you came in. I am very glad, more glad than I can say, Robert, to see you so.'

This speech was a great deal more sweet to Robert than Hirell had intended to make it. It made him happier than she had any idea of ; and enabled him to talk to her with less restraint than there had been between them for a very long while.

She was greatly interested in all the Nytimber gossip that he brought, and felt as if it came from a place in which many years of her life had been spent.

Elias welcomed Robert a great deal more warmly than he had taken leave of him when he had last left Bod Elian ; and even smiled slightly several times, during supper, at Robert's accounts of Mr. Wrigley's blunders with his new machines.

It was not till just before prayers that Kezia told him of the visit they were daily expecting, and then all his happiness seemed gone like a dream, and he could not tell how it had taken possession of him. He had know, he told himself—he had known, ever since Hirell came to Kent, that she would marry Cunliff at last, whatever happened to make him think otherwise.

The next day was Friday, and Robert spent it with his old tutor at the Abbey Farm. He went to church in the evening, and saw Mr. Rhys alone in the Dola' Hudol pew—looking so much older and less strong than in the old days, that Robert scarcely at first knew him.

He got back to Bod Elian too soon to evade the ministers

who had been there to arrange with Elias certain matters connected with the next Sunday's meeting. When he saw Elias taking leave of some one at the door, in the twilight, Robert's heart grew cold and heavy. It must be Cunliff. He had been, then. All was settled ; and how ?

When he went in, after watching the retreating figure in the dusk, he thought he had never heard such music as the voice of Elias, when it said to him rather reproachfully—

'I would you had come a minute sooner, Robert Chamberlayne, that you might have met our gifted young friend, the Reverend Griffith Griffiths, who has but just now left us.'

Robert was so greatly relieved that he was able to express quite a lively regret at having lost the chance of making the young minister's acquaintance.

The evening was concluded by the usual prayers, and an additional one for a blessing on the great undertakings of to morrow.

CHAPTER LIV.

HIRELL'S CALL.

ALL at Bod Elian were stirring early on the morning of the great day.

Robert was out in time to help Hirell with her little farm-yard duties, as, indeed, he had been every morning since his arrival, making Hirell half pleased, half vexed.

On that Sunday she had risen earlier, on purpose to avoid him ; and when she saw him sitting on the kennel playing with the dogs and waiting for her, she returned his 'good-morning' with a something so like a frown that it perplexed Robert ; and made him steal an uneasy, inquiring glance at her, which Hirell returned with a very bright, impatient, almost angry one, and they went to their work in silence— Hirell finishing nearly everything Robert tried to do.

One of the cows was ill, and Hirell had to see it take something her father had prepared for it. While they were waiting, Robert ventured a word of advice, but Hirell instead of answering, pulled her hymn-book out of her pocket, and began studying it.

'Well,' said Robert, losing patience, 'if I'm not wanted, I'd better go.'

'Do, Robert,' answered Hirell, almost sadly, 'and be ashamed of me as I am of myself. You thought better of me, I thought better of myself, than that I should hate you seeing all our wretched little contrivances and meannesses, because I've seen how different your place is. I ought not to feel it —I ought not to mind you seeing me do things that you set your ploughboys to do. Go in to breakfast, Robort, and don't be hurt—I'll pray to-day for my pride to be broken, and a better spirit given me, so that I can bear to have a fine gentleman opening and shutting doors and lifting pails for me, and bear to know he's thinking—" and she expected to be Lady Cunliff." There, go along, Robert, I know you are going to say something kind, but I won't hear it. I'm wicked, but I'm not a child—I won't be petted out of my wickedness—I'll get rid of it; I'll humble my spirit to-day by taking to myself the harshest condemnations that Ephraim Jones hurls at the miners.'

Smiling with tears in her eyes, she pushed him gently out of the shed, then shut herself in.

Robert, after a moment's hesitation and perplexity, went in, and as usual told his troubles to Kezia, who took his assistance at the same time gratefully enough.

At breakfast a minister came in hot haste with a letter which he had received from the Reverend Ephraim Jones, who sent word to say that he should not be able to get to Capel Illtyd in time to address his dear brethren there after the morning service, as he had intended. He gave up his task, he said, to no one save Elias Morgan, the founder of the chapel, himself; whom he solemnly commanded to take his place, and not to heed the promptings of Satan to shrink from his duty, but to speak out of the fulness of the truth within him.

Elias was much disturbed by the unlooked-for summons, and retired to ask Divine aid and countenance for such a task.

He returned in a little while, looking calmer and resigned, but anxious.

'I am willing to undertake the trust which is given so suddenly into my hands,' he said to the young minister, ' but I have a weakness to contend with, which our reverend friend has overlooked. I know not how to express myself freely in the English language.'

A A

This was a fact which no one present could doubt. Though Elias spoke English correctly, it was in a slow and rather stilted manner, that must spoil any eloquence he might be inspired with, while taking Ephraim Jones's place.

Hirell had been thinking of it ever since the minister's message had been delivered, and wondering how the difficulty was to be met, for she knew that by far the greater part of the open-air meeting after the service consisted of English and Irish miners.

'Could you, friend Evans, render my words into English as I go on, if I preach in my own tongue?' inquired Elias.

The young minister looked very dubious, and said he did not think it would do—no, he did not at all think it would do.

Hirell felt greatly relieved when she heard brother Evans refuse the task, for she knew it was quite impossible he could do justice to her father's thoughts. He was an amiable, industrious young man, yet he had by no means a strong or original mind; but was, as Ephraim Jones had once described him, 'one of the many who stood forth to smite Satan, but could never do more than tickle him.'

'Could the gifted Griffith Griffiths?' Elias asked.

No. Brother Evans knew he had to hurry away directly after the service, as he was to preach at Aber in the afternoon. Besides, brother Evans thought it decidedly would *not* do; nobody could translate quick enough.

As Elias looked along the table, from one face to another, his eye fell suddenly on what appeared to him a message from Heaven that put an end to all his difficulty. It was Hirell's face looking towards him full of light, and wistful, solemn inquiry. He knew it said to him—

'Father, shall *I* do?' and he answered instantly aloud, and with glad emotion—

'Hirell, beam of light indeed, your call has come! this work is yours—no other's. Be at peace, brother Evans, the multitude shall be spoken to in two tongues at once.'

When Hirell rose with changing colour and trembling hands from her place, Robert, who had not been able to understand the whole of what had passed, the minister and Elias having spoken in Welsh, began to suspect something of the truth, and asked Kezia what it was. When she told him, he turned quickly to Elias, exclaiming—

'No, no, surely, Morgan, you would never let her do that.'

Elias looked at him with calm contempt.

'If you choose to come with us, Robert Chamberlayne,' he said, 'it may be you will be glad the mission has been sent to her. Come, Hirell. We will go and pray together. Brother Evans, your time is precious—we will not keep you.'

'I should never have believed it of Elias,' cried Robert, walking about indignantly, when he was alone with Kezia. 'It wouldn't matter so much for any other woman—but Hirell! Hirell to be stared at and talked over by hundreds of tipsy miners.'

'Ah, Master Robert, leave it to Elias,' said Kezia soothingly. 'He knows what is best. He has wonderful lights; and ah, dear Hirell! it will be a sight to see her giving out her father's sayings, and crowds and crowds looking at her. I always said she was one of the holy women, such as the blessed Paul loved and sent greetings to by Phebe, and now I must get my bonnet on, and be all ready to help the dear child.'

CHAPTER LV.

AT THE MARTYR'S OAK.

They went out together, Hirell walking with her father, Robert with Kezia.

Hirell had since 'her call' changed her dress for a very old black one of Kezia's, and wore black gloves and bonnet.

'Is this part of the humiliation of the day, Hirell?' whispered Robert, touching her sleeve as she waited with him and Kezia, while her father was talking to a group of friends just arrived from Dolgarrog.

She looked down at her rusty dress, and answered—

'No, Robert, this is not humility, this again is pride.'

'How's that?'

'Don't you see that, as the bearer of good tidings, it would better become me to put on cheerful colours, to remember myself only as the Lord's servant, doing His will, and forget myself *as* myself, timid and startled by the gaze of many eyes. But I cannot do this, Robert, so I've put on black, that I shan't be much noticed as I stand with father and the others, who'll all be in black too.'

As they approached the simple, gray little chapel which

Robert remembered so well in its unfinished state, they saw already a large number of miners in straggling groups on the Aber road.

The chapel stood on a mound towards the centre of the stony field that sloped towards Bod Elian.

The morning was warm and sunny, the ascent difficult, and those who came from great distances sat down on the broken walls and heaps of stones, wiping their faces, and waiting for the chapel doors to open.

When they were open, Elias, Hirell, Robert, and Kezia were respectfully made way for; but no sooner had they gone in, and sat side by side on the first long seat, which was for the special use of Elias and his household, than the push and tumult for places began. In an almost incredibly short time the little building was filled.

After this there was still a noise and confusion at the door, and several English jeers and jests about the smallness of the chapel reached Robert's ears, and made him feel more and more irritated at the thought of Hirell addressing such a rabble.

Without waiting for the confusion to stop, the Reverend Griffith Griffiths began the service, and before many minutes those close outside the door, either from curiosity or from despair of distracting the attention of the congregation, became very quiet, though the vast and still increasing number outside and around the chapel made a strange, buzzing, uneven sort of murmur.

Hirell's heart beat fast as she heard it, and thought how soon the service would be over, and her novel and formidable task begin.

At last she knew the time had come. The Reverend Griffith Griffiths was shaking hands with her father, and a cry was raised outside the door of—

'They are coming out—make way, they are coming out.'

There was a noise, as of eager feet, a great movement and bustle within, and soon Hirell found herself out in the strong noon-day sun, her hand held firmly in her father's.

She heard her father give the order that the crowd should draw together, and proceed to the Martyr's Oak higher up the valley, singing as they went a hymn which he gave out, and which he led himself.

The Martyr's Oak was the only tree to be seen from the chapel. It was of great size and age, and held in extreme veneration far and near. Under its branches, said tradition, in tho days of Laud and Whitgift the persecuted flock of Christ had come to worship; and, at times, in the dead of night, when the search was too hot for them to meet in the light of day; and on one occasion a young minister had been captured and hanged upon its branches.

There the people spread themselves out in a kind of half-circle. Many in the front sat down, till row after row was formed, so as to admit those standing behind to share in the expected feast.

Just in front of the broad trunk of the oak rose a short stunted stem, as if some other and younger tree had grown there and been cut down to make a pillar on which a man might stand; and that, with its overshadowing and waving canopy, was the Martyr's Oak.

Elias declined at first to mount to so conspicuous a position, but waving his hand for silence, began to explain that he and his friend had experienced a great disappointment in the absence of the Reverend Ephraim Jones, who had promised to be with them. But God, he said, was no respecter of persons; and had prompted him, Elias Morgan, their humble friend and neighbour, to determine to address them to the best of his ability.

He did this first in Welsh, then in English; and then, also in both languages, explained to them that as it was difficult to him to think in English, and as also there were many there who would not understand him if he used that tongue, his daughter, an earnest child of God, reared from infancy in the one true faith, would endeavour to lift up her voice and translate for them into English what he spoke in Welsh.

Hirell trembled as some English cheers—some mocking, but mostly earnest—were raised as her father ceased speaking. She saw, too, a decided swaying of the crowd, a vehement pushing forward, and heard a few loud English remarks on her appearance, and invitations to stand upon the tree and show herself. She saw Robert standing alone, for he had been deserted by Kezia, who had told him, to his amusement and contempt, that the men and women must separate on leaving the chapel. Hirell saw him standing looking towards her with eyes full of tender vexation.

Her cheeks were very hot—the crowds of familiar and strange faces swam before her eyes. As she tried to look steadily around her, she suddenly laid the other hand on her father's and pressed closer to him.

He looked down at her, and met her eyes looking up at him full of tears, and passionate entreaty.

'What is it, my child?' he whispered in Welsh.

'Pray, pray let me go. I cannot speak. *He* is there, father, I saw him.'

'Sir John Cunliff?'

'Yes.'

Elias gave one stern, hurried glance in the direction the little fluttering hand on his seemed to indicate, and there he saw indeed Sir John Cunliff, looking wonderfully like 'Mr. Rymer,' in his tourist dress.

He did not hesitate a moment after looking at him and around upon the crowd.

'Hirell,' he said, sternly, 'the welfare of all these children of the Almighty Father assembled here must be more regarded by me than the suffering of my own one child. You must not shrink—you shall not—send forth your voice and trust to Him to make it heard. Now follow me instantly.'

And he cried in a loud voice—

'Gweddiwn.'

Immediately a piercing, plaintive tone followed like an echo with the English,

'Let us pray.'

And throughout all that long prayer it never failed, but like a silver bell struck by the same hand that had just sent the deep sonorous sound from one of iron, rang out clearly, thrillingly, and sweetly.

At first the fair young face, with auburn hair pushed back under the black bonnet, and sweet eyes clouded and wandering as if they saw nothing, provoked much rude staring and admiration; but before many minutes the short sentences thrown out by that grand, sonorous base and sweet treble of repetition, began to strike home in many a wild, wicked, and miserable nature, till the air grew more and more silent and clear for the passage of the two voices.

At last the attention of the crowd became rapt and unbroken; smoking, nutcracking, orange-eating, orange-peel-throwing, everything seemed forgotten, but the grand crowding mountain of heads, and God's double-voiced messenger, who spoke as with the mouth of archangel and seraph.

A time had been when Hirell would have looked and acted very differently under such circumstances, and several who listened to her and watched her now knew it. Once, and only a little year ago, she would have spoken to those crowds of men in a way only to make them stare and wonder and forget. Strong in her own purity, and in the purity of all she loved, she would have stood before them coldly radiant, like some angel immeasurably separated from them and their sorrows and their sins and their despairings by her own ignorance of pain, her own calm, cold innocence, and her own unquestioning certainty of her salvation.

But now the pride of her supposed sainthood was gone from her. She no longer looked proudly, as if conscious of its crown, no longer stood proudly as if its spotless robes were on her limbs. In spite of her father's words, which she repeated, her voice and eyes and gestures were full of a passionate humility, which seemed to bid all souls to fall with hers, and own His laws beyond all understanding, and implore the mercy none might hope to deserve.

Elias also had undergone some of this change. The past year had tended to break down his spiritual pride as well as Hirell's. They both were conscious of it—both felt it as a token of divine displeasure, and bowed under it with a meekness and humility that to other eyes than their own became as a crowning glory to their simple and pure natures.

Sir John Cunliff dimly perceived something of this. He noticed, too, how strange and mysterious a sympathy there was between the truly good and the utterly wicked. There was a frightfully depraved-looking fellow near him—ugly with mental and physical deformity—he had been jeering at Hirell longer than any of the others, but had been quiet now for some time, and Sir John noticed that he and many—more or less like him—became most moved by the very sentences which most strongly affected Hirell, while the self-righteous and respectable part of the crowd remained scarcely touched. Perhaps the bond between them was the sense of the immeasurable distance of Him to whom they prayed.

'Poor publican,' thought Sir John, as he saw the heavy, disgusting-looking eyes near him blink, and look down, at sentences that made Hirell's weep. 'How comes it that you are nearer to the angels than to the Pharisees?'

The 'poor publican,' who was in truth a poor navvy, emitted something between a groan and an oath, that Sir John trusted might be taken in Heaven as an 'Amen,' when Elias concluded his closing prayer with these words—which Hirell repeated in English with a pathos and yearning indescribable—

'My God, my God, let it not be that I have forgotten Thee too long ever to find Thee again!

'Let me not go a stranger into the land of death, or the worm find its way to my heart before my spirit hath come unto Thee!'

A cry of exultation from the Welsh broke the silence following the prayer. There was a newcomer seen, recognised as the Reverend Ephraim Jones.

Elias and he met very near to where Sir John Cunliff had moved, making convenient use of the oak-tree's trunk, or descending limbs, for the shelter he needed from time to time, while only seeming to be one of the scattered crowd that clung closely to the vicinity of the pulpit.

The minister was hard-breathed with the hurry of his walk, and in a most profuse sweat, and it was as much as he could do to let out a few words of explanation, while wiping his face, opening out his coat, and throwing back his waistcoat to seek air and coolness.

'Friend Elias, thou dost make me rejoice greatly, yea, and thank God even for my great trouble—this breach of a solemn engagement—when I see and hear of all thy doings in the Lord. And thou also, Hirell Morgan, "Blessed art thou among women!" Would I had myself been a listener! But all in good time I shall hear thee—God willing.'

If a blush was ever detected on Elias's face, it was then. He valued greatly his friend's ability and judgment, and was troubled to feel how sweet to him was this appreciation of faith.

He ought, perhaps, to repel the honour to himself, but his old delicacy of perception forbade, lest he might seem to be reproving his chief.

The two men stepped a little aside from the crowd, and so came still nearer to Cunliff, who could only evade them by turning his back.

Suddenly, to his extreme annoyance, he caught the Rev. Ephraim Jones's eye full and stern upon him.

Cunliff turned at once full face, and lifted his hat.

Elias's attention was now caught, and he, too, saw Sir John, and received his salutation. Before these two could speak or determine whether they should speak to each other at that moment, the minister plucked his friend by the sleeve, and said something in a low tone, which Cunliff only partially heard, but which was enough to send the blood in a rush to his cheek. The words he heard were these :

' As I expected, friend Elias, a mere juggle ! An imposition, for what purpose she best knows—though thou too mayest guess.'

Then with some difficulty the minister reduced his voice to a whisper, a tone he neither loved nor was accustomed to, and Cunliff could hear no more, except the phrase ' spoiling the Egyptians,' which seemed to be uttered by the minister with great unction, and produced a grim smile on Elias's face.

But he saw them glance at him, and felt certain his trick about the five hundred pounds had been discovered.

' Well, what could they make of it ? ' he thought defiantly, but felt horribly annoyed.

The two men moved away as if to evade him.

Presently he saw a considerable portion of the congregation gathering once more together about the Martyr's Oak, and lo ! on the pillar or pulpit, stood the big, unlovely, but not unmajestic figure of the Rev. Ephraim Jones.

'Friends and brethren,' he said in a voice of portentous strength, ' it is not my purpose to-day to weaken by diluting the admirable address that I hear friend Morgan has given you. I shall have another opportunity to talk to you, but I should like to give you yet something more to carry home before you go. Have you not had to-day joyful tidings respecting God ? I know you have. I hope your hearts are full with it ; but you must make room there for yet one crumb of comfort more relating to God's house—yonder chapel !

' It is not for me to tell you its history ; you know it even better than I do. Are there not among you many who, poor as the Scripture widow herself, have given their mites in and for it ? Are there not among you men who, after toiling the whole day for bread for their families, have come here into the dark night, and toiled to make a place where yet another kind of bread should be always found ? But I am not here to praise you, I have little gift that way. I want to tell you how God has raised up for us in his own manner,—do you hear me? in his own manner, which is often not our manner —succour sufficient to finish the good work. All its debt will now be paid off; friend Elias will have the mill-stone taken from his neck, nor that only, for I have the satisfaction to inform you that there will be left, after its entire completion, enough money to form a permanent fund for its repair.'

He was interrupted by the usual Welsh hum of approbation, then by cheers which the English understood better than hums, and then by cries of—

'How? how? how?'

'Five hundred pounds have been sent anonymously—ah, brethen, how sweet charity can exhibit itself!—to our friend Elias Morgan; who, knowing no other just or manly purpose for which it could be sent, accepts, on my advice, the idea that it is for our chapel! hurrah!'

The minister perhaps forgot himself when he waved his hat, and gave that loud hurrah, which set off the whole body of listeners; or perhaps he thought he had a right once to forget ministerial formalism in sheer enjoyment of the punishment he inflicted.

'Name! name! name!'

'Don't give it; there's enough done,' said Elias in a low but earnest tone, as he saw Hirell pale as death, and felt her trembling hand resting on his arm for support.

'Not give it!' said the minister looking grandly round, while there was a rich twinkle of light in his eye: 'Not give it! I would not omit it for the world. Does not our benefactor deserve the gratitude of his fellow-men? At least,' and here suddenly he changed his tone, 'do we not know he ought? Brethren, put up your prayer this night for our benefactor, Sir John Cunliff, Baronet; and pray as heartily as I do, that whatever he may need in this life, or in the life to come, will be vouchsafed him in measure as abundant as his practical generosity to us. Sir John Cunliff, Baronet. Amen.'

There was a pause, and Cunliff breathed again as he found there was no intention to make known his presence.

But he was furious, and moved about uneasily for a few seconds, wondering whether or no he ought and dared to disclaim the gift and the honour.

No, he saw that was too dangerous; he was tied hand and foot by the past, a helpless captive of the bow and spear of the Reverend Ephraim.

They advanced.

'You are pleased to make merry with me, gentlemen!' he said.

'Why not, sir? The Lord loves a cheerful giver; he can hardly be wroth with one who also receives cheerfully,' was the minister's response.

'Mr. Morgan,' said Cunliff, 'will you favour me with a few minutes' conversation?'

'May I first ask, Sir John, if this visit is an accidental one?'

'No. I come now from London expressly to see you.'

'Then you are welcome to Bod Elian, Sir John Cunliff. We are ready to turn homeward with you now. Hirell!'

She was standing still by the oak with Kezia and some other women, who had come about her, praising her, some to her comfort and pleasure, some to her humiliation and annoyance. But during that last minute or two, she had had but scant attention to give to any of their praises.

When her father called her, she turned a little paler, set her lips close, and with a quick imploring look at Kezia, glided to him and stood at his side, acknowledging and stopping Sir John's eager advance towards her by a slight bend of the head.

'Hirell,' said her father, 'go home with Kezia, and prepare to welcome Sir John Cunliff with what hospitality is within our power.'

They hurried on in advance of Sir John and Elias, who followed.

Without either mentioning his name, both looked round for Robert, and saw that he had disappeared.

He had waited till he was certain as to whether Sir John was going to be permitted to enter Bod Elian and then took himself off to the Abbey Farm, to wait there till the visitor should be gone. He had no wish to receive Sir John's thanks, or to let him see by his behaviour how little he cared about his gratitude. So he thought it on the whole wisest to be absent.

He felt there was a time now come for him, that however long, or however brief, would contain the most bitter moments of suspense he had ever known.

CHAPTER LVI.

THE BITTER CUP.

HIRELL had no time to think of changing her dusty black dress or to bathe her eyes that ached with the strong sun which had shown before them so blindingly at the Martyr's Oak.

She could not even obey her father in helping Kezia to prepare some refreshment for Sir John. Directly she got into the house she went straight to her father's room and sat down between the bureau and the window—very still—so still, that Kezia, coming anxiously from her preparations, to look at her, thought she had fainted. But when she called to her and touched her, Hirell looked up with a sweet, wild kind of smile, and taking Kezia's hand, locked it tightly in both her own, then put it from her saying—

'Don't mind me—don't hinder.'

As Kezia left the room, she met Sir John and Elias coming towards it, and turning back looked at Hirell to warn her.

She remained very still, but Kezia knew she was aware of their coming, and quickly went out.

'Hirell,' said Elias, 'Sir John has said that to me, which I think entitles him to say it also to you. Hear him patiently. My child, I leave you in God's hands. Whatever you do, be sure of His blessing, and I have nothing more to ask.'

She turned her head then, and looking at Elias, answered almost in a whisper—

'Yes, father.'

Then she heard him go out and close the door, and knew that Sir John was close to her, one hand on the back of her chair, the other on the table before her.

'Hirell!'

She was silent and motionless.

'Oh, Hirell, forgiveness has come for me, at last, has it not?'

'Yes, Sir John; you know it.'

'Do I know it? may I trust that I know it?'

'You may.'

His hand trembled—she saw it tremble at the sound of her voice, which was cold and forced.

'I may—ah yes—I know I have your *Christian* forgiveness,

Hirell, but it is not that I mean, it is your own heart's full forgiveness that I need.'

' And—that you have.'

'If I have that, Hirell, I am blessed, indeed, for I know that you cannot give me that without giving me back with it all that was mine before. I am here to offer you all that God has given me, sincere repentance for what has been—my name—my wealth—my devoted love—my eternal care and cherishing—'

' Sir John Cunliff ! '

She spoke so coldly that involuntarily he took his hand from her chair, and drew back a little way as if stung. He stood more directly facing her now, and she looked up at him with heavy, mournful eyes as she spoke.

'I can give you nothing but the free forgiveness that has long been yours, and my heart's best wishes for your good. I can take nothing from you but *your* forgiveness and good wishes, which I ask for, Sir John.'

He looked at her with eyes full of passionate, tender incredulity. He said to himself that there could not be such cruel strength of purpose in such a fair, childish face—more childish now, strange to say, in its thinness and delicacy than he had ever seen it. Was Elias, after all, untruthful in telling him no one had tried to influence her against him? He thought of her early love and its utter guilelessness and humility, and felt it was impossible she could mean indeed to refuse him.

He did not answer very soon, and his silence affected Hirell far more than any words could have done. Though her eyes were still tearless and her lips closed firmly, he saw her fingers fluttering nervously near her slender, swelling throat, as if there was rising in it words or cries she would fain repress.

'Oh, Hirell,' he cried, suddenly kneeling by the table where she sat, and laying his hand on her wrist, 'You haven't quite ceased to love me, have you?'

She was startled—startled into tears, but not out of her coldness.

'I have ceased to love you well enough to become your wife,' she answered, in a very low, firm voice.

'No, no,' cried Cunliff, 'give me what little love you have left, Hirell, I will be content ; I will make it more. You have pledged yourself to me—you have *your* pledge to remember whatever I have done.   Can you dare to break your solemn promise to be true to me?'

At this a little strange gleam of fire came into the wet eyes.

'I gave my solemn promise to be true to Mr. Rymer—I was true to him, till the last,—but, Sir John Cunliff, from the first minute *you* were made known to me, I felt— I felt the one that I had loved before was gone.   *You* were left, but you were not the one that I had loved—I do not wish to love you. I do not understand you—I will certainly never marry you; I am not fit for you, nor you for me.   You saw it all so truly, if you would but remember.'

He stood regarding her in bitter silence.   Those words, 'you saw it all so truly, if you would but remember,' were as gall to him!   and it was as if the cruel light they threw upon his heart's secrets was reflected back on Hirell's, for he suddenly saw, or thought he did, the one taint of her nature.

'Hirell,' he said, in a voice such as she had never heard from him before, 'you are not so perfect as you think, after all your anger against me.   Your suffering, which keeps alive your anger, is all not because I sinned against your womanhood, but because I sinned against your sainthood; and you cannot bring back the old glory and halo, the *sense* of unapproachable light and goodness of which you were so proud.'

Her eyes, fixed on the table before her, were filled with anguish; he saw that he had indeed stung her—but, when she spoke, he knew the sting had only made her heart close up from him the more.

'Perhaps you are right, Sir John Cunliff,' she said, 'perhaps I am guilty of the thing you say, but if so I have never withdrawn myself from God's hands, and He knows what He is doing with me.   I am sure, too, that He knows I ought to keep the one thing you *have* left to me—my faith in Him, and this I could not do if I married you.'

'Hirell, forgive me.   How dared I say what I have said!'

'I have no doubt but that it was true—too true, Sir John.'

Again he stood silent, in fierce self-reproach and suffering.

'Hirell, Hirell,' he cried suddenly, 'this is too much!   It cannot be that I must drain this bitter, bitter cup.'

'May God make it less bitter for you, sir; I cannot.'

He rose, and walked the length of the little room twice with head bent down, hands linking, and eyes looking helplessly round as in a vague search for hope.

At last his eyes resting on Hirell's little Bible as it lay by her black gloves and bonnet, he stood still a moment looking at it. Suddenly he went to the table, took up the little book, and came to her with it.

'Hirell, I cannot play the patient lover after this, and offer to live on hope when no hope seems to exist. I know you too well, and I know I have already given you too much time for consideration for this to be any mere caprice, and yet I cannot —I cannot bring myself to believe, Hirell!'

She looked at him with cold, questioning eyes.

'Hirell, my darling! my only hope and love! you do not mean me to take your words for solemn truth—not for truth so solemn that you could swear it upon this book. You could not do that?—say you could not, and I will wait—and hope—and come to you again.'

She rose up, she put her hands upon the book as he held it, but though her lips opened and moved, she could not speak.

'No, Hirell, no,' he pleaded, shudderingly trying to draw away the book; but following his entreaty came the words, low, but clear and distinct—

'I swear upon this book that I will never marry Sir John Cunliff.'

His hands were slowly withdrawn, the Bible slipped from hers, and fell on to the floor.

Both knew that the vow, the first she had ever made, was irrevocable. Both knew, as she sank into her chair, and he knelt beside her, that they were severed as utterly as two sailors on an iceberg, when it breaks, and they are being borne away on its different parts by different currents.

He scarcely seemed to feel her hands, or she his, as they were clasped in that last clasp. They seemed rather to be stretching them towards each other in the distance they felt spreading so fast between them.

And then the real parting came, and they saw each other no more.

CHAPTER LVII.

THE SOLITARY.

As a man stunned by a blow which deprives him of all sensation beyond a confused dull pain, which he does not even attempt to understand, will go blindly groping along, so that a bystander may not even guess his state, Sir John Cunliff, after carefully closing the door of Bod Elian behind him, descended the hill into the valley.

He stood for a minute or two on the Dolgarrog road, upon the long, old, stone bridge that crosses the valley, and leaned over the parapet, as if studying the Roman pavement of the ancient ford below. But the head sank more and more, till it and the hand rested on and pressed closely to the cold stone.

A bird sang high in the air, and began to descend, singing deliciously as it did so. He lifted his head, as if from old habit, to listen; broke out into a passionate but unintelligible exclamation ; climbed over the wall of the bridge, and went on through the marshes, up to his knees in water occasionally (for the tide overflows here), nor did he stop till he reached the ferry.

The ferryman was on the other side, and Cunliff gazed as if in perfect helplessness towards him. Perhaps, the sound of his own voice, raised just then in a shout, would have been too horrible.

He waited in a dreadful calm till somebody should come. A tramp, with tracts in his hand, as a pretence for a vocation, was the first comer : he shouted lustily.

The boat and boatman soon crossed, and soon took them both over ; the tramp neither annoying Cunliff by looking at him, nor by offering his wares, to the latter's great relief.

' Is the river deep ? ' asked the tramp.

' Deep enough to drown a man last week,' replied the boatman, ' who got in for a swim, and couldn't get out again.'

' I wonder what he thinks of his luck, now ? ' said the half-jesting, half sepulchral voice of the gentleman-passenger ; but the boatman looked as though he'd be glad when he'd got rid of such a reprobate : and the tramp himself looked on in a spirit of grave reproof.

Cunliff, as he jumped out of the boat, threw them a shilling a-piece, and called out with a laugh—

' Even the devil, you see, is not so black as he's painted,' and passed away from their wondering eyes.

It was the solitude of the mountain that evidently tempted him. Criba Ban in all its majesty rose before him ; its highest peaks rising steeply up from where he stood ; while its mighty arms were prolonged far away, right and left, for many miles in each direction.

He was mad enough to think he could ascend from this part. When, after some half hour of vain effort, he saw he could not, he determined to ascend from the side opposite to Dolgarrog; a place that just now he seemed bent to shun.

A tremendous sweep had to be made to accomplish this, but after two or three hours of exertion that would have been simply impossible had he been in his ordinary senses, he found himself at the top of one of the minor crests that hang about the breast of Criba Ban.

He was now full two thousand feet above the valley. The afternoon was yet sufficiently light for him to see the glorious scenery. Never yet had he ascended to a place like this without a vivid sense and keen enjoyment of the beauty and sublimity thus made visible. Yet now, the moment he stood on a little level platform, which he seemed to know familiarly, he lay down, without casting even a single glance around.

He lay on the hard, bare rock—now with his face to it, now, in his writhings, with his face to the sky, the eyes shut, and the teeth fixed, as if with a vice. He seemed above all things to dread that unpacking of the heart with words, of which Hamlet speaks.

Gradually the light decreased, and a thin white mist crept stealthily up. Had any friendly voice been near, it would have been raised in warning. To be on Criba Ban, or Snowdon, in a mist, is about the most promising condition in which a man can place himself who would like to have the benefit of suicide without its responsibility.

Sir John may be acquitted of any such thoughts; he had found the solitude he yearned for, the one only thing that in all this world offered even a gleam of relief; and if the word luxury can be applied to any condition annexed to the bed of tortures on which he lay, that luxury was his—the luxury, the relief to be alone.

Still more dim grew the afternoon, but he saw it not, saw nothing, till a faint light began to twinkle out on the slope of the opposite hill. He saw that, and sprang to his feet as if an electric shock had passed through him.

It was Bod Elian; there was no other house there.

He stood as if turned to a pillar of stone, watching that light for some minutes. Did its radiance—the undefinable sense of comfort suggested by it—kindle the possibility of hope, of yet another effort to win Hirell before it should be too late?

Some mechanical impulse caused him to take out his watch, look at the time, knowing nothing, however, about it, and put the watch back. Then quite unconsciously he again took it out, and did notice, though with some difficulty, through the increasing gloom, that it was near six, and then came the full remembrance of where he was, and of his danger if he remained.

Before he had stirred a dozen paces it was again all forgotten, and he threw himself upon the rock so carelessly as to cut both his face and hands with the sharp prominences; but he felt nothing of the hurt, but began to give way to the heaving, maddening chaos within, to the bitter loathing of himself, of his life, of the world, and of all created things that he felt.

Passages from Scripture, used by Elias, came from time to time athwart this seething, sweltering hell, into which he struggled not to look, but which would not be denied his countenance. When he had covered all over as with the black ash of ruined hopes, and strove only to be at rest in a blank torpor, there would be a sudden light, and roar, and he and all the fiends of hell seemed once more to be in company.

The growing darkness seemed to be as welcome as sleep to wayfarers in the Arctic regions when suffering from intense cold, the sleep that foreruns death.

Is it with the cruel inconsistency that suffering forces upon us, that he cannot leave the place from whence he sees that far-off light gleaming, even while every particle of strength he possesses is given, and has been given for hours past, to the one effort that can alone save him from insanity—the effort to shut out the actual picture of Hirell from his sight, and to exclude every thought directly leading to her from his mind?

The darkness is still thickening about him, the wind moaning and sobbing vehemently, so that he can see nothing distinctly in the valley below; and at last, the light that he has watched as a drowning mariner on a raft at sea might watch a similar indication of the place where he yearns for his foot to rest, fades, fades, and disappears.

The sense of the extreme cold now strikes upon his senses for the first time, as though that poor light had been sufficient sun for him while it lasted.

He rises slowly, goes to the edge of the precipice to estimate better his way down. Growing more conscious at every step, his footsteps begin to quicken. He understands perfectly his danger; he has often ascended, and alone, not simply to this height, but to the very loftiest peak of Criba Ban.

He sees that the gathering mist has already shrouded all the lower part of the mountain, but he also sees a certain spot on the way down, which once reached, he would be safe, even if moving through a deeper than Egyptian darkness afterwards. The way to that spot is fortunately also sufficiently clear at present, and may remain so to enable him to pass through its dangers, if he does not lose a moment. Once the mist covers that route, he sees it is death to go down; and probably for him, in his present state, worse than death to remain on the mountain through such a night.

The prospect of danger does him good, brings back some instinct of mental health, and best of all, gives him work that may shut out, at least for a few minutes, or perhaps more, the sense of his intolerable sufferings.

He moves carefully. Between him and the goal to be reached are black tarns of soundless depth, sudden, precipitous descents, ridges, crossing which, under such circumstances, is apt to appear to the bewildered wanderer like walking along the edge of a gigantic knife; these, and a score of lesser but confusing obstacles, he has to deal with.

The fast-rising wind increases the cold and the danger. The mist comes every now and then as if in dense patches; he is obliged at a certain point to pause for breath, and to take counsel with himself as to a choice of the routes that offer over a particularly dangerous chasm.

It was during that pause he heard something which induced him to prolong it, even though conscious life now might be a question of minutes, nay, even of seconds.

He heard it again, but half fancied it was the wind, and determined to heed it not, but go on.

Some inexplicable impulse of humanity however stopped him again to listen, and then he heard clearly a low wail come by him borne on the wind.

Full of wonder as to the human being who could be here at such an hour, and desirous to save time, he went back a few yards, and there saw a shadowy something, just a little denser than the enveloping mist, advancing towards him.

The wail came again, a piteous one, and very feeble. He had evidently been seen. What was he to do? A few minutes lost now might compromise him hopelessly. The thought of 'hope' was sufficient. He went back.

The form suddenly disappeared. Cunliff stood transfixed with horror; he ran on, and found what seemed to him at first sight a heap of rags. Stooping, he touched it, and a groan came from beneath.

'What in the world is it?' he said aloud: then some of the rags were pushed aside, and a wizened, old hatchet-face looked up at him with cap-frills shaking round it, and tooth-less jaws moving as they uttered what appeared to him a jargon he had never heard before. Certainly, he thought, if this were Welsh, it was very different from the Welsh they talked at Bod Elian. Suddenly the poor old soul stopped her incomprehensible complaint, and said sharply, and with in-effable disgust and despair, in Welsh:

'No English!'

'No English!' echoed Sir John, 'I understand that. But what the devil are you doing here?'

'No English!' again answered the old woman, with a piteous wail.

'Well, up with you,' he said, energetically speaking, though he knew she could not understand him, but feeling as as if his words must make his signs more comprehensible to her. 'Up with you,' and he tried to lift her.

He managed to get her to stand, then seeing that she had a bundle hanging by a string round her waist, he tried to take it from her. 'Come, away with this; it's as much as I can do to save you, you poor silly old creature, staying here till this time of night.'

She looked at him bewildered at first, as to what he wanted with her bundle, but when she understood by his tugging at it that he meant to take it from her, she pushed him off with her long, stiff-knuckled-hand, and hugged her bundle to her, shaking her head emphatically at him.

'Come, away with it, I say; why what the deuce is in it, you miserable creature?'

She understood by his touching it, and perhaps by the tone of his voice, his curiosity, and making her stiff, trembling old limbs bob a curtsey, undid a corner of her bundle, and respectfully showed him it was full of sheep-wool.

'And you come up here for this?' he said; and she, seeing him look round again, understood him. She saw that the ever-inquisitive Englishman—inquisitive even at such a time and place as this—desired to be informed as to where she got it from, and immediately picked some bits from a bush close to her, bits which the sheep had left clinging there. She also pointed to the east, then to the west, by which Sir John understood her to mean she had been here at her work from sunrise till now.

'Well, come,' he said, putting his arm round her, and half lifting her along.

He looked for the goal of safety. It had passed out of sight.

Still, he reflected, the light might be sufficient for the way to be traced step by step, if only they could but go faster.

The poor old woman strained her little powers to the utmost to keep up with the gentleman, but her pace slackened, rather than increased, her weight to him grew more serious every minute.

He began to think this was only risking both lives. Had he not better lay her down in some sheltered corner, then go at his greatest possible speed to Dolgarrog, and send off ample assistance? How exquisitely ridiculous to good society would seem the fate of Sir John Cunliff, when reported as perishing in attempting to save a wretched old woman, whose wits, like his own, had gone wool-gathering on Criba Ban!

The person in question saved him all further trouble about this problem; she suddenly slid to the ground moaning with the pain of her sprained foot, mutely refusing, with all the obstinacy of age, to move any farther.

Fortunate chance! But Sir John Cunliff seems no longer himself, is evidently losing his self-possession, and growing childish. Somehow, this poor, exhausted life has swelled to him into something of value, something that he cannot afford to lose, something that suggests to him he knows not what, but that he means to look to by-and-by

'Now, mother, I am an obstinate man myself, and therefore your obstinacy is of no use. Tell me, can you or can you not walk?'

All the answer she could give him was to lay her head more at ease on the slaty earth, and murmur meekly in her cracked voice—

'N's da!'

'No, no—not "Good-night," yet. Now for your bundle! Hark! do you hear it going down? I wish I could roll you with as little harm down the same crag—but as I can't, I must do this.'

He knelt, raised her up, half sitting, turned his back to her, slid his arms under hers, and in a trice he was again on his feet, and labouring along under his load; which, happily for him, was not heavy—had known too little nourishment to be in danger of such a state.

And in that position there came into his thoughts remembrances of old Dalilahs of his experience and imagination, and the contrast seemed to him delicious in its bitterness.

He speculates upon her, and finds relief, in so doing, from speculations nearer home. Had she a soul to be saved? He could not tell! but by the living God he would save her body, if the thing was to be done. He felt thankful that such a thing as even this poor life was intrusted to him.

The wind was now coming in fearful rushes, so that to cross particular spots became at times impossible without delay.

On one such occasion he put down his burden for rest, and gazed about till he forgot alike her and himself in the extraordinary phenomenon that presented itself. The day was yet light enough to see the valley but for the mist. Where he now stood on an isolated height, the fury of the wind kept the mist in a perpetual boil, but every instant it would open, the world beneath would be seen, then instantaneously close again, and so all round, towards every point of the compass. Anything more awful than the continued glimpses of the infernal caldron in which they seemed to stand—or than the mad dance that the world itself seemed to be performing round him, Cunliff had never seen. His imagination, which just then drank deep of horror, soon pictured it all as a Cambrian Walpurgis night, a saturnalia for witches and devils, and for aught he knew, here he was hugging one of the supernatural hags to his very breast.

When he took up his burden again, at the first lull of the tempest, he found her all but lifeless.

He began to find his own strength—which hitherto he had recklessly drawn upon—now fail; and with that came the thought he too would fail in what he had set himself to achieve.

The damp sweat is on his face. The obstacles are too tremendous. He glances for a single moment up to the sky—where nothing but mist meets his gaze—he utters in words no prayer, but the pleading, passionate cry of his soul is not the less heard.

It is for the poor old creature's life to be saved.

He ventures now upon the last of the really serious difficulties, the passage across an open, sloping space, on which the whole fury of the wind seems bent on expending itself.

Steadying his own and her weight at every step, ready at any moment to drop to the ground, he passes two-thirds of the way in safety, and with something like exultation at his heart for that bit of conquest simply, when the two forms are caught from behind as by the power of a gently-touching, yet irresistible hand—the hand of the spirit of the giant mountain evoked for their destruction—which lifts him and his burden, gives no time for thought, or cry, and sweeps him and her along as but mere human straws.

'Hirell!' That is his last thought, hope, and aspiration, believing that the hour had indeed come! when lo, the dangling feet of the old woman strike against some projection of rock, that enabled Cunliff to stay the rush for a single moment, and that moment Cunliff used for his and her bodily salvation, by hugging the ground, as children might hug their mother, fresh from the most imminent danger.

He waits now for rest, as well as for the chance of a fresh lull, vainly striving to comfort the old woman by a few genial words from time to time; but at last he ventures the rest of the transit, succeeds, and all the remainder of the way is but fatigue, bodily pain, and assured success.

He leaves her at a little stone hut that he knows of, under shelter; reaches Dolgarrog; sends off a carriage and a couple of men for his late companion; waits in the dreadful solitude of his chamber for the news of her safe arrival and recovery, thankful he has that yet to engross him; then lies down in his clothes on the bed, not expecting long to stay there, even if to sleep at all, but he does sleep in spite of fate.

His last words as he was sinking into sleep were:

'Men sleep, they say, before execution; the devil's in it if I can't after.'

CHAPTER LVIII.

THE AWAKENING.

It would have been well for Sir John Cunliff if from that sleep there had been no awakening; at least, such was his own conviction, when the first faint light of day met his opening eyes on the following morning.

It were useless to attempt even to indicate the sufferings of which such a man is capable, when every element of his nature is called into preternatural activity, his every faculty of perception into the most vivid life, but only to enhance the anguish over a blow struck at the most vital part.

He saw no one, locked and double-locked his door, and then tried to persuade himself that the worst had passed, and that it was time for him to live a little more rationally.

The relief he felt might be such as the unfortunate Montezuma may be supposed to have experienced during those moments when the fire beneath happened to burn a little less fiercely, as the miscreant tormentors ceased for a moment to feed the flames.

He knew it not as yet, but this was the day for him of that vital revolution which all men of powerful and comprehensive natures experience at some time or other of their lives; and which seems destined to enable them to go back to instincts, and first principles; to cast off the slough of the world, as a serpent casts its skin; and then to recover, and to unite with the experiences and strength of manhood the ideal aspiration of youth, without which the world is indeed but a valley of the shadow of death, a place of desolation and of dry bones.

On the dreadful yesterday, which already seems divided from him by some inconceivably vast gulf, he *felt* only To-day he *thinks*, and though it seems but a change of suffering for suffering, it is progress.

Round and round the same set of thoughts go on perpetually circling, like that horrible devil's dance he had seen on Criba Ban, and leaving him no rest for the sole of his intellectual foot. His love, from which he must turn as Lear turns from his peculiar danger, for ' that way madness lies ;' his humiliation ; the cruel irony of fortune that he—a passionate

lover of the ideal—should destroy such an ideal as Hirell
would have made a reality of, for him; his weakness in crying as a child might cry that first will, then will not, then will
again; the exposure before Elias, Chamberlayne, Kezia, and
that bloated Puritan, the Rev. Ephraim Jones, such are the
component parts of the hideous glimpses he gets on one side
of his mental horizon.

Sick and dizzy with the whirl and confusion, he turns to
another, his early, hopeful life, so full of worth, of promise, of
brightness, of faith, of earnest will, of everything that could
foreshadow a life of manly vigour and usefulness, alike for
himself and his fellow-men. Was all this utterly gone?
Had indulgence eaten out the very heart of his manhood, so
that he could only drop into the world's stream, and go where
that went?

To stop thinking, while thinking led to nothing but chaos,
he took up a newspaper that had come with some letters by
the morning's post, none of which had he opened. Had he
thought it possible that any conceivable thing he might see
there would tempt him to feel the least interest, he would have
flung it into the fire. It was a purely mechanical action, one
his fingers had long been used to.

He saw his name, allowed his eye to run down the column,
pausing here and there, with a new and fierce light rising in
his glance as he did so, then dropped his clenched hand on
the damp paper, and told himself aloud, in conscious irony of
his assumed quiet, the substance of what he had seen.

'My cottages at——, the subject of a special local inquiry,
unknown to me or my agent, a report sent to the Government—filth, overcrowding, nuisances, delicate suggestions of
incest, hot-beds of fever, death placed at my door—and this,
the editor, my Tory assailant during the election, knowing
how I have been violently opposed at every step in rebuilding
—knowing what I am about to do for a thorough reformation,
hastens to contrast with the sensation, so he calls it, everywhere excited by my maiden speech, which prepared everyone
for some new social apostle; and here he is, the Radical M.P.
and Baronet, Sir John Cunliff!

'Of course, since this is *here*, it is also in every British
newspaper, regaling every hearth in the three kingdoms with
the spectacle of me, hung out as it were—a spectacle to gods
and men—the arch-hypocrite of my age.'

He stopped. No fit of violence now offered even a temporary relief. Literally, the man's heart seemed broken. It might be a pitiful thing to say, but somehow he had a sort of sacred respect for his name, for his reputation. It was in its stainlessness as regards men, a kind of bond by which he held some security for the future. That was gone. He might build and reform as he pleased ; spend as he pleased ; toil as he pleased. Never again would there be any verdict for him, but that he had been simply driven by the outraged voice of public opinion no longer to violate public decency.

He tried to walk about his room, tried to eat, tried to read, raised and lowered the blinds again and again, found an old chair in a dark corner of his long apartment, and there sat for a long time staring at vacancy.

He saw a book on the sideboard, fetched it, found it was a Bible, opened the leaves and began ; then, stung by something, hurled the book back towards its place. Seeing it fall to the ground, and lie there sprawling in an unseemly fashion, he took it up, went back to his chair, and tilted up the legs, keeping his knees together to make a place for the book.

With a sort of half-scorn, a quick, impatient hand, he turned over the leaves once more, restlessly and aimlessly, as if after all he were thinking of something else. By accident he thus left the book open opposite the first of Corinthians, and read aloud in that abstract kind of voice which indicates an effort to recall the thought from some more tempting theme :

'And whether one member suffer, all the members suffer with it ; or one member be honoured, all rejoice with it.'

This he read a second time, then remarked :
' Why the whole spirit of true government is summed up in that,! '

He began now to hunt for things that might be similarly noticeable, and lighted upon this, from the Romans :

'We then that are strong ought to bear the infirmities of the weak.'

He made no remark, but pondered long before he again turned over the leaves, and read from Revelation :

'Because thou sayest, I am rich, and increased with goods, and have need of nothing : and knowest not that thou art wretched, and miserable, and poor, and blind, and naked : I counsel thee to buy of me gold tried in the fire, that thou mayest be rich ; and white raiment that thou mayest be clothed, and that the shame of thy nakedness do not appear ; and anoint thine eyes with eye-salve, that thou mayest see.

When he again read—still continuing to read aloud, as if disputing with the fear that he could not—his voice broke with emotion, which was instantly checked, and he read the next in silence :

And the fruits that thy soul lusted after are departed from thee, and all things which were dainty and goodly are departed from thee, and thou shalt find them no more at all.'

He could for some time read no more, but closed the Bible with a gentle touch, set it down, and paced his chamber silently for perhaps an hour. Then again he took the book up, saying in a low voice—

'God help me ! I don't understand all this ! No mortal man could have spoken more directly to me, and so anatomized me.'

He was soon made to understand it when he lighted upon the text :

'For the word of God is quick and powerful, and sharper than any two-edged sword, piercing even to the dividing asunder of soul and spirit, and of the joints and marrow, and is a discerner of the thoughts and intents of the heart.'

'To what end, O God,' he cried in irresistible passion, ' to what end, if Thou wilt not show me the path out of this my intolerable shame and anguish ? '

He could read no more, but went to bed, not to sleep, but to try once more to shut out the light that wounded alike body and soul.

Futile effort. He was soon poring over the Bible again, knowing well what he wanted to find, and which he had chosen not before to see. He found it, read it to himself many times over in silence, then once aloud, and once only :

'That which is born of the flesh is flesh, and that which is born of the Spirit is spirit.

'Except a man be born again he cannot see the kingdom of God.'

To the last days of the world's existence, men like Cunliff, however powerfully moved to the regeneration of life, to the sense of the necessity of something that can only be worthily described by the words, New Birth, will still differ in the mode of manifesting their experience, from the mode of those who have led simpler, less artificial lives, whose natures are less complex, though possibly even still more strong. Whatever of the nature of conversion Cunliff was now to know, it was not the conversion of Christian in Bunyan's immortal allegory.

The pride of knowledge, of culture, of intellect, is exceedingly adverse to the straightforward, noble simplicity, and uncompromising earnestness which characterize truly religious men; and make them accept the new light and faith without a murmur, except as to their own profound unworthiness.

He had often before now amused himself by taking up one by one the cardinal points of religious belief—new birth, atonement, faith, confession, and so on, in order to show the natural elements in each, which all reasonable men would acknowledge. And thus he explained the doctrines away till they might be very perfect logically, but leading to no earthly benefit for any human being.

He saw now with surprise it was possible to reverse the process to a precisely opposite issue, and began to mount by the well-known familiar steps.

Our space, and the nature of our book, forbids further development. But, to illustrate the action of Cunliff's mind, let it be briefly observed, that he found on recalling by the aid of his superb memory the lives of great men, it was almost always to be discovered that they had passed through that memorable phase, which Dante calls 'new life,' and which turned Cromwell from gambling and other dissolute courses, into one of the greatest of the world's men. Seeing *that*, Cunliff found to himself *now* the courage to treat at its exact value the ridicule, the knowingness of society, and to think only of his real need.

Two other texts there were which affected him strangely:

'Eye hath not seen, nor ear heard, neither have entered into the heart of man the things which God hath prepared for them that love him.'

'For I am persuaded that neither death, nor life, nor angels, nor principalities, nor powers, nor things present, nor things to come, nor height, nor depth, nor any other creature, shall be able to separate us from the love of God, which is in Christ.'

The inconceivable beauty and grandeur of all these passages, which he placed before him carefully copied out—of these and many others—filled him with something that was not hope, nor pleasure, nor desire of life, but that was at least likely again to lead to such things when the awful period of transition should be gone through.

They suggested, also, powerfully to him the inner harmony between them and the life he had always vaguely yearned for in spirit; and so the harmony between the life of this world, and the life of that to come, which it is the true work of the statesman, the philosopher, the poet, the artist, the philanthropist to restore. As to Cunliff, while the very thought of hoping or caring for aught personal was simply in its present state revolting, he found himself drawn irresistibly to hope and care for others ; and note with wonder how all his wanderings seemed somehow or other to lead finally to this.

He summed up the results of his life, having first asked if he could do it truly, that is, justly and inexorably.

In the light, whether lurid or pure, of those facts, he studied his own character—what it had been, what it should be.

Then he scanned narrowly his aspirations, and the quality of his own powers to realize them, if indeed he were about to realize anything.

Finally he asked himself—Could he thenceforward consecrate his life, fortune, and whatever of health, heart, strength, and ability God might have given, or have left him, to the service of his poorer countrymen, at a moment when it seemed to him that a social revolution impended, of the gravest—possibly of the grandest—character.

To quiet the anxieties of his kind landlady, as well as from apprehension of her gossip, he admitted her to his room with food, and ate.

The next few days were spent in silent, continuous study and labour. Many letters were written, much business got through. And, although he went no more abroad than he could help (especially when he found how popular the episode of the old woman had made him), still he would walk out occasionally ; and it was noticed by those who had known him ever since his first arrival among them a year ago, how changed he was in manner. He spoke to no one of his own motion, but if spoken to there was a strange gentleness in the tone of the voice, a pleasant, though sad light in the eye, which threatened even to place him among the simple-hearted Welsh on a pedestal high and peculiar as Hirell's own ; but of which he knew nothing, suspected nothing.

All this while he had been discussing within himself a certain act of duty which it seemed to him he ought to perform, and just one week after the collapse of all his hopes and worldly strength, he set out for Dola' Hudol. He had heard that both Mr. and Mrs. Rhys were at the house, and that the lady was very ill.

CHAPTER LIX.

MIDNIGHT AND DAWN.

The first thing that made Elias aware of Sir John's departure, was the opening and gentle closing of the house door.

At that sound he and Kezia looked at each other with eyes full of tender fear, then went together to the room, where they found Hirell with her arm and face on the bureau, white and senseless.

Together they revived her and carried her up to her own room.

When Robert came back from the Abbey Farm there was an almost deathly silence in the house. He found no one in the kitchen, and as he sat there waiting he felt himself punished for the joy that had almost made him tremble when he had seen Sir John Cunliff crossing the little bridge at Capel Illtyd. He had seen him do this as he stood at the refectory door giving his opinion on the merits of a new horse the master of the Abbey Farm had just brought home from Dolgarrog fair. Then Robert when he saw him, was assured of the truth; and it had amazed him and filled him with a strong irrepressible hope, and a gladness of which he was too much ashamed to go back at once to Bod Elian. He could not stay at the Abbey Farm, his excitement was too great to be concealed; so he went for a walk on Moel Mawr, and did not return till he was thoroughly tired, and his shoulder was paining him, and forcing him to think more of Cunliff and less of his own suddenly revived hopes.

When he found himself so long alone in the lower part of the house, and heard no sound anywhere about it, his heart sank within him. He had so schooled himself, his look, his voice, before he entered, that his untimely joy might not show itself too plainly, and then there he sat alone, his hopes growing fainter and fainter, his fears stronger, as the slow minutes passed.

At last, nearly an hour after he had been in, Kezia came down stairs.

The first thing he saw her do, as he lifted his eyes in almost timid inquiry to her face, was by no means comforting. She sat down in a chair, and putting her apron to her eyes, had, what she afterwards called, a good cry; but to poor Robert it was a bad and ominous one.

He sat looking perplexed and anxious till it occurred to him that the poor woman had probably touched nothing since their early breakfast, and now it was past four.

She had brought a little tray with tea on it downstairs with her, and seeing this on the dresser, Robert made use of his housekeeping experiences at the hooded house to pour Kezia out a cup of tea, which he brought her as gallantly as if she had been one of the finest young ladies in one of the best drawing-rooms at Reculcester.

'Indeed now, Master Robert. Only to think!' said Kezia as he took her apron out of her hand, and put the cup of tea into it; then, after sipping it, she added:

'It's just that beautiful I'll take it up to Elias, for not a bit or sup, Master Robert, has passed his lips since breakfast.'

'Nor yours either. You'll do no such thing,' said Robert, laying his hand on her shoulder. 'You shall take him some afterwards. Drink this yourself, and here's some cake in my pocket Cicely Lloyd sent for you.'

Sitting on the edge of the high table, he watched her in silence a minute or two, then said:

'Is it very sad up there, Kezia?'

'Oh, Master Robert, her suffering is very sad to see. She has given him up: you know that she has vowed she will never marry him?'

'And now, Kezia, now you think the act is costing her—her life perhaps? Is it not, Kezia?'

'Oh the poor lamb!' cried Kezia, setting down her cup and resuming the apron, 'to see her on her knees, Master Robert, to hear her, ever since she came to from her faint, calling herself the cause of all her father's troubles, and asking forgiveness for all her false pride, and I can't tell you all. Her father has prayed with her, and comforted her now, a bit, and they are sitting talking beautiful to hear, Master Robert. But oh, she is that white and cold! and when we try to make her lie down she says she cannot rest till her heart is more at peace.'

'Yes, it will kill her, Kezia, don't *you* feel it will kill her?' said Robert, almost fiercely; then in voice suddenly softened, he said, as he took her hand:

'Kezia, *I* am nothing now, of course. I may do nothing, may not see her, perhaps, for many days, may I?'

Robert had always been a great favourite of Kezia's, and now when he stood looking her ' through and through' as she said, his eyes questioning her so much more beseechingly and wistfully than his lips had done, she was moved a second time to use Elias's confidence in her in a manner with which he would certainly not have been pleased.

'Oh, Master Robert, you must not expect things to be different—not yet, if ever,' said Kezia. 'I ought not to tell you, but I would not have you hoping with that hope that maketh the heart sick. They have talked about you, Master Robert. Her father asked her in their talk how her heart was towards you, and she cried very much, and called herself ungrateful, but begged and prayed of us to let her stay with us, and say no more about you, and she knew you would find one more deserving, and all that. Oh, Robert, the truth is, she feels her heart is broken.'

'Thank you, Kezia; I will keep all this a secret, and I will go away to-morrow. I'll cause her no distress—God forbid I should do that if I cannot comfort her—which I would cut off my right hand to do.'

'Ah, Master Robert, you have been faithful to her, and always so tender in saving her any pain, the Lord will reward you at His own time—in His own way.'

She went up then to Hirell's room, and Elias came down.

Robert and he did not speak; but Robert when he came in set a chair for him, and waited upon him with a woman's care and gentleness. He was filled with gratitude too deep for words for what Elias had tried to do for him—too deep for words even if he had not been compelled to be silent for Kezia's sake. He was so surprised, too; for he had little thought that Hirell's father considered him so worthy of her as to be induced to overlook the differences of their religion, though he certainly knew Robert was not one to interfere with Hirell's faith.

Elias was in a very silent and absorbed mood when he came down, and did not speak for a long time or take any apparent heed of Robert's attention; but when at last he awoke from his sorrowful obliviousness to the fact that he was eating food of which he stood in great need and was being waited upon and supplied with every comfort, and saw, too, Robert's own dainty wool-worked slippers on his feet—he looked up at Robert, then down at the slippers, then at the table, and the toast cut and buttered on his plate, and then he turned his eyes again on the handsome, subdued face bending down near the fire, and gazed upon it with a look of deep, solemn regret and sorrow. Robert felt rather than saw the look, and understood it to mean—'My lad, thy fate is fixed. I cannot alter it.' He understood it so well that he felt he should make some reply to it, but all the reply he could make was to answer Elias's gaze with a look manly and cheery, and a smile shortlived as lightning, but it made Elias's eyes glisten as he withdrew them.

He spent the rest of the evening at his daughter's side at the request of Robert; who made Kezia tell him all there was to see to indoors, and who did ever so much more than was necessary, or than Elias would have approved of his doing on a Sunday evening, had he known.

Kezia and Elias never once left Hirell alone till prayer-time, and then when they and Robert were on their knees, came a cry of wild restlessness and pain—

'Father! Father!'

It thrilled Elias to his heart's core, but he would not rise till his prayer was ended. But Robert could not bear it—could not have her call left a second unanswered. He rose and crept up to the foot of the stairs and called softly, but with his whole heart's love and yearning breathing in his voice,

'Hirell, dear Hirell, what is it? He is coming—he is coming instantly.'

It was not till the middle of the night when he had heard Kezia go from Hirell to her own room and Elias leave his second watch beside his daughter, it was not till then, when the house was very still and he found himself yet sitting cold and reluctant to move in the great kitchen, that Robert knew to the full how bitter his disappointment was to him.

He felt like a man who sees himself being fast overtaken by a black devouring tide, from which he tries vainly to escape. His life had so little fitted him to know how to endure a prospect of long years of joylessness and hopelessness, such as he saw before him, that he felt himself to-night rebelling against fate like a passionate coward, as he called himself. Other men had to face such things, and why should not he? And yet he felt as if he would rather that the wound in his shoulder should open afresh, and let him bleed to death—or that he should fall from the Major's coach on his way to Llansaintfraid, over Criba Ban, and be dashed to pieces in some slate quarry—or come to any end, rather than go back home to live under this new and frightful feeling of gloom and despair.

Until that long and wretched night Robert had scarcely known what real suffering was, but he had it then in its very essence.

Once when his fears for Hirell's life sickened him so that he could not remain still, he crept up the stairs, and listened near her door. He heard her voice and her father's talking very quietly, and he heard with a deep emotion his own name uttered by her. It calmed him wonderfully. He became filled with shame at his own self-pity, now that he knew she had a pitying thought for him.

Welcoming that one bit of sweet faint comfort in his heart, he went back, and sitting down at the long table, and laying his head on his arms, fell into a calm, dreamless sleep.

It had been very near dawn when he fell asleep, and in less than an hour the light and the twittering of the birds woke him.

At first the sight of brown bare oak everywhere he looked, made him fancy himself at the Hooded House; and the remembrance of where he really was, and how he was to return home that day, came to him bitterly enough.

He heard steps on the stairs, and started, for he wondered what Kezia would say to him at finding he had been there all night.

As he rose and was looking towards the door, grasping his chair, he was filled with astonishment to see Elias come in holding Hirell's hand.

As he looked at them and saw them coming straight towards him—Hirell in one of the fresh light dresses his mother had made her wear at Brockhurst—Robert doubted if he were indeed fully awake.

'Robert Chamberlayne,' said Elias, 'my child and I have this night wrestled with her sorrow, as Jacob wrestled with the angel; we have talked of and considered with much prayer for divine guidance, how best we may bring back to her the peace of her mind, and the happiness of her heart, both of which have even thus early been lost to her. We have considered, too, that it will be well to save her from having her soul tempted to break a vow she has vowed before God never to marry the erring, but I trust repentant man you once called your friend, John Cunliff. We have considered, too, Robert, that you, having been faithful in your love for her as Jacob to Rachel, generous to her in her time of trouble and exile, as Boaz to Ruth—we have considered that to you more than any other should the work of comfort and cherishing belong; and to that end I give her to you, and she gives herself to you—not now with the love that you deserve, but in the full trust and belief that it will come.

'She said to me, Robert, that last night when you rose even from addressing your Maker to answer her call, your voice went unto her heart with a strange warmth and comfort. Was it not so, Hirell?'

Robert, as he listened to these words, had been looking upon the sweet chastened face of Hirell, with eyes that at first were doubting and perplexed; but that soon had vied with the early morning skies outside, in glistening light and depth.

When Elias said, 'Was it not so, Hirell?' he placed at the same time her hand in Robert's, and Hirell answered faintly, 'Yes.'

Then Elias gently unwound the clinging fingers of her other hand from his, and drawing her nearer to Robert, said—

'Take her then, Robert, and be not impatient with her sorrow, which I have strong belief will only cover her soul for a time; therefore regard it only as the veil with which the women of the Scriptures veiled themselves when they were first brought before their husbands, even as Rebecca veiled herself when she beheld Isaac coming to meet her. I have judged it best that the marriage should be very soon, for the sake of both you and of another.'

Then Robert drew her to his heart and kissed her, and in his smile she seemed to see a reflection of the great peace and sunshine of that home of his, where she was to spend her life. As she closed her eyes upon his shoulder, a sense of rest came over her, she stretched her hand towards her father, and as he gave her his she held it close to hers and Robert's.

'You will love him very soon, Hirell, and dearly,' said Elias; 'he is not a gifted man, but he is what the Lord loves better, an honest man in whom there is no guile.'

'Father, I know him.'

CHAPTER LX.

LETTER FROM SIR JOHN CUNLIFF TO ELIAS MORGAN.

'Dolgarrog.

'DEAR SIR,—I fear I am again going to make you angry—but shall be content if your anger does not also extend to my companion and friend, Hugh.

'We have again met, and to me unexpectedly. I find he has come down here, hoping to be of service some way or other to me, and specially in undoing an impression that he fancies his letters may have given Hirell, about his disposition towards me. I was fortunate enough to meet him on his way to you, to convince him his errand was ended, and—

'Why make a short story long? We understand each other too well in all things to be inclined just now to separate. I have made him abandon Tidman's, and promise to accompany me on a short tour abroad; hoping to send him back to you when we return, as sound of body as he is of mind; and prepared to enter on his vocation as a musician in a more earnest spirit, and with more deliberate care as to the means, than have hitherto been possible to him.

'Forgive him, then, if he needs forgiveness. As to myself, I shall wait till you see what the next few months do for him before asking an opinion on my conduct.

'I know, sir, and respect your fear; but I have not been so successful in tampering with my own faith to be at all inclined to repeat the process with another. That which has made him —you—Kezia—Hirell—what you all are, I bend before in true humility; and would rather ask that your belief might be imparted to me—were that possible—than mine infused in him. If that, then, be your only fear—as I cannot but hope it may be—dismiss it, I entreat you, as baseless.

'You will hear from Hugh shortly. He will keep you regularly informed of all our movements, so that it will not be at all difficult for you to answer some, at least, of the letters he proposes to write you weekly.

'Before this reaches you we shall have started. Farewell.

'J. C.

'Hugh has written to his friend the Rev. Ephraim Jones.'

CHAPTER LXI.

DIES IRÆ.

AVOIDING tho ostentation of a carriage, Sir John walked tho distance to Dola' Hudol, and on reaching the mansion, sent in his card.

A painful incident occurred. The servant had gone away, and he was mechanically reclosing his card-case, when some memorandum on the back of one of the cards attracted his eye. He turned the card, and saw written, 'Mr. John Rymer,'—and felt once more, in all their bitterness, the sad degrading incidents that had brought him to this place. A sudden passion of disgust overmastered him, and he tore the card to pieces. Then he prayed in his soul for patience, to face the dreadful ordeal before him.

The servant returned instantly, and bowing with marked respect, led him to the drawing-room.

There he sat for some minutes, before the door opened, and Mr. Rhys entered ; stiff, and stately ; but with a kind of emphasized courtesy in the reception of his visitor, which agreeably surprised Cunliff, as soon as he realized the fact.

After the first formal greeting, and Mr. Rhys's request that Sir John would be seated, a request which was unattended to, there was a pause, a very painful one to Cunliff ; and Mr. Rhys was sufficiently accommodating to begin to speak words of congratulation on his accession to—when he was interrupted.

'Congratulations, sir, of any kind, are out of place to me here, and from you. Allow me to explain my presence. When a man is conscious of wrong-doing, and has reason to fear that others have been deeply injured by his acts, I beg you, sir, to tell me how he may best discharge his duty, and case his conscience. Tell me that, sir, and I shall, if it be humanly possible, make you the amends you yourself appoint. Meantime, I beg to express my most profound regret ; and to say that I know few things henceforward that I more care to obtain than your forgiveness.'

He ceased. Mr. Rhys gazed at him, as a man gazes who lacks faith in the exterior presented, and is trying to see behind the screen, while doing it politely.

He then handed Cunliff a lady's card, on which he saw written with a pencil in a handwriting so tremulous that it thrilled him to see, words to the effect that Mr. and Mrs. Rhys, having heard of Sir John Cunliff's presence in the neighbourhood, would feel obliged by a call at his leisure.

Knowing not what to make of all this, except that it seemed to say Mrs. Rhys was better, and, probably, reconciliation come to, Cunliff felt a great spirit of thankfulness in his heart, and waited in silence.

'Would you like to see my wife?' asked Mr. Rhys, with the same calm manner.

Sir John hesitated to reply. He could hardly say no, and yet his judgment and feeling alike warned him there could be no good in such an interview, and might be danger to his secret resolves, his new impulses, the altogether new life he desired to enter upon when he repassed this terrible threshold.

'I may remark, Sir John, that this is probably the last time my wife is likely to receive you,' said Mr. Rhys.

'She is no worse, I trust?' asked Cunliff, casting about him for some mode of escape.

'I hope not; I believe not. But you shall judge for yourself who have known her in health. Will you go with me?'

Mr. Rhys hardly waited for an answer, but passed to another door, leading to a corridor that was strangely darkened.

'Will you step in, Sir John?'

'Is he going to murder me?' was Cunliff's agitated impulse of inquiry, but he was angry with himself a moment afterwards that he was not more even in mood. The peace he yearned for, alas, had not yet come.

He did not hesitate, but walked on into the darkened corridor, Mr. Rhys closely following him, and so they walked right through to its end.

Again Mr. Rhys, with formal politeness, opened the door, bowed, and waited for his visitor to go in first.

The moment he had entered the room, he turned fiercely upon Mr. Rhys who was still closely following him, and seemed as if he would fly at his throat.

But the terror that had seized him soon froze the blood it had sent rushing so hotly to his brain.

His hand fell powerless, his chest heaved, there was a chair near the door—he felt for it—groping blindly with out-stretched hand and drooping head ; and thus standing, heard a voice speaking quietly, very quietly—

' I am glad to bring together the artist and his work.

As if a blinding light pained his eyes, Cunliff shaded them with his cold and shaking hand, while he looked towards the bed where the body of Catherine Rhys lay, resting in all tho sad pomp of death.

Fearful was the still beauty of the closed eyes with their large, blue-tinted lids, and golden lashes ; fearful the marble smile ; fearful the never-to-be-broken muteness of the sweet pale lips. The head rested on a cloud of gold—that wonder-ful hair which loving fingers had spread out wide over the pillow ; and which tho dimly burning watch-candles lit with a faint, unearthly radiance.

Then the waxen hands—how perfect, how motionless ! One holds, with meek obedience, the jasmine flowers that have been placed within it, while the other, pale, faultless as an artist's model, lies straight at the side of the young form, full and regal of outline as that of some Scandinavian princess.

There was no daylight in the room. The windows were covered with black hangings, and the bier with its lights its awful whiteness, and pure, cold beauty, shone like a star in a black sky—frosty, lovely, blinding—oh how blinding to the eyes of the man who tottered a step or two forward, and knelt by her !

For a long time it was all chilling, all agonizing to his soul, but at last its beauty began to be felt there, not only as a terror, but as something that in its effect upon him was almost a hope. Like the star that led the wise men of the East to the light of the world, so it drew his spirit from its deadly anguish and its darkness, and made it look where there was light. The mysterious beauty and glory that seemed to radiate from that still form was like a message —a token, left for him by one who had seen farther than human eye might see, and whose seeing had been sublime and joyous, and who bade him look up from his depths of misery, to live, repent, strive, conquer.

At last the silent watcher, who had been standing with folded arms at the door, apparently obeying, as he looked on, a foregone purpose of stern, terrible, overwhelming duty, touched Cunliff's shoulder, saying—

'Rise, sir, and come away'

He rose submissively, but as he half turned to follow, the fierce tide of human passion hitherto subdued and awed by the solemnity of this sudden meeting with the dead, burst forth and shook him like an ague.

Supporting himself by holding with both hands the chair by which he had been kneeling, he gazed at the bier in uncontrollable anguish, and forgetting that there was any one near, cried out—his voice rising and sinking in quick gasps—

'Oh, what a life should have been here—to be worthy of this exquisite form—this entrancing beauty—this sweetness —of the soul it lodged—of the love that throbbed with every pulse of her heart!'

'Will you oblige me by following me now, sir?' said Mr. Rhys.

'Sweet, most sweet face! Why does it smile? So great a sufferer, and smiling, Catherine? Does she smile because she thinks the excess of her punishment may be taken to lighten mine, which is greater than I can bear?'

'Come, sir, even the voice of repentance is a desecration in this room.'

'Yes, forgive me, forgive me,' said Cunliff, his awe returning upon him.

Mr. Rhys opened the door and saw him pass out, followed, and closed it gently, turning his head away as he saw Cunliff remaining to touch the panel with his lips.

He then led his visitor to the library.

There was an old Elizabethan chair at the foot of the long library table, where Hugh used to sit when he copied manuscripts for the antiquarian. He motioned to Cunliff to seat himself in it, and when he had obeyed, placed ink and paper before him, then remained standing, resting his fingers on the table.

'You asked me,' he began, in a steady, cold voice, 'to appoint what amends I think you can now make. They are very slight: First, Sir John Cunliff, I demand that for which my wife wrote you the invitation you see on the card I gave you—I demand a letter from herself to you. You will know it, she said; she wished me to obtain it of you.'

It was something to be permitted the comfort of obeying her once more—he valued it even more than what he was asked to resign.

'Do me the justice of believing, sir, that it was in order to show you by that letter,' he said, 'that I alone was seriously guilty, that I came to-day.'

'You are welcome,' replied the cold voice, 'though I have long been aware of the fact you mention, and it is in regard to my wife's wishes only that I ask for the letter.'

'This is it, sir.'

Mr. Rhys took it from him with a formal bow of acknowledgment. No other thanks did Cunliff receive for his valued treasure, and it was valued more dearly than he had before known. But he felt himself to be undergoing a kind of mental death, the bitterness and darkness of which he must face without hoping to bear with him one of his heart's dearest possessions.

Its new owner took it to the window to read.

In a few minutes, having placed it in his desk, which stood open at that end of the table, he returned to Cunliff, his face more pale and stern than before.

'It was my intention, Sir John Cunliff,' he said, 'after my wife's funeral, to seek you in whatever part of the world you might be, and request you to favour me by writing on this paper a few words I should have dictated, I ask you now to do so. If you refuse—of course I can permit no altercation in this house of mourning—I must wait ; but if you consent, you will be released of all fear of my trespassing on your time hereafter.'

He placed a sheet of note-paper before Cunliff, who, looking at it, read these words in the widower's writing :

'*Died at Dola' Hwlol, North Wales, the 13th of September, 18—, Catherine Rhys, aged 20, wife of Owen Rhys.*'

'And what is it you wish ?' asked Cunliff, looking at it with dim eyes. Oh, that little score of years, what a summer of sunshine, bloom, thunderstorm, and utter ruin, had it been ! His whole soul was mourning over the vivid little life, when he was startled by the cold, monotonous voice beside him, saying,

'An unpunishable criminal, like yourself—be seated sir; no vehemence can be permitted within these walls, while she from whom we have just come still hallows them with her presence ; and if *I* am calm in speaking of these matters, surely *you* should be. I repeat, an unpunishable criminal like yourself, unless he be no longer a man at all, but a very devil, must consider he owes something to his victim's mourners in their bereavement.'

'To what end, sir, do you inflict this torture? Could my life, could a thousand such lives as mine pay you for hers?'

'Your life, Sir John, is safe enough for me; the laws of this kingdom forbid my injuring it, as well as the laws of that in which I hope to meet my wife, and to regain the priceless treasure of her love which might now have been mine, had you not come between us, and seen the folly of so sweet a blessing crowning the gray hairs of so old a man. We knew *some* happy days before you came—if you can condescend to believe so apparently preposterous a fact—but you did come, you played your part in the tragedy of this old and once honoured house, and from thence its doom was sealed.'

He here became aware that he was allowing the icy calmness he had maintained hitherto to become disturbed. He paused, and, when he spoke again, his voice was once more level, cold, almost courteous.

'I have not been wandering from the subject of my request, Sir John, though you may think so; I wish you to be perfectly aware that I had faith in my power of making my wife happy—rather, perhaps, by virtue of her generosity than my own merits—before you came between us; I wish you to be perfectly aware that I have watched the effects of your influence over her—that I have seen it gradually killing her. I know all this, and I wish you to be aware that I know it; but, sir, I am an old man, I shall spend many lonely hours here—I may grow morbid—I may sometimes forget the truth to my own torture—I may, perhaps, be tempted to listen to what the world will say; "she was unhappy through her marriage—she died broken-hearted." In my loneliness, and morbidness because of it, I may take this view of her death, and madden myself with it. I have thought, sir, that at such time it will be well for me to have the criminal's own acknowledgment of his guilt, in his own writing, and this is what I ask you for—here, upon this paper. Here is the date of her death—you will please write beneath it your acknowledgment that it was caused by you—and sign your name.'

Cunliff raised his eyes to the face belonging to that hand which was steadily moving the inkstand towards him. The face was calm—grave now, rather than stern—but implacable.

'Sign, sir. This paper will be seen by no eye but mine. It is a poor satisfaction—it is all I shall ever ask of you.'

Then the widower stood again at Cunliff's side, resting his long fingers on the table and watching him.

It was the only drop of sweet revenge he had allowed himself to look for. He had told his frenzy when it raged within him beyond control—this much it should have and no more. This much—though it were bought dearly—ever so dearly—this, and no more.

He waited very patiently for him to begin. The silence was long and almost breathless.

'And you call me unpunishable, Mr. Rhys,' was said at last in a strange sepulchral voice, 'while you rack my soul thus? A pen, if you please.'

One was placed in his hand ; both hands as they touched were very cold and damp.

Cunliff seized the pen and wrote ; Mr. Rhys watched.

They were interrupted by a heavy drop of water falling on the paper, and running into the ink, and obliterating the words that had been written.

Mr. Rhys quietly took the paper, and copying into another sheet the record of his wife's death, replaced it before Cunliff.

Again the writing was begun, but it so happened that the freshly-traced words in his host's writing took a more than ever pathetic meaning ; again unbidden and unwelcome drops of agony fell, and deluged the clean fair page, till it was impossible to write on it.

Again the stern and ever-watchful eyes saw and noted the accident, and the quiet hand, scarcely this time so firm as before, took the paper gently away, and with wonderful patience re-wrote the sad words on another sheet, and placed that before his visitor as he had done the other two.

This time he did not remain standing at his side and watching him, but walked to the window.

As he stood there some repulsive sound seemed to meet his ear, for he remained listening with his face strongly expressive of annoyance and surprise.

He opened the window. As he did so the sweet church-bells of Capel Illtyd filled the room with vehement joyous music.

Mr. Rhys called to a gardener at work near, and asked him in a voice terrible in its intensity, what so untimely a jubilee could mean.

The man answered him that some one had already been sent up to have the bell-ringing stopped. Mr. Lloyd was away, and he supposed the clergyman who had taken his place for the time had yielded to the solicitations of the village people up there, to have the bells rung in honour of Hirell Morgan's wedding to-day. Though she was a chapel woman, Mr. Lloyd had always said they should be rung on that occasion, if she married his pupil, which she had done.

The man was English, and though he spoke in a subdued voice, he was heard at the farthest end of the library.

Mr. Rhys was aware of this—was aware, too, by degrees, of the effect the man's words must be having upon his visitor at the library table. He had heard enough of Sir John's recent history to know this. And he felt with an unholy passion, that the work of punishment was being taken out of his hands into mightier ones—Cunliff was being made insensible to his efforts by this new calamity. For the moment his thirst for revenge became fiercer for being baffled.

He shut down the window, and slowly returned to the table to see how the confession was progressing.

This time it had been nearly completed, but now—as Mr. Rhys looked down upon it—nothing but a watery, inky blister met his view, and moreover the writer's hands were clenched upon it, and his head was so bowed as to nearly touch them.

Drawing his hand again and again down his long gray beard, Mr. Rhys stood regarding him, full of thought and perplexity.

Suddenly his eyes lit with a generous fire worthy of those valiant Celtic princes from whom he was so proud of tracing his descent.

Gently he laid one hand on the blistered paper, and said, pointing to the door with the other—

'Go, Sir John Cunliff, go bearing with you my full forgiveness, and the thought that her last tears were shed for you. May they baptize your soul anew. You need not write what I asked you. Since nature blots out the record, may God blot out the sin.'

APPENDIX.

'*ARE THE ENGLISH ANGLO-SAXONS?*'—*A SKETCH WHICH
IMPATIENT READERS MAY PASS BY UNREAD.*

THE cry of Anglo-Saxon as a distinctive mark of nationality,
and Teutonic origin, is one that I verily believe no other
people under the sun would raise under similar circumstances.

Suppose it for a moment strictly true, as applied to the
greater part of England, what then? Is it true as applied to
Devon, and to Cornwall; and to Manx Islands, to the Channel
Islands, or to the Highlands of Scotland? Is it true as applied
to Wales? Above all is it true as applied to Ireland, which
alone *has had* a Celtic population of more than six millions?

Reflect then, by the aid of these plain facts, on the good
taste, the good sense, the patriotism, the chivalry, the honest
regard for truth of the predominant race in ignoring such
immense numbers of their fellow-citizens whenever the grandeur of the empire is in question, by the summing up all in the
self-glorifying phrase, ' Anglo-Saxon.'

It is quite impossible to acquit English writers and politicians
of a disregard for truth in their treatment of this subject.
Facts in every direction stare them in the face, if they will but
take note of them, and point to exactly opposite conclusions to
those which they eternally parade, as if in full faith, before the
world.

For example: If the European character of England as a
military power were to be traced back to the influences that
most powerfully tended to its formation, we should all, I think,
revert to that wonderful series of battles fought in France—
that is to say, to Crécy, Poitiers, and Agincourt, as the events
that impressed indelibly upon the imaginations alike of the
English and of Continental nations, the idea of a prowess to
which thenceforward everything was humanly possible. Now
mark!

Those very battles were, in all probability, due as much to Celtic as to Anglo-Saxon valour. The connection between the earlier English Princes of Wales and the Welsh people was marked by special tokens of royal trust and honour, and especially by the gathering of a large number of Welshmen under the Prince's own command, for the French expeditions. At Crécy, in the Black Prince's own division, there were, apart from the archers, who played the part allotted to sharp-shooters and skirmishers in modern battles, just one thousand Welshmen to eight hundred men-at-arms, presumably English, but who may have contained many persons from Ireland and other Celtic districts. These men-at-arms and Welshmen had the severe business of the hand-to-hand fighting to undertake, after the archers had created as much confusion as possible in the ranks of the enemy. To which body did the Prince give the precedence? To the Welshmen; who, advancing under the flag of the Red Dragon of Wales, struck the blow that not only disorganised the whole French array by the slaughter of so many of its leaders, but, it is said, offended even the king, Edward, inasmuch as that they did not preserve the richer men for ransom. The gallant Welshmen thought their business was to hit hard, and not trouble their heads about money-making. So much for Crécy.

Now for Poitiers. The Black Prince himself commanded there; and it is certain the Welsh, as well as the Irish Kernes, were largely represented; and the former being in his own favourite and tried division, we may be sure played their parts at least on an equality with the Anglo-Saxons.

As to Agincourt, less I believe is known as to the numbers present of the Welsh; but the special brilliancy of their deeds and position is most suggestive. Henry the Fifth, who commanded in person, sent to reconnoitre the overwhelming masses of the confronting French. Probably, the choice he made was a superb piece of diplomacy, as between himself and his small army in so tremendous a conjuncture. That peculiar property of Anglo-Saxons, in their own estimate, phlegm, did not it seems shine out in the moment of supreme danger from an English face, to the king, but from a Welshman's. It was his favourite Sir David Gam, who went, saw, and brought back the report, that, when re-echoed through the camp, was almost equivalent to a new division for the army. The enemy he said were enough to fight, enough to be killed, and enough

to run away. Cæsar's *veni, vidi, vici* was scarcely happier than
this; with the difference in his ease of the ease of speaking
epigrammatically after victory, and the difficulty of Gam's
venturing to do so before.

But this is but the comedy-prologue to an awful tragedy.
Eighteen French gentlemen banded together that day in a
solemn determination to kill or to capture the English monarch,
or die in the attempt. They failed. The king was saved.
How? By the rampart which the devoted Gam and his
officers made around him of their breasts. They saved him, but
died in the process. Was there ever, in all military history,
a more touching incident than that of Henry coming to his
dear brave-hearted Welshmen, after the battle was won, and
knighting them in their moments of death, as the only mode left
him to show alike to them and the world his heartfelt gratitude?

And then Englishmen, of this day, *not of that*, go blowing a
brazen trumpet about the world, in memory of the Anglo-
Saxon deeds, that made England great.

It may be thought this is a mere exception in our military
history, however brilliant. Judge ye. Is it or is it not a fact
that all or nearly all the great modern battles of England,
whether fought in Flanders, in India, Egypt, Spain, or Belgium,
have been fought by armies in which the Celts of the empire
predominated? Why the Irish alone, I believe, even now,
form something like half the British army. Was I then unjust to use the word 'honest' in connection with this cuckoo
cry of Anglo-Saxon?

The mention of the conquest of Agincourt, and of the Irish
elements in the British army, remind me of other facts worthy
our attention. After the death of King Henry, his widow
married again; and from the issue of that marriage sprang
one of the greatest of English sovereigns. And the mere
name of her dynasty makes the author of it, Owen Tudor, a
household word, wherever the English language is spoken.
Was Queen Elizabeth Anglo-Saxon?

The other instance to which I referred is that of the greatest
of modern military commanders—an ·absolutely perfect representative, I imagine, of Anglo-Saxons, in their own estimation
—the Duke of Wellington; who, born in Ireland, and related,
by the maternal side, to the illustrious Welsh family of the
Tudor-Trevors, is not much more Anglo-Saxon than Queen
Elizabeth herself.

I see you smile, and no wonder. But this is a far more serious matter than at first sight it may appear. British statesmen seek unity. They are ever ready to put in operation the extremest powers of government to coerce differing national elements into unity. We refuse, even to the death, the right of self-government, say for instance to Ireland, in the name of unity. Nothing, in English opinion, can be more criminal than for non-Anglo-Saxon elements to oppose unity. No punishment is too bad for the rebellious spirits that will not lovingly kiss the hand of authority in unity. And while all these things are so, amid the ceaseless strifes and heart-burnings thus produced, there rises, alike for those who yield and for those who struggle, the same eternal songs of triumph for Anglo-Saxondom.

WHAT BECAME OF THE ABORIGINES?

But are the English Anglo-Saxon, after all?

I think not, and hope to show they may look to a much nobler ancestry.

Does it ever occur, I wonder, to the more thoughtful and cultivated men among them, to ask themselves as they read the spirit-stirring records of their very earliest history, what became of the Aborigines?

Of course, I know, as they know, the babyish story, which even learned men have been content to accept as history, that the Britons were all killed off, or driven away into Wales, by the early Saxon invaders. I will deal with that presently. But there must have been other ideas and influences at work to strengthen and maintain such a conception of the origin of the English people through so long a period of time, accompanied, as it was, by a reversal of the usual order of things; for whereas we find in history generally the memory and influence of great ideas or events gradually fading away, till at last they are little more than a recollection and a name; here, on the contrary, the original idea has gone on growing with the country's growth, till at last it has become one of the more conspicuous standing phenomena of the world.

What, then, have been these influences? I think they may be thus enumerated:

First, as regards the earlier state of things, there would be the hate felt by the successful invaders for those they had so deeply injured, who had struggled with them so long and so well, and whose civilisation they were unable to appreciate.

Then, as regards modern times, I note—

The notions about the very limited numbers of the aboriginal British population;

Their supposed barbarous character, which seemed to suggest how easily a more cultivated race might displace them, and which made the English unwilling to think them their progenitors;

The very weighty fact of the language; and lastly· –

That peculiar trait of the Teutonic race, the belief in its descent from gods, no matter that they were pagan gods, which makes each man resent, as a personal offence, everything that opposes his god-like ideas and will; and which, when he is in the position of absolute conqueror, commanding the lives, liberties, customs, education, marriages, etc., of a mixed race, may gradually through a favourable combination of circumstances extend through the whole; leavening even the non-Teutonic blood with the pleasant titillating fancy of the whole of humanity ranged as in a circle before the Superior one's eyes, humbly bending like the sheaves of corn of Joseph's brethren, while his own particular sheaf stands erect in the centre, lord of all.

The British population then, according to the popular notion, was very limited. Indeed! Julius Cæsar did not think so. If he, speaking from his own personal experience, may be supposed to know anything about the matter, ‘the population’ was ‘infinite, the houses very numerous.’

At a later period (the time of Nero), and after immense losses by fighting against the Romans, Tacitus, speaking of tributary British chiefs in council, says they were reminded that ‘if the Britons would but consider their own numbers, they would find that the Roman troops who were among them were but a paltry and inconsiderable force.’

But the fact of the long continuance of the wars between the first military power of the world, and this despised British population, before a final conquest was achieved, ought to have shown the absurdity and shamelessness of the theory. To conquer Britain became with the Romans the culminating point of national glory. For this triumphal honours were granted by applauding senates, imperial coins stamped. Think of a Roman Emperor changing his name, in order to call himself Britannicus, in memory of the Roman Conquests. Tacitus says of one of the decisive battles, in which the Britons under

Boadicea were defeated, ' the glory won on that day was equal to that of the most renowned victories of the ancient Romans.' We can easily understand that when we hear of such an incident as a Roman Legion being almost annihilated by a single and sudden stroke, while on its way to reinforce its besieged countrymen; when we recall Severus's loss of fifty thousand men in a single campaign; or when we remember that the Roman conquest was not finally completed in less than a hundred and thirty years; though if the time of the last actual fighting be the limit, then more than two and a half centuries were required.

Judge then how curiously untrue is the notion of the aborigines being few or weak. Let me add two portentous facts. When the revolted Britons under Boadicea attacked London and St. Albans, which were occupied by the Romans, and Roman-British, and British in submission or alliance, they killed seventy thousand persons. And then when the Romans were able to retaliate effectively by a tremendous battle, victory, and slaughter, they killed, according to Tacitus, some eighty thousand British men, women, and children, on the field, or afterwards. And all these came from only two of the seventeen tribes by which South Britain was occupied. Let us finish this part of our theme by the mention of a pleasanter incident. It refers to the year 359, when the bloodshed between Roman and Briton had ceased; when 'arts' had again taken the place of 'arms;' when a prolonged peace reigned—never again to be broken by the same combatants; and with as much of dignity for the dependent race as was compatible with the military, political, and tributary submission. It was when the Roman colonies on the Rhine, having been pillaged by the barbarians, were left in imminent danger of starvation. Eight hundred vessels of unusual size were in consequence sent to Britain for corn, and brought back a most abundant supply. Such was the state of agriculture at that time among us; such was the population on which the abundance depended.

But the Roman dominion ended by the Romans' own act, through the general decay of their power. And then followed what no doubt every wise and patriotic Briton had mournfully foreseen, his country became a prey for the hordes of robbers who were drawn to it by the knowledge of the unprotected state in which it had been left. For several generations

the art of war must have died out among the Britons, unless
we make an exception in favour of the many men of mixed
blood, Roman-British, who must by this time have come into
existence; and who may have been trusted with arms and
trained as Roman soldiers, without being, like other British
recruits, sent abroad.

The Picts were the first—and the most unnatural of these
invaders—for in all probability they were of Celtic blood.

To save themselves from this influx of barbarians, who
could have had no motive but the superior wealth, and, therefore, superior civilisation in many respects of the Britons, the
latter, it is supposed, appealed to the Saxons for aid, who
came—drove off the Picts—and then turned upno the unhappy Britons treacherously; and after another frightful
period of anarchy and war, which lasted some hundred and
fifty years, were 'exterminated and driven into Wales.'

The simplicity, neatness, and completeness of this theory
is certainly charming, if only it is true.

But why is Wales made a receptacle for destitute Britons?
She had her own and powerful tribes, her own interests, her
own land to care for and guard. No doubt she might in cases
of necessity receive a limited number of refugees, whose
characters as warriors, or whose local position on the borders,
when flying as houseless wanderers from the vengeful Saxon
sword, might give them a claim to the hospitality of the
Kymri (a distant branch, remember, of the Celts), who
possessed Wales. But anything like a wholesale reception of
such fugitives would have been simply suicidal. They must
all, guests and hosts alike, have perished by famine; to say
nothing of the endless additional complications of absurdity
into which we are plunged by the hypothesis.

No great numbers then of the Britons of England could
possibly have been received in Wales, or existed there if
received. Nay, we may even ask, how could they ever have
got there?

If the Anglo-Saxons were in such absolute mastery as to
achieve the result spoken of, they must also have been able to
stop the wandering masses of Britons, who might attempt to
march through or across the country, and therefore slaughter
them at once, rather than risk the most dangerous of all
results—their junction with men of their own blood in or near
Wales, who were still free.

The alternative, then, is that the Anglo-Saxons killed them off—which makes the theory probably neater, more finished than before—but also not a little startling.

What, kill all those warriors, of all those tribes, within a very limited space of time, who had previously made alike Roman and Saxon measure their rate of progress towards conquest by centuries rather than by years? The idea is a bold one, and takes one's breath away! But let us accept it and go on.

The warriors gone at one fell swoop, what about the labouring population, scattered over every part of the interior of the country, and without whom warriors and war would alike soon have come to an end? How were they to be got at even to be killed? Did the Anglo-Saxons send a deputation of a couple or half-dozen armed men to every township, village, and hamlet, of the whole of England, that they might there call the rustic Britons together, as the memorable mistress called her ducks, 'Dilly, dilly, come and be killed?' Or did they, less confidently, send armies to march through the whole length and breadth of the land to perform the job, having previously sent a polite request that the natives would be kind enough to stay at home till they came?

But I am inclined to be generous and allow the possibility, as a bare theory, that the whole labouring population might have been killed off, but I am arrested by a little difficulty in going farther. Did the Anglo-Saxons not want corn, or pork, or beef? Or did they object on principle to make other men labour for them? Or were they so enamoured of industry, after a long and successful career of pillage and slaughter, that they preferred not to be lords—not to be masters—but do everything, down even to the humblest offices, for themselves? Certainly that would be a revelation of Anglo-Saxondom for which the world is hardly prepared.

But it is in argument as in love; once begin to yield to your antagonist, and you must go on. So, I give up the whole labouring population to indiscriminate slaughter, as well as the warriors.

But what about the women? Did the Anglo-Saxons not want *them*? Or is it supposed that one, two, or three hundred thousand virgins were fetched from the wilds of Germany?

And if so, how did they come? In those fleets of 'three' and 'five' ships, of which we hear so much? Or did each batch, in first coming, bring with it, stowed away below as ballast, a reasonable proportion of sweethearts, wives, sisters, and daughters to profit by the change of country, when their lords and masters should have taken undisputed possession, in periods of time varying probably from a few to more than a hundred and fifty years?

And even if the ascetic, spiritual-minded Anglo-Saxons forswore the charms of British women, and with heroic self-sacrifice killed them all, what about the children?

Suppose only those children left alive who were under twelve years of age, how many would there be? Look back at the series of facts I have detailed and judge whether it is humanly possible that they could have been—roughly speaking —less in number than the whole of the Anglo-Saxon invaders, excluding of course those who had been born on the soil; who would assuredly be Celtic on the mother's side, and whose true designation was, what all Englishmen's ought to have been, Anglo-Celt.

Of course, having admitted so much as I have done, I may be now asked to admit finally the wholesale slaughter of even the innocent young children. And if the idea can be accepted and looked at even for a single moment as true, what an infamous set of barbarians must the ancestors of the English people have been! And yet Englishmen are to call themselves Anglo-Saxons! To glorify themselves as Anglo-Saxons! Why they should rather have a day set apart of solemn humiliation, renunciation, expiation, and pledge; a kind of political baptism to wash them clean, and put an impassable barrier between those Teutons and these.

But again, I say the English, with that charming modesty that so becomes them, mistake themselves; neither they in their notions of the past, nor their presumed ancestry in their actual deeds, are so bad as they seem.

The whole basis of this incredible story rests upon one man —Gildas—to whom may be applied the Eastern fable of the tortoise that supports the world, and the question the fable provoked, what supports him? Nothing.

He is supposed to have written his book in the year 550-- 560, to have been a monk, and to have obtained his materials not from Britain itself, nor from original British documents, but from the Continent, probably from British refugees devoted like himself to Roman ideas and interests. But the value to be attached to his writings may be judged by two facts; one, that where independent and more trustworthy evidence can be placed by the side of his, it is generally to contradict him ; the other that Mr. Stevenson, in his preface to a recent edition of Gildas, says:

' We are unable to speak with certainty as to his (Gildas's) parentage, his country, or even his name, the period when he lived, or the works of which he was the author ! ' In other words we really *know* nothing about him.

But the most amusing part of the business is that even this half-mythical personage does not say what is almost supposed he did say, but rather the very reverse. Here is the passage that has been made such wonderful use of, and which I transcribe from Dr. Giles's translation in his 'Six Old English Chronicles : '

' *Some* therefore of the miserable remnant being taken in the mountains were murdered in great numbers ; others, constrained by famine, came and yielded themselves, to be *slaves for ever to their foes*, running the risk of being instantly slain, which truly was the greatest favour that could be offered them ; some others passed beyond the seas with loud lamentations, instead of the voice of exhortation,—" Thou hast given us as sheep to be slaughtered, and among the Gentiles hast thou dispersed us."

' Others, committing the safeguard of their lives, which were in continual jeopardy, to the mountains, precipices, thickly-wooded forests, and to the rocks of the seas (albeit with trembling hearts), *remained still in their country.*'

So that, instead of saying the Britons were all killed, Gildas really says some went abroad (who must have been very few), some were killed, some made slaves, and some driven for shelter to the forests, mountains, etc., who thus, as he points out, remained still in the country. Exactly ! Just what one might have anticipated beforehand.

Strange to say, looked at in this simple natural light, Gildas's story becomes not only probable, but is beyond question substantially true. He says nothing whatever to contradict the idea that the great mass of the British remained alive and under Saxon rule. Large numbers may have been killed, but the interesting question for us is as to how many remained alive, and in what state. And that question may be briefly and summarily answered from the Saxon Chronicle.

Eleven years after the dates mentioned for his book (550–

560) Saxons and Britons fought at Bedford; and Aylesbury and other towns were *then taken from the Britons.* Six years after that Gloucester, Cirencester, and Bath were *found in the hands of the Britons,* and three British kings slain in dispossessing them. And yet again, seven years later, we find it recorded that *many towns were taken from the Britons.* And now for the crowning fact:—617. This year Ethelfrid, king of the Northumbrians, was slain by Redwald, king of E. Angles, and Edwin, the son of Alba, succeeded to the kingdom, *and* [then] *subdued all Britain*—THE KENTISH MEN ALONE EXCEPTED.

It is most important here to note that where the invaders first landed there they first always strove to make for themselves strongholds or places of safety; and from these marched into the interior of the country, often only to be driven back.

All their tactics must have been framed with a view to the permanent retention of the strong places on the coast; consequently the British strength must have been in the interior. And the known historical facts confirm this. Caractacus, in his ever-memorable speech, speaks of his nation as the most renowned one of Britain, dwelling in the very heart of the country, and out of sight of the shores of the conquered, so that their eyes were unpolluted by the contagion of slavery. Cæsar, distinguishing between the maritime people (formerly invaders from Belgium), refers to the interior as peopled by the natives; and the latest of the battles between Britons and Anglo-Saxons were, as we have seen, in the interior.

Really one is ashamed to reflect how clear, after all, is the matter, if looked at without prejudice, in the light of common sense.

Here is a people consisting of many distinct tribes of nations (Kent alone had four kings) overpowered, not at once, but by successive and very slow steps, and with alternations of fortune and of feeling on both sides. Now one grows weary of the strife, now the other. Thus spring up the two parallel ideas —hateful at first, but gradually growing irresistible—first, of the native yielding to the foreign force that presses so heavily, and seems capable of endless reinforcement; and, secondly, of the conquerors accepting submission without making it too humiliating and hopeless for the conquered. And this state of view as regards the more independent-minded of the Britons would be constantly forced upon their unwilling thoughts, by the sight of so many of their countrymen in different parts of

England already enslaved through the superiority of the Saxon strength in those particular localities.

A still more potent element would be the amalgamation of the races through the marriages of Saxon men with British women—forced probably at first. And it is easy to see how large a number of such women there would be after the terrible slaughter of the British warriors in the latter years of British independence.

Here, I think, is the key-note of the whole. The Saxons could have—as a general rule—no women but those they obtained from among the Britons ; and when once that process had gone on for a few years on a scale of considerable magnitude, as in the nature of things it must have done, the very heart of resistance was plucked out ; the two enemies were fast becoming friends by the law of inexorable necessity.

Two or three facts will confirm, I think, the truth of this my theory. Bede shows us that in 603 Ethelfrid gave the Britons the alternative of becoming tributary, or being driven out. If one of the worst of the ravening ' wolves,' as he was called, found it necessary to offer such terms as these, after the period when it is supposed the Britons had altogether disappeared from the land of their birth, we may judge how less ruthless spirits would deal with them. And here is a striking commentary :—Cœdwalla, a British Prince, actually reigned over one of the newly-formed Saxon kingdoms, Wessex, A.D. 634. How can that fact be explained, except on some such hypothesis as I have suggested ?

It was a compromise, I conclude, between the politically powerful but less numerous Saxons with the less powerful but more numerous Britons ; the latter accepting the Saxon arrangements, in return for the personal respect shown to their race ; the former yielding the post of sovereign for the certainty that all further opposition within the new kingdom would cease. I shall leave this part of my subject with one later glimpse of Saxon and Briton together in amity. At Exeter, in 940, there was a British part of the city and a Saxon part, the two having equal privileges.

You will be prepared now to receive, I hope, as it deserves, a few words from our Welsh Triads, which really, in many senses, are historical documents of the utmost value—

' *The Lloegrians* [*i.e.*, the people inhabiting what we now call England] *become as Saxons.*'

To the suggestive simplicity and straightforwardness of those words, written probably in the same century as Gildas wrote in, one can add nothing.

But the poet Taliesin, living in that same sixth century, has also left his record. He says (I quote from Mr. Borrow's 'Wild Wales'):

A serpent which coils,
And with fury boils,
From Germany coming with armed wings spread,
Shall subdue and enthrall
The broad Britain all,
From the Lochlin ocean to Severn's bed.

*And British men
Shall be captives then.
To strangers from Saxonia's strand ;*
They shall praise their God and hold
Their language as of old,
But except wild Wales they shall lose their land.

I cannot agree with my countryman Mr. Stephens, author of that very excellent work, ' The Literature of the Kymri,' who appears to include this prediction among the poems wrongly assigned to Taliesin, and to consider that it was made long *after* the Britons had been enslaved ; and for the rather obvious reason, that as the Britons have *not* kept their language any more than they have kept their land (except in Wild Wales), the prediction shows on the face of it that it was written when the ruin of the British power was impending, but not consummated ; and hence was liable to the fate of all human prophecies—mistake.

Partly then through actual amalgamation and the amity produced by intermarriage, partly through political compromises and alliances in moments of Saxon need, but chiefly through reduction to slavery, did the ancient British population become merged into the new England ; and in numbers that, according to all probability, must have greatly exceeded the numbers of the invaders. And thus we find Taliesin's prediction of what should be, in harmony with Mr. Hallam's view of what was, when the historian refers to the great proportion of the serf population of England as consisting of Britons.

But how, it may be asked, came the ancient Celtic language to be so completely obliterated in favour of the Teutonic ?

The ceaseless spirit of exaggeration that affects the Anglo-

Saxon advocates has misrepresented this, like every other part
of the subject. The ordinary notion has been that the language
is throughout Teutonic, alike in the vocabulary and the
structure. Both positions are now denied; and as to the first,
I shall merely point to the opinion of Mr. Max Müller, that not
one third of the words in English dictionaries can be traced to
a Teutonic source.

Still the language is the one specious argument that Anglo-
Saxondom can urge in favour of the idea, that the English are
Anglo-Saxons. How specious it is, is seen the moment we
cast our eyes across the Channel, to the descendants of the
Gauls, who were the very same people as our own Britons, who
now also speak the language of conquerors, not their own.

All the causes I have enumerated for the absorption of
Britons and Saxons into one race of Englishmen, but under the
dominating influence of the latter, acted with equal effect in
producing one language, and that the English, under the des-
potism of the conquerors.

They of course dreaded the tongues of the oppressed, for
they might at any time bring about a new alliance of the
tribes, a new struggle, a new conquest, if not even a reversal
of the conquest by defeat.

The British poets, and the poets of Wales, who came by
degrees to represent the former (helped, no doubt, by many
of the choicer spirits who fled to them for hospitality), were
at the time full of predictions of the restoration of British,
and the destruction of Saxon power; as you will find in Mr.
Stephens's book.

The native language therefore was put down: not in one
year, nor ten, nor perhaps in a century, but still put down.

And the process may not have been as barbarous as at first
sight one might fancy, nor so difficult. It was only to see
that the children were all made to learn Anglo-Saxon. And
how could they help but learn, when their own fathers in a
vast number of cases were the teachers? The amalgamation
of the Saxon men with the British women clears away every
difficulty.

But is it not a pitiable spectacle to see a knot of learned
men eternally squabbling about race and language, as if the
mightiest interests of humanity were bound up in proving
some impassable barrier between these men and those; while
all the while, they themselves show us that Celt and Teuton

in blood and language alike draw the line of descent from one common stock or parent, the Indo-European ?

Well does Sir F. Palgrave remark :—'Britons, Anglo-Saxons, Danes, and Normans were all relations, however hostile. They were all kinsmen shedding kindred blood.'

Is there yet need of further demonstration ? If so, glance at the faces of Englishmen wherever you meet them, and ask them what story they tell. Do fair complexions, blue eyes, broad faces, flaxen hair—such as we have been told to look on as characteristic of the Saxon race—predominate ? Or as Mr. Pike puts the matter in his valuable and interesting book, ' The English and their Origin,' [1] which goes deeply into this part of the subject (and putting aside in fairness what may be merely the exaggeration of a truth), do men of darker complexions and hair, oval faces, and long heads, predominate or no over men of less dark complexions, broader faces, and shorter heads ? It is impossible for there to be any doubt as to the answer : the former greatly predominate. And yet the types thus summarised are precisely the accepted types of Briton and Saxon.

But I do not agree with Mr. Pike, as to an actual predominating Celtic influence in English society looked at in its broadest aspect; and for this, to me, all sufficing reason,—if there was ever a nation of 'imagination all compact,' it was that of my countrymen before the destruction of their independence by England; and what they were, the Britons previously had been in all essential qualities ; while, on the other hand, there never was a nation, perhaps, in which imagination was so deficient as in the Anglo-Saxon of the middle ages, and as at present in the bulk of Englishmen.

I do not doubt that there are stupid Celts and brilliantly endowed Teutons among us ; but no fair observer can question the statement that the predominant *character* among the English is Teutonic, and the predominant *population* Celtic

---

[1] The author wishes to mention in connection with this work, and one on a similar subject by Dr. Nicholas, that his own views as conveyed in the text were formed long before he had seen either of these books. It was during a protracted residence in Wales for the purpose of this novel, he first began to ask himself the question and to obtain the answers, he has put into the mouth of another. This refers simply to the general theory of the above sketch. Its tone and peculiarities must be considered in connection with the fact, that it is a Welshman who is the speaker.

—the rural elements of the latter constituting probably the largest proportion of the whole—having suffered to a ruinous extent by the original slavery of their condition, then by serfdom, and lastly by their modern state, as agricultural labourers, earning too little to nourish either body or mind properly.

But with the Celtic town population it has been different. They might there be inferior in numbers to the Anglo-Saxons, and hence have been beaten in the race for material things, but they have also been the winners probably in those greater achievements, which give glory to the nation. Chaucer, and Spenser, and Shakspeare, and Milton, have little or nothing in common, so far as their genius is concerned, with the unimaginative masses of the English (rich or poor) of our time, but they have everything in common with the bards and romantic heroes of early Welsh and British history. At all events I please myself by thinking that we have the greater right to them—while we resign to our old antagonists the material conquests of industry—and the past influence over legislation.

BRITON OR SAXON, WHICH NOW SHOULD BE OUR EXEMPLAR?

Can there be a doubt? asks some impatient Anglo-Saxon, contemptuously thinking only of painted Britons on the one side, perhaps, and of a King Alfred on the other.

What will he say then to my assertion that the Saxon invaders were mere pagan barbarians? and that they came to attack, stifle, or destroy a civilisation and a religion too high for them even to understand?

The Englishman admires antiquity, yet takes care to stop short before an antiquity to which his antiquity is but a thing of yesterday. As Bishop Percy, long ago, told the English, the hills, forests, rivers, of their country retain to this hour the names that British forefathers gave them, and, perhaps, innumerable centuries ago. Everything of the grandest antiquity we possess is Celtic.

So again of the British laws and customs, however difficult it may be to trace step by step the links, and show what remains. Sir John Fortescue in his *De Laudibus Legum Angliæ*, writing so late as the fifteenth century, and referring to the excellence and duration of those in his own time, enumerates the conquerors who came to rule over the country, Romans, Saxons, Danes, Saxons again, and Normans, then says, ' if these ancient British customs had not been *most excellent*, reason, justice, and the love of their country, would have induced some of these kings to change or abolish them, especially the Romans, who ruled all the rest of the world by the Roman laws.' So spake one of the very highest English legal authorities on British laws and customs, not from his reading or theories, but from his own actual living experience.

Is it in individual heroism that the Saxon surpassed the Briton ? Excuse the smile with which I ask. I suppose if the world's suffrages could be collected, there would be but one opinion, that a grander specimen of heroic humanity never glorified our planet than Caractacus. And the British woman was only less grandly represented in Boadicea. Here are two figures who are yet to the imaginations of men living, actual beings never to be forgotten.

Or do we wish for yet another variety of hero ? Take him then in Arthur, the representative alike of the actual and the ideal—here each personified in the most glowing and enchanting of all antique individualities. Do you know that while his deeds rank him as among the greatest of patriotic kings and warriors—a man who side by side with Alfred would make even that most noble, most magnificent monarch shrink in the comparison, *were those deeds only as well known as the Saxon's*—do you know, I ask, that the mere light and glory shed from his life have sufficed to fill Europe from that time to this, not vaguely and egotistically, but generatively with the most precious fruits of our literature ? From the Arthur legends sprang the romantic poetry and fiction of modern Europe. At this moment England's greatest living poet finds his grandest opportunities in the dealing with the British King Arthur.

Yet even these things seem to me for the moment trifles when I contemplate another feature of that early time, and the fratricidal contest of the two races. One can hardly believe one's senses when we read English history, to see how the introduction and reception of Christianity to this land appears to be thought the merit of Anglo-Saxons. Why, the barbarians found the religion of Christ flourishing among us, and destroyed it for us so far as they could. Tertullian, about the close of the second century, boasts that the Gospel had subdued the very tribes of Britain *that were still unconquered by the Romans.* Was there ever a more magnificent compliment paid to the courage, the intellect, and the divine instincts of a nation? Why, the Church in Britain was in full organisation by the end of the second century, and sent bishops and others to represent it at the great councils held on the Continent, as for instance at Arles in 314. And then those delicious Anglo-Saxons, after having choked everything like religion out of the hearts of the people, re-discovered it; and other would-be Anglo-Saxons, centuries after, boast of the grandeur of the exploit!

Before I try to illustrate the culture of the 'painted barbarians' at the time of the Saxon invasion, let me show the Saxon culture by one pregnant fact. Even in Alfred's time there was no Anglo-Saxon literature: all the treasures of the past remained to be translated into the Anglo-Saxon tongue, and he himself laboured to begin the work.

How, on the contrary, was it, centuries earlier with the Britons? I will not dwell vaguely on the knowledge of the Druidic times, great as that certainly was, but refer you simply to existing evidences.

There are specimens of the intellect and philosophy of the Britons, Triads, so called, which are among the oldest things preserved in Welsh literature, and which date probably from the very time of the Druids. Take the subject Genius, and compare, for instance, with Wordsworth's view of the poet's genius in the Preface to the 'Lyrical Ballads:'

The three foundations of genius:—the gift of God, man's exertion, and the events of life.

The three primary requisites:—an eye that can see nature, a heart that can feel nature, and boldness that dares follow nature.

The three supports:—strong mental endowment, memory, learning. And again:—prosperity, social acquaintance, and praise.

I may deceive myself, but it seems to me that here is an absolutely perfect analysis of the subtlest thing in the world, not only in its diviner spiritual aspect, but also in its worldly aspect; so that to-day, as so many centuries ago, it remains absolutely true, and you can neither add to it, nor take away.

Consider again these themes from the Triads, godliness and social duty, so finely melting into each other:

The three characteristics of godliness:—to do justice, to love mercy, and to behave humbly.

There are three actions which are divine:—to succour the poor and feeble, to benefit an enemy, and courageously to suffer in the cause of right.

One more triad, and I have done. It is a glimpse of the ancient Briton's speculative philosophy:

The three priorities of being—which are the three necessities of Deity:—Power, Knowledge, and Love. And from these three are strength and existence.

Hugh, don't forget to ask your new Anglo-Saxon friends to put by the side of these things whatever they think may best stand the comparison in connection with their cherished exemplars, of the sixth and seventh centuries, and tell me the result.

But our forefathers acted out what they thought; whereas the Saxon nature seems almost to fear thinking, lest it might be tempted to act. Look at the treatment of the artisan as shown to us by his treatment in Wales in the very earliest periods. He could travel where he pleased, and enter what house he pleased, sure of hospitality. The Mabinogion presents to us a knight knocking at the gate of a castle, and being told the knife is in the meat, and the drink is in the horn, and there is revelry in the hall of Gwyrnach the Giant; and except for a craftsman bringing his craft, the gate will not be opened to-night.

Even in trade the Britons preceded and taught their conquerors. Himilco, the Carthaginian navigator, described them long before the Roman invasion as a numerous race, endowed with spirit, with no little expertness, *all busy with the cares of trade*.

Herodotus and Aratus also speak of their export of metals to the East.

Could you not fancy it would be a most interesting thing to be able to look into the home of one of the early Britons? Well, you may do so. You may judge of the domestic state and culture of the Britons in the sixth and seventh centuries, by the anecdote quoted above, and by that which Giraldus Cambrensis found in the year 1204 in Wales; which could have had no external lights or influences of any kind in the interim, to change the substantial character of its civilisation. It may have improved or deteriorated, but not fundamentally changed. Consider then this charming picture, and especially its bearing upon the condition of women, and then think of the wreck that was made when these things were destroyed in England:

'The strangers who arrive in the morning are entertained until evening with the conversation of young women, and with the music of the harp; for in this country (Wales) almost every house is provided with both   . In the evening, when no more guests are expected, the meal is prepared according to the number and dignity of the persons assembled, and according to the wealth of the family which entertains. The kitchen does not supply many dishes, nor high-seasoned incitements to eating. The house is not furnished with table-cloths or napkins; they study nature more than splendour; for which reason the guests being seated in threes, instead of couples, as elsewhere, they place the dishes before them all at once, upon rushes and fresh grass, in large platters or trenchers. They also make use of a thin and broad cake of bread, baked every day; and they sometimes add chopped meat, with broth. Such a repast was formerly used by the noble youths from which this nation boasts its descent, and whose manners it still partly imitates. While the family is engaged in waiting on the guests, the host and hostess stand up, paying unremitting attention to everything, and take no food till all the company are satisfied.'

Music is the only thing, alas, in which we now seem able to indicate our former quality. Pray listen, Hugh, for this should be very interesting to you. The same authority says:

'By the sweetness of their musical instruments they soothe and delight the ear; they are rapid yet delicate in their modulation; and by the astonishing execution of their fingers, and their swift transitions from discord to concord, produce the most pleasing harmony.'

And again: 'It is remarkable that in all their haste of performance, they never forget time and musical proportion; and such is their art, that with all their inflection of tones, the variety of their instruments, and that intricacy of their harmony, they attain perfection of consonance and melody, by a sweet velocity, an equable disparity, and a discordant concord. .   .

'They enter into a movement, and conclude in so delicate a manner, and play the little notes so sportively under the blunter sounds of the bass strings, enlivening with a wanton levity, or communicating a deeper internal sensation of pleasure, that the perfection of their art appears in the concealment of it: for—

> Art profits when concealed,
> Disgraces when revealed.

'It is asserted,' adds Mr. Stephens, 'that the Welsh were acquainted with counterpoint prior to Guido's supposed discovery of it, as one of the twenty-four ancient games, in which Welshmen were ambitious to excel, was to sing a song in four parts with accentuations.'

The position of the Bard-musician among such a people must indeed have been enviable. His order was erected into a hierarchy. Going back so far as the tenth century, we find his position as supreme bard was next but one to the patron [i.e., the chief, prince, or king] of the family. His land was free, a horse from the king was in attendance for him. When the office was first secured to him he had a harp from the king, and a gold ring from the queen. Hugh, lad, does not thy soul expand at the thought of the things such bards did? Imagine thyself in the position provided for the bard when he was ordered to sing the Monarchy of Britain in front of the battle !

Before I draw to a close I must remember that I have said nothing of the chiefest glory of those olden days. Yes, you understand me—the poetry which we have still in possession, linking the Britons of the most ancient days with my own countrymen, the Welsh, down to a period before the advent of England's morning star in Chaucer.

The wealth at my disposal embarrasses me. But at the very same period English poetry—the poetry of the Anglo-Saxons—had literally no existence. Uncouth thoughts, in still more uncouth rhymes, crop up every now and then ; but from the sixth to the fourteenth century, when Chaucer wrote, there is scarcely a gleam of anything that even looked like fancy, imagination—in a word—poetry.

Now for the contrast. What shall I give you first? A Bacchanalian hymn; not, however, in honour of the juice of the grape, but of that from honey; of which, by-the-by, the Anglo-Celtic queen, Elizabeth, was very fond.

Listen to an extract from the Mead Song of a very early time :

THE MEAD SONG.

To him who rules supreme; our Sovereign Lord,
Creation's chief—by all that lives adored,
Who made the waters and sustained the skies,
Who gives and prospers all that's good and wise;
To him I'll pray that Maelgwyn ne'er may need
Exhaustless stores of sparkling nectrous mead;
Such as with mirth our hour has often crown'd,
When from his horns the foaming draught went round.
The bee whose toils produced it, never sips
The juice ordained by Heaven for human lips,
Delicious mead, man's solace and his pride;
Who finds in thee his every want supplied.[1]

Can you believe that such a poem was written in Wales a century or two before Chaucer was born? yet that is the latest period assigned to the poem. But here I am again at issue with Mr. Stephens, who thus dates the poem, in direct contradiction to the popular tradition and belief, and to the very name attached to it, Taliesin. If it was his, it was written by a Briton in the sixth century, *i.e.*, the very period of the struggle of the Britons against the Saxons. And why does Mr. Stephens doubt its antiquity? Simply because the language (in the Welsh) is so smooth, pure, and lucid. But he forgets that the original poem may easily have undergone slight verbal transformation as the language became modernised, without any vital change whatever in the essential character of the original. Meantime the poem testifies beyond all question to my mind that it belongs to the earlier date, and to the supposed author. Note this :

To him I'll pray that Maelgwyn ne'er may need, etc.

Who was Maelgwyn? Why, a celebrated king of the Britons, contemporary with Taliesin, and his personal friend and patron.

[1] Stephens.

So much for the Mead Song. Now take a specimen from what I may almost call a splendid dramatic poem of the twelfth century, the Hirlas. The prince-poet who wrote it imagines himself presiding over a banquet with his warriors, on the eve of a day of battle. ' Fill, cup-bearer!' he exclaims at the beginning of every verse; and then taking his chiefs in succession, he reviews their deeds, managing with admirable skill to vary the praise bestowed on each. In the list he comes in turn to Tudyr and Moreiddig.

> Fill, cup-bearer, as you would avoid death,
> Fill the horn of honour at our banquets,
> The long blue horn of high privilege; of ancient silver
> That covers it not sparingly;
> Bears to Tudyr, eagle of slaughter,
> A prime beverage of florid wine.
> Thy head shall be the forfeit if there come not in
> The most delicious mead.

The cup-bearer goes, as the poet-prince supposes, with the mead to the heroes he names, in whose praise the song again rises—

> To the hand of Moreiddig, encourager of songs,
> May they become old in fame before they leave us.
> Ye blameless brothers of aspiring souls,
> Of dauntless ardour that would grasp ev'n fire,
> Heroes, what services ye have achieved for me !
> Not old disgustingly, but old in skill;
> Unwearied, rushing wolves of battle ;
> First in the crimsoned ranks of bleeding pikes,
> Brave leaders of the Mochnatians from Powys,
> The prompt red chiefs to use their arms,
> And keep their boundaries free from turmoil :
> Praise is your meed, most amiable pair !

He now turns to greet them, but their places are vacant; he recollects they fell in the morning conflict; he hears their dying groans—his triumphant exultations cease—his hilarity flies—and the broken tones of mournful exclamations suddenly burst ont—

> Ha—the cry of death! and do I miss them ?
> O Christ ! how I mourn their catastrophe !
> O lost Moreiddig—how greatly shall I need thee.[1]

I can add to this only two pieces more, extracts from love poems, a class of which I could find a hundred other examples,

---

[1] Stephens.

in the poetry of Wales, before the Anglo-Saxons of England had obtained a single poet.

The first is a literal translation by Mr. Stephens, from Rhys Goch, who died in 1340. Of course the charm, the aroma of the original verse, is not to be hoped for in such a guise. But take it as it is:

> Above us streamed the rays of the summer sun,
> And long green grass covered the fields,
> Trefoils in great numbers and leafy trees adorned the scene;
> There lay I and Gwen in perfect bliss,
> Reclining both among the flowers,
> Surrounded by troops of trefoils;
> Lip to lip we spent the time.
> From the lips of the maid I obtained a feast,
> Like that of saintly David in the choir of Hodnant,
> Or Taliesin at the court of Elphin,
> Or the Round-Table feasts of Caerlleon,
> Or angel joys in paradise.
> And we both feasted thus
> Without a care for what had been,
> Without a thought of what would be;
> This height of bliss was never ending
> For we were both of one intent,
> And all that day we only sang
> That we would live and love together!
> Living sweetly upon kisses,
> And both dying on the same.

The second is a love-song by Howell, Prince of N. Wales, who died in 1172, and who has written other exquisite things:

> Give me the fair, the gentle maid
>   Of slender form in mantle green
> Whose woman's wit is ever staid,
>   Subdued by virtue's graceful mien.
> Give me the maid whose heart with mine
> Shall blend each thought, each hope combine.
> Then, maiden, fair as ocean's spray,
> Gifted with Kymric wit's bright ray,
>   Say, am I thine?
>   Art thou then mine?
>   What? silent now?
>   Thy silence makes this bosom glow,
> I choose thee, maiden, for thy gifts divine,
> 'Tis right to choose; then, fairest, choose me thine.[1]

---

[1] Stephens.

Judge now of the true characters respectively of Britons and Anglo-Saxons, and of our debt to each in blood and culture.

Judge also whether, as I said at the onset, the time has or has not come to put off the false and put on the true designation. To banish the word Saxon—the most hated word to be found, perhaps, in any language—so far as it concerned Britons, Welsh, Scots, and Irish, in past times, and by the Irish people even now. Banish it for ever, with all its bloodthirsty and egotistical associations. Oh, banish it! Be content to take precedence with your own favourite word—that which gives name to England—and then, instead of a kind of repetition of your own notion of your own exceeding excellence, substitute a word that may allow your fellowcitizens to have also a position, a share, a satisfaction, in whatever affects the happiness, the honour, or the welfare of the whole empire. Let us have no more Anglo-Saxon—but let Anglo-Celt henceforward be the national watchword.

In conclusion, let us not forget that, in the scheme of God, we may be very sure that all qualities are interchangeable between all races. Perhaps, because they all came from one; or if not that, then because they are yet to become one; one people, one language, one government, but comprising in that sublime trinity in unity, endless diversities of people, tongues, and governments; with a wealth of all kinds, mental and material, inconceivably beyond aught we at present know, but without that incessant war of interests and bigotries which at present makes the whole world but groan like a creation in travail; and renders even the wealth we do possess valueless in the eyes of a Christian philosopher, except as materials for the future to which the spirit of progress must lead us on ; that progress itself being but the law which is evolved from the interchanges of which I have spoken.

LONDON: PRINTED BY
SPOTTISWOODE AND CO., NEW-STREET SQUARE
AND PARLIAMENT STREET

BOOKS FOR PRESENTS.

LYRICS OF LOVE,

From Shakespeare to Tennyson, Selected and arranged by W. Davenport Adams, jun., fcap. 8vo, cloth, extra, gilt edges, price 3s. 6d.

"A most careful and charming compilation."—*Standard.*

HOME SONGS FOR QUIET HOURS,

By Rev. Canon R. H. Baynes, M.A., Editor of 'Lyra Anglicana," etc., Third Edition, fcap 8vo, cloth, extra, price 3s. 6d. This may also be had handsomely bound in morocco, with gilt edges.

"Of a very high standard of excellence."—*Standard.*

POEMS.

Red-line Edition, with 24 Illustrations and Portrait of the Author, by William Cullen Bryant, post 8vo, cloth, extra, price 7s. 6d.; small crown 8vo, price 3s. 6d.

"Of all the Poets of the United States, there is no one who obtained the fame and position of a classic earlier, or has kept them longer than William Cullen Bryant."—*Academy.*

ENGLISH SONNETS.

Collected and arranged by John Dennis, Elegantly bound, fcap. 8vo, cloth, price 3s. 6d.

"A selection which every lover of poetry will consult again and again with delight."—*Spectator.*

PRELUDES.

A Volume of Poems, with Six Illustrations by Elizabeth Thompson (Painter of "The Roll Call"), by A. C. Thompson, 8vo, cloth, price 7s. 6d.

"It is altogether a choice little book, which not a few will welcome and find delight in."—*Nonconformist.*

OUR PLACE AMONG INFINITIES.

A Series of Essays contrasting our little abode in Space and Time with the Infinities around us. To which are added Essays on "Astrology," and "The Jewish Sabbath," by Richard A. Proctor, B.A., Second Edition, crown 8vo, cloth, price 6s.

"Mr. Proctor has the happy faculty of describing ascertained facts, in such a manner as to make them intelligible to all."—*Examiner.*

THE EXPANSE OF HEAVEN.

A Series of Essays on the Wonders of the Firmament, by Richard A. Proctor, B.A., with a Frontispiece, Second Edition, crown 8vo, cloth, price 6s.

"A very charming work; cannot fail to lift the reader's mind up ' through nature's work to nature's God.'"—*Standard.*
"A very charming work."—*Standard.*

HENRY S. KING & Co., LONDON.

ALFRED TENNYSON'S WORKS,
THE CABINET EDITION,
COMPLETE IN TEN HALF-CROWN VOLUMES.

Each Volume with a Frontispiece, fcap. 8vo,
cloth, price 2s. 6d.

VOL.

I.—EARLY POEMS, Illustrated with a·Photographic Portrait of Mr. Alfred Tennyson.

II.—ENGLISH IDYLLS, AND OTHER POEMS. Containing an Engraving of Mr. Alfred Tennyson's Residence at Aldworth.

III.—LOCKSLEY HALL, AND OTHER POEMS. With an Engraved Picture of Farringford.

IV.—LUCRETIUS, AND OTHER POEMS. Containing an Engraving of a Scene in the Garden at Swainston.

V.—IDYLLS OF THE KING. With an Autotype of the Bust of Mr. Alfred Tennyson, by T. Woolner, R.A.

VI.—IDYLLS OF THE KING. Illustrated, with an Engraved Portrait of "Elaine," from a Photographic Study by Julia M. Cameron.

VII.—IDYLLS OF THE KING. Containing an Engraving of "Arthur," from a Photographic Study by Julia M. Cameron.

VIII.—THE PRINCESS, with an Engraved Frontispiece.

IX.—MAUD AND ENOCH ARDEN. With a Picture of "Maud," taken from a Photographic Study by Julia M. Cameron.

X.—IN MEMORIAM. With a Steel Engraving of Arthur H. Hallam, Engraved from a Picture in possession of the Author by J. C. Armytage.

THIS EDITION COMPLETE, IN HANDSOME ORNAMENTAL CASE, price 28s.

For particulars of the Author's Edition, see third page of cover.

HENRY S. KING & Co., LONDON.